Khan Elias Crichell thought to himself. The man who stood before him wore a gray jumpsuit with Clan Wolf markings. His flesh had gray and yellow tones to it as befitted a man who had been fighting for months and living the last few days on survival rations.

Crichell looked down at the man at the foot of the dais. "Your message indicated you had valuable information for me."

I served ilKhan Ulric Kerensky as aide during the Trial of Refusal." Vlad smiled in a lopsided way that made Elias feel uncomfortable. "What I saw will give you the means to destroy Khan Vandervahn Christu. I will even kill him myself. Your path of ascension to ilKhan is clear."

"If you are right, you will want something of me in return."

"I will, but we may speak on it after I have fulfilled my half of the bargain. When he is gone, you will not deny me what I desire."

"How can you be that certain?"

"I am willing to kill a man to avenge a dead leader from a dead Clan whose policies I found repugnant and opposed with every fiber of my being." Fire burned deep in Vlad's eyes. "Deny me what I want, and you will discover how truly dangerous I can be...."

"In the tradition of Gordon Dickson's *Dorsai*, Stackpole's battle clans swash and buckle with style and vengeance."—Simon Hawke

BATTLETECH®

MALICIOUS INTENT

Michael A. Stackpole

A ROC BOOK

ROC
Published by the Penguin Group
Penguin Books USA Inc., 375 Hudson Street,
New York, New York 10014, U.S.A.
Penguin Books Ltd, 27 Wrights Lane,
London W8 5TZ, England
Penguin Books Australia Ltd, Ringwood,
Victoria, Australia
Penguin Books Canada Ltd, 10 Alcorn Avenue,
Toronto, Ontario, Canada M4V 3B2
Penguin Books (N.Z.) Ltd, 182-190 Wairau Road,
Auckland 10, New Zealand

Penguin Books Ltd, Registered Offices:
Harmondsworth, Middlesex, England

First published by Roc, an imprint of Dutton Signet,
a division of Penguin Books USA Inc.

First Printing, March, 1996
10 9 8 7 6 5 4 3 2 1

Series Editor: Donna Ippolito
Cover: Roger Loveless
Mechanical Drawings: Duane Loose and the FASA art department

Roc REGISTERED TRADEMARK—MARCA REGISTRADA

BATTLETECH, FASA, and the distinctive BATTLETECH and FASA logos are
trademarks of the FASA Corporation, 1100 W. Cermak, Suite B305, Chicago,
IL 60608.

Printed in the United States of America

To Richard Garfield

A creative genius and innovative game designer
who proves that nice guys don't have to finish last
and, in special cases, can finish way out in front.

The author would like to thank the following people for their contribution to this work:

Sam Lewis and Bryan Nystul for story direction; Donna Ippolito for pinpointing those areas where I get lazy and making me fix them; Liz Danforth for not killing me every time I interrupted her painting to share something I thought was brilliant; John-Allen Price for the continued loan of a Cox; Lisa Koenigs-Cober and the members of the Crazy Eights for donating generously to charity in return for their appearances herein; and the GEnie Computer Network over which this novel and its revisions passed from the author's computer straight to FASA.

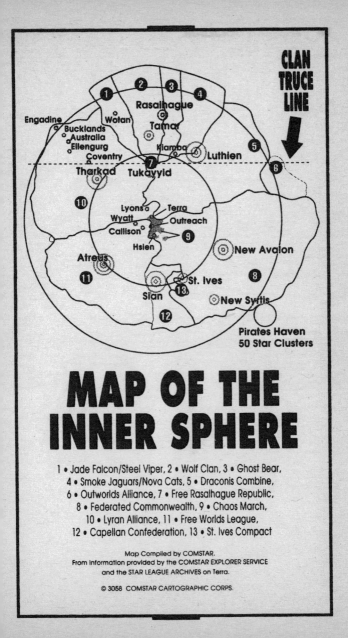

CLAN TRUCE LINE

MAP OF THE INNER SPHERE

1 • Jade Falcon/Steel Viper, 2 • Wolf Clan, 3 • Ghost Bear,
4 • Smoke Jaguars/Nova Cats, 5 • Draconis Combine,
6 • Outworlds Alliance, 7 • Free Rasalhague Republic,
8 • Federated Commonwealth, 9 • Chaos March,
10 • Lyran Alliance, 11 • Free Worlds League,
12 • Capellan Confederation, 13 • St. Ives Compact

Map Compiled by COMSTAR.
From information provided by the COMSTAR EXPLORER SERVICE
and the STAR LEAGUE ARCHIVES on Terra.

© 3058 COMSTAR CARTOGRAPHIC CORPS.

BOOK I

Unfinished Business

1

Borealtown
Wotan, Jade Falcon Occupation Zone
11 December 3057

Now the Wolves belong to me.

As he regained consciousness, this was the first thought that came to him. It worked its way past the fiery ache in his left forearm and the scattering of other stinging annoyances on his arms and legs. He clung to that thought and made it the core of his life and universe. *The rest are all dead, now the Wolves belong to me.*

Vlad of the Wards slowly turned his head, alert for any pain in his neck that might signal a spinal injury. It seemed unlikely, what with his arms and legs faithfully relaying their discomfort to his brain, but with so much responsibility facing him he could take no chances. As he moved his head, dust and gravel rattled off the faceplate of his neurohelmet, pouring more grit down into the collar of his cooling vest.

Through the dust Vlad thought he could see his left forearm, but it looked distorted and odd. He brushed the viewplate clean with his right hand and was able to correlate the bump on the top of his arm, and the bruise surrounding it, with the lightning-like shooters of pain emanating from that spot. Glancing up he saw the hole made in the viewport of his *Timber Wolf* when Wotan's Ministry of Budgets and Taxation building had been blown to bits and buried Vlad in a smoking pile of bricks.

One of those bricks must have struck his arm and broken

the bone that ran thumbside up the forearm. The bump meant the break was dislocated. Unset and unhealed, the injury rendered the arm all but useless. As a warrior buried beneath a building in an enemy zone, Vlad knew the crippling injury could easily be fatal.

For most warriors it would have been cause for panic.

Vlad smothered the first spark of fear rising in his breast. *I am a Wolf.* That simple thought was enough to forever tame his panic. Unlike the freebirth warriors of the Inner Sphere, or even those of the Jade Falcon and other Clans, Vlad refused worry or anxiety. Such emotions were, to his mind, for those who abandoned all claim on the future—those who preferred to exist in a state of fear instead of pressing on to a point where fear was banished.

For him there was no fear because he knew this was but one more twist in the legend that was his life. His existence could not end so ignominiously, with him dying of exposure or starvation or suffocation in the cockpit of an entombed BattleMech. Vlad refused to let that possibility exist in his universe.

The Wolves belong to me. That fact alone was vindication and confirmation of his destiny. Six centuries earlier, Battle-Mechs—ten-meter-tall, humanoid engines of destruction—had been created and come to dominate the battlefield just so that he might one day pilot one. Three hundred years ago Stefan Amaris had attempted to take over the Inner Sphere and Aleksandr Kerensky had vanished into the Periphery with most of the Star League's great army precisely so Vlad would one day be born into the greatest of warrior traditions. The Clans had been created by Nicholas Kerensky to further his father's dream, and Vlad had been born a warrior among them expressly so he could guide the Clans to the ultimate realization of that dream.

Such thoughts allowed him to soar beyond the pain in his body. Vlad cared little how someone else might view this vision of himself as the end product of six hundred years of human history, for he saw no other way to interpret his life. He shied from the mysticism of Clan Nova Cat, and examined the events with cold logic. Occam's razor sliced his conclusion from events cleanly—his reasoning, as extraordinary as it might seem, had to be true because it was the most simple explanation that wove everything together.

If his view were wrong, the Clans would have returned to

the Inner Sphere a century before or after his lifetime. If it were not true, he would never have suffered humiliation at the hands of Phelan Kell—a humiliation that allowed Vlad to see the true evil the man represented while the ilKhan and Khan Natasha Kerensky had not. The trauma of that defeat had left him immune to Phelan's charm and made Vlad the last true Wolf in the Clan.

Ulric knew that, which is why he entrusted the Wolves to me.

A cold chill sank into Vlad. He had come to Wotan with ilKhan Ulric Kerensky and had led him to a battlefield chosen by Vandervahn Chistu, Khan of the Jade Falcons. Ulric and Chistu were to fight a battle between them, a battle in which Ulric would have prevailed had Chistu not cheated. The last Vlad had seen of the Wolf leader was the fire-wreathed silhouette of a *Gargoyle* pressing one step closer to the enemy despite the withering missile firestorm engulfing him.

Lying on his back, Vlad glanced up at the dead instruments in his cockpit and smiled. Not only had he witnessed the Falcon Khan's treacherous murder of Ulric—he had recorded it. Chistu had to know that the incriminating evidence existed in the cockpit recorder. Had it been Vlad, he would have recognized the threat immediately and poured fire into the midden that had swallowed Vlad until all that remained of him or his *Timber Wolf* or the building was a huge crater. That Chistu had not done so marked him as even more a fool than Vlad had thought.

This means they will be coming for me. Chistu would not order the destruction of the building now—*though he should.* Vlad decided Chistu would send people to look for the 'Mech and recover the recorder—under the pretense that the medical data recorded there would provide information on how Vlad of the Wolves had died. It would also allow Chistu to view for himself Ulric's destruction from another angle, and to see how handily his marksmanship had buried Vlad under the bricks and mortar of a huge building.

They will be coming and I must be ready.

With his right hand he unbuckled his belt and pulled it free from around his waist. Inserting the end back through the buckle, he then slipped the loop around his left wrist. He slid the buckle down until it snugged against his flesh. Pain shot up and down his arm, leaving him weak for a moment and nauseous.

Vlad waited for the nausea to subside before pushing on with his plan. He pulled his right knee up to his chest and hooked the heel of his boot on the edge of the command couch. He fumbled with the buckle at the top of his calf-high boot and undid it. He slipped the end of his belt through backward, stabbing the tongue through one of the holes at the very end. He thrust the tip of the boot-belt back over his other belt and fastened it in place. He tugged on the waist-belt until he was sure it would remain in place and would not pull free.

He lowered his leg again and his foot hit the pedal at the bottom of the command couch without using up all the slack in the belt. He took a deep breath, then gently pulled his left leg up and hooked the heel of that boot over the belt. He eased his left forearm into his lap and let the intact bone rest on his thigh. With his right hand he took up all the slack in the restraining straps that crossed his chest and lap to keep him in the command couch.

Sweat began to burn into his eyes. He pulled the medi-patch wires from the throat of his neurohelmet, then unbuckled it and tossed it off back over his head. He heard the helmet clatter against some debris, but he didn't care. He shook his head violently, spraying sweat into a vapor that drifted back down like cold fog over his face.

He knew what he had to do, and he knew it would hurt unbearably—worse than any physical pain he had endured till now. The wound that had torn open one side of his face and left a scar that ran from eyebrow to jaw had been just as painful, but the medics had him so dosed with painkillers that he wouldn't have felt a 'Mech tap dancing on him. Those same drugs all existed in the medkit located in one of the cockpit's storage areas, but if Vlad used them he'd never be able to set his arm.

Pain is the only true sign you are alive.

The light brush of his fingertips over the break felt as heavy as stone and started agony rippling out in waves that seemed to liquefy his body. His breath caught in his throat and a sinking sensation threatened to suck his guts down into his loins. Icy slush filled his intestines, and his scrotum shrank as his body recoiled from the pain.

Vlad smashed his right fist against the command couch's

right arm. "I am *not* a Jade Falcon. This pain means *nothing!*" His nostrils flared as he sucked in a lungful of chill air. "I am a Wolf. I will prevail."

He slowly straightened his left leg, his vision blurring as the belt tightened on his wrist. He tried to lean forward to give the belt slack, but the restraining straps held him in place. His left arm extended and the elbow locked. Shimmering bursts of pink and green exploded before his eyes, and blackness crept in at the edge of his vision.

He continued pushing and then dropped his right hand over the break. The fiery agonies consuming his left arm magnified what his right hand felt in incredibly fine detail. Millimeter by millimeter, bone slid against bone as the belt tightened and the break began to slide into place. Each little bit of motion sent seismic tremors through Vlad's body, wrapping him in pain that seemed to have existed his entire life and promised to engulf his future. Yet, despite that, he knew from the sensations in his right hand that the ends of the bones were still kilometers apart and would never slide into place despite eons of torture.

The squeak of teeth grinding together echoed through his brain and almost drowned out the first faint click of bones beginning to slide into place. He almost let the tension on the belt go, convincing himself that everything was repaired and that what his right hand felt could not be right. A firestorm of pain flared up and through him. He felt his resolve begin to melt in its inferno.

Then he remembered the image of Ulric's 'Mech taking just one more step.

I will not *surrender.*

Screaming incoherently, Vlad straightened his left leg. Bone grated on bone, the lower half pulling even with the break, then slipping past it. The gulf between the ends of the break seemed to stretch on forever, but he knew that was an illusion. He clenched his right hand over the break, clamping it down. Bones snapped into place.

The argent lightning storm that played out from the break bowed his spine and jammed him hard against the couch's restraining straps. He hung there forever, his lungs afire with oxygen deprivation. He wanted to scream and his throat hurt as if he were, but he could only hear the wheezing hiss of the last of his breath being squeezed from his chest.

His muscles slackened and the restraining straps slammed

him back down into the couch. He felt more pain, but his nervous system had not recovered from being overwhelmed and could only report faint echoes of it to his brain. He took a shallow breath, then another and another. Each one came deeper, and as his body learned that breathing would not hurt him, it gradually returned to normal functioning.

The break throbbed, but the bones had been slid back into place. Vlad knew he would find a splint in the command couch's medkit, but he didn't have the strength to get free from the restraining straps and go digging around for it. He let his head loll to one side and then the other to drain sweat from his eyes. It was not much, but along with breathing it was enough.

As strength gradually returned, Vlad wasted a bit of it in a smile. He had passed the first test in his ordeal, but he knew there would be many more. There would be enemies to be destroyed and allies to be used. The war—technically a Trial of Refusal—between the Jade Falcons and Wolves would have left both sides devastated. Vlad knew, based on the fact that he had not been rescued immediately, that the Jade Falcons had won. That meant he would have to appeal to the Falcons who shared his disgust with the Inner Sphere if he were to have any help from them. *Better I seek aid from the Ghost Bears, as they have long been allies to the Wolves.*

Vlad nodded slowly. *There are many matters with which I will have to deal. I can use the time here, waiting in my cockpit, to consider them all. Those who come for me will believe themselves scavengers, only to find themselves rescuers. Little do they know they will be midwives to the future of the Clans.*

2

Eleventh Lyran Guards Temporary Headquarters
Elarion City, Wyatt
Isle of Skye, Lyran Alliance
12 December 3057

This is going to be a disaster, he thought as he snapped to attention and clicked his boot heels together. "Hauptmann Caradoc Trevena reporting as ordered, sir."

Without rising from his chair, Kommandant Grega flipped Doc a two-fingered salute, then pointed to the heavy wooden chair opposite the desk. "Sit, Hauptmann."

For a half-second Doc almost refused, choosing instead to stand at ease, but the weariness of fourteen years in the military bore down on him. He sat, but forced himself to sit straight instead of slumping in the uncomfortable seat. He looked up, seeking some sign that things weren't going to be as bad as he feared.

Grega popped a gray data disk from his computer and tossed it onto the middle of his Steiner-blue desk blotter. "I've been reviewing your file. It's rather remarkable, Hauptmann. You joined the service in 3043, just after the 3039 festivities." The multiple ranks of battle ribbons on the left breast of Grega's jacket showed that he hadn't missed that war. "And despite being in the Armed Forces of the Federated Commonwealth during the Clan invasion, you have never served in a unit that has seen combat. How is that?"

Doc shrugged. "Luck?" He knew that was the wrong answer before he said it. To people like Grega—those who'd been under fire—he was a paper-veteran. He'd served *during* a conflict, not *in* the conflict. Even in the most recent fighting, when the Free Worlds League invaded the Federated Commonwealth and took back worlds lost a quarter century before, his unit had opted out of the fighting. The Eleventh had decided to abide by Katrina Steiner's proclamation of neutrality. They'd left their station on the embattled world of Calliston and returned "home" to Wyatt.

Grega slowly exhaled. "Luck? That's exactly the sort of attitude that has us concerned here, Hauptmann. Yours is not a military record many would want to emulate."

I bet the dead ones would love to have my record. Doc leaned forward and clasped his hands together on the desk. "I'm not certain I understand that assessment, Kommandant. All of my evaluations have been satisfactory."

"Yet you've been passed over for promotion twice now. And if not for the Clan invasion, you'd have been mustered out long ago." Grega tapped the disk with an index finger. "At this point your chances for promotion are dead."

Yes, but it's not my service record that dooms me. The Eleventh Lyran Guards had been a linchpin unit in the AFFC, holding the line against possible Free Worlds League aggression in the Sarna March. When it pulled out and joined the newly formed Lyran Alliance it became a key unit in what was now known as the Lyran Alliance Armed Forces. The irony of the resulting acronym—LAAF—had not been lost upon him, yet to make a joke about it appeared to be akin to treason in the minds of most LAAFers.

Those who found the joke appropriate were usually warriors hailing from the Davion half of the Federated Commonwealth. Refusing to help her brother defend against the invasion of the Sarna March, Katrina Steiner had seceded from the Federated Commonwealth, baptized her new realm the Lyran Alliance, and called all loyalist troops home. Those who answered the call, like the commanders of the Eleventh Lyran Guard, were staunch Steiner loyalists who showed a certain teutonic lack of humor about life in general and the unit in specific.

Grega leaned back in his chair and patted scattered strands of brown hair across his balding head. "I know this isn't an easy time for you, Hauptmann. It must have been quite a shock when your wife chose not to leave Calliston when we evacuated. Your career is stalled, and with the Clan truce in place for another ten years, the chances of you seeing combat and reviving your prospects are nil."

Doc shrugged. "Just my luck we fled from Calliston."

"Marshal Sharon Byran *chose* to honor Archon Steiner's request for the return of Lyran forces to the Alliance. It's your *bad* luck that her compliance ended any hopes you had of advancement." Grega's gray eyes hardened. "However, I have a bit of good luck for you, Hauptmann. The Lyran Alliance Armed Forces is prepared to offer you a generous compensation package if you choose to resign. Your fourteen years of service don't qualify you for a pension per se, but we're willing to give you 20,000 Kroner and an honorable discharge, which will make you eligible for full veteran medical and occupational training benefits. I should think you would find this offer more than fair."

"Would that include passage back to Kestrel?"

Grega opened his hands. "I'm afraid transport is limited right now, but you are free to pursue the possibilities on your own."

"Which means that 20,000 Kroner will get me about as far as Terra."

"A bit further, perhaps."

"But isn't the Lyran Alliance paying the full expenses of people who want to repatriate themselves from the Federal Commonwealth?"

Grega made a vain attempt at hiding his smile. "Different government department, I'm afraid. A bit of bad luck."

Doc sat back. "All my luck's been bad luck."

The Kommandant nodded. "So it seems."

"Yeah, well, I believe in sharing, Kommandant." An edge crept into Doc's voice and he fought to keep the volume below a shout. "Let's get down to the trenches here, shall we? You're moving every paper-veteran you can out of this unit and filling it with Steiner heroes to make this a showcase unit. It's a purge, nothing more and nothing less."

"We're a military organization, not a political party."

"It shouldn't surprise me that you're short-sighted enough to think I'd believe politics and the military don't mix—I'm not a fool." Doc reached out and tapped the disk on Grega's desk. "If you'd taken a serious look at my record, Kommandant, you'd have noticed something important. The reason all my evaluations have been good is because I've been assigned to company after company filled with MechWarriors who'd earned only substandard evaluations. Every unit I've every worked with was deficient before I arrived, including your Third Striker Company, but they were sharp and battle-ready by the time I was done with them. I may not be the guy who forges the knife, but I'm the one who puts an edge on it, and our superiors have seen my value in that. Promoting me would have moved me out of that role, and that was the role to which they thought I was best suited."

Doc's dark eyes narrowed. "You've also made two assumptions about me that were unwarranted, sir. The first is that just because I've not seen combat and not been promoted, you assume I'm a slack warrior. You think I'm substandard and that I can't fight. I can. You're sure I'd fall apart in combat, but you ignore the performance of units I've trained—they've done damned well. And if I'd been leading them, they'd have done better because I've studied our enemies. I know them, their tactics, and how to defeat them. All things being equal, I'd have no second thoughts about taking on either the Falcons or the Wolves."

Grega slowly shook his head. "My, my, perhaps I should send a message to the Archon and have you appointed her advisor."

She could damned well use one. Doc held his tongue. While he was willing to toe the line between dissent and treason, he didn't want to step full on it. "Perhaps you should, Kommandant, because she'd tell you all about Archon's Order 5730023—Reorganization of the Lyran Alliance Armed Forces. I've read it. Because a state of war technically still exists between the LAAF and the Clans, company and field grade officers cannot be dismissed from the service through anything less than a court martial. You have nothing on me that would warrant you bringing legitimate charges against me. Unless I resign, you're stuck with me."

Doc folded his arms across his chest. "You thought this would be easy. No way. You figured my wife leaving me, my poor career prospects, and the rest would make me go meekly because I've got nothing to live for. Well, I do have something to live for, sir, and that's making sure *nothing* is easy for you. If I let you jerk me around, you'll end up mangling the life of someone who actually *has* a life."

Grega raised an eyebrow. "Are you finished?"

"Wasn't I finished before I stepped in here?"

"Perhaps, in fact, you were." Grega shrugged. "Exactly *how* you were to be finished was not cast in ferrocrete. You aren't the first officer who's cited AO-5730023, though I hadn't expected *you* to protest. I do find your arguments about your performance quite self-serving and indicative of an overblown ego, but I also find the irony of your making this point rather delicious."

Grega's precise pronunciation of the word "delicious" was disturbing. He fit his mouth delicately around each syllable, as if the word were a razor he would use to carve Doc up. *He's taking great delight in this, and I don't like that.*

"You see, Hauptmann Trevena, there are units that have been carefully chosen as repositories for warriors such as yourself."

"Units on the line with the Clans?"

"You would like that, wouldn't you?" Grega shook his head. "Of course, those worlds have to be guarded by units of unquestioned loyalty and superior abilities. I would be negligent in assigning you to such a unit, despite your self-assessment. No, you'll be sent to command a company in the Tenth Skye Rangers on Coventry."

Doc kept a defiant smile on his face, but inside he felt something dying. The Isle of Skye was a hotbed of anti-Davion sentiment, and the Rangers had been formed from some of the region's most loyal sons and daughters. Duke Ryan Steiner had used Skye as his power base for an attempted coup that would have torn the Skye March away from the Federated Commonwealth, and he had been the brains behind the Free Skye Movement that had fomented open rebellion on several of the worlds just last year. Victor Davion had put the rebellion down and, some believed, had given the order for Ryan Steiner's assassination on Solaris. The Gray Death Legion had slapped the Tenth Skye Rangers down on Glengarry, and Doc guessed that restructuring the unit was LAAF's way of keeping it benign.

Filling such a unit with people who had not seen combat, like him, or had little aptitude for combat would certainly accomplish that goal. If his luck were to turn good, Doc knew he'd have six difficult years before he could resign with a pension. After leading such a Skye unit, anything would seem an improvement, so retiring on half-pay wouldn't be that bad. *If I can stand it for that long.*

Being killed in a training accident looked like the only

early release he could hope for, largely because of the unit's posting. Coventry was a key world within the Lyran Alliance, so the posting seemed honorable, but in reality it was a sham. Coventry was deep enough inside the Lyran Alliance that only a serious Clan push would ever reach it. Moreover, the Coventry Academy had its Cadet Corps and the Coventry Militia was known to be one of the most highly trained units in the Alliance—largely because it was staffed with warriors who also served as test pilots for the Coventry Metal Works 'Mech production facilities.

We'll never see combat, and we have two ultra-loyalist units there to watch over us. Putting him on a JumpShip and targeting it for a black hole was about the only other way they could have consigned his career to an even more ignominious end than a resignation bought for 20,000 Kroner would provide.

Doc nodded once. "I hear the weather on Coventry is nice. I'll send you a hologram of me sunning myself."

"Please, do that, Hauptmann." Grega stood and waved Doc toward the door. "You know they say it's better to be lucky than good. It's a real tragedy to be like you, because you're neither."

"That's a historian's judgment, sir."

"The victors write the history, Hauptmann."

"No, sir, *survivors* write the history." Doc gave him a salute. "Given my record, I think you should hope I remember you kindly."

"And you, Hauptmann, should hope I choose to remember you at all."

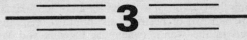

= 3 =

Using the command couch to shield himself, Vlad hunkered down in the darkness of the cockpit as gravel and voices drifted down from above. Even as 'Mechs had labored outside to uncover his *Timber Wolf*, he'd dug a great deal of the debris out of the back of the cockpit and piled it on the command couch to fortify his position. The lasers the searchers would be using would take some time to burn through the bricks and stone with which he'd armored his haven.

Vlad had spent his last two days constructively. Using one of the lasers in his survival gear he'd burned a hole up through the stone above his 'Mech. The rubble burying him had enough holes in it to provide him ample air—the laser-burnt hole was meant to give searchers a clue that he'd survived the collapse and, at some point, had been alive. Shooting the laser off at night, letting the red beam play out into the air, would have been an easier way to summon help, and one he'd been saving for when his food ran out. While it would bring rescuers, it would also let them know he lived. And that, Vlad decided, was not necessarily conducive to his continued survival.

Vandervahn Chistu's murder of ilKhan Ulric Kerensky must surely have been a move to preempt the other Jade Falcon Khan in the race to become the new ilKhan. Khan Elias

Crichell, the senior Khan, was a consummate politician—as evidenced by the fact that he'd retained his rank long after abandoning the cockpit of a 'Mech for an office and data terminal. Crichell had orchestrated the political crisis that had culminated in the war between the Falcons and Wolves, leaving Chistu to prosecute that war.

Though Crichell had a lot of power, including many favors owed him by the Khans of other Clans, Chistu had killed Ulric Kerensky, a deed that could easily win him enough standing to claim the title of the Khan's Khan, the leader of all the Clans. The luster of Chistu's single combat with Ulric might let him eclipse Crichell when the Clan Council met on Strana Mechty to elect a new ilKhan. Ulric had opposed a repudiation of the ComStar truce and Vahn Chistu had killed him, making Chistu the logical choice to carry the war again to the Inner Sphere.

Unless I can tell the true story of what happened here on Wotan. Were the truth about Ulric's death to come out, Chistu's hopes of becoming ilKhan would fare worse than Ulric had on Wotan. The other Khans would expel him from the Grand Council, and the Jade Falcon Council would surely strip him of his rank. If he was lucky they would assign him to a solahma unit. He would live out the rest of his days hunting bandits and other scum unworthy of a true warrior's attention. *Most likely they will just kill him—the Falcons are rather inflexible in matters of honor.*

Chistu could not chance Vlad living to tell what he had seen. Any searchers would surely be coming with the intention of seeing that he never left the cockpit alive. His only chance of survival would be to neutralize the first people down into the hole, then escape before anyone on the surface could call for help. Vlad was sure the rescue team would be composed of relatively few people so that Chistu could preserve his secret.

Light filtered down into his cockpit and played around. Vlad could see the round beams as they slashed across the cracked and holed viewports. That was a mistake. They had cleared enough debris that he would be able to get out if he somehow got free.

The dangling tail of a rope descended through the hole in the canopy. "Star Captain Vladimir, can you hear me? This is Star Captain Marialle Radick. Are you hurt?"

Vlad's eyes narrowed. Marialle Radick had been his partner in bringing treason charges against ilKhan Ulric in the Wolves' Clan Council. Ulric had even transferred her from the Sixteenth Battle Cluster to the Eleventh Wolf Guards for the war with the Jade Falcons. That she had survived the fighting did not surprise him—she was a good Mech-Warrior—but her participating in his rescue did puzzle him. *Could we have won after all?*

"I am here, Star Captain."

"I am coming down."

"Alone."

"As you wish."

"And unarmed."

A faint tremor of fear ran through her reply. "As you wish, Star Captain."

Vlad raised his left hand and gently pressed it over his left eye. That way any flash device they dropped would blind only one of his eyes, and he could still return fire when they came in. At his feet lay the gas mask from his survival kit. He could have it on before they could fill the cockpit with an anesthetic or irritant gas.

The dangling rope danced a bit, then the silhouettes of two booted feet appeared on either side of the hole in his 'Mech's windscreen. A second later the canopy sagged, then peeled away and crashed against the interior of the cockpit. Vlad remained hidden and safe as dust billowed up in the small enclosure.

"Are you unhurt? I did not expect it to collapse."

"Keep coming."

Marialle Radick lowered herself into the 'Mech's cockpit. Small and slender, wearing a dark jumpsuit that hugged her narrow waist, she looked more child than adult. Her blond hair had been gathered at the back of her head in a tight knot. Her amber eyes glowed gold in the light reflected from above. "Are you hurt?"

"I have injuries, but none grave."

She nodded. "I have a light, if you do not."

"I have light, both focused and unfocused. I would prefer to use only the latter, but only after I have determined what the situation is outside. Today is the thirteenth, *quiaff?*"

"Aff. Ulric died on the tenth."

"I know. I saw him die."

"But he died several miles north ... What are you doing here?"

"Let me ask the questions, please." Vlad coughed lightly. "And I assure you I am in my right mind—I suffered no head injuries. Did we carry the day?"

"No."

"And there have been no reprisals against the Wolves?"

"There was a Ritual of Abjuration carried out against those of our brethren who retreated from Wotan and those who fled with Khan Phelan."

"Abjuration." Holding that ritual made sense because it exiled all those who had fled. Abjuration was seldom invoked, and then only in the case of gross cowardice or dereliction of duty. An abjured warrior surrendered his bloodname, if he had one, and any chance of his genetic material becoming part of the Clan's breeding program.

Vlad would not have pursued abjuration against the fleeing Wolves because he would not want to relinquish jurisdiction over those who had gone to the Inner Sphere. At some point in the future it might be possible to bring them back into the fold, but after abjuration that would be difficult. *The ritual was held prematurely. Another sign my leadership is needed.*

"Abjuration was believed to be the best choice, given the circumstances. The Wolves defeated at Morges will be in no way associated with us."

"That would not do." Phelan and a goodly number of Wolves had run for the Inner Sphere. They faced Jade Falcons on a world known as Morges. Vlad was not as confident as Marialle of the Wolves' defeat, but preventing backlash caused by the fighting on Morges was a wise idea.

"Who sent you to find me, Star Captain?"

"Standard salvage detail. Aerial survey picked up a lot of battle damage in this area. The way this building had collapsed did not suggest bomb damage, so we were sent out to check."

"You weren't sent here to kill me?"

"Kill you?" She blinked in astonishment. "We didn't even know it was you until we uncovered enough of your cockpit to see that this was a *Timber Wolf* assigned to the Eleventh Guards. Your name is stenciled on the side."

Is Chistu that stupid? "Star Captain, I am going to turn on my light." Vlad scraped the flashlight taped to the barrel of his laser pistol against the edge of the command couch. The button clicked on and he pointed it at her. *"Freebirth!"* he cursed.

"What is it?"

The woman at whom he pointed his laser wore a green jumpsuit with Jade Falcon insignia on the shoulders. He recognized her face and form, for he knew Marialle Radick well, but seeing her dressed in the emerald green of a Jade Falcon warrior threw him utterly. He almost pulled the trigger, then he raised the gun and hid her in darkness again.

"Why are you dressed as a Falcon?"

"Because that is what I am."

That is impossible. He could not conceive of Marialle surrendering to the Falcons. Even if she had, they would have made her a bondswoman first and then, sometime later, they might have allowed her to become a MechWarrior again. *And she called herself Marialle Radick, but the Jade Falcons do not possess blood from that line. It is a Wolf bloodline only.* "How are you a Jade Falcon?"

"That is what we all are now, Vlad. The Wolves lost a Trial of Absorption. We are all Jade Falcons now."

Vlad's mouth hung open. "What?"

"Khan Chistu told us, the survivors, that we had been absorbed into the Jade Falcons. This is why he undertook the Ritual of Abjuration—he would not have Jade Falcons fighting Jade Falcons on Morges."

"But this was never a Ritual of Absorption."

"Not formally, no, but Khan Chistu said that when Natasha and Phelan pledged everything the Wolves had to fighting the Trial of Refusal, it automatically became a Ritual of Absorption." Marialle leaned forward slightly. "I did not like it at first—none of us did—but the logic is inescapable. Our war with the Jade Falcons hurt them badly, and hurt us badly. Alone, neither of our Clans is strong enough to stand, but together we are a fearsome force. The warriors who have survived are the best on both sides. Khan Chistu says this was a crucible in which the impurities of both Clans were burned away."

Vlad scowled. "The Trial of Refusal occurred in response to charges of genocide and treason against Ulric. The Wolves defeated the Jade Falcons on every world where we fought, save here."

Marialle threw him a sharp look. "It was closer to a draw. The Falcons offered us terms after Ulric's death. The terms were honorable and we accepted them. Some of us ran to Phelan, others stayed here."

"And Phelan still fights. The Wolves have not been defeated yet, Star Captain Radick."

"What are you saying?"

"The chronology of events you presented gives me the impression that Khan Chistu announced our *absorption,* then he initiated the Ritual of Abjuration to exile the Wolves who oppose his Jade Falcons on Morges, *quiaff*?"

"That is how it happened, aff."

"Yet the Wolves could only be absorbed if defeated, *quiaff*?"

"Aff." Marialle's eyes narrowed. "You are saying that if Phelan defeated the Jade Falcons, he could return and challenge Khan Chistu to a Trial of Refusal concerning the absorption and abjuration."

"Chistu would not have to acknowledge Phelan's claim because he has been abjured. It would take a Wolf to challenge the Absorption, but all the Wolves here on Wotan have become Jade Falcons."

"Except you."

"Except me. Come, Star Captain, help me from this tomb." Vlad smiled and stood slowly. "Tell me more of this fiction Khan Chistu has created about the death of Ulric. Do it, and I will show you how our honor may be redeemed. Do it and you will see why the Wolves were entrusted to me."

4

*ComStar Military Headquarters, Sandhurst Military
   Academy, Berkshire
British Isles, Terra
13 December 3057*

Precentor Lisa Koenigs-Cober rubbed sleep from her eyes
and stifled a yawn as she was shown into the Precentor Martial's office. The room, with its paneling of dark walnut and
shelves crammed with antique leather-bound volumes,
seemed very warm to her. Through the high arching windows she could see snow drifting down through the night,
and her stomach grumbled as she recalled the turbulence her
plane had encountered passing through that storm over the
Atlantic.

The demi-Precentor holding the door announced her. "Precentor Koenigs-Cober to see you, sir."

"Thank you, Darner, that will be all." The Precentor Martial, a tall, slender man, surrendered nothing to old age but
the color of his hair and some lines on his face. When she
had seen him before, at staff meetings or at troop reviews,
he had always been dressed in a simple white cassock belted
at the waist with a golden cord. That uniform belied his role
as the supreme military commander of the Com Guards, and
she had always assumed he wore it to prompt others to underestimate him.

The fatigues he wore now were white, but had obviously
been chosen in keeping with the weather conditions and not
for any symbolism of ComStar. His tunic bore no rank insig-

nia, but the black eye-patch covering the empty socket on the right side of his face identified him as someone no Com Guard could mistake.

The Precentor Martial rubbed his hands together, then held them out toward the fire blazing in the huge hearth on one side of the room. He turned his head to look at her and she saw reflections of the dancing fire in his one good eye. "I apologize for summoning you at this hour. I had hoped to let you get some rest before I required a report from you, but there is urgent business that will take me to Morges in a couple of hours."

Lisa stood watching him for a moment, hands clasped behind her back. "Morges is where elements of Clan Wolf and Clan Jade Falcon are fighting. The Kell Hounds are there as well."

Anastasius Focht nodded, then pointed to one of the brown leather chairs facing the fire. "I'm pleased to see that you remain current on events outside the Terran system."

"Any Clan moving troops closer to the truce line is of concern to me, sir. I've not forgotten that their ultimate goal is the conquest of Terra. Forewarned is forearmed." She walked over to the chair he'd indicated, but paused before being seated. "Is it possible I might accompany you to Morges for a chance to observe more of their fighting—more than I saw at Tukayyid?"

"That would be a splendid idea, but no, I'm afraid it's not possible. Even though this trip is an emergency, I doubt I'll make planetfall before the end of the month. There's already been some combat on the southern continent. Given the way the Clans fight, the battle will no doubt be decided before I arrive." The old man looked down for a moment. "I expect Christmas there to be a rather bloody affair."

The Precentor Martial stared into the fire for a moment before turning back to her. "But that is not the reason I can't allow you to come with me. You have too much to do here. Brion's Legion has left North America?"

Lisa sat on the edge of the seat, not daring to lean back and let the warm, soft leather lull her to sleep. "Yes, sir. With the Sarna March balkanizing, the price of a mercenary contract has skyrocketed. The Legion is traveling to Pleione, to become one of the key units in the Tikonov Reaches."

Focht lowered himself into the chair opposite her. "I hope you know I tried to get the First Circuit to match the offer

Pleione made Colonel Brion. I know you were close to Major Iljir."

"I appreciate that, sir." Lisa held her hands toward the fire, though she knew the chill in them came from inside not outside. Rustam Iljir had asked her to leave ComStar and go with him to Pleione, and she'd asked him to join ComStar and stay with her, but both of them knew those requests were impossible for the other to comply with. *We each asked because we had to ask, and we each declined because we had to decline.* "The truth is, though, sir, we'll be getting a better unit in the Twenty-first Centauri Lancers. The Legion got a bit complacent here on Terra. The Lancers can use some light duty after skirmishing with the Second FedCom Regimental Combat Team on Hsein. Colonel Haskell is a good commander and I think her troops will benefit from the time spent here."

"Are they still set to arrive in early January?"

"Yes, sir. Alpha and Beta Battalions of the Terran Defense Force will take them through orientation ops."

The Precentor Martial sat back in his chair. "Then they should be fully operational in late February or early March?"

"Perhaps sooner. Colonel Haskell is prescreening replacements for the pilots she lost in battle or by taking this assignment. We're running security checks on all of them, of course, but we should end up with a squad that's more seasoned than the Legion was when it took this assignment seven years ago."

"Good. That leaves Terra vulnerable for only a month or two."

Something about those words sent a shiver down Lisa's spine. "You'll forgive me, sir, but are we really in much danger here? I know there is unrest among the Clans, but that's a long way from seeing the truce violated, isn't it?"

Focht fixed her with his one good eye. "I negotiated the truce with ilKhan Ulric Kerensky. It was to run fifteen years, from 3052 to 3067. While he lives I have no fear that it will not be honored."

"And he is still ilKhan."

The Precentor Martial shook his head and his shoulders sagged a bit. "I hope that is true, but I don't even know if he's still alive at this point. The message I received today was sent less than a week ago and its contents lead me to believe that both Ulric's life and the truce are in jeopardy."

Lisa's mouth soured, for news of turmoil affecting the Clan truce could not come at a worse time. The Federated Commonwealth was engaged in open warfare with the Capellan Confederation and Free Worlds League in the Sarna March. In a protest over the catalyzing event that prompted the Free Worlds League to attack Prince Victor Davion's Federated Commonwealth, the Lyran Alliance had seceded from the Federated Commonwealth. To keep peace and maintain political stability in the Inner Sphere, Draconis Combine troops—serving as peacekeepers under the ComStar aegis—had occupied worlds trapped between Victor and his sister Katrina, angering the Lyran Alliance and making some of Victor's subordinates nervous about Combine aggression.

Just when the Inner Sphere needed to be united it was falling apart.

Focht sighed wearily. "I hope my mission to Morges will help clarify what's going on with the Clans. If Ulric is alive and still in control, we have no need for alarm. It he's not, then the next leader the Clans choose will have the power to repudiate the truce. Fortunately for us, the Clan Khans will have to return to their homeworld—a place they call Strana Mechty—to elect a new ilKhan. That bought us nearly a year of peace during the invasion."

"But we can't count on them doing that this time, can we?"

Focht shifted his shoulders uncomfortably. "Anticipate, yes, but rely on, no."

She nodded. "Then would it be imprudent for us to begin to rotate my more experienced troops forward and bring the green troops back here for training? The orientation ops with the Lancers would provide some solid work for our people."

"True, but that would leave the defense of Terra in the hands of the Lancers, the Sandhurst Training Regiment, and your green troops. You will forgive me if that does not contribute to my peace of mind."

"But the Clans will have to work through the rest of the Com Guards in the Free Rasalhague Republic to get here. If they can do that, the number and nature of troops we have warding Terra will be largely immaterial."

"The Clans are not the only threat we face."

Lisa blinked with surprise. "You can't mean you think any of the Houses of the Inner Sphere would attack Terra."

Focht shrugged. "What Sun-Tzu Liao will do is anyone's guess, and Katrina Steiner is not proving to be terribly predictable either. My concern, however, is less over the aggressive tendencies of the Inner Sphere's rulers than with the possible actions our former brethren might take."

"Word of Blake."

"Exactly."

The resolution of the war against the Clans had split ComStar as seriously as it had allowed the Inner Sphere to fragment. Under the direction of Primus Sharilar Mori and Precentor Martial Anastasius Focht, ComStar had gone from being a cultish organization steeped in mysticism to a largely secular organization that maintained interstellar communications and used the bulk of its troops to secure Rasalhague's border with the Clans. This reversed centuries of tradition—tradition begun when Jerome Blake founded ComStar back in the 2700s.

The reactionary element of ComStar broke away and fled to the Free Worlds League. Thomas Marik, the League's ruler and a former ComStar Precentor, had welcomed the refugees. He had kept them and their actions from getting out of hand, but he did use Word of Blake agents to supplement his anemic intelligence agency, SAFE. Word of Blake members made noises about declaring Thomas "Primus in exile," but had yet to do so. ComStar's analysts assumed that would wait until Thomas made the League a Blakean theocracy or the Blakers somehow took control of Terra.

"I can see them as a threat, sir, but I think you would agree that the Clans are the more immediate and more likely one. Taking steps to deal with them should be our paramount concern."

Focht gave her an approving smile. "You're right, Precentor, but premature with your ideas of troop rotations. A decision on that can wait until after I visit Morges. I will send you what reports I can, including combat video and battle analyses. Perhaps you will find something you can use to surprise the Lancers."

"I would hope so, sir."

"So would I, Precentor. I have considered moving you into a command position with our Invader Galaxy, if you would like that."

Lisa hesitated. The Invader Galaxy was a Com Guard unit configured to fight like the Clans, using their doctrines and weapons. Technically speaking the move would be a demotion, for commanding the defense of Terra was a high honor. *But the Invader Galaxy is the unit that will hone the rest of the troops for the day when the invasion begins again.*

"Your offer is an honor, sir." She glanced down for a moment. "I would like time to think on it, if I might. I would want to be sure Terra's defenses are secured before considering such a move, but it is very inviting."

"That's a fair answer to a difficult question. We will speak more on it at a later date."

"Thank you, sir."

Focht looked toward the fire. "You know, there was once a time, ages ago—in another life entirely—when I would have spent a night like this with people I thought were my friends. Safely tucked away in the warmth, a snifter of brandy filling our middles and firing our brains, we'd plan and scheme and dream of what would happen when we managed to influence events to place us at the center of the universe. We looked at gathering power as if it were an end unto itself.

"In those days, at those times, I never thought I would be in this position." The Precentor Martial hesitated, something sparking in his eye. "Or, rather, I assumed that if I were old and able to sit before a roaring fire it would be because I had failed. I saw this as the repose of a powerless man—one who had failed to reach his full potential."

Lisa stared into the fire and saw phantom shapes and shadows immolate each other. "And now?"

"Now I am an old man who succeeded in defeating the greatest threat the Inner Sphere has ever known. I had hoped, in winning a truce that lasted fifteen years, that it would give us time to match the Clan's technological advantages, possibly even exceed them. In the last few years we've made strides, great strides, but now I'm not certain they're enough. And I'm not certain, faced with the threat resurrected, that I'll be able to stop it again."

Lisa looked over at the man who controlled the military might of ComStar. "The Clans will not prevail, Precentor Martial, because they cannot be allowed to prevail."

"A valiant sentiment, Precentor, but hardly armor against their BattleMechs."

"It's not meant to be that, sir." She straightened up and tapped her own breastbone. "The Clans believe in the superiority of their machines and their breeding, but those two things are but aids to the real core of battle inside a warrior. At Tukayyid you made sure we knew that surrender was not possible, so we fought far beyond what anyone would have expected was our capacity to fight. We *had* to win, so we did. So will we win again, with you as our leader, or with another, if need be. You showed us how to win, and in that you realized as much of your potential as any human has a right to realize in one lifetime."

The Precentor Martial unfolded himself from his chair and took Lisa's hand as she stood. He raised it up and lightly kissed her knuckles. "You will forgive me this contravention of military protocol, but you honor me with those words, and a salute seems a cold reward for such thoughtfulness."

She smiled at him and gave his fingers a squeeze before he released her hand. "The man you described yourself as once being was a destroyer. You, sir, are a defender and preserver. I know enough to honor that. And to set it as a goal for myself and my people."

Focht nodded slowly. "The Clans *are* still the greatest threat we have ever faced, but with warriors like you to oppose them, it will never be an insurmountable one, and in that the Inner Sphere should rejoice."

5

So, this is the last of the Wolves, Khan Elias Crichell mused to himself. *He is a wretched beast.* Standing before him was a warrior in a gray jumpsuit with Clan Wolf markings and the left sleeve slit to accommodate the plaster cast encasing his forearm. His flesh had the sallow gray tone befitting a man who had been fighting for months and living the last few days on survival rations.

But his eyes. Vlad's dark eyes burned with life and anger—enough to fill even the large chamber Crichell used for audiences. That anger had been easy to see, even in the holodisk the man had sent to request the audience. Crichell had been tempted to refuse the request, and Vandervahn Chistu had been quick to agree with that. That made Crichell wary, not because of his junior Khan's agreement but because he even deigned to pay attention to so trivial an administrative matter. Normally Vahn seemed bored or even contemptuous at the mention of such things. That it sparked interest of any kind was remarkable.

Crichell leaned back in the tall wooden chair and looked down at the man at the foot of the dais. "Your message indicated you had valuable information for me. How is it that a Wolf who has been buried like a turtle could know something of use to me?"

"I served Ulric Kerensky as aide during the Trial of Refusal—a trial still being waged on Morges."

"Renegades and mercenaries, led by a foundling—they will be swept away."

Vlad smiled in a lopsided way that made Elias feel uncomfortable. "You can wish that, Khan Crichell, but I do not think it will be so. And it would be best for you if it were not." The Wolf bowed his head—less, it seemed, as a gesture of respect than a performer's acknowledgement that he stood before a potential patron. "This is but one of the many things I know that could be of use to you."

"How could it be better for me if the Jade Falcons on Morges lose?"

"Khan Vandervahn Chistu sent the troops that are fighting the exiles there. He sent them over your protest, or so I have learned since my resurrection. If they win, you appear to be a fool. Chistu, having slain Ulric Kerensky, having destroyed the renegades, will win all the glory. He was the one who proclaimed the Absorption of the Wolves into the Jade Falcons, therefore he is seen as the one who subdued the most haughty and arrogant of the Clans. He will have the gratitude of other Khans for this."

Crichell felt the hairs rise at the nape of his neck. He had seen Chistu's maneuverings and knew their import, but he had viewed them as isolated events, not as stages of a single process. With the death of Ulric at Chistu's hands the true extent of his subordinate's planning had crashed in on him. Chistu had obviously gained momentum. It was a foregone conclusion that the next Grand Council would choose an ilKhan from the Jade Falcon Clan. Elias Crichell had assumed he would be the one chosen to lead the Clans in the conquest of the Inner Sphere, but now it looked as if Chistu was more certain to win that honor.

"This is nothing I did not know, and I do not find your insights particularly valuable."

Vlad shrugged. "I did not mean *that* to be valuable. If you had found it valuable you would be too stupid to see the value of what I *can* offer you."

"And, aside from insolence, that would be . . . ?"

The Wolf's smile broadened evenly, and Crichell did not find it any more pleasant than before. "I will give you the means to destroy Khan Vandervahn Chistu. Utterly and completely. From this moment forward, he is no longer your rival. Your path to the position of ilKhan is clear."

Vlad's words came so coldly and precisely that Crichell almost let the spark of joy in his heart show, but he restrained himself. "The only way you could do that is to kill him."

"No, there is another way, but I do prefer the more lethal alternative." The Wolf tapped himself on the chest with his right hand. "I will eliminate Khan Chistu for you, and do it in a manner that will raise no questions of impropriety. In return you will give me two things."

"And those are?"

"The first one is this: I ask of you the right to challenge Khan Vandervahn Chistu to a Trial of Refusal. Because I do not have a bloodname, my challenge to do combat with a bloodnamed warrior of a Clan must have the sanction of a Clan Khan." Vlad balled his right hand into a fist. "You see, I was there when Ulric was slain, and I dispute Khan Chistu's account of the circumstances surrounding his death."

Elias Crichell leaned forward, barely able to believe his ears. "You are saying that Vandervahn Chistu lied about killing Kerensky?"

"I am, and I have proof of my accusation. I recorded the battle—the ambush, the *murder*. That proof has been hidden well away and will be made available to you if I do not succeed in slaying him in single combat." Vlad's eyes glittered coldly. "You must understand why I make this request. I was there to ward Ulric and I failed in that duty. I should have anticipated treachery and I did not. The only way I can remove this blot on my honor is to kill the man who put it there."

Elias Crichell sat back and gave Vlad the hint of a smile. Aside from the obligatory formality of an annual Trial of Position in a 'Mech that qualified him as a warrior and allowed him to maintain his rank within the Clan, he had long since forsaken combat. Even so, he was not so old that he could not remember when the passion for vengeance had burned in his veins. This request by a Wolf to redeem his honor surprised Elias, for he had long believed that no Wolf clung to the true ways of the Clans—the way exemplified by the Jade Falcons and their strict code of conduct and warfare.

"You speak more like a Falcon than a Wolf, Star Captain Vlad."

"Is that not what all Wolves have become?" Vlad opened his arms. "This last act by a Wolf should be one based on honor, *quiaff*?"

"Aff." Crichell nodded. "I grant you permission to challenge Chistu, but beware. Because you do not have a bloodname and he is a Khan, he is within his rights to name a surrogate to fight you in his place."

"I understand the rules governing this sort of challenge and will abide by them."

"Good." The Jade Falcon Khan shifted in his seat. "And the second thing you will want from me?"

"If I succeed, you will know what it is."

"And if you fail?"

"Then you get what you want at only half the cost." The Wolf had let his arms drop, but he stood tall. "You will be meeting with Khan Chistu here, later today?"

"I will."

"Good, I will challenge him at that time." Vlad gave Crichell a salute. "I will see you then."

The Jade Falcon Khan raised a hand. "Wait."

"Sir?"

"Once you have slain Khan Chistu, what reason have I to uphold the other half of the bargain we have struck—the half I know nothing about?"

The lopsided grin returned. "You will uphold it, sir. You will see the wisdom in doing so."

"How can you be so certain?"

"Khan Crichell, I am willing to kill a man to avenge a dead leader from a dead Clan whose policies I found repugnant and opposed with every fiber of my being." Fire burned deep in Vlad's eyes. "Deny me what I want and you will discover how truly dangerous I can be."

Vlad found it curious that upon his return to Khan Crichell's headquarters he felt less like a bleeding man diving into a shark tank than he did an executioner come to dispatch a wretched prisoner. Two towering Elementals opened the doors for him. Vlad entered the room, setting his feet on the strip of red carpet leading to Crichell's throne, then waited for the doors to close behind him.

He executed a sharp turn to the left—turning away from

the empty throne—and offered a salute to Elias Crichell and the other three people seated around the Khan's desk. Though he had never met any of the trio, he recognized them all. Kael Pershaw, head of the Jade Falcon arm of the Watch, was the misshapen humanoid thing sitting at Crichell's left hand. More machine than man, Pershaw had been a legend among the Falcons for as long as Vlad had been aware that Clans other than the Wolves existed. That the Falcons had repaired and replaced so much of him suggested that Pershaw had value, but Vlad believed that if the man had truly been legend material, he'd have no need for all the cybernetics keeping him alive.

The woman, who had been seated with her back to the door, turned and stood. Marthe Pryde's high forehead and sharp chin gave her face a triangular shape softened somewhat by the fullness of her lips. As tall as he was but decidedly more slender, she had the greyhound physique the Jade Falcons favored in breeding their MechWarriors. The youngest of the Falcons at the table, she also had the most promise. *And her eyes promise the most danger.*

The final member of the quartet was regarding him curiously. Khan Vandervahn Chistu's steel-gray hair and matching goatee bracketed a broad-featured face with a nose that spread out from numerous breaks. His cold eyes looked dead, which struck Vlad as a positive omen. Shorter than Marthe Pryde and thicker of limb, he sat back, seemingly without a care in the world. *He already believes himself to be ilKhan.*

Chistu smiled casually. "So this is the last Wolf?"

"It is good to meet you again, saKhan Chistu."

The Falcon's junior Khan slowly straightened up in his chair. "We have not met before."

"Face to face, no, but on Government Hill here in Borealtown, we did. I was there. I survived. I know what you did." Vlad nodded toward Khan Crichell. "This morning I asked Khan Crichell for permission to challenge you to personal combat to settle our differences."

"Our differences?"

Crichell laid a hand on Chistu's shoulder. "This last of the Wolves disputes your telling of how Ulric Kerensky met his death."

Blood drained from Chistu's face.

Vlad nodded slowly. "That is the least of the differences I have with you, Khan Chistu. I demand a Trial of Refusal."

"Disputing Ulric's death?"

Vlad watched the fear in Chistu's eyes, thinking the man was probably plumbing the depths of his predicament right now. In ambushing Ulric Kerensky he had broken any number of the strict mores that defined honor for the Jade Falcons. The ambush in and of itself was a gross violation of their code of conduct. Added to that was a transgression that only the Falcons recognized: he had used an entire unit to destroy one foe. While Vlad and the Wolves might view the tactic as a suitable use of military resources, the reactionary Falcons thought one-on-one combat the soul of military dignity.

Disclosure of these sins threatened to do more than prevent Chistu from becoming ilKhan. The Jade Falcons would, very likely, strip him of Clan and military rank. The House of Chistu might even undertake a Ritual of Abjuration and expel him from it. Worse yet, his genetic heritage would end with him.

Vlad slowly nodded. *The problem with grasping for a prize placed so highly, Khan Chistu, is that the fall that results from failure is that much more tragic.* Fighting Vlad for his honor in this matter would be taken as an admission that there had been, in some way, irregularities in the Khan's report of Ulric's death. Chistu had to know that Vlad would only have been granted permission to fight him because he had been able to substantiate his claim, so he already found himself poised and teetering on the brink of oblivion.

Chistu looked up. "You said that was the least of our differences."

"I did."

"And the greatest of them is?"

Vlad smiled slowly. "You made a Trial of Refusal into a Trial of Absorption."

Chistu's eyes sharpened. "And you dispute this as well?"

"I do."

Vandervahn Chistu stood. "Then you shall have your Trial of Refusal. We shall fight to settle the issue of the Absorption."

"No!" Crichell pounded a fist on his desk. "I granted permission for this battle based on the accusation concerning Ulric's death. I revoke that permission and without it you cannot challenge a Khan."

Chistu smiled all teeth at his superior. "But, Elias, you forget, *I* am a Khan as well. *I* grant his request to challenge me—to challenge me over the issue of the Absorption." The junior Khan looked at Vlad. "Is this acceptable to you?"

"Bargained well and done, Khan Chistu." By fighting Vlad in dispute of Absorption, Chistu was admitting to a much lesser offense, one involving interpretations of Grand Council regulations, not the customs that defined the Jade Falcons. His shifting the trial to the Absorption also made conspiratorial confederates of all the other Falcons who had welcomed the co-opting of the Wolves, shifting the blame from Chistu alone to the Clan as a whole.

"Well bargained and done, Vlad of the Wolves." Chistu clasped his hands at the small of his back. "I am the challenged party, so I choose to fight you from a BattleMech. And I even waive the right to have a second represent me."

The Wolf smiled. "You waived that right by accepting my challenge yourself, Khan Chistu."

"So I did. Where will you have us fight?"

"Government Hill suited your purposes before." Vlad opened his arms. "I will await you there."

"Done."

Vlad nodded, then looked at Crichell. The outrage in the man's eyes almost prompted a laugh from Vlad. *Yes, now you know what the second half of our bargain is—I rid you of your rival and you give me back my Clan. You sought to use my ambition as a means to further your ambition, and now you will pay a price for your arrogance.*

Admiration and loathing mixed in Marthe Pryde's eyes, making her that much more interesting to him. She had apparently pieced together how Vlad had successfully played one Khan off against the other. This impressed her. The hatred in her expression, though, he could not so easily fathom. *Is it me she has no use for, or the political jostling that left her Clan's leaders open to a challenge by the last Wolf? The latter, I hope, for she will be an implacable enemy.*

Vlad spun on his heel and marched toward the doors. *An*

implacable enemy, but still no more than a Falcon. One of their Khans shall die for getting in my way. More Falcons can follow as easily as not, and I will be pleased if many more do.

6

Borealtown
Wotan
Jade Falcon Occupation Zone
14 December 3057

Vlad shifted on the command couch of the *Warhawk* he had borrowed from a former Wolf. He felt uneasy in the cockpit, though not because of the cast on his arm. He had broken away the plaster around his palm so he could grasp the portside targeting joystick in his left hand. He felt occasional twinges of pain when moving the hand—and he knew his arm would have to be rebroken and reset after the fight—but he anticipated no difficulty in fighting Khan Vandervahn Chistu.

His discomfort came at seeing how quickly all traces of Clan Wolf had been erased from Wotan and, presumably, the rest of Clan territory. The *Warhawk* had seen action on the tenth, yet four days later was already repaired and repainted with Jade Falcon colors. His own neurohelmet had been cracked in the fighting, so now he wore one painted green. He knew it was identical to the gray one he'd left in the carcass of his *Timber Wolf,* but somehow it didn't feel right.

He forced such thoughts from his mind as Chistu marched his *Gladiator* to the top of Government Hill. The Battle-Mech looked exactly as it had the moment Vlad first saw it on the night Ulric died. Pristine and daunting, the humanoid 'Mech had a blockiness to it that reminded Vlad of Chistu himself. Its left arm ended in the muzzle of its most powerful weapon, an Ultra autocannon capable of spitting out enough ordnance at close range to rip any of his *Warhawk*'s limbs clean off. The right arm carried the extended-range particle projection cannon that provided the 'Mech's longer-range punch. The extended-range small laser completed its weapons inventory. The small laser was virtually useless in combat—at least to cause serious damage. In the battle against Ulric it had been converted to provide targeting data used by other Falcons to launch multiple missiles at the ilKhan.

The *Warhawk,* by contrast, did not even begin to approximate humanoid in appearance. The legs bent backward at the knees and the torso thrust forward over the heavy, clawlike feet. Slender, short arms supported weapons' pods that hung parallel to the 'Mech's prominent torso. The pilot rode in the 'Mech's head, set more toward the center of the torso, taking a position that put him closer to his enemy than his weapons. The inhuman form of the 'Mech left no question that this was anything but a machine created to thrive in the inhumanity of warfare.

Vlad had chosen his 'Mech carefully. It carried more armament than Chistu's *Gladiator* and had a somewhat tighter targeting profile. Its twin extended-range PPCs gave it double the *Gladiator*'s long range power. It also carried two large pulse lasers, which again increased the 'Mech's ability to strike from a distance. If Vlad could keep the fight outside the range where the autocannon could devastate his 'Mech, and manage to disable the extended-range PPC on the *Gladiator*'s right arm, Chistu could do nothing serious to hurt him.

And I have a targeting computer. The targeting computer would let him concentrate the damage done by his weapons, *if* the program came up with a correct firing solution. In the heat of battle, with both 'Mechs moving and reacting to a legion of inputs, getting a successful firing solution was not a sure thing. But if the computer kicked in at the right time, the fight would end quickly.

If not, it will just take me longer to kill him. Vlad keyed his radio. "I am Star Captain Vlad, of the Wolves. I am here to challenge Khan Vandervahn Chistu to refuse the Absorption of my Clan into the Jade Falcons."

"And I am Khan Vandervahn Chistu of the Jade Falcons,

here to answer this challenge. Let the outcome of this battle establish the truth in this matter."

"Seyla!" Vlad hit a switch and his targeting system reduced a 360-degree view of the area surrounding his 'Mech to a 160-degree holographic arc hanging in the cockpit before him. Red bars defined the edges of his forward firing arc. Golden cross hairs hung in the middle of the hologram, then drifted down to cover Chistu's *Gladiator*.

Chistu's voice crackled through the speakers in the neurohelmet. "Somehow it is fitting we fight here." The previous fighting had blackened the entire hilltop and had leveled the various government buildings surrounding what had once been a circular park. When Vlad had first seen it, the Hellenistic architecture had made the area look like an Olympian paradise.

And the ambush that killed Ulric reduced it to a charnel field. Vlad smiled as a red dot pulsed in the middle of his cross hairs and a tone sounded in the cockpit. "Indeed, Vahn Chistu, for this is a place already anointed with the blood of a Khan."

As the *Gladiator* took a step forward, Vlad hit his triggers. The PPCs' azure lightning stabbed into the right side of the *Gladiator*'s chest and played along its right arm. Molten ferro-ceramic armor bubbled up and dripped off the 'Mech, gushing down its side. The *Warhawk*'s twin large pulse lasers shot volleys of green energy darts at the distant target. They lanced through the armor froth on the *Gladiator*'s right arm, stripping away the last of the armor. Their energy unspent, they began frying both the ferrotitanium bones and myomer fibers that made the arm useful.

A wave of heat flooded the *Warhawk*'s cockpit. In firing all of his weapons Vlad had strained the 'Mech's capacity to shunt away excess thermal energy. The stink of hot plastic filled his nose. He knew his choice of tactics was risky, and that it could do as much damage to him as to his foe, but the harder he hit Chistu initially, the shorter the fight would be overall. And the less chance Chistu would have of hurting him.

The Jade Falcon Khan somehow managed to keep his 'Mech upright, despite the gross balance shift caused by losing nearly three tons of armor. The PPC in the *Gladiator*'s right arm flashed back at the *Warhawk*. The blue beam devil-danced up the right arm, flensing off nearly a ton of ferro-fibrous armor. That reduced the armor on that part of Vlad's 'Mech by more than fifty percent, but still left it protected against another onslaught.

Taking care to manage the heat in his 'Mech, Vlad shot at the *Gladiator* with only his PPCs while pulling his 'Mech back to keep it at his optimum range. Both beams slashed through armor on the *Gladiator*'s chest. One peeled layers of armor from over the 'Mech's heart, while the other cerulean lance pierced the 'Mech's right flank. Hideous flashes of light lit the interior of the torso and a puff of smoke surrounded the ER small laser mounted on the 'Mech's right side.

Vlad smiled as his computer indicated Chistu's 'Mech was suddenly putting out a lot more heat. *The shot inside the torso must have damaged the shielding on his engine. It's over and he knows it.*

Chistu shot back at the *Warhawk* with his own particle projection cannon, a bolt of synthetic lightning striking the 'Mech's left side. Ferro-fibrous armor plates cascaded down toward the ground from the wound, leaving a smoking trail to mark the 'Mech's line of retreat. With damage done to the left side and the right arm of his 'Mech, Vlad couldn't shift to present an unblemished target to Chistu. *Tactics be damned, I have no desire to contribute to Vahn Chistu's conceit by even suggesting he has hurt me with his attacks.*

Vlad slid the gold cross hairs over to cover the tattered outline of the *Gladiator*. When the red dot pulsed in the middle of the cross, he tightened down on his triggers and fired all four weapons. Only one of the PPCs and one of the lasers hit, both sizzled into the blackened hole on the right side of the *Gladiator*'s torso. Explosions spat out half-melted bits and pieces of the 'Mech's internal structures. The 'Mech's right arm, bereft of support, pulled away and fell smoking to the ground. Armor over the 'Mech's heart began to boil away, all but stripping the 'Mech's center torso of protection.

More devastating than that was Chistu's inability to compensate for the loss of the 'Mech's arm and the collapse of the right side of the chest. The *Gladiator* lurched forward, then stumbled and fell. It crashed down on its chest, then rolled over to the right before sliding to a stop with a mound of burned turf and earth hunched up on its shoulder.

Vlad waited for the suffocating heat in his cockpit to begin to drain away, then he spitted the downed 'Mech's left arm with his cross hairs. He hit the triggers on his lasers twice in quick succession. As the stricken *Gladiator* tried to use that arm to lever itself up off the ground, burst after burst of green laser needles blasted through it. They vaporized all the armor, then tore the arm off at the elbow. With it went the autocannon, leaving the *Gladiator* utterly defenseless.

The last of the Wolves walked his 'Mech forward. He configured his radio to tight-beam messages to Chistu's 'Mech, then he keyed the mike. "You must have known you would not prevail—or did the Jade Falcon's legendary arrogance insulate you from reality?"

Chistu laughed. "I handled you well enough four days ago."

Vlad tensed for a moment, then smiled. "True enough, but I was taken as much by surprise that night as you were today. On the tenth I came here to watch Ulric kill you. Today *I* came to kill you. I already knew what your 'Mech could do, and that is why I chose this 'Mech and this battlefield. You had lost before the first shot was fired."

"A Wolf would be foolish enough to believe that is true."

"And a Falcon is foolish enough to believe it is not."

"So now you think you have won your Clan's freedom." Vlad could hear muted mirth in Chistu's voice. "How long do you think it will be before some other Clan is granted a Trial of Absorption?"

Vlad's *Warhawk* came to a stop ten meters from the prostrate *Gladiator*. "It is of no consequence to you, Vandervahn Chistu, because the Grand Council will never let the Jade Falcons win the bidding to absorb us. I still have the guncamera video of your treachery and cowardice in murdering Ulric Kerensky. If I make that available to the Grand Council, the Falcons will win no bids for a very long time."

Vlad paused, letting the words sink in. "And if I couple it with evidence that Elias Crichell let me kill you to eliminate a rival to his becoming ilKhan, well, that ends his career, *quiaff*?"

Fatigue slowed Chistu's reply. "You have thought long on all this."

"I have thought long on many things, but how to deal with the Jade Falcons is not one of them. You Falcons require little thought."

"Oh, I think you underestimate us. You are a fool to think you and your Clan can dismiss us so easily."

"Perhaps, Vahn Chistu, but I will have plenty of time to learn how to deal with the Jade Falcons."

"But will your Clan have time enough to let you learn?" Chistu's voice took on a sinister edge. "Time is what you may not have, but you do have other means at your disposal."

"I do?"

"Let me be your advisor."

"What?"

"Think of it. Elias Crichell delivered me to you, and I can do the same to him. I know his secrets and his weaknesses. With me as your advisor, he would be as nothing to you. You could destroy him in an eyeblink."

Vlad's smile grew. "But how can you become my advisor?"

"You have defeated me. Make me your bondsman."

"You, a Jade Falcon Khan, would be willing to become my bondsman, *quineg*?"

"Yes. Together we can destroy Crichell."

"Interesting."

"You will find me very useful and resourceful."

"I already know how resourceful you are, Vandervahn Chistu." Vlad reached out with his 'Mech's right arm and tapped the cockpit canopy gently with the muzzle of the arm's large laser. "I have already seen how resourcefully you dealt with Ulric, remember?"

"But you can have my skills for your own."

"I think my skills are sufficient, Khan Chistu."

"And so you will just kill me?"

"Aff, as I have ever planned to do."

"Then why all this talk?"

Vlad dearly wished Chistu could see the smile on his face. "I wanted to know how far a Jade Falcon Khan would sink to save his life. You have offered to become my slave and betray your Clan. I think that is low enough."

"You need me, you can't trust Crichell."

"No, Chistu, I know I cannot trust *you*." Vlad triggered his large pulse lasers, unleashing a torrent of green energy bolts at the *Gladiator*'s head. The popping and cracking of armor plates and the hiss of super-heated steam drowned out any final scream Chistu might have made.

The *Warhawk* stepped back, and Vlad looked down at the black smoke pouring from what had once been the *Gladiator*'s face. "You see, Khan Chistu, Elias Crichell has yet to prove himself unworthy of my trust. That is why he still lives. I suspect, though, he will not live long."

7

Borealtown
Wotan
Jade Falcon Occupation Zone
15 December 3057

As he waited at one end of the grand hall of Khan Elias Crichell had chosen for the ceremony, Vlad's face burned. The warriors who ringed the hall had all been Wolves and most could claim to be bloodnamed. They had once stood as he did now, awaiting the first battle in the Trial of Bloodright to win one. Those who were close enough to see Vlad's flush might have wondered if he shied at being the focus of so much attention, or at having the Khans of Clan Jade Falcon presiding over the ceremony.

Those things were not what gave birth to the color rising in his cheeks.

Once before he had entered a bloodname contest. He had slain the four foes he faced as the field of candidates narrowed from thirty-two to two. His final enemy was a man he had defeated in combat, and who had defeated him, both in 'Mechs and in hand-to-hand combat. Their final fight would decide who was supreme between them, and the bloodname of Ward would be the prize won in that battle.

Phelan Kell, a freebirth whom Vlad had captured and brought into Clan Wolf, had risen from bondsman to warrior and been declared eligible to compete for the Ward bloodname. Vlad had hated Phelan and everything he represented. The other's successes put the lie to the Clans' belief in the superiority of their warriors. Phelan was the antithesis of the Clan way, and Vlad had wanted to kill him even more than he wanted the bloodname for which they competed.

Vlad did not prevail that day. Defeated, battered, and bruised, he'd lain in the dust of Tukayyid and had asked Phelan to kill him. "You are a warrior. Kill me."

"You do not get it, *quiaff*?" Phelan had looked down at him with abject pity. "I am *more* than a warrior. Maybe you will understand what that means by the time you win your bloodname."

Oh, I do understand, Phelan. Though it shamed Vlad to admit it even to himself, Phelan had been right. Being warriors was what the people of the Clans were bred and born to be. Vlad could no more *not* be a warrior than he could sprout wings and fly. The essence of warrior was impressed into every fiber of his being, tangled in the strands of his DNA. Being a warrior was as natural to him as breathing.

Becoming *more* than a warrior called for something else, the calm of vision and a sense of destiny. Vlad had never doubted that he had the makings of a great leader for his Clan, and perhaps for *all* the Clans. Realizing that destiny meant taking aim at what he dreamed with clarity and determination. Slaying enemies to guarantee his genetic material a place in the breeding program was not enough. He had to look beyond, to shaping the future in which his genes would be bred, and that meant identifying and eliminating all who stood in his way.

But the first step is winning my bloodname.

On the dais at the far end of the room, Elias Crichell stepped forward and away from Marthe Pryde, newly named as saKhan of the Jade Falcons. "I am the Oathmaster and accept responsibility for representing House Ward here. Do you concur in this?"

The word *seyla* echoed through the hall as all present answered his question. At another time, in another place, the acknowledged head of the Ward bloodline would have presided over the conclave, but Phelan Kell Ward had been exiled through the Ritual of Abjuration. Crichell had insisted on acting as Oathmaster, and Vlad had not gainsaid him.

"Then what transpires here shall bind us all until we shall fall." Crichell's expression sharpened and his speech slowed as he worked his way through the Wolf formula for the ritual instead of the more formal rite used by the Jade Falcons.

"You, Vlad, represent the best of House Ward and your Clan, yet it is not for your Clan you battle here today. You fight for the right and honor of bearing the name Ward, and it is a Bloodright especially revered. The Ward name is exalted, as were those of all who remained loyal to Aleksandr Kerensky's dream. Do you understand this?"

"Seyla," Vlad replied. Every child in every sibko knew how Aleksandr Kerensky had believed he could end the conflicts that had destroyed the Star League and devastated the human race by leading his people far from the Inner Sphere to make their home in distant, uncharted regions of space. But conflict had followed them. Nicholas, Aleksandr's son, saw the solution. Six hundred warriors joined him in pacifying their warring people and thus were born the Clans and their ways. The name of each of those six hundred loyal warriors was transformed into an honorific that could be bestowed on his progeny, though only twenty-five warriors at any one time could claim a Bloodright.

The pedigree of a particular Bloodright was very important, for it formed the tradition that each new holder of that line tried to further. In some cases a Bloodright had a poor Bloodheritage because of a disgrace—much as Vandervahn Chistu's Bloodright would now bear. Crichell had chosen to let Vlad fight for the Bloodright last claimed by Conal Ward, a bold Wolf warrior who had shared Crichell's political views and who had been murdered by Phelan Ward.

Crichell nodded solemnly. "In accepting your part in this battle do you realize that you sanctify, with your blood, Nicholas Kerensky's determination to forge the Clans into the pinnacle of human development? That you have been chosen to participate marks you as elite, but victory here will rightly place you among the few who exist as the zenith of what the Clans hold sacred."

Vlad nodded. "Seyla."

"Tell us, Vlad, why you are worthy of this honor."

Vlad tugged at the edge of the gray gloves he wore and let the gray Wolf Clan leathers squeak mutely, to remind the former Wolves dressed in Jade Falcon green that he alone remained faithful to their roots. "I am worthy because I have been denied. I am worthy because I have persevered in the face of adversity. I have slain our enemies and followed the commands of our leaders. I have effaced blemishes from our honor."

Crichell appeared a bit puzzled by his answer, and Vlad assumed this was because Jade Falcon candidates were well known for reciting a long list of combats and victories extending back even to their days in the sibko, long before they had attained the rank of warrior. The list of conflicts was meant to identify each warrior, and tended to be unique, like fingerprints. Vlad's response was unorthodox, even by Wolf standards, yet there was no question among those in attendance about who he was or why he was being so honored.

"Your claims have substance and have been verified." Crichell casually waved Vlad forward. "You shall now face your first foe."

Ten meters in front of Vlad a young man stepped from the crowd and took up a position on the red carpet linking Vlad and the dais. He wore a green jumpsuit and towered above Vlad. His hulking, muscular form marked him unmistakably as an Elemental, though Vlad did not recognize the man. In keeping with Elemental tastes, he wore his fair hair in a long queue, with his head otherwise shaved.

Vlad approached and stopped with barely a meter between them.

Elias Crichell's voice filled the hall. "Why are you worthy?"

The Elemental's eyes tightened. "I represent sixteen who are not worthy."

Because of what Vlad had done to free the Wolves from the Falcons, no one in the House Ward wished to stand against him in the Trial of Bloodright, yet Clan tradition would not permit the bestowing of a bloodname without some sort of contest. Each person he faced would stand as surrogate for all those who would have lost in the five rounds of the contest. All Vlad was required to do was to tap his opponent on the shoulder and he would be allowed to pass.

Vlad reached down and slipped a wolf's-head-pommel dagger from the sheath in his right boot. Straightening up, he took the Elemental's queue in his left hand and pulled down roughly on it, tilting the man's head back. As the Elemental's chin rose he exposed his throat. Vlad pressed the dagger's silver blade to the pale flesh below the Adam's apple. He used enough pressure that a slight slip of the blade left a slender crimson line in its wake.

Vlad released him abruptly, and the Elemental stood aside.

Next in line came one of the small, frail-bodied, large-headed warriors who piloted the Clan's aerospace fighters. She announced that she stood for eight who were not worthy, and Vlad similarly bloodied her throat. After her came a MechWarrior who took the place of four who were not up to the challenge of winning Vlad's bloodname.

Vlad moved on and unsurped Crichell by asking the next foe, "Why are you worthy?"

The MechWarrior shook her head. "I am surrogate for two who are not worthy." Even before Vlad could grab a handful of her black hair, she raised her chin and presented her throat to him. He pressed the tip of the blade to her throat long enough for a single incarnadine droplet to flow down toward the hollow between her breasts, then he let her withdraw and continued on to his last foe.

Vlad again overrode Crichell's with his own. "Why is it you are *not* worthy?"

The Elemental's eyes grew wide at the question, then his face hardened. "I am not worthy for you alone, Vlad, are a Wolf in heart, mind, and soul. My life is yours to take." The taller man tore open his jumpsuit, bared his chest, and solemnly closed his eyes. "Still this unworthy heart and assume that which is rightly yours."

Vlad reversed the knife in his hand, then raised it, poised to plunge it into the man's chest. A few voices rose in shock as the dagger hovered at the apex of a fatal arc—Khan Elias Crichell's voice foremost among them. Vlad waited, letting the thrill running through him send a vibration into the knife. The blood already gathered on the blade ran toward the tip and dripped off to join the red of the carpet.

Flipping the dagger around, Vlad brought his hand down and thumped the wolf's-head pommel against the Elemental's breastbone. Shocked, the man collapsed and Vlad pounced, straddling his chest before he could even open his eyes. Vlad took hold of the man's black braid and raised his head up off the floor.

"Were I *just* a warrior, I would have slain you. I am *more*." Vlad brandished the dagger and, turning it back and forth, looked past its bloodied tip at those assembled in the hall. "Today I am become Vladimir Ward. I am more than I was, yet less than I will become. Mark this day. Mark these events. From this point forward Nicholas Kerensky's designs will be fulfilled through me and my people."

He released the Elemental's hair, then stepped over him. As he looked up he saw Elias Crichell staring hard at him. Marthe Pryde's eyes were on him as well, but her gaze showed none of the anger and surprise of Crichell's. *She watches me as I have watched enemies. Just as I know Phelan to be the antithesis of the Clans, so she knows me as the antithesis of the Jade Falcons. She sees what Crichell will not allow himself to see.*

Elias Crichell descended to the first of the three steps leading to the top of the dais. Vlad swept past him, then turned. He took the hand Crichell had extended in congratulations and used it to guide the Jade Falcon Khan back up on to the dais. Vlad raised the bloodied dagger above his head.

Crichell freed his hand from Vlad's grip, then turned and backed away a step, but did so without seeming to escape or flee. "Trothkin near and far, seen and unseen, alive and dead, be of brave hearts. Another of your number has been blooded. I present to you Vladimir of the Wards."

"Seyla," shouted those in attendance.

Crichell held his hands up to silence the scattered applause. "Your Bloodright, Vlad, is one of especial honor. It is the only one unsullied by the Abjuration—it has forever been loyal to the Clans. It has been open since its previous holder was brutally murdered by a Wolf Khan. I knew Conal Ward. Despite Clan enmities, he was a friend of mine. It makes me proud to think of you inheriting the Bloodright that was meant for you."

Do you think you will exert control over me so easily, Elias? Vlad stared at him blankly, then shook his head. "That is not the Bloodright for which I fought."

"But, the others . . ."

Vlad nodded slowly. "Yes, you thought I sought a Bloodright untouched, untainted by the departure of disloyal Wolves. I can see how this would be of concern for you and the Jade Falcons, for you cling to your honor most tightly. Where you would avoid even the hint of taint, I have chosen to wallow in it. It is my intention to fully redeem a soiled Bloodright."

The Wolf slowly lowered his right hand and thrust his dagger home into his boot. He straightened up, then looked out at the audience before him. "It was my intention to fight for and win the Bloodright I was denied before. I claim the Bloodright of Cyrilla Ward, the Bloodright owned by Khan Phelan before he betrayed us all."

Gasps and nervous laughter dissolved into applause. Color flooded Crichell's cheeks and Marthe's face became an unreadable mask. Vlad smiled and opened his arms, which increased the volume of the cheers.

The elder Falcon Khan snarled at him. "You have won a bloodname, Vlad. You should not act as if it has made you a Khan."

"It has not. Yet. It has merely opened the door for me." Vlad raised an eyebrow at Crichell. "Fulfilling *your* half of our bargain is what will make me a Khan."

Marthe's eyes narrowed. "The Jade Falcons already have two Khans."

"So they do, Khan Marthe." Vlad looked back at Crichell. "I fought to refuse the Absorption. To become a Khan I need a Clan of my own."

Crichell nodded. "The second half of your price."

"Exactly."

"What!"

"Not now, Pryde, not now!" Crichell snapped, then to Vlad, "As you wish it, you shall have it. Actually, you shall have it better than you wish. I will see to that."

Vlad raised his hands, then lowered them, bringing the din to silence. He looked to Crichell. "The floor is yours."

The Jade Falcon bowed his head almost respectfully in Vlad's direction. "Thank you, Vladimir Ward. As you all know, Vlad slew Khan Vandervahn Chistu during a Trial of Refusal over the absorption of the Wolves into the Jade Falcons. This absorption, which was unchallenged for days, was accomplished without protest until Vlad was discovered alive in the rubble of Government Hill. His action on behalf of a Clan that had ceased to exist is worthy of celebration and demands a reward."

Crichell pressed his right hand against his own chest. "I am but one Khan among thirty-two, and limited in my power. What I give Vlad now, what I give all of you in his name, is the most I can offer, and offer it I do, freely and willingly."

"Trothkin, near and far, seen and unseen, dead, alive and only dreamed of, hear me and be bound by what I say." Elias

Crichell seemed to smile, but Vlad read deceit in his eyes. "I renounce the Absorption. You who were once the Wolves and so recently became Jade Falcons, rejoice. I proclaim you all the founders of Clan Jade Wolf. All will abide by the rede given here—so shall it be until we all shall fall."

═══ **8** ═══

Borealtown
Wotan
Jade Falcon Occupation Zone
15 December 3057

The fury blazing in Marthe Pryde's eyes reminded Elias Crichell of a PPC beam. She stalked along beside him, breath jetting steamy streams from her nose, as they headed away from the hall where the Jade Wolves were calling a Clan Council to order. The old man smiled and kept his voice low so that the Elementals pacing them front, back, and to either side would not overhear.

"I cannot tell, Khan Marthe, who was more angered by my announcement: you or Vlad."

She looked down at him sharply. "You gave Vlad but one thing to be angry about. My reasons for anger are legion. I should challenge you to a Trial of Refusal over the creation of that new Clan."

"But you will not."

"No?"

"No." Elias smiled despite the edge in Marthe's voice. He knew she was very close to making good her threat, but he also knew if she had the strength of her conviction she would have challenged him, not warned him. "You know you would win, and I would die. A new Khan would have to be elected in my place and the Wolves—who would be Falcons because of your victory—would promote Vlad into that position. Though you hate politics, even you can see how perilous that would be. By destroying me you would risk destroying the Jade Falcons."

"Ha!" Marthe stared at him, disbelief replacing anger in her eyes. "You are a warrior in name only! You enter an alliance with an unblooded whelp to eliminate a Clan Khan—and you do this because Vahn Chistu had made himself a likelier choice to win the vote for ilKhan. That is *not* the way of the Jade Falcons."

"Perhaps not, Marthe, but it is the way to *preserve* the Jade Falcons."

"And stripping away the Wolves, cutting our strength in half, will preserve us?"

Crichell allowed himself to chuckle, then coughed into his hand as the cold air tickled his throat. "You and Vandervahn Chistu looked only at the military outcome of the war the Wolves waged against us. Yes, they hurt us gravely. We lost many warriors and much equipment. We have yet to pacify some of the worlds the Wolves liberated. Perhaps it would have been convenient to make up our losses with the troops and equipment left behind by Phelan Ward, but it would have destroyed us."

Marthe's brow furrowed. "How would that have come to pass?"

Elias stopped and pointed back toward the hall. "Were you not just with me, *quiaff*? Did you not see how much those Wolves rejoiced in what Vlad had done? Any of those five warriors who stood between Vlad and his Bloodname would have willingly given his life. Each one represented more than just the many foes in a Trial of Bloodright—they represented the shame of the Wolves who failed to step forward and protest the Absorption. With their leaders slain, their best warriors running off to Morges, they believed themselves abandoned and accepted our leadership because they wanted to belong to something instead of nothing."

Marthe folded her arms across her chest. "And so their something was becoming part of our Clan."

"No, they would never have accepted that. For all intents and purposes Vlad conducted his own ceremony in there. He took over as Oathmaster and the questions he asked the surrogates were questions he asked *all* those present. Even now they are electing him Khan of the Jade Wolves. Those people, his people, would never have been content among us. We view them as scornful of traditions that for us are the way of the Clan. They think us too hidebound and rigid to survive. The Wolves could never return to our way."

Marthe hunched forward against a slight breeze and started walking again. "Your words make the Falcons sound inferior to the Wolves."

"Not at all. We *did* win the Trial of Refusal. We beat Ulric. We proved we were superior to the Wolves." Elias nodded at one of the Elementals who held open the door to the building where the Falcons had their headquarters. "By holding to the traditions set down by Nicholas Kerensky we build on a strong foundation. As evolution has shown, most changes result in death. The Wolves might adapt themselves to fight well in rarefied situations, but that means they fight less well in others. Our strength is in our training and our insistence on honoring the fundamentals because when all goes awry—and there is no time in warfare where it does not—basic skills are what prevail."

"You would do well, Khan Elias, to think more on our fundamentals."

"How do you mean?" Elias preceded her into his office and pointed her to one of the chairs near his desk. "What have I done that you find foolish?"

Marthe stopped and looked utterly amazed at the question. "Vlad Ward is a dangerous individual, and you have allowed him to gain power, but not the power he wanted. In doing so you angered him. I believe doing that was not wholly wise."

Elias nodded as he poured himself some brandy to banish the chill of their walk. "You mean by creating Clan Jade Wolf on the spot."

"Indeed. He wanted you to bring back the Wolves and give them to him."

"I know." Crichell moved from the sideboard to his desk and sat. He breathed deeply of the liquor, then held a mouthful on his tongue a second or two before swallowing. "May I offer you some, *quiaff*?"

"Neg." Marthe remained standing with her hands touching the back of a chair. "He will have satisfaction from you over that."

Crichell shook his head. "I believe you are wrong, Marthe. The moment I realized he wanted the Wolves, I also saw the reason he could not have them. He will see it, too—he is not stupid."

"I never thought he was, just lethal."

"Lethal, yes." Elias smiled and sipped a bit more of the brandy. The warmth pooling in his belly slowly spread out to his skin. "Vlad is ambitious and he will realize that working with me, with us, is the best way to further his own ambitions. He will not like it, but there is little he can do about it. He will come to that conclusion soon enough."

Marthe's shoulders rose in a shrug. "I hope, for your sake, that you have neither over- nor underestimated his intelligence."

"I think not. I had not expected him to demand his own Clan—I thought he would ask me to appoint him to Vahn's place at the head of the Turkina Keshik."

"You never seriously considered that, *quiaff?*"

"Be calm, Marthe, don't let your Pryde blood run hot over what never happened." Crichell shook his head. *Valiant though you Prydes are, this preoccupation with the appearances of honor is limiting in the extreme.* "The reaction of the ex-Wolves at the ceremony tonight convinces me that the clan creation was the right thing to do."

Marthe's blue eyes narrowed. "And what convinced you that conspiring to kill Vahn Chistu was the right thing to do?"

Crichell's head came up. "Do not ask questions to which you do not want to know the answers, my Khan. You saw enough of Vahn to know he was positioning himself to supplant me. I assume this has you mildly disgusted. Allow matters to remain there and progress no further."

Her mouth opened, then snapped shut. He saw a shudder ripple across her shoulders, then she looked down at him. "Your agenda, from this point, is . . . ?"

"Simple." Crichell finished the last of the brandy and set the empty snifter on his blotter. "As the victor in the war against the Wolves, I have to report to the Grand Council. I have called a meeting for the second of January. At that time I expect we will elect a new ilKhan, and I shall be pleased to take my rightful place as Khan of Khans, at the head of the final campaign in our return to Terra."

It had taken all the restraint he could muster for Vlad to refrain from reaching out and snapping Elias Crichell's neck. A red curtain had settled over his vision and blood thundered in his ears with each heartbeat. At the pinnacle of his triumph, at the moment the Wolves should have been liberated and given to him, Crichell had spoiled the victory. Crichell had denied him his due.

He will pay for this temerity! Vlad would have struck right then and there, for the cheering and celebration of the Wolves urged him on and made him invincible. He knew he could have killed Crichell with his bare hands and not one of the Wolves present would bear witness against him. They would say that Crichell had attacked first, or that Crichell had been slain by person or persons unknown—whatever Vlad would have asked them.

Only the outrage flashing in Marthe Pryde's eyes gave Vlad pause and let him rein himself in. Her anger, burning so brightly in those blue eyes, was not directed at him but at Crichell himself. *She hates him, despises him. The enemy of my enemy is my friend.*

In control again, Vlad bowed graciously to the Jade Falcon Khan. "You are a most honorable man, Khan Elias Crichell. I bid you leave us now so we may conduct ourselves in a manner befitting a Clan reborn."

"As you wish." Crichell had inclined his head toward Vlad, then he and Marthe Pryde retreated from the hall.

Vlad drifted away from the dais as Marialle Radick assumed a position at center stage and sought to convene a Clan Council. Those Jade Wolf warriors who were pale—unblooded, as Vlad had been before the ceremony—were asked to leave. Others were sent to fetch the few blood-named warriors not already in attendance. Because of the Abjuration and casualties of the recent war, the Clan Council's membership had atrophied from 750 to barely more than 200, but with so many Bloodrights being vacant, the presence of just over one hundred individuals would constitute a quorum.

They can and will elect me Khan of this new Clan. His hands convulsed into fists. *I cannot believe Crichell was so stupid as to deny me the restoration of the Wolves.*

But as Vlad thought on that for a moment, he realized he had drawn a conclusion from insufficient evidence. Though he had no respect for Elias Crichell, the old man's long span as a Jade Falcon Khan suggested he was far from stupid. This, in turn, suggested that he had a reason for doing what he did. Vlad was almost certain Crichell had not anticipated what the other half of his price would be, so the creation of the Clan Jade Wolf would not have been premeditated.

The simple thing would have been to recreate the Wolves. The fact that he did not means there is something else here, something I am overlooking.

Vlad's victory in the Trial of Refusal over the Absorption should have cleared the way for the return of Clan Wolf. In fact, it called into question the legality of the whole Absorption, which the Grand Council had not sanctioned in any event. *They are probably awaiting the outcome of the fighting on Morges before reviewing this situation. With Chistu's death and the creation of the Jade Wolves, Crichell neatly sidesteps any hint of wrongdoing.*

Just as Clan law allowed for Clans to be absorbed, so it allowed for Clans to subdivide. It had never happened before because it would have encouraged the same divisiveness that had torn the Inner Sphere apart. Still, the fact that Nicholas Kerensky had envisioned a time when a Clan might want to undergo fission spoke to his wisdom. Crichell's use of this obscure provision in the regulations that governed all the Clans proved another measure of his understanding of the political side of Clan life.

Yet subdividing does not repudiate the Absorption, it only makes amends for it. Why? Vlad rubbed his forehead with his right hand, then he smiled slowly. *Of course, I should have seen it sooner!*

Khan Crichell could and would argue that the Trial of Refusal Ulric had waged against the Jade Falcons had been lost along with his life here on Wotan. Because Phelan and the other Wolves were fleeing Clan space, the outcome of the fighting on Morges was immaterial to the outcome of the fight on Wotan. The Wolves had been defeated.

Vlad, like so many other Wolves, had seen the Trial of Refusal as Ulric's way of preventing the repudiation of the ComStar truce. Everyone knew that was what the war had truly been about—just as they knew that when Crichell was elected ilKhan he would press for renewal of the invasion. War or peace had been decided by the battling between the Falcons and Wolves, and the Wolves had lost in their bid to protect the truce.

But the Trial of Refusal that had sparked it all was not one based on a decision to repudiate the truce. It was, instead, Ulric's refusal to accept the Grand Council's verdict that he was guilty of the charge of genocide. With the loss of the Trial of Refusal, the whole of Clan Wolf assumed Ulric's guilt. As the Grand Council had done once previously with another Clan, they had the right to order the extermination of Clan Wolf, ending, after so brief a time, Vlad's reign over the Clan he had saved.

So, in thwarting me, he has saved me. Vlad's lips pressed together in a grim smile. *I can learn from this—I have learned from this.*

Applause filled the hall and Vlad looked up. Marialle Radick beckoned him forward. "I present to you Vladimir Ward, the first Khan of the Jade Wolves. He created this Clan, and in doing so restored to us our honor. Long may he lead us."

"Seyla," chanted the Wolves solemnly, and as one.

To achieve this I became more than a warrior. Vladimir Ward smiled. *Now I will become more than a Khan.*

9

Borealtown
Wotan
Jade Falcon Occupation Zone
2 January 3058

Khan Elias Crichell smiled broadly, determined that Marthe Pryde's foul mood would not ruin his day. *The darkness of her thoughts shall make this day brighter by contrast.* "Khan Marthe, I can and *do* intend to see this course all the way through."

Marthe Pryde stared at him, her slender frame almost vibrating with restrained fury. "Elias, never before has an ilKhan been elected away from Strana Mechty. You are acting utterly outside precedent."

His blue eyes, only slightly darker than hers, flared angrily. "Precedent is what lesser men use to sanctify questionable activities. I would prefer to *set* precedent than follow it. We are Jade Falcons. We are meant to lead, and lead we will."

"An illegitimate leader is no leader at all."

"The legitimacy of my leadership is for the Grand Council to decide." Crichell thrust a finger at the door. "In that chamber our fellow Khans are assembling to decide whether or not I shall become the next ilKhan. That decision will be made here, today, and it is best for me, for you, and for our Clan that the decision places me in the fore."

Marthe turned away sharply, her shoulders hunched beneath a tunic of green leather. "Do not attempt to sway me with promises of personal glory, Elias Crichell."

"That was not my intent, Marthe, though personal glory will be yours if I am elected." Crichell refrained from smiling as she peeked back over her shoulder at him. "You know I am not suited to leading the Clans in battle—that I leave for fine warriors like you. When I am ilKhan and resume our crusade . . ."

"Two events that will happen at the same time."

"Hardly."

"What?" Marthe turned back to face him. The malachite and gold pectoral swung slightly out of line, but she shifted it back again with her left hand. "You would delay the start of the Crusade?"

"I would."

"But if you want to become ilKhan to lead it, why not take the time to return to Strana Mechty to make the election a proper thing?"

"Because time is not on our side." Crichell lowered his voice, and Marthe drew closer to hear him. "You are aware of how severely Ulric and Natasha Kerensky hurt us in the recent war."

"I am."

"And now the Wolves have devastated the force we sent to Morges. Star Colonel Mattlov disgraced herself and let her force be destroyed. Even more significant is that the exiled Wolves suffered far less crippling damage. They have retreated to the world of Arc-Royal—once the homeworld of Phelan Ward—and are prepared to defend the Lyran Alliance border against our predations."

"They are but the remnants of a Clan. We can overwhelm them."

Crichell shook his head. "No, we cannot."

"We were that seriously hurt?"

"Ulric did his work well." Elias frowned. "No one else, save you and I, has any idea of just how gravely the Falcons were damaged. Our brethren in the invasion force believe so fervently in the Crusader vision that they cannot conceive of a Warden force being able to overcome our best troops. Because they believe the Wardens' reluctance to press for total conquest of the Inner Sphere is an inferior philosophy, they also believe the Wardens to be inferior warriors."

"Fools."

"Yes, but fools we must use at this critical juncture. In recognition of defeating Ulric, I can be elected ilKhan. It is imperative that I assume the office so that we can buy the handful of years needed to rebuild to our former strength."

Marthe's jaw hung open for a moment. "A handful? We would need a minimum of *fifteen* years for our sibkos to mature sufficiently to provide us the warriors we need."

"Not so, Marthe." Crichell smiled slyly. "Remember, I once did my share of fighting, and it taught me well the destructive capacity of war. I looked ahead, nearly twenty years ago now. What I saw in the future let me plan for just such a moment as this."

"You sound like some dreaming Nova Cat."

"Not dreaming. Thinking. Seeing far and wide with the eyes of a falcon. Then I acted on what I saw." Crichell smiled confidently. "I am having the files sent for you to review and decide the best use of what my far-seeing produced."

"What have you done, Elias?"

"Calm yourself, Marthe, it is not as hideous as you seem to imagine, though I am sure your Pryde sensibilities will be offended at first. Perhaps you will find it more palatable to think of it like a storm front that rolls in and grounds your enemy's aerospace fighters. The weather is there despite your intentions or desires, but you can still use it to your advantage."

"Using weather is one thing, violating our honor as Jade Falcons is quite another." Marthe tapped the pectoral. "You have authorized some program that runs counter to our traditions and you expect me to vote for you as ilKhan? I should denounce you before the Grand Council!"

"You won't do that because my deed will preserve the Jade Falcons, Marthe." Crichell raised himself up to his full height. "What you threaten will destroy us."

She hesitated. "We are Jade Falcons. The other Khans must respect us for that."

"As the Wolves respected the Widowmakers when they absorbed them, and as we respected the Wolves when we absorbed *them*?" Crichell laughed harshly. "At this crucial juncture, we are fighting for *survival,* not respect.

"Think about it, Marthe. We have been bred to fly high and attack weakness where we find it. When the other Clans learn how weakened *we* have become, they will devour us."

Seeing her brow furrow, Crichell knew the shot had hit true. As rigidly as Marthe honored the way of the Clans and the traditions of the Jade Falcons, she could also see how a reluctance to adapt could doom them. Though she believed that honoring the fundamentals was their strength, without enough warriors to fill their ranks and defend their worlds, the Jade Falcons would perish. Given a choice between working with him and the death of the Clan, Marthe took the only logical path open to her.

"The decision whether to use this plan of yours is mine alone, *quiaff*?"

"Of course. All yours, Marthe. You will be pleased, trust me."

"I will never *trust* you, Elias, and never respect you."

"I will try to live without either."

"As ilKhan."

"I think you will find that unless I become ilKhan, your vision for the future of our Clan will wither on the vine." Crichell hefted the gold and green enameled falcon's-head mask he would wear in the Grand Council chamber. "I give you the Clan's future; you give me your vote."

Marthe nodded stiffly. "Bargained and done."

"As a Jade Falcon Khan, I respect you, Marthe. As ilKhan I will exalt you."

"None of that, I beg of you, Elias Crichell." She fixed him with an arctic glare. "It suffices you do not embarrass me."

Following Marthe into the makeshift Grand Council chamber, Crichell nodded at Kael Pershaw seated toward the front of the room. Pershaw rose from his seat behind the wooden desk and hammered his flesh and blood hand against the oaken desktop. "I am Kael Pershaw and have been chosen to act as Loremaster for this gathering of the Grand Council. I hereby convene this conclave under the provisions of the Martial Code handed down by Nicholas Kerensky. Because we exist in a state of war, all matters shall be conducted according to its provisions."

"Seyla," Crichell called out in unison with his fellow Khans. Fourteen Khans were present in person, the other twenty attending via holovid monitors stacked on desks, chairs, and tables around the tiered amphitheater. Of those who had not physically attended the last Grand Council meeting, only the Khans of Clan Diamond Shark had bothered to appear in person this time. Elias took this as a sign that his efforts to persuade the absent Khans to give him their votes had been successful.

Pershaw sat down again and glanced at the screen of the noteputer on the desk. "Today we come together to select a new ilKhan."

Removing his glittering helmet with the dorsal-fin crest, Khan Ian Hawker of the Diamond Sharks stood. Pale, of light eye and lighter hair—like so many of the Hawker line—his expression was severe. "This action is unlawful! The ilKhan has ever been elected on Strana Mechty. Calling an election here and now mocks our ways."

Crichell would have spoken in reply, but Vladimir Ward rose from his place at the far side of the room. He wore the gray leathers of Clan Wolf, though both he and Marialle Radick had added a mantle of jade-green leather over their shoulders. Vlad removed his enameled wolf's-head and set it down in front of him. "I would beg to differ with you, Khan Hawker."

"I am certain you would, *if* you had standing here."

The scar on the left side of Vlad's face burned bright red. "I *do* have standing here, Ian Hawker. As do my Jade Wolves. I have been given, these past two weeks, to studying the Martial Code handed down by Nicholas Kerensky. A fitting task for a newly elected Khan, *quiaff*? I have read carefully the passages providing for the creation of a new Clan—an action that requires *no* approval by this conclave."

Crichell saw fire in the younger man's eyes Vlad let his glance travel over the faces of the gathered Khans before speaking again.

"Neither did my studies turn up any directive that the Grand Council must convene in a specific place in order to select a new ilKhan." Vlad smiled slowly. "Perhaps I might also remind you that this conclave sanctioned a Grand Council meeting to be held on Tamar for the express purpose of unseating a sitting ilKhan. If an ilKhan can be demoted in the field, certainly he can be elected in the field."

Vlad finished speaking and looked directly at the elder Jade Falcon Khan. Crichell nodded in appreciation and Vlad took his seat. *You are learning to play the political game, Vladimir Ward. You have obviously puzzled out why I created a new Clan for you, and it seems you acknowledge yourself in my debt. That is good.*

Lincoln Osis, Khan of the Smoke Jaguars, stood. The

gray creeping into his tightly curled dark hair contrasted sharply with his dusky skin, but his heavily muscled body seemed to defy the ravages of age. Osis was an Elemental, and though standing a row below Hawker, still looked down on the man.

"Your scorn for the pragmatic, Khan Hawker, may make you a good leader among the Diamond Sharks, but it will not help us settle the urgent matter facing us here. The ilKhan is dead and one of us must take his place. Were we to return to Strana Mechty, not only would it remove us from the theater of combat, but it would also give our enemies even more time to prepare. To permit that is both unwise and unnecessary."

Osis turned toward Pershaw and called out for all to hear, "I offer Elias Crichell of the Jade Falcons as a candidate!"

When Severen Leroux, the ancient Khan of the Nova Cats, seconded the call, Elias wondered why. He'd not lobbied the Nova Cats for support because they tended to seek guidance in mystical visions and portents rather than logic. The Nova Cats often acted as if they were agents of fate, and right now he dearly wished he knew what they saw in store for him in the future.

Kael Pershaw punched something into the noteputer. "The name of Elias Crichell of the Jade Falcons has been placed before this conclave. You will each cast a vote aye or nay. If Elias Crichell obtains half plus one of the ayes, he wins the vote. I will poll you individually."

Crichell kept his own tally as the votes were cast. Neither Severen Leroux or Lucian Carns of the Nova Cats explained their votes, but both cast in his favor, so their reasons mattered little to him. Both Diamond Sharks cast against, which he had expected, but the Smoke Jaguars, Steel Vipers, and Jade Falcons voted for, establishing an early six-vote edge toward victory. The Ghost Bears cast against him, but they had long-standing ties with the Wolves and Diamond Sharks. The holo-vote split almost evenly, leaving him a positive two-vote margin when they came down to the newest Clan.

At Vlad's urging, Marialle Radick voted first. "It was I who first brought Ulric's treason to the attention of my Clan. It was I who took the first step on the road that led us here today. I, Marialle Radick, do vote 'aye,' for Elias Crichell."

The old man smiled. *That does it. Vlad's vote makes no difference.*

Vlad stood up, taking a moment to compose himself. "I welcome the selection of Khan Elias Crichell to the post of ilKhan of the Clans. It is my duty, however, to honor the memory of the ilKhan who led our glorious invasion—without whose leadership we would never have come this far in the conquest of the Inner Sphere. His thinking may have been flawed, but none can deny that Ulric Kerensky was a warrior born. I vote 'nay.' "

Pershaw hit one last key on his noteputer and twisted his ruined face into what might have been a smile. "By my tally the vote is seventeen in favor and fifteen against. Let it be proclaimed by the authority of this solemn conclave—Elias Crichell is today named Khan of Khans, the ilKhan of all the Clans!"

"Seyla!" the assembled Khans cried out, and began to thump their desks and tables in approval as Crichell descended to the head of the room and stood behind Pershaw. He removed his helmet and held it in front of him like a short podium. He smiled as the sounds died away, then bowed his head to the other Khans.

"I vow to prove myself worthy of your confidence. *Your* vision for the future is *my* vision for the future—the restoration of the Star League and the elevation of the Clans to our rightful place of rulership in the Inner Sphere, a place only we were born to hold."

He glanced down at Pershaw's noteputer. "And now we take up the crucial question of when to resume our invasion of the Inner Sphere. Yes, Khan Vlad?"

"Forgive my interruption, but there is another matter . . ."

"I thought you would be the one to see this." Crichell nodded indulgently. "You wish to postpone the discussion, *quiaff*? Because of the unexpected loss of my saKhan, I have had insufficient time to prepare an accurate survey of my resources. I assume the same is true for you and your Clan, Khan Vladimir. Shall we postpone the discussion until we have had time to prepare?"

Vlad stood. "I would appreciate that, ilKhan, but a delay is not the other matter I wanted bring to the Grand Council's attention."

"Then what is it?"

The younger man's face sharpened. "I, Vladimir Ward of the Jade Wolves call for a Trial of Refusal."

What? "See here, Vlad, we've had enough of your—"

"You are not fit to lead us, Elias Crichell. You are not fit to be Khan of Khans. I challenge your right to be ilKhan."

10

Borealtown
Wotan
Jade Falcon Occupation Zone
2 January 3058

"**W**hat?"

The incredulity and fear in Crichell's voice infused Vlad with power and made him smile. "You heard me, Elias Crichell. I challenge your qualifications to claim the title of ilKhan. I say you are unsuited."

"You cannot!"

Vlad nodded slowly. "I can. I have."

The older man straighted up. "On what grounds?"

Vlad ran a hand along his jaw. "Are you certain, Elias Crichell, that you wish me to answer that question?"

"He asked and you will answer," snapped Lincoln Osis.

Vlad turned on the Smoke Jaguar. "I am a Khan. You cannot order me to do anything."

Osis glared at him for a moment, then dropped his gaze toward the floor. "I intended no disrespect. Your accusation against the ilKhan is of more import than any ill will you bear him. If he is not fit to serve, we must know why."

"Then know you shall." Vlad pressed his hands against the smooth wood of the table in front of him. "I could point out that Elias Crichell conspired with an unblooded warrior to destroy his rival for power. I could point out that he knew of evidence that proved Khan Vandervahn Chistu murdered Ulric Kerensky, but did not demand it be brought forward in the Jade Falcon Clan Council. Both of those things reveal a serious lapse of honor, but that is not the heart of it."

He pointed at Crichell. "My challenge is based on the most fundamental qualification for the title of ilKhan: Elias Crichell is not a warrior."

Crichell's face flushed crimson. "This is absurd! I have tested out in a Trial of Position just as any warrior must. The proofs are there for all to see."

"Yes, ilKhan Crichell, the *results* are available, but there are no holovids of your tests." Vlad smiled coldly. "I took the liberty of obtaining the maintenance records for your BattleMech and those of the 'Mechs that tested against you. Your techs have fired more shots in your 'Mech than you have, and the 'Mechs you fought have required no more than the replacement of ejection seats afterward."

Crichell folded his arms across his chest. "I cannot control the actions of my foes. If they fear death at my hands, is that a fault to be laid at my door?"

"It surprises me, then, ilKhan, that so fearsome a warrior as you did not take his own BattleMech against the Wolves in the fighting last month." Vlad shook his head. "Your explanation matters not—my challenge stands and you must respond to it."

"Very well, you will have your Trial." Crichell looked over at Kael Pershaw. "Summon Taman Malthus—he will be my second in this."

"Kael Pershaw, ignore that request."

Crichell stared coldly at Vlad. "What do you mean in giving my man orders?"

Ian Hawker laughed aloud. "He means to prevent you from further proving yourself unworthy, Elias. He has read the rules and has you trapped. He challenged *you,* not the vote. Had he contested the vote, you might have named a second to fight for you. But he challenges your qualifications as a warrior, and only you can defend the Trial of Refusal against them."

Vlad bowed his head toward the Diamond Shark Khan, then turned back to face the gathering. "A Khan of the Khans must be able to handle any type of combat. As the challenged party you would normally have the right to choose how we would fight: augmented or unaugmented. As ilKhan you abide by a random choice. Kael Pershaw, randomize a number, one or zero. One is augmented, null means we use nothing."

Kael Pershaw hesitated for a moment and only moved to the noteputer when Marthe Pryde nodded to him. He tapped something into the noteputer, and a green zero flashed up into the holographic display. "You will fight unaugmented."

Vlad vaulted over his desk and landed solidly on the main floor of the amphitheater. "I am the challenger. I say we fight *now!*"

Crichell lifted his chin. "We fight unaugmented, but you are wearing a club on your left arm."

Vlad whirled and smashed the cast against the table with a thundercrack. Plaster chips flew off in all directions, peppering Marialle Radick and the Nova Cat Khans. Vlad felt an ache start in the middle of his forearm, but he pushed the pain away. With his right hand he pried the cast apart and dropped it to the floor.

Bits and pieces of it crunched beneath his boots as he walked toward Crichell. "I allow you to strike the first blow, Elias Crichell."

The older man's right fist arced at his head. Vlad felt the impact and tasted the blood flowing from mashed lips. He felt himself losing his balance and moving involuntarily backward, then going down, but none of that mattered to him. With that first punch Crichell had confirmed Vlad's accusation: he was no warrior.

A warrior would have gone for a killing blow. Vlad rolled to a stop against the legs of the Smoke Jaguar table. As he stood, leaning heavily against the table, he swiped blood away from his mouth with the back of his left hand, then smiled. *And a warrior would have followed up his attack, giving me no chance to recover.*

Crichell waited for Vlad in the center of the floor. The younger man staggered toward Crichell, as if still addled by that one punch. Confidence blossomed on Crichell's face, and Vlad could see the man anticipating how this fight would add to his myth. Crichell had already begun to look beyond this moment to future times, and started to shift his weight around in preparation for the blow that would put Vlad down and out.

Vlad's jerky movements flowed fluidly into a sidestep that gave Crichell's uppercut no target. As the older man recovered himself, Vlad jabbed twice, connecting with quick punches that crunched Crichell's nose and split his lips. Vlad followed them with an overhand left feint at Crichell's head. The older man brought his hands up to protect his head, opening the way for Vlad to bury his right fist in Crichell's middle.

As Crichell jackknifed forward, Vlad snapped his right knee up, catching Crichell in the face and straightening him again. Then he grabbed the back of Crichell's neck to keep him close, and pounded the man's midsection with his right fist. While raining blows on Crichell's stomach and ribs, Vlad added a knee to the belly just to break things up.

He could tell from the gasping sounds Crichell made that the man couldn't draw a full breath. Barking a harsh laugh, Vlad released the older man, then gave him an openhanded slap across the face. Crichell spun away and crashed into the desk in front of the Nova Cat Khans. He clung to it, keeping himself off the ground, then levered himself up and moved back into the fight.

Crichell's cheek burned crimson with Vlad's handprint, and blood covered his chin. He made a feeble attempt to strike quickly at Vlad, but the younger man merely melted away from the punch. Crichell kept his fists up and elbows in to protect his body as he closed with Vlad. He was playing the warrior, but the glazed look in his eyes told Vlad and everyone else in the room that his body was responding unconsciously with things he had learned long ago.

And those lessons were obviously not learned well.

Vlad darted forward and slapped Crichell again with his left hand, this time across the stomach. Crichell's hands made no attempt to cover his midsection, but instead he grazed a left jab past Vlad's right ear. That brightened the old man's eyes, but only for a second before Vlad slammed his right fist home against the old man's left temple.

Crichell's knees buckled and his legs turned to water. He dropped to a kneeling position, then sagged back on his heels. His hands fell to his lap and his head lolled on his neck as if it were only balanced there precariously. Vlad knew the man wasn't thinking—he was in shock, both physical and mental. The fight was over.

It is not over until I decide it is over!

Vlad prodded him with a toe. "Is that *all* you have, Elias Crichell? Even Vandervahn Chistu gave me more of a fight. And before that, Ulric Kerensky gave Chistu more of a fight. Can you do nothing more? Are you like all the Falcons—bold in peace and bled in war?"

Crichell struggled back to his feet. "I am a Jade Falcon. I was a warrior before you were spawned."

"And I shall be a warrior long after you are dead." Vlad whirled and lashed out with a spinkick that would have taken the older man's head off had the kick not glanced from his shoulder first. As it was, the boot lacing cut the scalp over his right ear, and crimson began to leak into his gray hair. The force of the blow spun Crichell again to the floor, where he rolled to a stop at Marthe Pryde's feet.

She made no move to help him rise, but neither did Crichell make an appeal for her assistance. Though staggering as he rose to his feet, he looked a bit more clear-headed as he approached Vlad warily. He moved around in a circle, leaving Vlad at the heart of their arena.

Vlad was content to wait. All the advantages were his. Reach. Skill. Courage. And, above all, hunger. *Crichell has come to believe it is his right to be ilKhan, but it is a right he has never earned. The ilKhan must be the warrior of warriors. This man does not fulfill that requirement.*

Crichell closed and threw a torpid right fist at Vlad, who instantly brought his left hand up and caught the fist. He applied pressure for a moment just to watch the pain on the older man's face, then twisted Crichell's hand over, locking the arm and elbow. He brought his own right elbow up and held it poised above Crichell's arm. One quick blow and he'd shatter the locked joint—which was exactly what the other Khans expected of him.

They winced as his elbow fell, but Crichell's arm did not shatter. At the last moment Vlad whipped his elbow out and around, crashing it against the left side of Crichell's head. As the old man started to go down, Vlad contemptuously watched him fall. Crichell flopped onto his back, blood streaming from his lips and nose. He rocked back and forth, cradling his head in his hands, but made no attempt to rise from the ground.

Vlad watched as Crichell slowly curled his body into a ball, then the younger man looked up to stare boldly at the rest of the Khans. He read the reactions on their faces, a full spectrum ranging from admiration to outright fear. Osis looked disgusted, while the Nova Cat mystics seemed to have been transported to a whole other plane, as if they were seeing things no one else could see.

"Behold the leader you have chosen to represent us."

Lincoln Osis looked away from Crichell. "It is done. He is ilKhan no more."

Vlad shook his head. "The fight is not over."

"Leave him, Vlad. He is finished."

"For the second time you try to give me orders, Lincoln Osis." Vlad took a step forward and delivered a sharp kick to the middle of Crichell's spine. The man cried out, arching his back, then rolled onto it and lay staring up at the ceiling and the man looming over him. "You have forgotten I am a Khan and a warrior, just as Crichell has forgotten what it is to be a warrior. It is time I give you both a reminder."

Vlad lowered the heel of his boot to Crichell's throat. "A warrior is one trained in the art of killing." He pressed his heel down until Crichell began to gurgle.

"A warrior is one who kills his enemies without regret." He added more weight until Crichell's voice became a harsh, scratchy hiss and his hands closed around Vlad's ankle.

"A warrior is one who leaves broken enemies in his wake because he knows the dead can never harm him." Remorselessly Vlad ground his heel into the man's throat until the crackling of bone drowned out the thumps of Crichell's thrashing. He continued to apply pressure, fracturing vertebrae with pops and snaps until even Lincoln Osis turned away. With one final push he forced a last convulsion out of Crichell's body, then he stepped back and viewed his handiwork.

When he finally looked up, he saw only Marthe Pryde watching him. He imagined it was because she wanted to make certain Crichell was really dead.

Vlad of the Wards opened his arms above the limp corpse. "*Now* it is done, my Khans."

Osis's dark eyes glittered like ice. "You now expect us to elect you in his place?"

"By no means." Vlad wiped blood from his face with the back of one hand. "This is neither the time *nor* the place to choose a new ilKhan. Elias Crichell was right about the need for new assessments of Jade Falcon and Jade Wolf strength. It will take a minimum of six months to complete the necessary work."

The Smoke Jaguar shook his head. "You stand closer to the office now than you will in six months."

"That, Khan Osis, says more about your lack of imagination than it does my standing. I have been an aide to an ilKhan. I know what the job requires and I have no desire for it."

"At this time," Marthe Pryde spat out.

"You may be right, Khan Marthe." Vlad shrugged noncommittally. "I do, however, have clear ideas on what must qualify a Khan for that position—and being a warrior in name only is not one of them. Perhaps a delay of six months will give any Khan who harbors ambitions a chance to prove he or she *is* truly worthy of leading us."

Ian Hawker pounded a fist on his desk. "Six months is reasonable, more would be prudent."

Marthe looked at Kael Pershaw. "Loremaster, tally the vote."

The Khans agreed to a delay, with no dissent. Vlad nodded grimly, then tugged on the green mantle he wore until it came loose. "One last thing, my Khans. I hereby create a new Clan. I consign everyone who was a Jade Wolf to it." He tossed the green mantel down onto Crichell's mangled face. "We are, once again, Clan Wolf."

Hawker looked up. "There is a verdict of genocide against your Clan."

"Those Wolves are dead. We are a new breed of Wolves. You will find us quite similar to those you once knew, but to mistake us for them would be a grave error."

Silence was the only answer to Vlad's words. He looked around the room, willing to accept any challenge, but none came. Lincoln Osis met his stare for a moment, then dismissed it with a curt shake of his head.

Vlad clapped his hands once. "I would say, then, that our business here is concluded."

Marthe Pryde moved to the door and opened it. The Khans filed out of the room in Pershaw's wake. Then the door closed behind them, leaving only Marthe Pryde and Vlad staring at each other above Crichell's body.

"His death was not necessary for you to win your challenge."

Vlad watched her carefully. "You do not regret his death. Perhaps you wished to be the instrument of it."

"Was your charge of concealing evidence of Chistu's crime true?"

"It was. The evidence is worthless now, though I will make a copy available to you, if you so desire."

"Yes." Marthe looked down at Crichell. "His fate should have been decided by the Jade Falcon Clan Council. That evidence would have unseated him. We would have dealt with him."

"Perhaps."

Anger flashed through her blue eyes. "You doubt our honor?"

"I doubt the list of crimes for which you would have punished him would have matched the list of crimes he committed against me."

"Crimes against you?"

"He bargained in bad faith and denied me my Clan." Vlad shook his head. "Even greater than that was his stupidity."

"What do you mean?"

The Wolf leaned back against his table. "When I first came to Elias Crichell, he asked what I would do if he denied me my due. He knew I would kill him for it."

Marthe's eyes narrowed. "But in denying you the Wolves, he saved you from death."

Vlad laughed aloud. "That was his mistake, wasn't it?"

"There is no need for vulgarity, Vladimir Ward."

He was surprised when she bristled at the use of contractions. "Are you that rigid, Marthe?"

"I respect the way of the Clans."

"You cling to a past that saps your strength and makes your Clan feeble."

"We defeated the Wolves, *quiaff*?"

"*That* depends on who is keeping score. The Falcons beat only part of the Wolves. And you won here on Wotan only because of treachery. Phelan Ward humiliated the Falcon warriors that were sent after him—and even your own warriors have admitted that Inner Sphere *mercenaries* defeated them." He pointed at Crichell. "Your ways produce imitation warriors."

"*He* was not a true Jade Falcon warrior."

Vlad let himself chuckle. "Ah, a display of the famed Pryde pride."

"Better that than Wolf hubris."

"Hubris?" Vlad shook his head. "Better to be bound for a

fall than to have already suffered one, Marthe. Your ways and your actions form a paradox you cannot resolve. If the old ways were so good, so true, then you would not have embraced new technology. You would be fighting with the 'Mechs of the Inner Sphere, and losing to Inner Sphere warriors even more often than you did in the invasion."

Her hands convulsed into fists. "Use of new tools does not warp tradition."

"And what are tactics but tools, Marthe?"

"Tactics are based upon tradition and honor—murder would be pragmatic, but we restrain ourselves from that."

"Chistu did not."

"And he was a fool! Had I known what you knew, I would have challenged him and killed him. He was more of a threat to the Jade Falcons than either you or the Inner Sphere. I would have dealt with him. And I would have dealt with Elias Crichell."

"Unable to compete, the outdated devour each other in an orgy of recrimination!" The Wolf forced a huge smile on his face. "You should find a more constructive outlet for your frustrations."

A calm consumed the anger on her face, and Vlad felt a cold chill as she spoke. "I have found such, little Wolf. The ways of Crichell and Chistu were not the true way of the Jade Falcons. I know this, and I will prove it. You will see, as will all the rest, that our tradition makes us strong."

"You will have to do much to prove that to me."

"And I shall." Her eyes sharpened. "I shall begin by granting you *hegira*."

Shock and outrage thundered through Vlad's brain. "You what?"

"It is the right of the victor to allow the vanquished safe passage."

"The Wolves were never defeated by the Jade Falcons."

"Ah, but they were. Your fight only repudiated the Absorption, not the outcome of the Trial of Refusal." Marthe regarded him through half-lidded eyes. "You may make any claims you want about your Wolves not being Ulric's Wolves, but you and I know there is no difference. I grant you *hegira* because you were beaten. Accept it. It is a tradition that has value, though you do not see it."

Vlad almost snarled at her, but her last words burrowed through his anger at her presumption. *The traditions of the*

Clans are the foundation of all that we are. In denying this one I would distance myself from our way just as Crichell and Chistu had. Going to war again right now would be stupid. She knows it, just as she knows I would have left Wotan gladly and peacefully. By offering hegira *she seeks to remind me that the Jade Falcons are worthy of respect.*

What I remember is that I must find a way to pay her back. A traditional way. Vlad nodded. "I accept *hegira* and will leave Wotan at the earliest opportunity."

"Good." She pointed at him. "This is the last you will see of me for a while, Vladimir Ward, but I will keep you informed of my activities. I will not tell you everything, of course, but enough that you will know I am the rightful leader of the Jade Falcons."

"I wish you luck, Marthe Pryde."

"I would not, if I were you."

"No?"

Her smile failed to ease the chill sinking into Vlad's heart. "In six months or eight or whenever we are called to Strana Mechty to elect a new ilKhan, the other Khans will know how weak or strong we are. At the least sign of weakness, we can expect another Clan will attempt to absorb us. I know a way to prove the Falcons strong, and I will use it. I wonder what you will do to prove that your Clan is hearty and able."

She turned to walk away, then glanced back over her shoulder. "Fare well, Vlad Khanslayer of the Wolves, but not too well. I do not look forward to having you as a rival in the future."

"I can imagine you would not."

Marthe laughed once, then shook her head. "Then again, perhaps I will enjoy it."

BOOK II

Blood, Sweat and Tears: Misery, Treachery, and All Our Fears

═══ 11 ═══

Tharkad City
Tharkad
District of Donegal, Lyran Alliance
5 January 3058

Tormano Liao bowed respectfully in the direction of the Archon of the Lyran Alliance. He smiled at her, more because she expected it than out of consideration for her beauty. And he did consider her beautiful—though his personal tastes ran more toward Asian women than tall, lithe ones with icy blue eyes and long blond hair. The smile let her think that her physical appeal gave her an edge over him.

And I must never let myself underestimate her because of her beauty. "Archon, I have completed my survey of reports coming from Clan space and have a summary for you."

Katrina Steiner waved Tormano to one of the white leather wingback chairs around her desk. "I have read some of the reports. We can compare conclusions."

"Indeed, Archon." Tormano settled himself in the chair and tugged at the crease of his dark trousers as he sat back. He'd done it to buy himself another moment or two of peace, but the distant look in her blue eyes told him the subterfuge was unnecessary. *She is lost in thought, which does not bode well for what I have in mind. Then again, perhaps she is thinking of nothing more adventurous than redecorating again.*

In the three weeks since Tormano had come to Tharkad, Katrina Steiner had completely redone the Archon's office, stripping out all the dark woods and antique furnishings, replacing them with deep carpeting, stark white furniture, and synthetic laminates covering the walls, her desk, and shelves. Little splashes of color appeared here and there, but anything meant to reside in the office for long tended to be plated in gold or tinted in a very light shade of Steiner blue. Even Katrina's silk suit was white over a royal blue blouse and accented with gold jewelry.

Tormano was uncertain why she'd made these changes. The press release put out by the Interior Ministry had used the word "virginal" to describe the color of the decor, and Tormano did understand enough about religion and Lyran folklore to realize that white symbolized purity and virtue. For him—a product of the more Asian culture of the Capellans—white was the color of mourning and he found the room cold and clinical.

"Archon, the reports coming out of Wotan are, at best, confused and confusing, but combined with reports from throughout the Jade Falcon Occupation Zone, and reports from Morges, we've been able to piece together the story. Apparently, the Jade Falcons and the Wolves recently went to war with each other. The reason for the conflict is unclear, but seems to have centered around a power struggle for leadership of the Clans as a whole."

"A struggle between the Crusaders, who want to repudiate the truce and continue the war against the Inner Sphere, and the Wardens, who want to halt the invasion."

Tormano nodded. "You seem to have a good grasp of Clan politics, Archon."

Katrina smiled sweetly. "I have had occasion to speak with Khan Phelan Kell about such, and the Precentor Martial has been equally generous in sharing his thoughts on the subject."

"Indeed. The situation on Wotan involved a last-ditch effort by the Wolves to destroy the Jade Falcons. They failed, or so it seems, when ilKhan Ulric Kerensky was killed in Borealtown on the tenth of last month. Almost immediately all signs of Clan Wolf vanished—it appeared that all the surviving Wolves had suddenly become members of the Jade Falcons. Then, almost as quickly, a Wolf challenged and killed one of the Falcon Khans. Subsequent to that a new Clan, the Jade Wolves, made an appearance."

The Archon plucked a gold letter opener from her desk

and tapped it against the blotter. "The death of that Khan liberated the Wolves, at least partially, from the Falcons."

"So it would appear. By the first of the year the Khans of the other Clans had arrived at Wotan. The various intelligence services of the Inner Sphere had expected the Clansmen to return to their homeworlds to elect a new ilKhan, as they had done before, but I think the arrival of these Khans may have been for the purpose of staging such an election on Wotan. We are not privy to what went on in their council, but certain external clues suggest another upheaval. Signs of the Jade Wolves have vanished and the Wolves appear to have reemerged as a Clan."

"Significance?"

"Unknown at this point, Highness." Tormano shrugged. "We can speculate that both the Wolves and the Jade Falcons were hurt by their war. Reports of the damage done on Morges to the Jade Falcon force are impressive. If those attrition figures hold true for other worlds where the two Clans engaged each other—and scattered reports support this conclusion—the Wolves and the Jade Falcons have both suffered severe losses."

Katrina sat back in her overstuffed chair. "What does this mean for the force Phelan Kell has at Arc-Royal?"

"Reports from Arc-Royal are rather spare, Highness. The people seem to have intense loyalty to the ruling family, and the Kells are preferring to operate covertly. Even so, there is said to be much activity on the subcontinent of Braonach. That island had been relatively undeveloped because of the strict environmental regulations the Kells put in place long ago, so it appears the Wolves will have their own world within the Inner Sphere."

Irritation whipped across Katrina's face like storm clouds being chased by a swift wind. "Damn them. How dare they defy me?"

Not this again. "Highness, Morgan Kell's declaration concerning the Arc-Royal Defense Cordon is a blessing for you. It absolves you of responsibility for a huge portion of your border."

"I cannot abandon the defense of the Alliance border to Morgan. In doing so I would legitimize his rebellion against me." Katrina slowly slid the blade of the letter opener between the fingers of her left hand as if it were a dagger being thrust through ribs. "People will begin to wonder why

Morgan is rebelling, going from loyal vassal and blood-kin to a bandit king creating his own realm."

Tormano Liao shook his head. "I cannot believe that you, of all people, do not see that the reasons for his actions do not matter. His declaration was simple and straightforward: he laid claim to the worlds along the Jade Falcon border. He gave no reasons."

"Others will supply reasons."

"Only if you do not supply them first."

The irritation knotting her brow smoothed away, and the intelligence that always impressed him flowed back into her eyes. "If I issue a statement thanking Morgan for accepting the enormous responsibility for the border and cite it as one more instance of how all the worlds of the Alliance must do all they can to safeguard our realm, his defection becomes something I allowed and welcome."

"Precisely, Highness." Tormano nodded solemnly. "It also gives you a chance to withdraw troops from that area and reassign them elsewhere."

"But why would I do that?"

"Because it pins Kell and Phelan in place. Since they have pledged themselves to defend the area, they cannot move away from it to attend to other things. They have trapped themselves, which gives you greater latitude in other areas, without fear of intervention by Morgan Kell."

"I see." The Archon sat forward and lightly stabbed the letter opener against her desk blotter. "Where would I move these troops to?"

"I would move them to the border with the Free Worlds League, to discourage Thomas Marik from becoming adventurous."

"Wouldn't that antagonize him?"

"He needs to see you are strong." Tormano killed the smile that threatened to creep onto his face. "It is important he sees this before he asks you to marry him."

The letter opener thumped on the desk. "What?"

"The logic of it is unassailable, Archon. You are beautiful and available, with a handsome dowry. As your mother's marriage with your father brought two realms together, so would a union between you and Thomas Marik. More important, it would establish you as a viable ruler of this newly unified realm over either his daughter Isis or my nephew Sun-Tzu. Subsequent to your marriage, of course, he would let Sun-Tzu marry Isis and bring the Capellan Confederation into the alliance."

Katrina shook her head, but disbelief still clung to her face. "He would have to be mad to think I would marry him."

"Not at all—the union would be to your advantage as well. You will outlive him. He is swiftly approaching the life expectancy of rulers of the Inner Sphere, and once before barely survived an assassination attempt. With Sun-Tzu waiting in the wings, one cannot be certain how much longer he will live. As a result, you stand to add the Free Worlds League to your Lyran Alliance. We mustn't forget either that the League's industrial capacity has been the backbone of the Inner Sphere's resistance against the Clans. By marrying Thomas you will be able to divert all that production, and most of the League's military, to the defense of your realm.

"Diverting League production to the Lyran Alliance would further weaken the Draconis Combine, which should not cause you to lose too much sleep. If the Combine collapses, we both know Victor will do what he can to salvage chunks of it, just as he will offer the Kurita royals safe haven in the Federated Commonwealth. He might even wed Omi Kurita, which would cause all manner of internal difficulties in the Commonwealth."

Katrina's eyes narrowed. "Such unrest would allow me to press my suit against Victor, and ultimately depose him and take over."

"Making you de facto First Lord of a new Star League."

"Provided someone does not make me a gift of flowers as they did my mother."

"That's a risk, but one we can minimize." Tormano smiled. "The main thing is that Thomas will not try to take by force or arms what sweet words and kindnesses might win him. Whether or not you accept or reject his suit, allowing him to pursue you gives you time to strengthen your realm and plan for the future."

"Your point is well taken." She arched an eyebrow at him. "This campaign to win my heart will begin when?"

"It has already begun through some very low-level diplomatic channels. League consuls are sending out feelers for your reaction to a possible visit from Thomas. The middle of June will see the first anniversary of his wife's death and the nominal conclusion of Thomas' self-imposed year of mourning. He would visit to thank you personally for your kind messages to him in his time of grief."

"Six months. Good. That gives me the time I want." Katrina blinked once, then flashed Tormano a quick grin. "You will handle the preliminary negotiations, of course. Play for time."

"Yes, Highness, but time for what?" Tormano always felt rather uneasy when he couldn't guess what she had in mind. Though Katrina was intelligent, her immaturity and inexperience often made her believe that certain things were possible that could never happen or exist. *She is too clever by half sometimes.*

She got up and begin to pace—a bad sign, as far as Tormano was concerned. "Your analysis of what my brother would do in the face of the Combine's collapse echoes my thoughts about it exactly."

"Good." *I hope.*

She smiled at him. "You have heard the expression, 'the enemy of my enemy is my friend'?"

"It is an old, old, saying."

"And has survived for so long because it is true. It strikes me, Mandrinn Liao, that I have multiple enemies who share the same enemy. That *shared* enemy should be my friend."

Tormano failed to suppress a wince. "Perhaps a more expansive explanation is in order, Highness."

"Of course." She waved one hand as if to say the explanation was all too obvious. "The Draconis Combine has suffered much at the hands of the Smoke Jaguars. Morgan Kell and his Hounds were on Luthien and helped defeat the Smoke Jaguars. Phelan Kell is a Wolf, and according to the Precentor Martial, the Wolves and the Smoke Jaguars have never gotten along very well."

Tormano's jaw dropped. "You propose an alliance between your realm and the Smoke Jaguars?"

"Yes! The simplicity of it is staggering, is it not?"

His mouth went dry, and Tormano was suddenly glad he was sitting down. "Highness, the Clans want to destroy the Inner Sphere."

"No, Mandrinn, they wish to conquer it, and I can provide them the means to do so much more quickly."

"But . . ."

"But what, Tormano?" She opened her arms and stared

down at him. "You outlined a simple way for me to become First Lord of a new Star League. I have found another means to that end. The initiation of relations and negotiations does not mean I will betray the Inner Sphere."

"But consider the implications."

"I have." Katrina folded her arms across her chest. "And I have made a decision. Within the week I will head out from Tharkad for the Smoke Jaguar Occupation Zone. In roughly five weeks I will enter negotiations with the Smoke Jaguars for an alliance."

She looked beyond him and Tormano knew there was nothing he could do to change her mind. "I have recorded a number of messages that you may release on the appropriate dates to conceal my absence from Tharkad. I am cutting down on all my public appearances because I am working closely with you to put together a package of reforms that will change forever the nature of the Inner Sphere, and so on and so forth. You will be my liaison with my advisors on this project."

"And if there is an emergency that requires your attention?"

Katrina stared at him, the blue of her eyes icier than ever. "Handle it."

Tormano opened his mouth, then closed it again. He waited until enough saliva had accumulated to cut the bitter taste in his mouth. "You would turn your realm over to me? What if I don't want to give it back?"

"If you refuse to relinquish control, it will become known that you had me kidnapped and shipped to the Clans as a peace offering. The people of this world will tear you apart." Katrina's smile froze his heart. "Does that answer your question?"

"Quite sufficiently, Archon."

"Good." Archon Katrina Steiner sat down again at her desk. "You may think my taking such a risk is mad, but I assure you it is not. In ten years the Clan tide will rise again, and my realm will be swept away unless the conquerors see a reason to leave it intact. I will give them that reason, and the Lyran Alliance will thrive while all the others whither and die."

=== 12 ===

Tenth Skye Rangers Headquarters
Coventry
Coventry Province, Lyran Alliance
6 January 3058

Doc Trevena took it as an omen that it rained on normally sunny Coventry on his first full day with his new unit. He'd been given command of the First Battalion's Second Company, nicknamed the Titans of Doom, though he'd already heard the unit called the Dwarves of Dumb. This spelled big trouble and the performance records corroborated that conclusion rather harshly.

He stared at the holographic display of records scrolling up in mid-air over his desk. Like him, Second Company's personnel had all been transferred in from other units. Hauptmanns Dorne and Wells, the commanders of First and Third Company, respectively, had arrived a week earlier, and like kids choosing up teams, they'd scooped up the best of what was a fairly pathetic crowd.

Doc didn't think it surprising for any unit to have a few duds in it. Truth to tell, he considered it a fact of life in the military. He tended to think of the duds as "mascots"— people long on heart and desire, but a bit shy on skills. They gave the unit a heart, and often became a rallying point for everyone in it. Usually it was some green kid, or a guy who was physically small, or someone who really didn't grasp the full seriousness of being part of the army.

Now I've got a unit with all *duds in it.* From the reports it looked like the only way his troops could hit a 'Mech with a shot was if they were *piloting* the 'Mech that got hit. They all looked like a recruiter's bonuses, or at least the ones that got him his quarterly quota. They weren't blind or lame, but not very far from it.

Doc sighed, then looked through the holograph at the skinny, goggle-eyed kid standing in the doorway to his office. "What is it, Corporal?"

Andy Bick's Adam's apple—after his nose, his most prominent feature—bobbed up and down. "Sir, Hauptmann Dorne has sent a message inviting you to meet her and Hauptmann Wells at the Officer's Club for dinner?"

Doc rubbed his eyes. "Who's buying?"

Bick immediately looked stricken. He glanced at his noteputer, then blanched. "I don't know, sir."

"Take it easy, Corporal, I didn't expect you to."

Bick's smile seemed somehow wider than his face. "Was that a reticle question, sir?"

"Rhetorical question, yes, Mr. Bick." Doc sat back in his chair. "Come in for a second and close the door. I want to ask you some questions about Two Company."

Bick's nervous smile flared for an instant, then died horribly. He closed the door, then perched himself on the edge of the chair across from Doc's desk. "Y-yes, sir?"

"What are your thoughts about the unit? You don't need to name any names—I'm not looking for people to watch out for. I just want a feel for things, and you've met everyone so far, right?"

Bick's brow wrinkled, his reddish eyebrows almost touching. "Well, sir, we're all from different places and we don't know each other. We've been confined to base since we got here . . ."

"Yet some people have managed to get lost . . ."

"Yes, sir, but I'm sure it was just an accident."

"It *is* a big base."

Bick nodded enthusiastically. "Everyone has been squared away with a bunk and most of us have had our equipment make it to Coventry. Those who did get their stuff are sharing things with those who didn't—folks have been good about that."

Doc raised an eyebrow. "No fights? No one playing the bully?"

Andy Bick became church-solemn. "No, sir, none of that at all."

Not only can't they fight, they're all nice guys! "And what about equipment? Have you been able to requisition what you need?"

"No, sir. I mean, I have the forms in order, at least I think I do, but the battalion quartermaster still hasn't delivered any of it." Bick looked up. "I'm trying, sir, really, but . . ."

Doc nodded. A note in Bick's file indicated his promotion to Corporal had been a field promotion made by Hauptmann Wells when he and Dorne discovered that the unit had nothing in the way of officers prior to Doc's arrival. Bick had drawn the short straw, though his experience as a clerk-typist before he got 'Mech training probably made him the best choice for the position.

"Don't worry about it. I think we can handle that problem." Doc killed the holographic display and leaned forward. "Do we have 'Mechs?"

"Yes, sir. Six *Locusts*, three *Jenners*, two *Valkyries*, and one *Commando.*"

Doc winced. "All lights?"

"Except for your *Centurion*, sir, yes, sir." Bick smiled hopefully. "We're a recon company."

"What a novel concept." *Perhaps if I have drinks with Dorne and Wells I can introduce them to Hemlock High-balls and get this regiment reorganized the way it should be.* Units composed of fast and light 'Mechs were invaluable for performing reconnaissance missions, but they never got as big as a full company, and seldom exceeded a lance in size. For reconnaissance to have any value, the rest of the unit had to be able to deliver the firepower required to eliminate whatever targets the scouts located. A company comprised entirely of light 'Mechs couldn't supply anything but a continuous stream of targets for a heavier unit.

The reasons Dorne and Wells would have purged their companies of light 'Mechs was obvious—heavier 'Mechs saw more combat. While the Tenth Skye Rangers weren't likely to see much action on Coventry, other fighting units would always be needing officers who could command heavy 'Mechs. Though everyone getting tossed into the Tenth was in the same boat, Dorne and Wells were proving to be pragmatists with an eye toward getting out again. However many years they needed to put in until retirement, they wouldn't *all* be with the Tenth Skye Rangers on Coventry.

"Well, Mr. Bick, I think we've got our work cut out for us. Can I count on your help?"

Corporal Andy Bick straightened up smartly. "Yes, sir."

"Good. For starters I'm going to need you to call everyone together at 1900 hours in the barracks. I want you to get me a holovid projector and a half-dozen Solaris holovids of matches featuring light 'Mechs—preferably the 'Mechs in our roster, got that?"

Bick made an entry into his noteputer. "Yes, sir."

Doc dug into his pocket and pulled out a K60. "Here's money—get some food, too—snacks and refreshments and that sort of thing. Or at least as much as sixty Kroner will buy. That's as much as I've got right now."

"Yes, sir." Bick frowned. "But if this is all your money, what are you going to do at the Officer's Club?"

"Dorne and Wells owe me buckets of dead Archons, so don't worry about me." Doc dropped his voice to a whisper. "Before you go, Bick, I need you to do one other thing."

"Sir?"

"You were a clerk-typist, yes?"

"Yes, sir."

"So you could hack your way into the quartermaster's computer and boost some stuff in our direction, yes?"

Bick's Adam's apple bounced like a rubber ball. "Well, sir, I might be able to get in, but, well, I'll probably get caught."

I expected that. "I'll cover for you. See if you can liberate marginal items and special stores, stuff like exotic beers and whiskey or something of value, okay?" Doc could see how much the idea pained Bick. "Consider it an order, Corporal. You're checking the security of our stores. If an enemy can break in and find out what you're going to find out, think how easily he can learn how many missiles and shells we've got—and we don't want that."

"No, sir." The skinny young man shrugged helplessly and his shoulders slumped. "What do I tell the quartermaster when he calls me in?"

"Tell him I gave you an order." Doc smiled broadly. "And tell him I'm in my office, but I've told you to tell him I'm out."

Bick frowned. "But—"

"Just do it, Corporal, then take care of the rest of what I asked." Doc winked at him. "Somebody's got to try to get this unit squared away, and I'm the guy who's going to do it."

Doc pretended he was surprised when Leftenant Ricardo Copley flung the door to his office wide open and stormed in. "What's the meaning of this?" he demanded.

Copley slammed the door shut, then marched over toward Doc and put his hands on the chair Bick had used earlier. "I'm thinking I should be asking you the same question. Sir." He stretched out the *sir* until it became a mockery of itself. "Your little clerk weasel tells me you ordered him to try to crack into my computer and funnel some goodies over here. That was a bad move, Trevena, and it's going to cost you and your unit. You don't know who you're dealing with."

"Let me hazard a guess." Doc pointed to the chair across from him. He kept his voice cordial, completely devoid of the outrage or fear Copley had obviously anticipated. "Please, Leftenant, have a seat."

Copley sat down cautiously. "Your boy was the one in the wrong here, not me."

Doc smiled evenly and stood. "All right, Leftenant, let's cut the bull. You're one of the few people who isn't new to this unit, which means either the LAAF has no use for you, or you've got enough juice to bounce any transfer. Either one of those things points to someone who's an ace scrounger. You're tied into the local black market and able to move a fair amount of merchandise. Since you've got no overhead, it's pure profit. Am I tracking well here?"

"I ain't saying nothing."

"You don't have to, Leftenant, I can see the pride in your eyes." Doc chuckled lightly. "You're a resourceful fellow. I think we can do business."

"How's that, Trevena? You got nothing I want."

"No?"

"No." The small man with slicked-back hair swayed like a snake as he sat there. "You got a pack of screw-ups and misfits to nursemaid around this planet in lightweight 'Mechs. A stiff wind and your unit's out of service." Copley laughed derisively and fixed Doc with a defiant stare. "Hell, a light breeze and your people are out."

"Exactly."

"Huh?"

Doc smiled. "Let me tell you a story. One of my first assignments was with a unit that was still using equipment that was old before the Fourth Succession War. We wanted new equipment—stuff that was lighter, more durable, more reliable than what we were using, but command wouldn't replace our equipment because we didn't need new stuff. To make matters worse, a lot of our inventory was just ones and zeroes in the computer. The equipment had walked or decayed or been mislaid."

"And you, being the officer in charge of the unit, would have had to pay for any shrinkage." Copley crossed his legs. "You're breaking my heart here."

"Maybe this will repair it. I ordered my clerks to move all that phantom material, plus the old antiquated stuff that really did exist, into and around one of the warehouses not being used on the base. Only our stuff was in it. Then we had a training *accident*—someone used the wrong coordinates for fire-support missions—artillery fired, and, *poof,* all that stuff was lost. Not a trace of it left. The accident got written up and we got replacement equipment for all of it."

Doc's smile broadened. "Of course, the warehouse we stored it in used to be a guardhouse at an unused gate—it was about sixteen meters cubed, but we had about twenty thousand metric tons of material jammed into it. Here on Coventry it would have to work differently, but you'd be surprised just how much stuff could be fitted into and onto a single hovercar that gets destroyed during an exercise."

Copley's mouth had slowly gaped open as Doc spoke, then he shut it with a snap. The quartermaster shook his head, but his brown eyes still looked slightly glazed over. "With your people's scores and records, no one would ever doubt how much got lost or destroyed by accident."

"Sixty-forty split."

Copley snorted. "Sure, my way."

"No, Leftenant, *my* way. You'll hold twenty of my points against getting me the equipment I want for my people on the black market."

Copley frowned. "Why buy when we'll be ordering direct from LAAF?"

"We're a dead-end unit—all they'll do is send me refurbished parts and partial shipments of whatever we order. My people may be screwballs, but they'll be the best-equipped screwballs I can pull together. You put my forty percent into something durable, with a nice high return value, got it?"

"Yeah, I gotcha."

"Good. I also imagine you're tapped into the local gossip networks. I want anything and everything that could be of use to me, right? I want to know what my superiors covet and how to get it for them ..."

". . . Or how to use it against them, right?"

"I can see we'll get along fine, Mr. Copley."

"I imagine we will, sir." Copley stood and gave Doc a weak salute. "I'll give you something for free right now ..."

"Call me Doc."

"Doc. Hauptmann Wells likes to play poker and will probably try to rope you into a game with the officers from Three Batt. When Wells is bluffing he tends to start blinking a lot."

"I appreciate that, but no poker for me tonight." Doc led Copley to the door and opened it. "I'll be getting to know my people tonight."

"I'll have more stuff for you tomorrow," Copley said with a sly smile, "including the coordinates for a couple of heavily laden aircars."

Doc arrived at his office before dawn the next morning and set about reviewing the records of the dozen people he'd met the night before. All of them had seemed to be pleasant enough and none were the total disasters suggested by their records. He found them attentive and a bit intense, but likable. *In any other unit they'd be perfect mascot material.*

Bick had done a good job in picking out the holovids, and Doc used them the same way he would gun-camera films in a post-mission debriefing. The questions his people asked were thoughtful, but a bit naive. Answers to his questions were tentative, but more right than wrong, giving him some hope for the ability of his people to improve.

He looked up as Bick knocked on the jamb of the open door. "Yes, Corporal?"

Bick crossed to the desk and dropped an envelope onto the blotter. "It's the money from last night, sir."

"Oh." Doc thumbed the envelope open, riffled the Kroner notes, then frowned. "There's sixty Kroner here. That's what I gave you to buy those snacks and to rent the holovids."

Bick nodded. "Yes, sir."

"Well?"

Bick shifted his weight from one foot to the other. "Well, sir, after we were done, after you left, I mentioned that you'd paid for everything with your own money. We didn't think that was fair, so we took up a collection and, well, there it is."

Doc shook his head. *They paid me back! These people are too nice to be stuck in this unit.*

"Is there something wrong, sir?"

"No, Corporal, nothing wrong." Doc sighed, then followed it with a smile. "You know what they say about nice guys finishing last. I guess we've got to make sure that doesn't happen with One-Two Company's Rangers, don't we?"

13

Victor Ian Steiner-Davion, Archon Prince of the Federated Commonwealth, sighed aloud as he reviewed his schedule. "It seems that for everything I *want* to do there are two things I *don't* want to do."

One of the other two men in the walnut-paneled office with him smiled, but the taller, ice-eyed one did not. Jerrard Cranston, Victor's intelligence chief, added a shrug to his smile. "I hope this briefing isn't one of the things you *don't* want to do."

Victor tapped a finger against the screen of his monitor. "We can put this in the *want* column. The unveiling of this year's selection of postage stamps is a *don't*, as is attending the Society for the Repatriation of Orphaned Animals luncheon."

"Don't forget that fuzzy little animals make for good holo ops for the newsgrids." Cranston's smile broadened. "And at the stamp unveiling you can wax eloquent about the joy of seeing your dear old friend Galen Cox memorialized."

That prompted a laugh from the Archon Prince. He marveled at how well Galen Cox had slipped into the Jerrard Cranston persona they'd created to cover his supposed death. He found himself thinking of Galen as Jerry more and more often, a phenomenon that disturbed him slightly. *Galen is a link to my life as a warrior and I don't want to lose that.*

Curaitis, the dark-haired giant from the Intelligence Secretariat, looked askance at Cranston. "That portrait of you looks too close. If someone with free time and a pencil darkened the hair and drew in a beard, your cover could be compromised."

Victor shook his head. "I doubt doodling will constitute a serious threat to Jerry's identity. Besides, Galen was far more handsome than Jerry has ever been."

"Agreed, but any leak could cause complications."

Victor nodded. The failed assassination attempt against Galen had revealed two things to Victor. The first was that Duke Ryan Steiner, Victor's rival for power in the Skye March, had ordered the hit. Victor repaid Ryan in kind, abruptly settling the Skye question.

The second thing was far more disturbing, yet something he couldn't act on without further, definitive proof. His sister Katherine—he refused to grant her use of his sainted grandmother's name—had possessed prior knowledge of the assassination attempt and had done nothing to warn Galen. In trying to investigate why, Curaitis had found circumstantial evidence that pointed to Katherine as a conspirator with Ryan in the plot to have Melissa Steiner Davion—Victor and Katherine's mother—killed in a bomb blast.

"I don't think my sister will look at a redrawn stamp and conclude that we know as much about her operations as we do." Victor shook his head. "And even if she does, any actions she takes to cover her tracks could finally lead us to the evidence we need to prove she was behind my mother's murder."

Jerry nodded. "The stamp is in the 'Heroes of the Inner Sphere' series—every one of them dead—so people will take that as proof of Galen's demise. The only doubters will be the scandal-vids, but having them make a big deal of the story will be to our benefit."

Curaitis shrugged as if their logic made no difference. "I can't stop you from dancing on the razor's edge."

"Your caution is exactly why I need you," Victor told him gently, then glanced over at Jerry. "Updates on the LAAF?"

Jerrard Cranston dropped into a chair. "Personnel are still being shuffled. The Fourth, Tenth, and Seventeenth Skye Rangers are getting a lot of rejects and folks presumed to be

Davion loyalists dumped into them. Tensions in some of those units would make them more likely to attack each other than any enemy they would possibly face."

Victor's gray eyes narrowed. "Someone is punishing those units for their part in the Skye Rebellion. Elements of all three fought on Glengarry against the Gray Death Legion. Is that Katherine's doing, or the influence of Tormano Liao?"

"Steiner sentiment runs high in the LAAF. Nondi Steiner is still in charge there, and revamping those units is likely her idea."

"Grand-aunt Nondi." The Prince frowned. "I never took to her, nor she to me. She *is* the wellspring of Steiner loyalty in the Lyran Alliance and seems to have transferred her feelings for my grandmother to my sister. It was a smart move keeping Nondi as commander of the Lyran Alliance military—she's got the necessary experience—but her hatred of the Draconis Combine means that anything I've done or will do in cooperation with the Dracs will offend her."

Jerry nodded. "She's publicly spoken out about the occupation of the Lyons Thumb by Combine troops."

"Under ComStar leadership and coming in as peacekeepers," Victor corrected sharply.

"You and I know that, Highness, but she sees it otherwise," Curaitis said. "They're reorganizing and streamlining LAAF, which has reduced the effectiveness of intelligence assets in the Lyran military. Right now, I'd put intelligence from those sources at minimal reliability."

"That I don't like, but there's little we can do about it right now." Victor frowned. "Has the schedule for getting back our JumpShips and DropShips improved?"

"Somewhat, and that's due to Tormano Liao's influence. A certain amount of the supplies and money we're paying to ransom our ships is flowing into the Chaos March to his old Free Capella forces. As that gives Sun-Tzu Liao and Thomas Marik something to think about, it's good; but paying to get our own materiel back isn't a precedent I like having set."

"Well, just make certain all the loot we're sending Katherine is listed as foreign aid. We might as well get a proper angle on the publicity for this debacle." Victor wrinkled his nose. "Thomas is meeting with our ambassador on Atreus today to iron out the details of the peace between us, right?"

"Yes, sir. We anticipate no problems there."

Victor glanced at Curaitis. "Your security check on the Intelligence Secretariat's forensic division found no leaks?"

"Clean, sir."

"So no one but the three of us knows that the man currently ruling the Free Worlds League is really someone made to look like Thomas Marik and substituted for him by ComStar back in 3037?"

The taciturn agent's head came up. "No one save Thomas himself, and others within ComStar or Word of Blake?"

"To the best of our knowledge, Curaitis."

"No, sir, no one else knows, to the best of our knowledge."

The Prince got up from behind the massive oak desk that had served his father before him, and began to pace. "I've tried to think of a way to use this information, but I keep coming up blank. Using it to extort concessions from Thomas seems to make the most sense, but he'd denounce the data as part of a ComStar plot to discredit him and Word of Blake."

Jerry smoothed his beard to a point at his chin. "Giving the information to Isis Marik would supply her with a lever to guarantee her remaining Thomas's heir—the Captain-Generalcy is hers by blood, after all."

"But she's engaged to marry Sun-Tzu Liao, and he'd be willing to kill Thomas to put her on the throne, especially if she had a legitimate claim to it and could show the current ruler to be an impostor."

"But letting Sun-Tzu get that much power isn't something we want." Jerry shook his head. "In a very real sense the fact that the Thomas Marik on the throne is an impostor doesn't matter. He's found a way to give his people what they want. He's more popular than ever, especially since taking back the worlds we took from the League back in 3028. Even if the truth came out, the people of the League might support him anyway."

Victor laughed. "Rather ironic, isn't it, that the most capable leader in the history of House Marik isn't a Marik at all."

Curaitis began to grin, which filled Victor with foreboding. "Wouldn't it be even more amusing if ComStar still had the real Thomas Marik on ice somewhere?"

"Is that possible?"

"Of course, Highness."

Jerry frowned at Curaitis. "But still only speculation. Very blue-sky."

The Prince nodded. "Give me the short form."

Curaitis sighed. "It took ComStar eighteen months to reveal Thomas's survival to the world in general, but the catalog of injuries suffered really doesn't seem to have required that much time for recovery. They did use words like 'complications' and 'rehabilitation' to explain some of the delay, but it wouldn't have taken that long to train an agent to take Thomas's place either. And it wouldn't have taken that long for the visible scars and alterations to the current Thomas to heal to the point where he could appear in public."

Victor closed his eyes for a second, then nodded. "I think I see what you're getting at. ComStar says nothing when they first pull Thomas out of the wreckage, because they aren't sure if he'll live or not. Then he makes some progress, so they're hopeful and know he'll be grateful for their saving him. Then he loses some ground, or his recovery stalls, so they need to find someone who can take his place against the day he can be put back on the throne. Who would have him now, if he *is* still alive?"

"We don't know. We think very few people were involved in the operation, and most of them are probably dead— Primus Myndo Waterly, for one. She might have had the real Thomas bundled off to any number of continuing-care facilities, on Terra or elsewhere, without letting anyone know who Thomas really is." Jerry shook his head. "But I don't think ComStar has him or knows they have him because he'd have been too useful as a lever against Word of Blake."

Victor nodded. "And if Word of Blake had him, the current Thomas would be a lot more toadying of them and their efforts, or risk exposure."

"That was my thinking, Highness."

"So, is there any way we can find Thomas, *if* he lives?"

Jerry shook his head. "The Inner Sphere is a fairly big haystack in which to search for one specific needle."

"I know. If it were easy, we'd have found and recaptured the man who killed my mother." Victor smiled weakly. "And if it were easy I'd not be asking you two to do it. See if there's any sort of a trail in any FedCom records. Myndo might have hidden him in my parents' realm as a safeguard against her Thomas going rogue—and we do have the best medical care in the Inner Sphere."

"We'll see what we can do, sir." Jerry Cranston fished a noteputer from his pocket and punched a few keys. "Last thing for today, sir, the Precentor Martial has sent a message asking to postpone the training exercise on Tukayyid until the middle of March. I'm coordinating with Shin Yodama to see how that will affect the Combine units involved. The delay is frustrating, but this operation was put together rather quickly, so problems like this are bound to crop up."

Victor Davion's face turned down into a petulant scowl, and he knew it. The year 3057 had been a disastrous one, and he blamed most of his problems on the ways he'd unconsciously been emulating his father. It was then that things started to fall apart. Even the Free Worlds League invasion of the Sarna March could be traced back to his approving Project Gemini, begun by his father—a project Victor had been more inclined to shut down totally.

To keep from ever repeating the mistake of trying to be Hanse Davion, he had decided to return to what had always been the core of his existence. Victor had been raised to be a warrior and, despite the internal turmoil in the Federated Commonwealth and the Inner Sphere, the Clans still represented the greatest threat to civilization. To reinforce that fact in the minds of everyone, and to get back to the life he knew best, he'd outlined and proposed to the Precentor Martial and the Coordinator of the Draconis Combine a joint military training operation to take place on Tukayyid, the world where the Clan invasion had been stopped.

Focht and Kurita had both agreed to the exercise, which had originally been scheduled for mid-February. Having to put things off for a month was frustrating, but it would allow Victor time to get more ships back from the Lyran Alliance. It would also let him move the Davion Heavy Guards Regimental Combat Team to Tukayyid without taking such a toll on the interstellar trade and transport resources in the Federated Commonwealth.

"This need for a delay is based on Focht's run to Morges?"

"Yes, sir. An unexpected turn of events. It also appeared that part of the Wolf Clan has traveled to Arc-Royal, with Morgan Kell's blessing. I imagine the Precentor Martial will have enough information about that situation to brief us when we get to Tukayyid."

"Well, I guess that means I can take care of a month of luncheons and dinners before I go." The Prince sat back down at his desk. "And make sure that month is full of 'Mech simulator sessions and actual training runs for me."

Jerry smiled. "In a two-to-one ratio?"

"At the very least, Jerry, at the very least."

=== 14 ===

DropShip **Lobo Negro**
Outbound from Wotan
Jade Falcon Occupation Zone
10 January 3058

The cabin he'd been assigned aboard the *Lobo Negro* as senior Khan of the Wolves felt to Vlad as if it still belonged to
Ulric Kerensky. *He haunts this place.* The spartan furnishings, the scant few mementos of a life glorious in service to
the Clans—everything seemed to press in on him, but less
because it reminded him of Ulric than because it reminded
him of what Ulric had left him.

As the Wolves had headed out for the last battles in their
war against the Jade Falcons, Ulric had entrusted Vlad with
the future of the Clan. *He bequeathed it to me.* Vlad had told
Ulric that if the Wolves lost and the ComStar truce were repudiated, he would take the Wolves and race ahead of the
other Clans, taking Terra and fulfilling the whole purpose
for the invasion in the first place.

Ulric had replied, "I think it would be best for all if you
die here with me today."

And I almost did—as did our Clan.

At the time he spoke, Ulric knew Vlad could never have
succeeded in such a plan. He had seen the troop strengths
of the remaining Wolf units. Whole Battle Clusters had
been wiped out. Galaxies were filled with broken 'Mechs
and mangled pilots. Many of the best and brightest had fal-

len—especially those who espoused Crusader views—while others had followed Khan Phelan into the Inner Sphere. *And took ten percent of our warriors with them.*

Ulric's intention had obviously been to form a Clan colony within the Inner Sphere. Just as obviously he'd intended to leave a shattered Clan behind. Ulric had believed that Vlad would take the survivors and follow Phelan into the realm of the enemy. The dominant Wolves would be Wardens, and would be opposing the Clans from without rather than within.

Ulric's jihad against the Jade Falcons had been very successful, but the price had been grievous. The numbers had begun to trickle in from the bits and pieces of units scattered all along the attack corridors Ulric and Natasha Kerensky had used to devastate the Jade Falcons. At best a Galaxy and a half of combat-ready Wolves existed, and that was only if Vlad suffered the indignity of counting solahma bandit-hunters as line units.

The paucity of warriors left to his Clan recalled to mind Martha Pryde's comments to him. In such a weakened condition, Clan Wolf would be a logical target for a true Trial of Absorption. The fact that Ulric's war had been mostly waged on Jade Falcon planets meant that the Wolf holdings in the occupation zone were quite attractive. If Vlad could not defend them, other Clans would take those worlds, leaving no hope of the Wolves ever becoming dominant again.

Vlad walked around Ulric's desk and sat in the canvas campaign chair from which he had been lectured on so many occasions. It was too much to expect that Ulric's wisdom would be inherited by whoever took his place. Even so, something about the spare surroundings seemed to help Vlad sort out and organize his thoughts.

His first problem seemed very clear—he needed to rebuild the Wolf warrior caste to fill the void left by the dead or defected. Though many of the most promising sibkos had gone into exile with Phelan, enough of the sibling-companies remained to guarantee a future supply of warriors. Expanding the breeding program would create more sibkos, and screening the current sibkos for precocious warriors would get some new blood into 'Mechs more quickly. Recalling warriors who were training sibkos to active duty would hurt the training program in the short term, but he needed bodies quickly.

The possibility of adopting likely candidates from the Clan's lower castes into the warrior caste occurred to him, but Vlad almost rejected it out of hand. He had a warrior's distrust of and distaste for the martial abilities of anyone—any freebirth—born outside the Clan's breeding program. The fact that Phelan had been a freebirth heightened his hatred for freeborns, but he stopped short of allowing emotions to close an avenue of opportunity for him.

I need bodies. The obvious place from which to pull reinforcements for his line units was from the various units garrisoning worlds the Wolves had conquered. But doing that would mean losing control of those planets unless he could find troop replacements. Much as he disliked the idea, Vlad realized he would have to start recruiting from the lower castes in massive numbers to release his best warriors for use in his line units.

All that would help the Wolves recover a year or two from now, but Vlad's second problem demanded an immediate solution. When the Grand Council met again, some Clan or other would request a Trial of Absorption directed at the Wolves. Such Trials had been granted only twice in the past because in all the other cases the weakened Clan had been able to muster a show of defiance that impressed the other Clans enough to buy them time.

To sit back and prepare to defend his holdings would only invite assault—no matter how costly it might be for the attacking Clan. *We are warriors. To be passive is to* deserve *absorption.* Though preparing to defend his holdings would make the absorbing Clan pay dearly—as the Widowmakers had done with the Wolves long ago—his efforts would not stop the Wolves from vanishing for all time.

Vlad realized that boldness was the only real hope of preserving his Clan. He had to gather what few military assets he had and strike out at another Clan. And he would have to hit hard so his prey would have no doubt the Wolves still had very sharp teeth. He would also have to wound their honor enough that they would bid hard to win the right to a Trial of Absorption. If he chose his target well, they might even bid away too much to win the right to absorb the Wolves, then be unable to conquer him.

The choice of target was crucial and he knew it. He also knew it had to be one of the invading Clans. The other Clans, by dint of the fact that they had not won the right to invade, were really beneath his notice. To prey on any of them might even be interpreted as a sign of weakness.

The Clan he attacked must be haughty and full of itself. The Jade Falcons immediately came to mind, especially as the shame of *hegira* still burned in his heart. But he rejected the idea most instantly because the strike against the Falcons would only further weaken both Clans. Though Vlad had no love for the Falcons, they would not be the most inviting target for Absorption.

The other Clan that filled the bill had the added benefit of being another old foe of the Wolves. The Smoke Jaguars and the Wolves had been rivals almost from the start, and the fact that a Wolf had replaced a Smoke Jaguar as ilKhan still ate at the Jaguars. More important, the Smoke Jaguars were solidly tied up fighting against the Draconis Combine, so they would be in a poor position to strike back at him.

And a strike against them would remind Lincoln Osis that I am his peer, not someone he can command.

The fact that the Ghost Bear Occupation Zone lay between the Wolves and the Smoke Jaguars also worked in Vlad's favor. He would not tell the Bears what he was going to do until after it was done. They would protest, but the Bears and the Wolves had been allies for as long as the Wolves and the Jaguars had hated each other. Though Vlad might have to make some concession to them, the Bears would fight against a Smoke Jaguar incursion into their space.

The Jaguars would be honor-bound to demand the right to absorb the Wolves. Others would dispute that right because allowing the Jaguars to absorb the Wolves would result in joining two of the most powerful Clans. That would make the outcome of the invasion a foregone conclusion, and none of the other Clans wanted to see the Smoke Jaguars elevated over them.

Vlad smiled to himself. "The Smoke Jaguars it shall be, then. Is that what you would have done, Ulric?"

Vlad did not really believe in shades of the dead speaking

to the living, but the heavy silence of the cabin seemed its own answer. "Then, without objection, here and now begins the rebirth of the Wolves. The goal from which you shied, Ulric, is now mine to realize."

15

ComStar Military Headquarters
Sandhurst Military Academy, Berkshire
British Isles, Terra
20 January 3058

Precentor Lisa Koenigs-Cober grunted with the impact of the panels against her back as her *Quickdraw* jetted up into the air on an argent trident of fire. Though she was seated in a simulator at Sandhurst Military Academy while the rest of the Terran Defense Force and the Twenty-first Centauri Lancers were using simulators in the complex at Salina, Kansas, the experience felt as real to her as if she were back in battle on Tukayyid. Had she stabbed her feet down that forcefully on the jump jet pedals in combat, inertia would have jammed her down hard into her command couch—and the panels in the back of the simulator's couch reminded her of that fact in the most firm manner possible.

Her BattleMech shot skyward as the ground beneath it exploded. A rising fireball toasted her 'Mech's legs, but the auxiliary monitor showed no damage. *There's a miracle. Had I stayed down, that salvo of long-range missiles would have ripped me to pieces.* Even though the damage would have all been in the form of zeroes and ones in the memory of a computer, she wanted to avoid it as much as if it were exacted in blood and bone.

The salvo had come from the far side of a line of hills. She knew a company of the Lancers had to be dug in on the reverse slope, but prior to cloudscraping she'd had no clue where they were located. As her *Quickdraw* reached the apex of its jump, she saw the irregular trench gouged out of the earth, and as much as it spelled trouble for her command, she knew there was a more immediate danger to her people.

They have a spotter calling in missile strikes by the Archers *and* Catapults *in that ditch. Where?* She punched her holographic image of the battlefield over from magnetic resonance scanning to ultraviolet. Two tiny lines, dark against the gold of the grassy prairie, met at a point further out along the foot of the hills. The spotter, using an ultraviolet laser, had marked her 'Mech, then used another UVL to relay the targeting data to the 'Mechs waiting to ambush her people.

"T-Def One to all units. Alpha Company, lay down suppressive LRM fire in and around grid coordinate 323,455. Beta and Gamma Companies, turn to heading 37.5, spread and move to speed. They're beyond the rise."

Feathering the jump-jet pedals, Lisa brought her *Quickdraw* to ground about a hundred meters in front of where she'd been before. Her 'Mech squatted as the thick myomer bundles absorbed the force of the landing. As it straightened back up to its ten-meter height, her Alpha Company's LRMs arced up overhead. A kilometer down-range they obliterated the target grid-sector and all eight that touched it.

The computer created a firestorm over where the Lancers' spotter had been. Beta and Gamma Companies were already charging across the open area toward the hills, and Alpha Company had begun to follow them. Alpha would hang back and direct suppressive fire at Lancer targets as Beta and Gamma requested it, providing an umbrella beneath which the Striker and Close Assault Companies in One Battalion could operate most effectively. *Now that's the way a unit is supposed to work.*

She brought her *Quickdraw* up to 40 kph, switched her display back to vislight, and started to follow Gamma Company as it cut around the end of the hills to flank the Lancers. Fear began to knot in her belly, but it wasn't the same dread she'd experienced when facing the Clans. That had been almost crippling, but she'd fought through it because the Clans had to be stopped. Back then, the fear had been born of death and failure.

Now embarrassment gave it birth.

The Twenty-first Centauri Lancers had been performing very well in their orientation exercises. The results hadn't bothered her at first, largely because the Precentor Martial had lately begun rotating green troops in to the Terran Defense Force from Tukayyid. She'd put the dismal performance of the Com Guard units down to fatigue from the travel to Terra, plus the fact that many commanders were still becoming familiar with their new personnel.

Things still weren't going well for her people, hence her decision to join them in a series of exercises. In this, the third operation she'd participated in, her troops had begun to perform at levels she'd expect from Com Guard units. In the first two, they'd been tentative, but they were following the lead of their commanders who, in turn, were uneasy about being watched by their boss. The Lancers had dealt with them rather handily in those engagements.

Lisa came around the hill and found a valley full of fire and smoke. Gamma Company had broken itself down into a trio of 'Mech lances that poured fire into the Lancer position. The mercenaries, while dug in, took fire from Beta Company as it came over the rise and Gamma as it came in on the flank, which gave them far too many targets to ever fight off effectively.

Scarlet laser darts burned into the head of a Lancer *Crusader,* then a PPC's blue beam impaled the cockpit viewport. The Cyclopean 'Mech pitched backward as the computers cut off all input from the pilot's simulator pod. Black smoke billowed up from the ruined face as the *Crusader* smashed into a flat-headed *Thunderbolt,* and both of them went down.

To her right a Com Guard *Centurion* reeled back from the Lancer line. The armor had been stripped from both legs, and the left one had lost everything below the knee. The pilot fought valiantly to keep the 50-ton 'Mech upright. A half-dozen short-range missiles plowed into its damaged back, blasting away armor. The added destruction and explosions were enough to knock the *Centurion* forward, sending it crashing down unceremoniously on its face.

Lisa stepped her *Quickdraw* into the breach created by the 'Mech's destruction. Catching a glimpse of the *Wolverine* that had finished it off, she dropped the red cross hairs onto its broad silhouette. As the targeting cross went green, she

riggered her two medium lasers and let loose with her one-
hot SRM launcher.

The ruby lasers sliced chunks of armor from the *Wolverine*'s right thigh and flank. Spiraling in on the Lancer
'Mech, two of the missiles hit one each of the 'Mech's arms,
nother its left knee joint, and the last slammed into the *Wol-
erine*'s cockpit. That last missile, which flaked armor from
he 'Mech's head, caused more trouble than damage as the
ilot shied and the *Wolverine* took a step back.

Lisa winced. On a head hit, the simulator pods tended to
hake a pilot around like a bug in a jar. She kept her cross
airs on the *Wolverine* and fired again without giving the pi-
ot any chance to recover. Lisa knew that even though her
Quickdraw massed five tons more than the *Wolverine,* she
vas undergunned and underarmored for a slugging match at
his range.

The spears of laser light boiled armor off the *Wolverine*'s
eft arm and flank, but she didn't like the way her shots had
cattered all over the target. Though she'd begun to nibble
way at the armor in a half-dozen spots, only being able to
mploy two medium lasers meant she'd be all day picking
he 'Mech apart.

The *Wolverine* settled back on its heels, but managed to
ring its weapons to bear. The ball-turret on the 'Mech's
ead whipped around, and the pilot fired a salvo of scarlet
nergy needles from the pulse laser, blasting the *Quickdraw*'s SRM launch pod to smithereens. Warning sirens
ounded in the cockpit and the auxiliary monitor showed
damage to the midline armor on the 'Mech's chest.

Pressing the attack, the *Wolverine*'s pistol-like autocannon
ipped flame and spat out a hail of projectiles that chipped
armor from the *Quickdraw*'s arm. Its left-shoulder SRM
launcher blossomed fire as it spat out a half-dozen missiles.
All six hit, peppering the *Quickdraw*'s torso and left arm
with a chain of explosions.

First, the simulator pod shot backward, then began twisting slightly to the right. When the missiles hit, it whipped
hard to the left. Little tremors coming up through the command couch felt exactly like the heavy footfalls of a 'Mech
fighting to stay up. Lisa threw herself forward against the restraining straps, then pushed off against the left arm of the
command couch to twist her body to the right.

The neurohelmet she wore translated her moves and sense

of balance into computer commands the *Quickdraw*'s control unit could understand. The computer shunted energy from the fusion engine to power converters. From there electrical impulses contracted and relaxed the various myomer-fiber bundles that served the 'Mech as muscles. Limbs shifted, feet dug in, and the 'Mech remained upright despite being the target of an assault that would have utterly razed a city block.

Lisa's lasers burned back at the *Wolverine*. The first slashed a molten scar down the 'Mech's breastbone, burning a path through the colorful blue and silver marking the Lancers used to decorate their 'Mechs. The second struck the 'Mech's head, vaporizing several layers of armor. The computer controlling the simulation made the armor gush down in steaming sheets over the 'Mech's shoulders.

Another head shot and he could go down hard like that Crusader did.

Before Lisa had a chance to line up more shots, another Com Guard 'Mech stepped between her *Quickdraw* and the *Wolverine*. She watched the *Wolverine* pilot making an effort to withdraw as the smoke cleared and he identified the 'Mech shielding her.

Precentor Victor Kodis's *Hunchback* had been designed especially for just this kind of close-in brawling. The boxy autocannon on its right shoulder vomited a gout of fire, the 'Mech twisting with the recoil. The stream of depleted-uranium shells it fired devoured the remaining armor over the *Wolverine*'s center torso, opening a gaping wound that revealed the ferrotitanium structural supports that were the 'Mech's skeleton.

As the *Hunchback*'s left-arm pulse laser melted armor on the left side of the *Wolverine*'s torso, Lisa waited for the 'Mech to go down. *That much damage almost always sends a 'Mech to the ground.*

The *Wolverine* stayed on its feet.

It even fired back.

Four SRMs hammered the *Hunchback,* one missile hitting the 'Mech in the head and the remaining trio shattering armor on the left arm. The autocannon clicked over into rapid-fire mode, doubling the number of shots, and sawing through half the armor on the *Hunchback*'s left leg. The *Wolverine*'s pulse laser bubbled armor off the *Hunchback*'s chest and, to Lisa's horror, sent the smaller 'Mech to the ground.

Her lasers shot out and hit the *Wolverine* in the left leg and in the chest, the leg hit vaporizing previously pristine armor. The coruscating beam that pierced the chest bored straight through the gap in the armor created by the *Hunchback*. Though scarlet light glowed in the dark interior of the *Wolverine*'s chest, she couldn't see what she'd hit.

Then smoke burst from the 'Mech's chest and it staggered. The *Wolverine* pilot tried to take a half-step backward, but the machine moved with none of the strength or grace it had previously shown. A convulsion shook it, then it stumbled backward, suddenly sitting down hard like a stunned child in the middle of some rough play. Then the 'Mech flopped onto its back and a smoky shroud closed over it.

Gyro hit. Lisa nodded as her secondary monitor informed her that her guess was correct. In front of her the *Hunchback* climbed back to its feet. "Thanks for the save, Kodis."

"Likewise, Precentor. With you at the head we're able to hold our own against these Lancers."

"Right. Let's continue."

"Roger." Kodis's *Hunchback* moved forward.

Lisa waited a moment before following him. In her mind she replayed the way the *Wolverine* had remained upright after the *Hunchback* laid it open, and compared that with her weathering the earlier assault by the *Wolverine*. She knew full well that she should have gone down, but only plenty of experience and even more luck had kept her 'Mech on its feet.

Lisa sighed. *Evelena Haskell said she accepted the contract on Terra because she wanted time to train up the new troops she'd recruited. If the rest of her recruits are as good as that Wolverine pilot, I've got the solution to the mystery of why my people are doing so poorly. But that solution brings up another mystery—where's she doing her recruiting?*

"Evelena, if you've got some source for naturally talented pilots, I'd like to know where it is." Lisa stepped her *Quickdraw* forward. "With people like yours on our side the Clans will never get any closer to Terra than we decide to let them."

=== 16 ===

Tharkad City
Tharkad
District of Donegal, Lyran Alliance
3 February 3058

Tormano Liao had trouble deciding if anger or fear was the predominant emotion in General Nondi Steiner's voice. Whichever it was, it only came through in tiny bits. She seemed to have the same steel-willed control over her emotions that her sister, the original Katrina, had always shown. "I'm afraid," he told her calmly, "that Archon Katrina is unavailable and has requested no interruptions. Whatever you would say to her you can say to me."

"Oh, I have every intention of saying it to you, Mandrinn Liao." The General's gray eyes narrowed suspiciously as her gaze darted around the white office. "I think I preferred the way this office used to be."

Tormano opened his arms. "We all prefer things of the past to those of the future until we become used to them. What brings you here, General?"

"Trouble. Big trouble." Nondi Steiner crossed to where a wide-screen holovid sat in the corner of the room, and fed a disk into it. "This came priority and encrypted with our most secret codes. It will take ComStar the better part of a month to crack it, *if* they can. Please, start it up."

Tormano plucked the remote control from Katrina's desk—marveling at how she'd managed to have it and the viewer itself cast in white plastic—and brought the viewer to life with the punch of a button. A field of gray static sank beneath a wall of black. Color slowly bled into the picture, but the scene had obviously been shot at night. The only light came from the retro-rockets being fired by four huge *Overlord* Class DropShips. The ovoid ships settled gently to the ground, then their 'Mech bay doors opened and Battle-Mechs began to pour out of them.

The camera panned upward and focused on the insignia splashed across the side of the ship. It depicted a green bird bearing a katana. Tormano felt his insides tighten. *Jade Falcons.*

He looked over at Nondi. "Where?"

"This holovid came from Engadine. The Twenty-second Skye Rangers are defending the world, but they're one of the units we've been using to house misfits and miscreants, so I don't expect much from them. The Ninth Lyran Regulars are on Main Street, which is only one jump away, and I'll move them over to help the Falcons."

Tormano concentrated for a moment. Each *Overlord* could carry three dozen BattleMechs. That gave the Jade Falcons a force strength of, at the most, 144. The Twenty-second Skye Rangers Regiment would have an operational strength of approximately 120 'Mech's, but they had older equipment, making them roughly half as combat-worthy as the average Clanner. *The Twenty-second Skye Rangers are dead.*

"Might not sending in the Ninth Lyrans be seen as throwing good troops after bad?"

Nondi Steiner thought a moment before nodding. "It might, but we've got to make a strong response to this ag=gression. Clan JumpShips and DropShips have showed up at Willunga, Neerabup, and Bucklands. That's a solid thirty-three light-year penetration of our border."

"Agreed, but that's barely more than one jump from theirs." Tormano would have dismissed the attack as border raiding—it was common enough on both the Clan border and down in the Chaos March that he knew the signs well. Even so, the double-jump required to hit Bucklands made him hesitate. A JumpShip equipped with lithium-fusion batteries could make two jumps before needing to recharge the Kearny-Fuchida jump coils. With the initial jump going into the Lyran Alliance, the second jump could be reserved for a quick retreat if things looked inhospitable.

At Bucklands that second jump had been sacrificed to

move deeper, which could mean the Clans intended to attack the world no matter what the opposition. "Bucklands is undefended?"

Nondi nodded. "For all intents and purposes. We have a veteran's group there who've fitted machine guns onto AgroMechs, but the Falcons will sweep that resistance aside in seconds. Neerabup has a militia regiment to defend it. Willunga, like Bucklands, has no troops stationed there. The Seventh Crucis Lancers are on Winter and can be moved to contest any of those worlds, but it will take two jumps and about as many weeks for them to arrive."

Tormano sat at the desk and used the integrated keyboard to call up a holographic map of the Inner Sphere. The initial Clan assault had entered the Inner Sphere at the top of the circle and then gone on to carve a decent-sized wedge out of it—if the map were seen as a clock face the wedge would run roughly from eleven to two. This new probe came in at ten o'clock. If more than a raid, it could be the preface of a renewed assault that would carve another sliver from the Lyran Alliance.

He typed in a command that expanded the map and isolated the Alliance. He further focused the map down onto the block of worlds that ran from Engadine to the Jade Falcon border, then down to the truce line. It ended at Coventry and Arc-Royal—two worlds well known throughout the Alliance. Coventry was home to one of the larger 'Mech-production facilities in the Inner Sphere and the Coventry Military Academy. The Kell Hounds made their home on Arc-Royal. Either world would be an inviting target for Clan aggression.

Tormano also noticed that the line from Engadine to Coventry, if continued past the truce line, skewered Tharkad rather neatly. *Would they be so bold?* A shiver started down his spine, then he shook himself. "Treating this as anything more than a border raid at this point is borrowing trouble."

"But we must still deal with it."

"Agreed." Tormano looked through the projected map at Katrina's grand-aunt. "You will be moving the Seventh Crucis Lancers to Bucklands, I assume."

"Hitting the Clans at their least defensible point is standard doctrine, yes. Bucklands also allows the Lancers to support Trentham, if the Clans shift their attack to that system. In coming from Winter they'll stop at Trentham first, then move to Bucklands." Nondi hesitated. "But dealing with this initial probe isn't the main problem we have here. Deciding how to react in case the Falcons mean to go further is."

She moved to the right, removing herself from the map's image. "The people of the Lyran Alliance are strong and dedicated to their nation, but we can't rely for help on Victor's military anymore. A renewed effort by the Clans against the Lyran Alliance could spark a panic that would make us unable to deal effectively with the threat."

Tormano smiled and pressed his hands together, fingertip to fingertip. "Even the suggestion of a new invasion could have devastating effects." *The merest hint of weakness might prompt Victor to move against the Alliance under the guise of safeguarding its people.* Looking from the map to Nondi Steiner, Tormano could sense that she feared the loss of the Alliance's independence in just such a scenario. *She knows she would be relieved of command of the Lyran Alliance Armed Forces—and she fears failing at her duties more than she fears personal disgrace.*

Nondi's smile came as a weak imitation of his. "Katrina would think to calm the situation by making a speech telling our people we have nothing to fear."

"Making meters out of microns, if this proves to be a raid."

"Precisely."

"You would prefer a total news blackout from the affected worlds until we have dealt with the situation?"

Steiner nodded, then crossed her arms over her chest. "Do you think you can convince Katrina that handling this situation with discretion is the best way to go?"

"I think I can say, without fear of contradiction, that you will encounter no opposition from Archon Katrina in this matter." He poked a finger at the holographic block of worlds in possible jeopardy. "I do want the troops in this area put on some sort of alert. If things do progress further, we'll want to be able to respond."

"Alerts will make sense for the troops on the border with the Jade Falcon Occupation Zone—they already function on a nearly constant alert basis." Steiner's face darkened. "Notifying the Kell Hounds, on the other hand, might be premature."

Tormano kept his surprise from his face. Morgan Kell had

always been known as a staunch Steiner loyalist, nearly as fanatical in his defense of Steiner interests as Nondi herself. The General apparently viewed Morgan Kell's forming the Arc-Royal Defense Cordon as an act ranking him right up there with the late Ryan Steiner in terms of being hostile. *She has a blind spot that could hurt us.*

"I would hope, General Steiner, that events prove you right. As it is, I think Morgan Kell will have his hands full with his ARDC duties. This could, after all, be a feint to draw troops from our border with the Falcons."

"My thoughts precisely." Steiner nodded toward the map. "The other troops inside your block will step up training. If the attack continues, we'll need to bring up all the troops we can to oppose the Falcons."

"I will open negotiations with several mercenary units and review troop-shifting plans." Tormano smiled at her. "I think, General Steiner, the Falcons will soon regret their audacity."

The Dales
Coventry
District of Donegal, Lyran Alliance

Doc Trevena could feel the noose tightening around him. He keyed his radio and sent a tight-beam message out to Leftenant Isobel Murdoch. "Head's up, Bel, they're coming."

"Then why are we sitting, Doc?"

"To see if they deal with the surprise of flushing us any better than they have before."

"Roger. I'll break north."

"I'm out west. Rendezvous at 325, 43, one hour."

"Wilco, out."

Doc smiled. *She'll give them a good run.* Murdoch's *Hunchback* moved into Doc's forward firing arc as she prepared to leave the little valley and head north. He shifted his scanners over to magres and caught a hint of metal moving to the west. *They're getting better.*

It had been readily apparent to Doc that he needed to fortify his people with some solid survival skills before he started working on anything tricky, like tactics. One rule in

'Mech combat was that a fast-moving 'Mech was a tough target to hit. Luckily for his company, the light 'Mechs they'd been assigned were among the fastest available.

Of course, a fast-moving 'Mech wasn't an overly reliable gunnery platform. While he needed his people to be able to move quickly, he also wanted them able to hit whatever they shot at. No light 'Mech carried sufficient firepower to bring down a heavy or assault 'Mech, but a lance of them could certainly hurt one of the large machines. If his lances could hit without getting hit back, they might be able to discourage pursuit and even turn a formation by harrying it endlessly.

Out in the region known to the locals as the Dales—the lightly forested foothills of the Schwartzswerter Mountains north-northwest of Coventry's largest city, Port St. William—Doc had put his people through a month's worth of hide-and-seek exercises. As per their agreement, Quartermaster Leftenant Copley had funneled software and hardware upgrades to Two Company first, improving the unit's equipment to the level of most LAAF line units. That boosted the outfit's proficiency somewhat, but they needed a lot more than just what technology could give them.

The progress they'd made had increased sharply after Doc had won Leftenant Murdoch from Hauptmann Wells in a poker game. He'd put up K2,000 against her transfer on a night when he'd folded in the face of Wells's previous bluffs. Murdoch hadn't wanted to come over to Two Company, but Doc managed to talk her into it by letting her meet his people, then telling her that she was all that stood between them and death. Giving her a slice of his private retirement fund cinched the deal, and since that time she'd pushed Two Company to the limits of their abilities and beyond.

Catching another blip on his holographic display, Doc started his *Centurion* heading west. The 'Mech's huge feet churned up the turf and squashed shrubs. He used its enormous arms to bat aside trees, then to keep the 'Mech's balance as he started it up a green hillside. Reaching the crest, he cut to the right and swept the autocannon built into the *Centurion*'s right forearm from left to right.

The autocannon whined almost deafeningly as it spat out under-powered marker shells. They exploded against the armor of a *Locust*, covering the green and black plates with a reddish-orange dye. The *Centurion*'s scanners picked up on the stains and translated them into damage on the *Locust*'s computer image on the secondary monitor. The damage was minimal, but for a lightly armored *Locust* minimal damage could be substantial. In this case the shot blew through the armor on the 'Mech's right torso and tore up most of the support structures there. In actual combat the hit would have all but crippled the *Locust,* so the onboard computer would hobble it accordingly for the exercise.

Despite Doc's popping into the middle of their formation, Two Company's Second Lance didn't panic. The *Valkyrie* and *Jenner* both missed him with medium laser shots, but they also had to shoot past the two *Locust*s blocking the path to his *Centurion.* The *Locust*s were luckier, both hitting with their medium lasers and three of their four small lasers, burning armor from over a half-dozen places on his larger 'Mech.

More important to Doc than their marksmanship—he'd congratulate both Eagan and Nugent on it at the debriefing—was the unit's reaction to his attack. All four light 'Mechs shifted away from his line of attack and turned to be able to fire into his rear quarter. The *Locust*s moved forward and out toward the flanks, prepared to pace him on either side. If he turned to bring his forward weapons to bear on one, the other had a clean shot at his weaker rear armor.

Doc cut to his right and brought the *Centurion* around toward Eagan's damaged *Locust.* He dropped the targeting cross hairs onto the other 'Mech's outline and got a red dot pulsing in the heart of the gold cross. Hitting the thumb button and first trigger, he blasted away at the 'Mech with both his autocannon and medium laser.

And missed cleanly. *Damn, they're getting hard to hit.*

The lance fired back and fared little better than he had, though Regina Walford's *Jenner* hit him twice with her medium laser—once in the back and another time in the head. The head shot depleted enough armor from his cockpit that another medium laser shot could kill him outright.

Doc kicked the *Centurion* to its full speed. Going full out he could beat John Lindsey's *Valkyrie* in a race. The *Jenner* and *Locust*s were faster than his 'Mech, but if they chased after him, they'd leave the *Valkyrie* behind. He noticed that Lindsey had pulled his 'Mech up short, forcing his lancemates to decide if they were going to abandon him or turn back well before they needed to make that decision.

He nudged the targeting cross hairs beyond the golden lines marking the forward arc of his weapons and swung it onto the form of Eagan's *Locust*. The *Centurion*'s back-mounted laser stabbed a red beam into the center of the small 'Mech's torso. The computer showed armor dissolving, but the *Locust* continued on. By choosing to stay on the *Centurion*'s right side, Reggie Eagan kept Doc from taking a clean shot at her damaged right flank—which was exactly the sort of fatal mistake she'd made only two weeks before.

The *Jenner* hit with one of its medium lasers and damaged the rear armor on the *Centurion*'s left flank. Eagan hit with one of her *Locust*'s small lasers, vaporizing armor on the 'Mech's left leg. Percy Nugent missed entirely with his spray lasers, and Doc smiled. *Almost away.*

Then the *Valkyrie* let fly with its weapons. Now that Lindsey was no longer moving, his ability to hit a target improved appreciably. The long-range missiles the *Valkyrie* packed in its left torso launched, and the computer resolved their impact on the *Centurion*. Doc winced as armor evaporated over the spine and right flank of his 'Mech. Then the *Valkyrie*'s pulse laser chewed through the last bit of armor on the right flank, touching off the LRMs stored in the *Centurion*'s chest.

Had this been actual combat, the missile explosion would have torn the *Centurion* apart from within. Doc knew without question that he'd never have had enough time to eject from the damaged 'Mech. *There wouldn't have been enough of me left to stain a slide in a pathologist's lab.*

The computer, sensing the 'Mech's destruction, brought the *Centurion* to a stop, then shut down.

Sitting there in the darkened 'Mech cockpit, watching one lance of his company assemble before him, Doc smiled. *I haven't taught them everything, but I've taught them something.*

He sighed. "Let's just hope there doesn't come a time when I have to find out if what they've learned is enough."

═══ 17 ═══

DropShip Barbarossa
Outbound from New Avalon
Crucis March, Federated Commonwealth
10 February 3058

Victor Ian Steiner-Davion looked back at the diminishing ball that was New Avalon. Though not the world of his birth, it seemed far more a home to him than distant, cold Tharkad. He had been born and raised on Tharkad, but he could no longer think of it as anything but the world that had murdered his mother.

Killed her, and now harbors her murderer.

He shivered, then forced his fists to unclench. Behind the *Barbarossa* he saw the ovoid forms of the *Tancred, Locrin,* and *Palamedes,* the DropShips bringing the Davion Heavy Guards Regimental Combat Team to Tukayyid with him. He knew them to be the finest combat unit in the Inner Sphere, yet even with a dozen units exactly like them he couldn't avenge his mother's death.

Were I to attack Tharkad in an attempt to bring my sister to justice, I would be seen as mad. He smiled weakly. *If I attacked Tharkad I would be mad.*

Not because he would lose—he wouldn't. As much as he respected Nondi Steiner and her abilities, he'd studied her during his time at the Nagelring Academy. She was good at set-piece battles, but her temperament wasn't well suited to the continually changing nature of warfare necessary to defeat the Clans. She sought decisive battles and seemed to have little patience for the long-haul attrition style of fighting that had permitted ComStar to finally stop the Clans after twenty-one days of grinding combat on Tukayyid.

While he knew he could beat Steiner, he couldn't say the same for the man who would be his host on Tukayyid. Precentor Martial Anastasius Focht was the commander who'd defeated the Clans—a total of seven of them—in the brutal battle on Tukayyid six years before. Victor had reviewed holovids and all manner of written analyses of the epic conflict, but some element of it all eluded him. What Focht had done amazed him in the same way as had a chessmaster he'd once seen taken on a dozen opponents while blindfolded. Each could do something he found incomprehensible.

Right now.

The desire to understand what Focht had done was the reason Victor had accepted the Precentor Martial's invitation to train of Tukayyid. The month's delay in getting the operation started had been regrettable, but it had given Kai Allard-Liao time to join Victor and Hohiro Kurita on Tukayyid in command of the First St. Ives Lancers Regiment. Hohiro would be commanding the First Genyosha Regiment, and Victor wondered if his two friends had accepted Focht's invitation for the same reason he had.

To answer the question of why Focht wants us there? It wasn't that long ago that ComStar had been obsessive about cloaking itself in mystery and mysticism. While Focht had stripped away much of the psuedo-theology surrounding the organization—thereby creating the splinter Word of Blake group as haven for fanatics—the organization still remained secretive about much of its activity. Reports from the Free Rasalhague Republic, which might as well have been a ComStar protectorate, contained a few details about ComStar's military strength and make-up, but the information was not always reliable.

Even now, with the resources of the greatest star empire known to man at his disposal, Victor could not pierce the mystery of Focht's true identity. That lack didn't bother him terribly, but the reasons why Focht would suddenly invite outsiders to see what ComStar could do did get under his skin. The sudden openness made no sense, really, except in one case.

The recent war between the Wolves and Jade Falcons must have Focht worried. The invitation had been issued before the extent of the split was known, and at first it was only for command staff to "observe" operations. After a portion of the Wolves fled Clan-occupied space and found haven on Arc-Royal, the invitation had been modified to include units and their participation in the exercises.

A chill ran up Victor's spine. He couldn't help feeling he was being brought to Tukayyid not so much to learn how to fight the Clans but to audition as Focht's successor. Obviously, neither Focht nor ComStar were going to name him Precentor Martial, but someone had to be ready to accept the mantle of Defender of the Inner Sphere from Focht. Jerry Cranston had put estimates of Focht's age as between seventy and ninety years. Though the average citizen on a civilized world lived to be a hundred years or more, seldom was their last decade spent under the constant stress of the Clan truce collapsing and war beginning anew.

If Focht is testing for an heir, how will I fare? The competition was stiff. Hohiro Kurita was a valiant and skilled warrior. He'd learned from his father to adopt the elements of the warrior tradition that made the Draconis Combine strong, and to adapt the weak parts so they would do no harm. Hohiro had fought hard against the Clans, at one point managing to keep his command alive behind enemy lines far longer than even the most optimistic of his kin had dared hope.

And Kai Allard-Liao was all that and more. The worst anyone could say about Kai was that he'd gone down and been trapped behind enemy lines during the Clan invasion. But even that had only been because Kai was stranded on Alyina after saving Victor's life and the F-C forces evacuated the planet. Left alone on Alyina, Kai had first eluded, then joined with Clan troops to defeat a ComStar attempt to take over the world. After that he'd gone to Solaris and in short order become the reigning Champion on the Game World.

As good as his two friends were, Victor knew he wasn't so bad himself. He'd fought the Clans too, and participated in two of the rare victories over them. Kai's contribution to the first, at Twycross, couldn't be discounted, but the second was a long-range relief mission to rescue Hohiro off the planet where he'd been trapped. The Tenth Lyran Guards, rebuilt and reconfigured to be the kind of unit best suited to fighting the Clans, had acquitted itself spectacularly.

It was also true he'd lost his first command to the Clans, but that was in one of their earliest assaults on the Inner Sphere. *We didn't know then what they were or what they could do.* In the eight years since, the Inner Sphere had made huge technological leaps, narrowing the gap that had made the Clans an almost unbeatable enemy. When tactical improvements were factored into the equation, a rough parity could be reached.

Very rough, though it seemed to work for Focht on Tukayyid.

A light knock on the bulkhead of his cabin brought Victor around. "Yes, Jerry?"

Cranston came in, closing the hatch behind him. "Two bits of news. First, ComStar relayed a message from St. Ives that Kai and the Lancers will rendezvous with us in the Raman system, just before we enter Combine space."

"That means they'll be with us for six weeks as we head to Tukayyid." The Prince gave Cranston a short nod. "It'll be good to see Kai again and to spend some time with him. He can fill me in on how married life is suiting him. Was there any indication his wife would be accompanying him?"

"None, though I tend to doubt it. She's pretty active in trying to restructure the delivery of medical services in the St. Ives Compact." Cranston grinned mischievously. "We also have sources that suggest Doctor Lear may be pregnant again."

"That's fantastic." Victor clapped his hands. "Do they know if it's a boy or girl?"

The Intelligence Secretary laughed. "Their doctor knows, but both parents have requested that information be kept from them."

Victor arched an eyebrow. "You know."

"You pay me to know things, Highness."

"Well, don't tell me. I don't want to spoil it for Kai." The Prince's eyes sharpened. "He *does* know his wife is pregnant again, yes?"

"That he does know. His delay in accepting the invitation to Tukayyid was because he didn't wish to leave his wife alone while pregnant. Apparently he began to get on Deirdre's nerves, so she sent him away."

"Remind me to send her a note of thanks. What else have you got for me?"

Jerry sighed. "Reports about the fighting on Engadine are

conflicting. All we know right now is that the Jade Falcons hit the world and severely drubbed the Twenty-second Skye Rangers. The Falcons pulled out as the Ninth Lyran Regulars were coming in."

Victor frowned. "Sounds like a border raid."

"Agreed, but given the response time for the Ninth Regs to get to Engadine from Main Street, the initial assault must have taken place on or about the first of the month. It's taken us over a week to get the barest of reports. The only reason we learned anything is because some of the Rangers were from the Federated Commonwealth, and ComStar transmitted a Next of Kin message after one of them died."

"We expected to have problems with our intelligence when Katrina walked away with the Lyran Alliance."

"True, but a report about a raid on Engadine should have been sent immediately to Nondi Steiner on Tharkad. It's true our spies in the LAAF have been compromised, but we still have plenty of agents on Tharkad. We should have known more than we do now by the fifth of the month, at the very least." Cranston shook his head. "More important, the newsvids and disczines coming out of that whole area are being censored. Based on the problems with getting solid intel, I have to assume the Jade Falcons raided the Periphery area in force. They've gotten as far as Bucklands and perhaps even Australia."

Victor's mouth went dry. "Australia? That's only about four jumps in from the border."

"It is, sir."

"But there's no evidence they're holding the worlds they take. I mean, could this be another Red Corsair series of raids?"

Cranston shook his head. "I've got too little data to make any sort of a determination like that, Highness. The force that hit Engadine was bigger than any force the Red Corsair used, and this group is making no pretense at being anything other than Jade Falcons. Still, they're not holding worlds. In fact, they could have withdrawn already for all we know."

Victor looked up at Cranston. "But you don't believe that, do you?"

"Belief has little to do with this job, Highness. *Knowing* is the essence of it and I have to admit I don't know what's going on in this situation."

"Well, I hope, for Katherine's sake, someone does." Victor glanced back at the viewport, thinking he'd never give his sister the satisfaction of being called Katrina. "At least we're heading in the right direction."

"You can't be thinking of intervening in this."

Victor shook his head. "I'm not, at least, not on Engadine. But you and I both know that if the Falcons are still raiding the Lyran Alliance by the time we get to Tukayyid, we might be in for more than training exercises."

18

JumpShip **Boadicea**
Nadir Recharge Point, MGC14239287
Uninhabited Star System, Wolf Clan Occupation Zone
12 February 3058

Katrina Steiner brought herself to the most dignified stop she could manage in the zero gravity environment of the JumpShip. Holding tightly to the edge of the hatchway leading to the bridge with her one hand, she reached back with the other to twist her hair into a queue she could tuck down the neck of her light blue jumpsuit. Glancing around, she saw that no one had noticed her unheralded arrival.

After a moment of pique, she decided that was a good thing. The dozen people in the spherical bridge all had serious duties to perform in preparing for the next set of jumps between this star and their destination. Using railings and handholds, they were able to twist this way and that to read the circular array of monitors surrounding them.

In the center of the bridge a slender pipe formed a base for a thick disk of a table at which three people floated. The surface of the disk contained a number of liquid crystal displays, and the core of it housed a holographic projection unit. Starfields floated above the table, and little red lines linked glowing dots as different course plottings were projected and reviewed.

When she cleared her throat to speak, a shock of surprise ran through the bridge crew. "Is there a problem, Captain Church?"

The portly man at the central disk brought his head up so quickly that his toupee strained against the tape fixing it to his bald head. "No, Highness, we have the course plotted. We were just checking to see if waiting here could bring us in closer to the third planet of the system."

A petite woman with closely cropped kinky black hair let her body slowly rotate until she faced Katrina. "Archon, *I* have a problem with this last leg of the journey."

Katrina nodded. "I imagined you would, Agent Jotto. You have had a problem with this whole journey, have you not?"

"Only in my capacity as mission security specialist, Highness." Like the rest of the crew, Agent Jotto had been sworn to secrecy concerning this mission Katrina had described as being of "vital importance to the future of the Inner Sphere." But Jotto was far too practical to let her devotion to Katrina and the Lyran Alliance blind her to the dangerous realities of the trip.

The Archon sighed, but didn't vent her ire. *At least Jotto's still with us and knows the value of discretion.* "Please, Agent Jotto, speak freely."

"Thank you, Highness. If we use the charge in the lithium-fusion batteries to carry us from here, across Ghost Bear territory, to Kiamba, we'll be forced to recharge at our destination. The Kiamba system is centered around a Class G4 star, which means it will take us one hundred eighty-five hours to recharge our Kearny-Fuchida jump drives. Add the transit time to reach a recharge point from where we come in and we'll have to spend two weeks in that system at the minimum."

Katrina planted her feet solidly at the lower corners of the hatchway, then folded her arms. "You would prefer to wait at an interim point and bring up a double-charge on the drive, so we can jump back out at the first sign of trouble?"

"I would."

Captain Church wiped beads of sweat from his upper lip. "The problem with that strategy is that if we wait to jump, we won't be able to get close to the third planet. We'd have a week's transit to the world, and then another week getting back to the *Boadicea* before we could leave. With recharge time at another star, we're adding a month to the trip."

"Unacceptable."

The security woman paled. "But, Archon, the risks here are considerable."

"I'm a Steiner, Agent Jotto. I was raised to thrive on risk." Katrina smiled slowly. "But I appreciate your caution, and I do bear it in mind as decisions are being made. In this case, however, the important thing is that we arrive at Kiamba as soon as possible."

Katrina pointed toward the rectangular viewing port. "We're now within the Wolf Clan Occupation Zone. From here we could jump to safety in the Combine, but that would reveal our plans to our enemies. If we're going to risk discovery, it would be best to do it in the Smoke Jaguar Zone."

The third man at the central table maneuvered his body to face her. As he turned, his long, silvery hair floated out from his head, giving him the appearance of being quite surprised. The droll, even disinterested tone of his voice belied that impression and drained tension from the room. "Highness, your thinking strikes me as correct. We're not likely to be safe anywhere on this trip, so we might as well put ourselves where our hosts will have the most to gain by dealing with us."

Katrina felt a trace of fear. Baron Erhardt Wichmann's analysis defined the problem very well. If they jumped into Combine space she had no doubt they'd be taken to Luthien and Victor would be consulted as to what her disposition would be. The Wolves had interests in the Lyran Alliance, so her capture in their space would give them a great advantage over the Alliance. Only the Smoke Jaguars, who could not conveniently get at the Lyrans, could benefit from a liaison with her, so everything possible had to be done to bring her journey to fruition.

"Your point is well taken, Baron Wichmann." Katrina graced him with a smile that might have inflamed the passions of someone who didn't share the Baron's sexual preference. Behind her ambassador, she saw Captain Church already beginning to puff up. "A decision has been made, then?"

Church nodded solemnly. "Helm, lay in course option KIA023."

Jotto shivered. "KIA—killed in action."

Wichmann smiled sweetly at her. "Not superstitious, are you, little Hodari?"

Jotto's face hardened. "This may be a pleasure jaunt to you, Baron, and your last great voyage into the unknown, Captain, but to me it's a nightmare. This ship is unarmed and I have an insufficient number of security personnel present to guarantee the Archon's safety." She shook her head. "And to think I told Curaitis he was a fool for accepting the assignment to safeguard Prince Victor."

He was, *Agent Jotto*. "When do we jump, Captain?"

"On my mark, Highness."

Two warning tones sounded throughout the ship. The floaters grabbed hold of the edge of the table, and Katrina used her hands to brace herself in the hatchway.

"Mark."

The energy pouring through the Kearny-Fuchida jump drives ripped a hole in the fabric of reality and allowed the *Boadicea* to slip through it to a point thirty light years from where the ship had been an instant before. Katrina watched as the JumpShip seemed to shrink around her, or she expanded to burst through the hull. She felt herself growing larger and larger—not bloating like some disease-ridden creature—but becoming so vast that she encompassed the universe. Every star system became but one amino acid in one gene of one chromosome of the cells of her body, and all that could be known about them flooded her brain with an infinite amount of data.

Just as she was beginning to coalesce back into herself, the second jump hit. Her consciousness swelled beyond what it had been before and pierced the bubble of what was known and knowable. On the other side of that barrier she saw her mother floating there, a titan to her dwarf, with arms spread to welcome her. Then those arms became pythons that coiled around her and crushed her while the flesh on her mother's face exploded, leaving in its wake a fanged skull with flaming eyes. As the snakes flung her broken body in toward the black maw, needle-sharp teeth pierced her every cell, filling her with pain.

Katrina didn't think she'd screamed, but her throat felt raw as she opened her eyes. Hodari Jotto had firm hold of her shoulder and thigh, anchoring her against weightlessness. The woman pulled her back to the passageway wall outside the bridge and pressed her solidly against it.

"Highness, are you all right?"

Warning klaxons blared loudly and insistently. "What's happening?"

Jotto's face darkened. "We're at Kiamba. We jumped into

the middle of a military formation, including a fighting War-Ship."

Katrina heard a distant explosion, then felt a tremor shake the deck. "We're under attack?"

"Yes, yes, we are." Jotto glanced back at the bridge and the viewport. "We'd be dead if they wanted us dead—the WarShips could destroy us. The explosions are shots from aerospace fighters that were already deployed."

Katrina swallowed and found it hard to do so. She'd imagined a number of scenarios concerning her arrival all during the trip, but none of them had including an attack. She'd been told—assured even—that the Clans always bargained before they struck. She'd counted on that initial communication to be able to make her case that the leaders of the Smoke Jaguar Clan should be brought to her, or her to them, so they could negotiate a mutually beneficial alliance.

"Did they not bargain first?"

"Bargain?" Jotto shook her none too gently. "We appeared in the middle of a formation, Highness. Kiamba is being attacked, and we stumbled into the midst of the fight."

"Attacked?" Katrina felt goose bumps rising on her arms. "The Combine is here? When did they get fighting Jump-Ships?"

"Who said anything about the Combine?" Jotto jerked a thumb at the viewport. "Those are Wolf ships out there, Highness. It's just my guess, but I'd say, as of now, your mission to the Smoke Jaguars is at an end."

=== 19 ===

JumpShip **Dire Wolf**
Kiamba
Smoke Jaguar Occupation Zone
12 February 3058

The ache of fatigue gnawed at Vlad's joints, but the sensation remained almost below the level of his conscious attention. The assault on Kiamba had gone quickly and well. The Wolves had arrived in close to the third planet, then burned hard into the atmosphere. Their strikes had been all but surgical, and the Smoke Jaguar garrison troops had fought poorly. He knew even before the bidding began that he could have taken the world from the Jaguars.

He also knew he could not hold it, so he had settled for winning bondsmen and breeding stock. That had been incidental to the purpose of the attack, however—salt in the wound he had opened in the Smoke Jaguars' pride. He and his people had prove they were not a broken Clan and that they were truly the rightful heirs to the Wolf Clan legacy. The threats of revenge beamed at him as his DropShip burned for the Wolf JumpShips had been a fanfare to mark his victory.

Then the Inner Sphere JumpShip had appeared in the midst of his formation. Though alerted to its presence immediately, he had expected it to immediately jump back out of the system. When it did not he knew something odd was happening. When his aerospace fighters reported that the ship was unarmed and bearing House Steiner markings, a tingle of anticipation tightened his scalp. He might have expected a Kurita scout looking over Kiamba before a raid, but a Steiner ship meant something special was going on.

His troops took the ship about the time the *Lobo Negro* had docked with the *Dire Wolf*. They reported no resistance, which did not surprise him overly. *Anyone traveling in an unarmed JumpShip had already conceded military superiority to his foes.* He'd learned enough about the Inner Sphere—from information Phelan Kell had given up during his interrogations—to know they considered JumpShips too valuable to pack with explosives and detonate in the middle of an enemy formation.

The capture of the Steiner ship had gone unremarkably, though one of the prisoners demanded to see the Wolf leader. She claimed to be Katrina Steiner, Archon of the Lyran Alliance, but such a claim could not be taken seriously. Her presence, unescorted, so far from her capital, would have been decidedly reckless or foolish.

Or both. Though Vlad had nothing but contempt for the Inner Sphere and its people, he did pay attention to intelligence gleaned from public holocasts. Though he scorned most of what passed for entertainment, the intelligence value of news programming was remarkably high. The freedom with which information was spread throughout the Lyran Alliance and other parts of the Inner Sphere was a bonanza for the Clans in their drive to learn their enemy's weaknesses.

He knew who Katrina was—hardly a newscast went by without some bit of frivolous gossip about her. He had, in fact, seen thousands of holographic images of her. The woman went around constantly in new fashions, and always with some new way of doing up her blond hair. He'd laughed at first, but also found it fascinating to see how craftily she changed her image to subtly influence the people of her nation.

The door to his cabin hissed open and Vlad rose to his feet. The gray jumpsuit he wore stood open at the neck, the fabric pulled taut over the muscles in his upper arms and thighs. He raked a hand back through his thick black hair, trying to sharpen his expression to one he hoped would seem harsh and cold. *Whoever this pretender is, she will regret her jest.*

An Elemental entered the room, dragging the woman by her upper arm. Her long tousled hair hid her face until she

suddenly wrenched her arm free of the Elemental's grasp.
She swept the hair out of her face, then turned her startlingly
blue eyes on Vlad with a stare full of fire. "I will not be
treated this way."

A jolt ran through him. Vlad wanted to say—intended to
say—"You will be treated as befits your status within the
Clans." In his mind he heard the growl that would have imparted threat to the words. Countless bondsmen and women
before her had trembled at that tone of voice. *But they were
weaklings who would have cowered at merely a stern glance
or upraised fist.*

He likened what he felt inside to fear—the tightening in
his stomach and a kind of ache around his heart. At once he
forgot all about the pain in his joints, which was instantly replaced by a curious sensation in the deepest reaches of his
belly. It brought with it thoughts he had never thought
before—thoughts beyond physical need and lust—and those
thoughts left him speechless.

Confused, Vlad hesitated. Even with the anger in her eyes
and the tension in her body, she was beautiful. What he was
feeling, what he wanted, went beyond physical attraction.
Many of the women of his sibko and his Clan could easily
be classified as beautiful. The worlds the Wolves had conquered likewise boasted legions of beautiful women. Both
within the Clans and without he had coupled with the
women he wanted, but never had one conjured up in him the
thoughts he now entertained.

Thoughts of procreation.

The second he was able to label the thought—the urge he
felt crying out to him on a nearly cellular level—Vlad felt
himself utterly outside his previous experience. It made no
sense to him, and that began to frighten him. He was a warrior, born and trained to become a dispassionate killer of the
enemy. Logic and intelligence were tools he used to define,
understand, and conquer the known universe, yet here was a
reaction that defied logic, undercut intelligence, and still had
the strength to shake him.

With the Clan system of genetic breeding, the act of cou-
pling was far removed from procreation for the warrior
caste. Vlad had felt affection for his partners, but no more or
less than he felt for other members of his sibko growing up
or the units in which he had served. Sex, for the Clans, provided pleasure and relief of tension. It was given freely—a

gift exchanged between comrades—with none of the emotional entanglements and jealousies that could tear a military unit apart from within.

He knew he could not be feeling this attraction, this compulsion, toward this woman. *I do not know* how *to feel such a thing.* The idea that there was a new sensation, a new experience he had not yet known, did thrill him. Then again, his physical body betraying his accustomed discipline and control over it was profoundly disturbing. *This is outside my understanding. How can I deal with it?*

Vlad recalled, dimly and distantly, Ranna describing a similar attachment to Phelan Kell, but Vlad had been unable to understand a word of what she had been trying to say. He had considered the freebirth Phelan beneath contempt and believed her involvement with him was at worst an infatuation or, more appropriately for one of the warrior caste, a way of enforcing her domination over the bondsman. It was merely some game of which she would soon tire—or so Vlad had thought.

This is impossible, yet it is real! All this passed through his being even before the last of her words had died. He looked over at the Elemental and pointed at the door. "Leave the prisoner here."

The Elemental squeezed past the woman, and Vlad thought for a second that she did not give way to make things difficult for the warrior who had brought her to him. Then he noticed that the tightness around her eyes had lessened slightly and that her mouth remained slightly open. She stared at him, but did so blankly—striking him less as prey frozen in the presence of a predator than as another predator discovering an intruder in her territory.

Vlad bowed his head slightly. "Welcome, Katrina of the Steiners."

Realization seeped over her face. "You are a Wolf, but you are not Ulric Kerensky." Her words came cautiously in a voice full of wariness.

"No, I am not. I am Khan Vladimir Ward of the Wolves."

"You understand who I am?"

"I thought I had some understanding of who you are." Vlad had paid little attention to Katrina Steiner and her exploits largely because she continually cast herself as a peacemaker. Her actions conjured up in him feelings of revulsion. Others might try to kill the Clans, but she with her peace-making would try to dissolve their society and scatter them, ending forever the practices and customs that made them strong.

But this woman before me is not the weakling I would have expected. Vlad could see that in the set of her shoulders and the way her stare never wavered. "Do you now present me with a façade, or has what I have seen before been mere illusion?"

Katrina tugged at the bondcord knotted around her right wrist. "No answer I gave could be verified. You will have to make your own judgment." She opened her arms and her blue jumpsuit snugged over her belly and breasts. "What do I seem to be to you?"

The fitting consort for an ilKhan, provided I *am that ilKhan* ... Vlad covered his reaction by turning away from her to gaze out a viewport on the void. *She is a* freebirth, *yet you would raise her above all others. This is madness.* "Your presence here means you are young and foolish."

"To the charge of youth I will agree, Vlad." Her voice filled with warmth as she pronounced his name. He knew some of it was intentional on her part, but the way her voice trailed off showed her own surprise at how she had spoken to him. "And perhaps I *am* a bit foolish."

"More than a bit." Composed now, Vlad turned back toward her. "Yours is obviously a unilateral mission to Kiamba intent upon opening a dialogue with the Smoke Jaguars. They would have been impressed with your taking the risk of appearing here in person."

"And are you impressed?"

"Does it matter if I am?"

"Only if you are."

"I am, a bit." Vlad shook his head. "However, I wonder at the wisdom of a leader who would leave her nation while it is under attack."

Katrina's head came up and anger filled her eyes. "Attack?"

"The Jade Falcons began an extended series of strikes against Alliance worlds at the beginning of the month."

Katrina Steiner's icy eyes closed for a second, as did her hands into fists, her coquettishness suddenly forgotten. "Where have they hit? How have they done?"

Vlad shrugged. "Falcon predations do not concern me. If they truly wished to prove themselves formidable, they would have dared strike at another Clan, not the Lyran Alliance."

Katrina's chin came up. "I must return to Tharkad immediately."

"Oh?"

"My nation needs me."

"The Lyran Alliance is no longer your nation. You are a bondswoman of the Wolf Clan."

"What?"

He pointed to the cord on her right wrist. "You were taken as a prize of war. You belong to me."

Her reaction to his comment seemed to mix outrage with a hint of curiosity. "You actually think you can own me?" She pointed toward the viewport. "I command the loyalty of billions of people. In my name, hundreds of thousands of individuals will take up arms against you and contest your claim."

He raised an eyebrow. "So far those people have been singularly unable to stop the Jade Falcons. Why should I believe they could wrest you away from me?"

"Why should I believe my people have not stopped the Falcons?" She planted her fists on her hips. "And why would you be foolish enough to believe my people won't yet stop them? If I had to guess, I'd say the Falcons were hitting and running, making themselves a difficult target. Tukayyid shows that when you Clansmen stop, you can be defeated."

"But the Wolves were not defeated on Tukayyid."

Katrina's blue eyes sparked. "The Wolves had Inner Sphere help at Tukayyid."

Vlad snarled, then caught himself and covered it with a smile. "You imply that without Phelan the Clans cannot win."

She returned his smile. "You might interpret it that way."

"And you believe Phelan and his people will save your realm from the Falcons?"

Her expression darkened slightly, then an impassive mask slipped firmly into place over her features. "His loyalty to his home is exemplary of my people."

Vlad nodded, analyzing her reaction to his mention of Phelan. *She is too impulsive. Her emotions run too close to the surface. This is a flaw, though an intriguing one.* "Phelan is your cousin, yet you do not like him."

"You know him, I assume." She regarded him frankly. "Do you like him?"

The Wolf laughed aloud, and Katrina seemed shocked by the sound. Vlad fingered the scar running down the left side of his face. "He has left his mark on me and on my people. And I blame our present plight on his undue influence over the ilKhan. His presence in your Lyran Alliance makes me view Arc-Royal as a special target when the invasion resumes."

"And that will be?"

He shrugged. "It will resume when we have chosen a new ilKhan."

She frowned. "But you met to elect a new ilKhan a month ago."

"Indeed we did."

"So the attack will be coming now."

"No."

"Why not?"

Vlad smiled. "We elected an ilKhan and I slew him minutes after his election."

"You what?"

"He was unfit to rule. I killed him for it."

Her eyes widened in open admiration. "But that was not your only reason for doing so."

"No. He was a Jade Falcon. I needed no other reason to kill him."

"I see."

Vlad nodded. "Perhaps you do."

"And you see the purpose of my visit here, *quiaff*?"

"An alliance with the Smoke Jaguars would give you leverage to press the Draconis Combine. That would distract your brother. The Jaguars might also be able to act as a brake on the Falcons or any other ambitious Clan with designs on your realm. From your incomplete understanding of how we work, doubtless they seemed a very good choice for you."

She gave no visible reaction to the mild rebuke. "You think there is a better choice for an ally among the Clans?"

"An open alliance with an Inner Sphere nation would be suicide for any Clan leader."

"As would an open alliance with a Clan power for any Inner Sphere leader." Her steely gaze met his. "You and I could reach an accommodation, I think. The enemy of my enemy is my friend."

Echoes of the original jolt trickled back through him. *The Falcons. Phelan.* He nodded. "An accommodation, perhaps, yes."

"Good." She held her right wrist out. "Free me of this bondcord and you will find me very accommodating."

"Bargained well and done, Archon Katrina." Vlad slipped a knife from his boot and sliced the white cord with a single flick of the wrist. The card fell to the deck between them, and he kicked it away. "Now let us speak as friends of those who will dread our coming together."

20

Tension petrified Tormano's neck and shoulders. The holographic map floating in the air above his desk had a jade green ice-pick stabbed deep into the Steiner-blue Lyran Alliance. The addition of strikes at Recife, Ellengurg, and Guatavita left no doubt that Coventry would be the next target.

And Tharkad lies only four jumps past Coventry. At the Jade Falcons' current rate of advance that would put them on Tharkad by April first. The significance of that date was not lost on Tormano. He would have shaken his head in confusion, but it hurt too much to do anything but leave his chin resting in the palm of his right hand.

What confused him was a yin and yang war of logic and illogic concerning the Clan aggression. Clearly the advance looked as if it was a drive to take Tharkad and thereby eliminate the Lyran Alliance from the fight against the Clans. That was good strategy on several levels. With Tharkad gone the various factions within the Lyran Alliance would be left on their own. They would either have to become Clan vassal states or hold on for as long as they could before the Clan tide sucked them down.

The loss of Tharkad would also force Victor Davion to turn his attention from the Combine's problems to those of a nation he claimed as his own. Davion would be forced to fight on his own territory to liberate a populace that had evidenced little love or use for him. If he did not defend the Lyrans, the Free Worlds League would have to push forward from their border up toward the Clan lines to create a buffer zone that would mean they'd not be fighting on their own worlds to oppose the invaders. If that happened, the chances of the Federated Commonwealth ever being united again were dead.

But there were also problems with viewing the Clan action as a brilliant bit of strategy. The first was that attacking to force Victor to shift support from the Combine to the defense of the Alliance would mean the Clans were working as one, since the Falcon action would also benefit the Smoke Jaguars and the Nova Cats. But the recent defection of Wolves to the Lyran Alliance was ample evidence that the Clans did not move together in lock-step.

With that little myth exploded, Tormano had to look at how the Jade Falcons benefited from the attack. Seizing Tharkad would take all the fight out of the Lyrans, to be sure, but the LAAF had not engaged in much cross-border activity. Nondi Steiner had concentrated on keeping the border quiet and on repulsing Jade Falcon incursions. She'd not struck back into Falcon space, and other than the Kell Hound operation a couple of years ago, Tormano knew of no strike launched from the Lyran Alliance into Clan-occupied territory.

What concerned him more than the lack of motive for the drive was its target. Tharkad was a logical one, to be sure, but the Clans had never made any secret that the goal of the invasion was the prize of Terra. Whichever Clan took Terra would supposedly be elevated above the rest. That Clan would establish and administer a new Star League, with the Clan way as the model for humanity. Only ComStar's defense of Tukayyid had stopped them.

Tharkad is not *Terra.* Tharkad would be a logical target if its capture would somehow put the Falcons closer to Terra or confer some other advantage toward taking Terra, but it would not. While bits and pieces of the Lyran Alliance did stand between the Falcons' most forward position and Terra, so did the Free Rasalhague Republic and a huge chunk of the Draconis Combine. Moreover, Tharkad stood one jump further from Terra than did Quarell. Traveling from Tharkad to Terra would bring the Clan troops along the Free Worlds League border, doubtless provoking action by Thomas Marik to protect his realm.

Nondi Steiner had argued that the Falcons planned to cross the truce line, triggering war between ComStar and *all* the invading Clans. That would tie up ComStar's troops while the Falcons made an end run through the Lyran Alliance to Terra. That made sense in a way, but Tormano doubted that Nondi had hit upon their strategy.

They aren't acting as they did when they first invaded. When the Clans first hit the Inner Sphere, they attacked, conquered, and held the worlds in their invasion corridors. In the current operation, the Jade Falcons landed on a world, beat the local defenders up, then departed. Unlike the initial invasion, they were defeating but not crushing, planetary defenders. The Falcons did take supplies from the worlds they hit, but less in the form of loot than in the way of an army living off the land through which it passed.

Nondi's theory was that the Falcons abandoned the worlds they attacked because they knew they couldn't hold them. She cited performance reports showing the Falcons to be less effective than in the first invasion eight years earlier. Tormano considered such statistics to be unreliable at best and thus insignificant. The fact was that the Falcons had kicked around everything the LAAF had thrown at them.

And just because he could see no logical reason behind the Jade Falcons' attack didn't mean there wasn't a good one. For all Tormano knew, the recently elected ilKhan could have decided that Terra was useless as a target and designated Tharkad in its place. The Jade Falcons could have won the bidding to be the Clan that took it. After it fell perhaps Luthien would be designated and targeted and so on until the whole of the Inner Sphere had been pieced out and picked apart.

Tormano closed his eyes to ease their burning, but he could still see the pinpoints of light he'd been staring at before. Even though he couldn't grasp *why* the Clans were heading toward Tharkad, he couldn't ignore the fact that they were. The security of the Lyran Alliance capital was paramount, for if it fell, no defense against the Clans could be organized.

He smiled. *And having Clan OmniMechs marching around the Triad isn't my idea of a good time. Decades ago was the last time I gave any thought to piloting a 'Mech, and those days are best forgotten.*

Opening his eyes again, he punched up a request for troop availability and locations. He wanted to call to Tharkad the best and most loyal of the LAAF units. Any counterstrikes could be staged from there, and such units would fight fanatically in defense of their Archon and her home. When the Clan foray did finally get to Tharkad, it would progress no further.

He made his selections and watched the mounting time it would take for the various ships to travel to Tharkad. Even in the best cases it would take two months for troops to arrive, putting them down approximately two weeks *after* the Falcons had attacked. While the delay was unacceptable, it was also inescapable—the laws of physics and the limitations of technology meant the fifteenth of April was the best he could hope for in terms of arrival of the force he wanted to defend the world.

If I cannot speed them up, perhaps I can slow the Falcons down. Coventry was the next obvious target for the Jade Falcons. He estimated their arrival time there at a little over three weeks, putting them down on the planet in the middle of March. The difference between Coventry and the Falcons' other targets was that Coventry had three substantial 'Mech forces already present: the Coventry Donegal March Militia, the Tenth Skye Rangers, and the Coventry Military Academy Cadre. While the Academy Cadre used only outmoded 'Mechs for its training, the cadets would surely make up in enthusiasm what they lacked in arms. The Militia was a mixed unit, with armor and aerospace elements in addition to 'Mechs. The Rangers, while a misfit crew, looked good in holograph.

With those three forces and the scattered personal guard units of the various nobles who made Coventry their home, the Clans would face a bit more resistance than they had so far. If the locals could hold out long enough, it would even be possible to drop reinforcements onto Coventry to further tie up the Falcons and perhaps make sure they never left the world at all.

The troops I send to Coventry are going to have to be very good and capable of independent operation. I would send the Kell Hounds, but I doubt they'd even answer my request, despite being closer to Coventry than my other choices. The

Eridani Light Horse were a mercenary unit with a history that extended back to the Star League, and a reputation that rivaled that of the Kell Hounds or Wolf's Dragoons. They had fared well in the fighting against the Clans' first invasion, and their presence near the Periphery could easily explain why the Falcons had looped around to their present attack vector. His figures showed they could arrive on Coventry in early April. If that were not early enough to engage the Clans on Coventry, the force could shadow the invaders and engage them on any other worlds they attacked.

The second unit he wanted to employ was Wolf's Dragoons. Though all five regiments were on Outreach, the Dragoons had enough JumpShips to send at least two of their regiments to Coventry by early April. Because Tharkad lay on a direct line between the two points, the Dragoons could stay on Tharkad if the Coventry situation resolved itself prematurely or push on to another world to fight the Falcons.

Bringing the other three Dragoon regiments to Tharkad would strengthen the defense of the world, but he wanted another unit that was more to his liking. Tormano knew that if the Clans *did* make it through to Tharkad, saving his life and evacuating him would be the last thing on the minds of loyal Lyran citizens. He could easily picture Katrina—if she made it back in time to see the world fall—exhorting her people to fight to the last for her, and he knew they would.

And would ultimately blame the fall of Tharkad on me or, more likely, Victor.

For that reason he would bring to Tharkad a mercenary unit that was personally loyal to him and would look out for his interests. For years he had paid them a retainer in case he should ever need them—either to fight for him or, more realistically, to engineer his escape if Thomas Marik or Sun-Tzu Liao had ever decided to have him killed. They were a competent unit with a good reputation, though their long-standing feud with the Dragoons still continued even though old Wayne Waco had retired. Putting the Waco Rangers together with the Dragoons on any world was a potential recipe for disaster, but the advantages outweighed the risk.

Reaching back behind his neck, Tormano shoved his thumbs into the knotted muscles there. *I'll have to run these troop adjustments by Nondi, but she'll approve them—as well as continuing the news blackouts from raided worlds.*

My actions will free her from having to worry about anything but direct action against the Falcons.

"I hope, Archon Katrina, your return brings with it good news. Actually, I hope it will be soon, good news or not." Tormano winced at the tightness in his neck. "It was not my aim, when I took this job, to preside over the death of the Lyran Alliance."

= 21 =

DropShip **True Word**
Boonville, Kentessee Administrative District
North America, Terra
28 February 3058

Precentor Lisa Koenigs-Cober tightened down the restraining strap holding her to the *Quickdraw*'s command couch, then keyed her radio. "Is there a chance, Mr. Archer, that you can fly around those downdrafts instead of through them?" She kept her question light, but didn't let it become entirely a joke. The *Leopard* Class DropShip had bounced around rather severely.

"Had I my choice, Precentor, I wouldn't be in the air right now. I could fly over this storm, but we're using the Lancers' beacon to bring us in on target."

"Acknowledged." Lisa sighed, not for the first time on the trip. Evelena Haskell had requested her presence as observer in a final set of exercises that would prove the Twenty-first Centauri Lancers ready to assume their duty station and thus trigger the contract clauses that started their pay at a higher rate. Lisa had tried to get out of it, even going so far as to plead the need to requalify on a live-fire range in her *Quickdraw* before the end of the month. Haskell pointed out that the Lancers had just such a range set up and would put it at her disposal, eliminating her last excuse.

Lisa finally agreed to join the Lancers outside Bowling Green, having realized that part of her reluctance came from the way her pride had been stung in the simulator exercises with the Lancers. She decided, without telling Haskell, that she and her lancemates would get additional qualifying out of the way by performing a combat drop into the live-fire range. She hoped that showing her skill at that would win back some of the face she'd lost when the mercenaries trounced her troops.

The arrival of one of the worst winter storms in recorded history almost scrubbed her plan. Warm, wet Caribbean and Atlantic air had collided with an arctic air mass over the North American midwest, and pushed on toward ComStar's headquarters at Hilton Head. It had already dumped several meters of snow on either side of the Mississippi River, promising floods in the spring, and then barreled on toward the eastern seaboard.

"I understand your reluctance to fly in this weather, Mr. Archer. Just try not to set it down too soon."

"Sure." The pilot's sarcasm poured into Lisa's neuro-helmet with digital clarity. "It would be nice if I could just see *where* to put it down."

The secondary monitor in her 'Mech's cockpit glowed white as Archer fed his external camera view to it. "It looks rather white out there."

"Yeah, and three meters deep, too."

"They've got a runway clear for you?"

"I guess so. They've got the beacons set up. We'll go on automatic approach in ten minutes or so. We're about a hundred and a half kilometers out. Hang on."

"Wilco."

Archer laughed. "I've got four Lancer aerofighters coming in. Either they're nuts, or they need adverse weather training."

Lisa smiled. "Follow them home, Mr. Archer."

"Roger, Precentor."

She punched a couple of buttons on her command console and shifted the view from the nose camera to the aerodynamic DropShip's radar. The storm clouds through which they were traveling created a lot of interference, but she could just make out four scarlet blocks marking the Lancers' TR-10 *Transit* fighters. They shot past the center of the screen, then came back around. As they pulled up onto the DropShip's tail, she expected them to move to the wings and out into the lead.

Just as she wondered why they did not, the ship bucked.

For a half-second she thought the DropShip had hit turbulence again, but the radar feed to the secondary monitor went dead. She almost ascribed that failure to the turbulence shaking loose her commline connection to the ship. She reconsidered quickly with the wet *thwap* of yellow-green coolant splashing against her 'Mech's cockpit canopy and the sudden addition of ragged patches of white where the 'Mech bay's black surface had been before.

Turbulence is the least of my worries.

Another tremor shook the ship, and the holes in the hull yawned open wide. The DropShip began to roll to the right and before she had time to react, it had inverted entirely. Wind howled through the 'Mech bay as the ship began to corkscrew in toward the planet.

Lisa punched the radio on—it had been off previously to keep from interfering with navigation, but the fact that she could bring it up meant the computer lockouts had been disabled. As far as the silicon brain controlling her 'Mech was concerned, whatever she was in was no longer a functioning DropShip. Obviously the pilot thought so too. As he activated the emergency system, the cargo doors blew away, giving her people one final chance.

"Get clear. Blast your way clear!"

She stomped full with both feet on the jump jet pedals, igniting three silvery jets mounted on the 'Mech's torso. They filled the 'Mech bay with fire. Above their roar she heard the scream of metal as the restraining brackets tore loose. She pushed back and away with her 'Mech's arms, propelling her machine forward toward the white crevasse in the ship's side. She felt the scrape of armor on the edges of the fuselage, then the ship lurched and her 'Mech was flung free.

The altimeter on the auxiliary monitor showed her elevation as two kilometers. *Higher than most combat drops.* Because her 'Mech was designed to use jump jets, it could support the stresses of landing from a jump. Normally that meant cushioning a descent of under a hundred meters, but in combat situations jumps from greater heights might be accomplished without serious damage to the 'Mech.

At one klick she hit her jump jets and cut into the velocity of the fall. The burn slowed the falling 'Mech slightly and managed to orient it so it would hit feet first. The altimeter continued to count down, the numbers blurring as they ran.

At two hundred meters she again stomped on the pedals and braced for impact.

It's not enough to slow me down. I'm going too fast. A split second before she could panic, invocations that ComStar used to teach its members flashed through her brain. On their heels came the regret that ComStar had abandoned its mystical training. Though utter nonsense, those prayers would have been more comfort than the cold, cruel logic of reality.

She felt something hit the 'Mech and start it tipping toward the left a heartbeat before its huge metal feet smashed down into the ground. Inertia slammed her into the command couch so abruptly that she felt blood gush from her nose onto her upper lip. The restraining straps dug into her shoulders and waist as she rebounded against them and the 'Mech started to tumble.

A world of white and gray and black whirled outside the 'Mech's cockpit. Hundreds of snow-demons beat against the *Quickdraw*'s armored hide as it rolled. Thunder played through the cockpit, vibrating straight through to her spine. The tempo of collisions between 'Mech and earth rose and fell with no pattern she could discern, but with an intensity that made her think it might never end.

She fought the temptation to fling the 'Mech's arms wide to slow the roll. The momentum of a 60-ton BattleMech in a losing war with gravity would snap an arm off in an instant. The fall from the DropShip and the landing were the worst of what she had to endure, so there as no reason to cause more damage to the 'Mech.

The *Quickdraw* hit hard once again. From the spin imparted to the 'Mech she assumed its shoulder had hit an outcropping of rock. The 'Mech's feet slewed around and the cockpit began to rise, as if the 'Mech were being propped up like a giant puppet by an invisible hand.

Then the collisions stopped.

The 'Mech went through a long, lazy somersault that filled the cockpit with silence. Lisa gritted her teeth and grabbed the arms of the command couch with viselike grips. Part of her knew that, given the pace of the flight, the next collision would be minor, but that intellectual assessment found no purchase in her heart. *This is going to be bad!*

The *Quickdraw* landed far more lightly than she'd dared to hope and, to her surprise, she barely bounced up from her seat. When she looked up at the cockpit canopy, all she could see was white as snow slowly floated down to cover it. At the corners of the view through the canopy she saw dark gray masses. It took her a moment to realize that the 'Mech had landed on its back and that the gray represented the forested sides of the mountains that cupped the valley where she'd ended up.

Or ended down *more correctly.* She flipped open the viewplate on her neurohelmet and pinched her nostrils shut with her left hand. With her right hand she punched a few buttons and ran system diagnostics on the *Quickdraw. Come on, be mobile.*

The computer came back and indicated that, aside from being nearly out of jump-jet fuel, the 'Mech was in decidedly good condition. *For a machine that just fell two kilometers through a blizzard.* The roll had damaged armor all over the 'Mech, lowering its protective value anywhere from ten to twenty-five percent. But the legs and actuators had weathered the landing in good shape. The *Quickdraw* would still walk just fine, and had lost only about fifteen percent of its sprint speed.

She flicked a switch and brought the weapon systems online. The computer showed them all functional with the exception of the SRM detachable launcher, which had detached during the roll. Lisa felt fortunate it had not exploded while still mated to the 'Mech's torso, though she did regret its loss.

Bringing the *Quickdraw* up into a sitting position, she discovered that it was half-submerged in what had been a frozen pond. Looking back to the right she saw a ten-meter-wide swath of flattened pine trees disappearing beneath a blanket of snow. Coming down onto a slope, the 'Mech had hit a tree, then started to roll until it came to a big rock outcropping that stood at the top of a thirty-meter cliff that overlooked the pond.

Lisa shivered. "I don't think I want to replay what my sensors recorded in that roll."

The numbers in the auxiliary monitor's Global Positioning System window showed her to be solidly in the middle of the Kentessee District. *I'm almost 750 kilometers northwest of Hilton Head and I have the Great Smoky Mountains between here and there. If I'm lucky I can hit fifty kilometers per hour. That's fifteen hours.*

She realized she'd decided to return to Hilton Head before she'd fully considered what had happened to her, and what she was sure to find at the ComStar headquarters. There was no question the Lancers had deliberately fired upon the DropShip with the full intention of killing her. They had no reason to assume she'd be buttoned up in a 'Mech. Even if the *Transits* had tried to follow the *True Word* down, chances were they'd have thought her 'Mech blasting free nothing more than a malfunction on a stricken ship.

Things began to slowly slip into place for her. The fact that the Lancers had tested as far more capable than what their service records indicated should have made her suspicious. Instead of wondering why they exceeded her expectations, she'd welcomed their precocious skill. It made her job of defending Terra easier.

I should have figured out that the Lancers we hired were different from the Lancers we got. The attack on her showed the substitution had been part of a plan to, at the very least, leave Terra defenseless. That made no sense since Terra was the Clan objective—unless, of course, the Lancers were really a Clan unit in disguise. Even so, if they were, how would they have been able to insert into ComStar computers the information needed to get the Lancers the proper security clearances?

Regardless of who the Lancers really were, only one group could have accomplished the substitution of records in ComStar files. Word of Blake had intimate knowledge of ComStar procedures and facilities, and everyone knew that some individuals in ComStar still had sympathetic ties to their former brethren.

And Word of Blake had long been making noises about reclaiming Terra and "driving the blasphemers from the temple."

Lisa brought the *Quickdraw* to its feet. She switched the scan mode to magres. *If anyone else made it out of the DropShip, or if the Lancers have sent ground forces to check out the crash site, I'll be able to pick them up. While they were hitting me, they must also have turned on the Terran Defense Force battalions training with them—provided they weren't infiltrated with Blakists, too.*

She sighed. "Their goal has to be Hilton Head and the Primus. I can't stop them, but if this storm delays them long enough, I may be able to surprise them." Lisa turned the

Quickdraw in a southwesterly direction. "Behead the snake and the body dies—but only if the head is truly dead. There's a fine line between winning and total victory, and with any luck I'll be able to pinpoint exactly where it lies."

22

Watching his friend's face as he studied the holographic star map projected into the space between them, Victor couldn't help but smile despite the gravity of the situation. The Kai Allard-Liao sitting across from him in the DropShip cabin seemed as sharp as ever, and his comments were as insightful as in the days of the Clan invasion, yet he'd changed in the six years since the truce of Tukayyid.

And in the six years, since I left him behind on Alyina. The two friends had met since then, but what little time they'd spent together had been on Arc-Royal. That had been only a couple of years ago, but Kai had changed significantly in that time—as much as he'd changed after the year behind the lines on Alyina.

Physically he was the same as ever: tall and on the lean side, but proportionately muscled. His almond eyes and yellow skin, along with his black hair, were all characteristic of his family's Asian background. He'd gotten his gray eyes from his mother, but the intelligence that shone in them came in equal and generous portions from both his parents.

Still, he looks different. "That's it," Victor said suddenly. Kai looked away from the glowing globes of the holo map. "That's what? You've found a solution for this Falcon raiding?"

"No, I've been trying to figure out what's different about you."

"Different?"

The Archon Prince of the Federated Commonwealth nodded. "You look happy. For the first time in all the years I've known you, you actually look happy."

Kai blushed. "I guess I am happy." His smile wavered for a second. "Not that I haven't been before, but, well, I always felt a lot of pressure trying to live up to what my parents expected. Of course, what *I* thought they expected had nothing to do with what their expectations really *were*—I was the one who decided I had to prove myself worthy of being heir to their reputations."

Victor laughed. "Their legends, you mean."

"Right." Kai shrugged. "It's odd, you know, but there are only a half-dozen people who I can talk to about this with any hope of their understanding. Being Hanse Davion's son, or Melissa Steiner's son, can't be any easier than what I faced, but you handled it differently."

"The situation wasn't exactly the same." Victor frowned. "Your parents were proud of you and willing to let you find your way in the universe. Mine knew I stood to inherit the family business, so they didn't have that luxury. As a result, my father would set up targets and I'd hit them, which meant I had a lot easier time figuring out how I was doing."

"Your parents had you hitting the kind of marks that would prepare you to rule the Federated Commonwealth one day, while mine let me pick my own—which happened to be marks they'd hit themselves." Kai rubbed a hand along his clean-shaven jaw. "Deirdre and I are combining those methods. She's already done a wonderful job with David."

Victor smiled. "I look forward to meeting him some day."

"You know Deidre is pregnant again."

"Really?"

Kai nodded, then his eyes sharpened. "You already knew."

"Well, yes, I did." Victor's smile turned sheepish. "I don't have my people spying on friends, but . . ."

"The impending birth of an heir to the throne of the St. Ives Compact is a matter of national security, I know. I have to keep telling Deidre that so she won't ditch the security detail my mother has protecting her."

Kai got up and crossed to the sideboard where he pumped a refill of *naranji* juice from a decanter into the zero-G suck-cup he'd been drinking from. He took a sip and smiled. "There's a bit of lime in this mix," he said appreciatively. "Just the way I like it."

"Thank Jerry Cranston, that's his doing."

Kai nodded. "I will. It's funny, he seems so familiar, but I can't place him."

"He did some graduate work at the New Avalon Military Academy in 'forty-six—you might have met him then."

"That's probably it." Kai gestured with the cup at the holographic map. "But back to this . . . Allowing for the sketchiness of the details, it does seem like the Falcons are probing rather deeply into Alliance space. But with the way things are right now, you can't really do anything unless Katrina invites you in."

"And that won't happen. *Katherine* hasn't even deigned to make a public statement about any of this. Nondi Steiner is moving troops around to try to deal with the raiders, but she can't leave the border undefended."

"Classic problem: how to defend everything that's valuable to you? An attacker can threaten more points than you can defend." Kai sipped some juice. "That's always been our disadvantage against the Clans. We're always reacting to what they do."

"Except when we hit Twycross and Teniente—they didn't know what to expect and we beat them." Victor nodded slowly. "I'd like nothing better than to have the opportunity to take the war straight to the Clans."

"Perhaps that's what Focht has in mind."

"What do you mean?"

The Duke of St. Ives set his cup down. "You, Hohiro, and I were all trained on Outreach back when the leaders of the Inner Sphere realized they had to unite against the Clans. It strikes me that Hohiro might be interested in continuing that kind of training in preparation for mounting some kind of strike against the Clans. I've been hearing about a war between the Wolves and the Jade Falcons, though it's been not much more than rumors. But if it's any indication of a general rift within the Clans, we might be able to start taking them on one at a time and do some serious damage."

"You might be right, Kai." Victor stood and glanced over at the door as a chime sounded. "Enter."

Jerry Cranston came into the room leading a woman wearing the scarlet robe of a ComStar demi-Precentor. The dark circles around her eyes and the paleness of her skin told Victor the shuttle that had brought her to his ship had pulled some serious G-forces in its race to get here before his ship jumped out. Moreover, since anything she would tell him in person could have been broadcast to the ship, he assumed the news was both bad and very private.

She bowed to him. "Forgive my intrusion, Highness. I am Precentor Regina Whitman."

"Please, Precentor, be seated." Victor nodded as Kai turned back toward the juice dispenser. "Would you like some refreshment?"

"Thank you, yes."

Kai handed her a cup of juice, and she sucked down half of it in the first go, then blushed when she realized they were all watching her. "Again, forgive me."

"No matter. Have you a holodisk for me?"

"No. The message came directly from the Precentor Martial, text only, no visual. It made for a smaller packet that traveled faster." The Precentor caught her breath. "We have lost contact with Terra."

"What?" Victor looked at Kai and Jerry, whose expressions showed they were as stunned as he was. *Was the raid into the Alliance only a diversion?* "Have the Clans taken Terra?"

"No, sir, I mean, Highness." She clutched the cup tightly and Victor could see the liquid inside it quivering. "According to some preliminary messages coming out of the Free Worlds League—both overt and covert intercepts—it appears Word of Blake has moved to lay claim to Terra. They struck on the last day of February—yesterday—because it was the 276th anniversary of Jerome Blake being given control of Terra and what would become ComStar. It was also the 38th month since the official naming of Sharilar Mori, and Jerome Blake had a 38-year reign—it all gets terribly complicated and bound up in their malignant theology."

Victor nodded slowly, his mind racing. Terra was the world from which humanity had spread out to inhabit the stars. Though he'd never been there himself, the fact that it existed and was held in trust for all mankind by ComStar had been a fundamental tenet of how the universe worked for him. Back during the Clan invasion he would have been ready and more than willing to fight to prevent the Clans from taking Terra. At this moment he realized that his willingness to defend the homeworld of humanity had not waned.

"Does the Precentor Martial want us to divert to Terra? Our flotilla here has two full BattleMech regiments, as well as artillery, armor, infantry, and aerospace regiments. We can reach Terra before we can reach Tukayyid."

Precentor Whitman smiled gratefully, and he saw that a little color had reentered her face. "The Precentor Martial asked me to thank you for that offer, but he said it would not be necessary. He said the loss of Terra is grave, but is the lesser of the two evils facing the Inner Sphere."

Victor nodded. "If we can't deal with the greater of those evils, Word of Blake can defend Terra from the Clans."

"The Precentor Martial's thoughts exactly." She stood and sipped the last of her juice. "If it would not be an imposition, I would travel with you to Tukayyid. I need to survey the situation in the systems where you will stop during your trip, and report on them when I reach our destination."

"Please, make yourself at home. Jerry, have someone find the Precentor a cabin."

"My pleasure, Highness. This way, Precentor Whitman."

Kai held a hand up. "One question, if I might?"

"Please, Duke Allard-Liao."

"The Primus. Where was she at the time of the attack?"

Whitman's shoulders slumped. "On Terra, at Hilton Head." The Precentor shook her head. "We've had no word and must assume she is dead."

= 23 =

The burning in her eyes came from more than smoke and fatigue, as did the tears welling up in them. Precentor Lisa Koenigs-Cober couldn't believe the destruction in the compound. Not a single building had gone undamaged. Fires burning in some of them rivaled the weak dawn light from the east. To the west the black smoke reinforced the dark clouds gathering to blast the island with the storm she'd so recently fought through.

The Primus's Bodyguard unit—light armor and jump infantry mostly—had managed to blunt the direct assault by the Lancers' armor battalion. The Lancers had retaliated by setting up their artillery battalion and using it to methodically bombard the First Circuit Compound. Their intention clearly had been to hammer the Bodyguards until just before dawn, then punch through their line with an armor assault.

And that would have happened if Crown and I had not arrived and spoiled their timing. After leaving the crash site Lisa had located one other member of her lance. Demi-Precentor Stephen Crown had managed to get his *Shadow Hawk* clear of the doomed DropShip. The other two 'Mechs aboard, a *Centurion* and a *Hunchback,* had been fitted with drop-assist jet packs that had either failed to work, or failed to work well enough to save their pilots.

Constantly goading each other to keep going, Lisa and Crown had made it to Hilton Head in thirteen hours. They'd systematically destroyed all the microwave dishes and communication lines they could find along the way, as well as taking down portions of the power grid. They assumed the interruptions to service would be blamed on the storm, and it minimized the chances that word of their approach would precede them.

Their caution paid off. They hit the Lancer artillery batteries from the rear, going for munitions first, then destroying hovertrucks packed with the stuff. The vehicles exploded like firecrackers on a string, filling the night with a false dawn and fiery death. Lisa chose to bypass most of the artillery and jump past the armor positions. She and Crown could have done significant damage to those forces, but it would also have destroyed their own 'Mechs, and thus any hope of accomplishing her main objective.

Glass and mortar crunched beneath her feet as she ducked through the doorway to the First Circuit chamber. She could see the gray sky through a hole in the southwest corner of the building. Dim light filtered into the room through the hole and the empty, semi-circular windows that surrounded the chamber. Smoke filled the upper reaches of the room, but down below in the wooden bowl, amid the Precentors' crystal podia, the air was clear. Standing in the center of the room was Sharilar Mori, Primus of ComStar. Worked into the polished floor under her feet was the golden insignia of ComStar.

"Primus Mori, we must go."

The Primus looked up, clearly startled. The hood of her golden robe slid back to reveal long, dark hair streaked with white. "Go, Precentor?"

Lisa descended the wooden steps, kicking debris out of her way. "Yes, Primus. The *Fond Memory* is ready to leave. We can link up with *Serene Wisdom* and leave the Terran system."

The older Japanese woman slowly shook her head. "I will not leave Terra."

"I have my orders, Primus."

Sharilar Mori's dark eyes sparkled with irritation. "I am Primus. Your orders do not concern me."

"I'm afraid they do." Lisa folded her arms across her

chest. "In the event Terra falls I am supposed to evacuate or destroy everything of value to our enemies."

"Then do your duty and leave me behind."

"I cannot."

"The Blakist rabble will not drive me from Terra."

"You'll be a martyr, then?"

"If they make me one."

Lisa shook her head. "I thought we'd abandoned such nonsense when the Blakists purged themselves from our midst."

The Primus stared up at her with hard eyes. Lisa braced for a brutal rebuke, but the anger in those eyes suddenly drained away. "The old ways die hard."

"The old ways here are dead." Lisa held out her hand. "Come, Primus."

Mori took Lisa's hand and let herself be led out of the First Circuit chamber. "How bad is it?"

"Oh, about as bad as possible. The Lancers are Blakists. I have to assume the 201st Division is gone: either destroyed from within or without."

"You don't think they went over?"

Lisa shook her head. "If the whole unit had mutinied, there'd have been no reason to shoot me and my command lance down. We represented a rallying point for resistance, so we had to be eliminated. Between turncoats and the Lancers, they're gone. I have no idea what's happened at Sandhurst, but I have to assume Blakist units are burning hard for Terra."

The Primus winced. "Two JumpShips did come into the system outside the moon's orbit."

"If not for the storm the Lancers would be waiting to welcome them right here on Hilton Head."

Sharilar Mori let her eyes travel over the savaged landscape, then shuddered. "They are welcome to what they find."

Lisa shrugged. "It won't be much, I'm afraid." She waved two soldiers over. "Take the Primus to the *Fond Memory*. Tell Precentor Konrad to leave immediately. Incoming DropShips are considered extremely hostile and are to be avoided at all costs."

"Yes, Precentor."

The Primus held her hand out. "Wait, aren't you coming?"

Lisa frowned, then tapped a toe against the ferrocrete

curb. "This island is honeycombed with research facilities, storage areas, and computer archives. We've loaded as much as we can onto the *Memory,* and your Bodyguards, save a squad or two, will also go with you. What's left of the rest of us will have to blow this place."

"But you will escape?" Mori's eyes narrowed. "I will not leave if my people are staying behind."

"A shuttle is waiting. We'll catch up with you before you link up with the JumpShip."

"Then I look forward till we meet again." The Primus turned toward the aircar parked in the middle of the boulevard, then looked back over her shoulder. "Remember, Precentor, martyrdom is nonsense we have abandoned."

"So I've heard, Primus." Lisa threw her a brief salute. "But you must make haste. The Blakists came for Terra, and we'll see to it that Terra is *all* they get."

24

McKenzy Molecular Smelters
Coventry
Coventry Province, Lyran Alliance
15 March 3058

Hauptmann Caradoc Trevena didn't know if he should be
thankful or angry about the urgent call to report to Second
Battalion's headquarters in the smelter's compound. Going
there would mean leaving his company in Leftenant Murdoch's capable hands. He knew she could handle their recon
sweep of the plateau's edge, but with Falcon DropShips out
there to the east, unloading their BattleMechs, anxiety would
be spiking among his people.

Better they're out there than stuck here.

McKenzy Molecular Smelters and the hills of smoking
slag surrounding it were the only visible feature on the flat
plateau from its eastern edge to the Cross-Divide Mountains
in the west. Off to the north, hidden from casual viewing,
lay the open-pit mine where they dug out the ore the smelter
refined. Doc couldn't figure out why he and his company
had been flown over to the Dunnigan continent to protect the
smelter. It was ugly as sin and of no military value whatso-
ever.

Beyond the Cross-Divides to the west lay the continent of
Veracruz, where the Tenth Skye Rangers had their home
base at Port St. William. From the few reports funneled to
him, Doc knew that the Clans had landed the main body of
their force there to face the Academy cadets, the other half

of the Rangers, and the Coventry Militia. The fighting over there would center around the Coventry Metal Works and would be decidedly nasty.

The Rangers dug in around the smelter perimeter challenged Doc as he approached, and he answered with the appropriate passwords. Bringing his 'Mech to a stop well inside their lines, he pulled off his neurohelmet and popped the hatch on the *Centurion*. He climbed down the left arm, jumped to the left thigh, then descended a bit further along the lower leg before leaping to the ground. Sharon Dorne and Tony Wells stood waiting for him in the 'Mech's enormous shadow.

He could tell from their faces, and the fact that they'd not briefed him over the radio, that things were bad. "What happened?"

"Duke Bradford called over here to personally express to Kommandant Sarz how important it was to defend the smelter. Old Horst took the call in the plant manager's office, where he happened to find the wet bar."

"Dammit, let's go." Doc followed them as they ran toward the smelter's offices. Like the rest of them, Kommandant Horst Sarz had been consigned to the Tenth Skye Rangers because of his unsuitability for service elsewhere. When he wasn't drinking, Sarz was an able commander, but a cloud appearing on the horizon was enough to make him look for a bottle. Doc had used his influence with Copley to see that no liquor got shipped out with the Rangers, but he'd not really expected Sarz to get through the operation sober.

We're closer to Port St. William than Horst is to sober. The Kommandant, a young man with thinning blond hair, sat slumped over the plant manager's desk. His head rested on the blotter and his tongue slowly flicked out as he licked at the mouth of the bottle that his hand couldn't quite tip correctly to pour out the last of the liquor.

Sharon Dorne's red ponytail lashed her shoulders as she turned back toward Doc. "He's a waste."

Doc nodded. "This is a nightmare."

Tony Wells pointed to Sharon and back toward himself. "We've been thinking. I'll take command of the unit. You'll pull your people back and hold the north flank. We'll make sure it costs them a lot to get this place."

"Say what?"

"Doc, it's the only thing we can do. Tony's got more combat experience than either one of us, so giving him command is logical."

"I don't think so." Doc tapped his chest. "I've got more time in grade than both of you combined. I'm happy as hell you've got the experience, but command of this unit falls to me, and I will command it. And we won't be defending this smelter."

Wells and Dorne just stared at him. "But, Doc, that's our mission. Tony and I heard what Duke Bradford told the Kommandant. This is a vital installation and it has to be held."

"Duke Bradford is thinking like a politician, not a military strategist."

Tony ran a hand through his unruly black hair. "I don't follow."

"It's simple." Doc gestured to the desk where Sarz had begun to snore. "See the nameplate."

"Sure, Ernst Rhuel. He runs the plant."

"And he's uncle to Chairman Gertrude Rhuel, leader of the Commonwealth Party. She's Duke Bradford's chief support in the Parliament of Governors here. We're guarding this plant because he wants to show her he's willing to look out for her concerns."

Sharon frowned at him. "This is still an important facility. The ore refined here goes over to CMW to produce 'Mechs."

"Right, this is a primary production facility. But, aside from some off-world shipments of strategic metals, it produces nothing that feeds directly into the economy. Everything this plant turns out has to be processed at least once more before it's useful." Doc opened his hands and looked at the other two officers. "This plant is of no use to anyone—especially Clan raiders—who are on Coventry to plunder and run."

Tony shook his head. "If that were true, the Falcons wouldn't have landed troops in the lowlands just outside the city."

Doc gently rapped his fists on his own forehead. "Tony, what the hell did they teach you at NAMA? The aim of modern warfare is to destroy the other guy's ability to wage war. The Coventry Metal Works is an obvious target for the Falcons. It gives them raw material and lets them blow the hell out of the troops defending it. That's why they're attacking in Port St. William. And the reason they landed over here in Idaway is because they're coming to get us. We're the only thing of military importance in this part of the world."

Tony was clearly stung by the tone of Doc's rebuke. "You sound paranoid. We moved while their DropShip scanners were blocked by the planet. They might know the plant is here, but not us."

"Think, guys. They know we're here because our position was given to them when they bid the battle out. They asked what we'd be defending with, and General Bakkish told them."

Sharon perched herself on the arm of a chair. "So what are we going to do?"

Doc hesitated. He'd read up on the Clans, studied their tactics, their victories, and their defeats. He'd trained people who'd gone on to fight against them. If the battalion was to survive, he knew he was capable of leading them away from destruction. A smile grew on his face with that last realization. *No dead soldiers have ever defeated anyone.*

"Okay, look, we're forty klicks out from the mountains. The Academy maintains some exercise grounds and live-fire ranges there. There are also supposed to be a lot of mines and natural caverns in the area. Find Copley—I heard he's been caving or something over there. We'll pull back to the mountains and set up in the Academy's prepared positions. We can use the gunnery range to protect our northern flank—it's got to be chock full of unexploded munitions. The Academy positions probably also have zeroed ranges for most of the passes."

Sharon nodded. "Sounds like a plan."

Doc looked to Tony. "What do you think?"

Tony Wells shrugged reluctantly. "I don't like the idea of retreating and abandoning our mission here."

"Okay, Tony, but think about this: what are the chances that a battalion—*our* battalion—can stop a regiment of BattleMechs? We've got no aerospace or artillery support. We're defending a wart on a plain, which gives the Falcons the advantage because their weaponry is far more effective at range than ours is. On Tukayyid the nastiest and most effective fighting done by ComStar occurred in the mountains, where all ranges are reduced to the point where the Clans lose their advantage."

"Yeah, you've got a point, but we're supposed to be defending this plant."

Sharon shook her head. "If we stay here the chance of this smelter surviving the defense are zero. If we pull back and the Falcons want the plant, they get it, then we take it back later. If they're really after *us*, they leave the plant alone. Doc's right, the situation here is suicide for us. The Cross-Divide mountains are defensible. Fighting from there will improve our chances of killing more of them before they get us."

Tony held his hands up in surrender. "Okay, but log my protest."

Doc nodded. "So noted. Now I have to ask you—how battle-worthy are your units?"

The other two refused to meet his gaze.

"Is it that bad?" he asked.

"We've got solid people," Sharon said, "but our training schedules aren't up to what they should be. I've got a Strike, Support, and Close Assault Lances."

"And I've got two Strike Lances and a Support Lance," Tony put in.

"Okay, I'll pull my people in and have them recon the mountains. The Support Lances and your Close Assault Lance go next, along with auxiliary, medical, and tech personnel. The 'Mechs will have to position themselves to cover the three Strike Lances as they pull out."

"As I said before, it's a plan." Sharon jerked a thumb at Sarz. "What about him?"

Tony shook his head. "Leave him."

Doc was inclined to agree, but shook his head. "Can't leave him—the Falcons could get a lot of intelligence out of him. We'll bring him with us."

Sharon glanced at Doc. "And you'll take his *Penetrator*?"

Doc smiled. The *Penetrator* was a 'Mech that had been produced specifically for combat against the Clans. While it was significantly slower than his *Centurion,* its jump jets did give it added mobility. The 'Mech's superior firepower and armor would make him far more effective in a fight. A whole world of possibilities opened up before him.

"I will—and I'll get some tech to start piloting my *Centurion.*" Doc nodded solemnly. "We're going to need every gun we can find to survive this thing. And make no mistake about it—that's what I want us to do."

Sharon gave him a thumb's-up. "Roger that, acting Kommandant Trevena."

25

Tharkad City
Tharkad
District of Donegal, Lyran Alliance
20 March 3058

Katrina relished the look of surprise on Tormano's face when he entered the office and saw her seated at her desk. "Good morning, Mandrinn Liao."

"Highness, I . . ." Tormano's expression and tone of voice hovered halfway between apology and anger. "When did you return?"

"Last night." She smiled, still tingling with the thrill of being smuggled back onto the planet. "Records of the landing having already been destroyed and the crew is being debriefed by the Ministry of Public Safety. Everything is in perfect order."

"You should have called for me when you arrived."

"I inquired. You had retired for the evening."

Tormano smiled and bowed his head. "I would have come . . ."

"No matter." She tapped the Enter key on the keyboard at her desk. "I wanted to review what's been happening in my absence."

The holographic map of the Lyran Alliance materialized between them. "I must congratulate you, Mandrinn, on your handling of the Falcon crisis. Even as I returned to Tharkad I was only beginning to hear of the raids on Engadine and Bucklands. Of course, in my absence, you had no choice but to stonewall news of the raids, but you did it in a way that our enemies in the Inner Sphere haven't an inkling of the trouble."

Tormano bowed a bit more formally. "I am happy that my work pleases you."

"Indeed." As Katrina studied him she found herself comparing Tormano Liao and the Wolf Khan she had met. Tormano possessed a sense of decorum that she'd also glimpsed in Vlad but that he seldom found reason to employ. The bigger difference was that Tormano might try to hide certain things from her, where Vlad would have proudly proclaimed what he'd done and why, confident of her approval.

And he'd probably get it. From the moment she laid eyes on Vlad of the Wolves Katrina knew she'd found what she hadn't even realized she'd been looking for. Not that she hadn't hoped to find someone to love one day, someone to share her life with. Galen Cox had seemed to be that man—his only flaw his unswerving allegiance to her brother Victor. Such loyalty to her most dangerous enemy had cost Galen his life, and from time to time she still mourned what she'd lost. Since then she'd found no suitable candidate— Thomas Marik did not interest her in the least—and so she'd given up the quest.

It is said that when you stop looking is when you find what you want. Her attraction to Vlad had been instantaneous and complete. She felt it in the pit of her stomach, hadn't even been able to breathe for an instant. He was certainly attractive enough—even with the scar on his face he was handsome—but it was something that shone through his eyes that drew her. Till now she'd jealously guarded her virginity and hand in marriage because of their value, but she wanted Vlad the moment she saw him. Nothing she had was too valuable to offer in exchange for a future with him.

Comparing Tormano and Vlad helped her to identify what it was she'd seen in the Wolf Khan's eyes. Tormano obviously had an attraction to and affinity for power. He had used and manipulated it all his life, but he was opportunistic and content to retreat from a source of power if opposed.

But Vlad—and she herself and her father before her— *hungered* for power. They preyed upon others, exploiting weakness for their own gain. Hanse Davion had coordinated the grandest assault ever seen in the Inner Sphere and succeeded in cutting the Capellan Confederation in half. Vlad and the Wolves had launched an assault on the Inner Sphere that dwarfed even her father's feat. Victor hated the Clans for that, but Katrina could only admire them for it.

Vlad and I are predators, the rest are prey.

"If I may ask, Highness, how went your mission? Have we an ally among the Clans?"

Katrina nodded and made no effort to kill the smile growing on her face. "We do indeed. I was prevented from reaching the Smoke Jaguars, but I have spoken with the leader of the Wolves and we have an understanding."

"An understanding." Tormano's tone seemed to soil the idea and layer it with innuendo. "The Wolves are split from Phelan's people, then?"

"Much as your sister's St. Ives Compact is split from the Capellan Confederation."

"And you are certain of this Wolf?"

"Quite."

She smiled again and Tormano waited for an explanation that she would never give him. During the return trip to the Lyran Alliance she had spent much time in Vlad's company, wanting to learn as much as she could about him. In many ways he was utterly alien to her, yet she found him more kin in spirit than any of her blood siblings.

With her brothers and sisters everything was a game of position, of taking power or surrendering it. With Vlad it was different because he accorded her an equality because of who she was, not what she was heir to. Oh, she knew that were she not the ruler of a star empire he would have left her a bondswoman, but his curiosity about her and respect would have been the same. Her position merely let him grant her the privileges to which she was born, while his feelings about her made him treat her as a peer.

They still played little games to seek and withhold information, and what games they had been. Katrina had ever been able to manipulate those around her, and even Vlad seemed susceptible to her charms. He, on the other hand, played by different rules. She had to learn how to deal with him and he with her, then both made forays into the other's territory, playing by the other's rules. She enjoyed the novelty of the blunt use of power, shredding the screen of polite manners that veiled her intent. Conversely, Vlad seemed to find amusing the intricate tangle of proper and improper social conventions that regulated life in the Inner Sphere.

By testing the other's methods they each learned how frighteningly similar they were. Those who had previously courted Katrina had either been so frightfully inept in handling power that she could only hold them in contempt, or so thoroughly afraid of offending her that they were completely bland and colorless. Even Galen had been flawed by his ties to Victor. Vlad's liking and skillful use of power made him virtually her twin.

Katrina pointed toward the holographic map. "I see, Mandrinn, that the Falcons have all arrived on Coventry. You have no clear idea of their strength."

"No, Highness. They are constantly shifting forces in and out. Their bidding only reveals to us the force they are using in a given attack, not all the force they have in the theater." He frowned. "The fighting in and around Port St. William is heavy and our people are holding, but casualties are high. There are shortages of ammunition in the Tenth Skye Rangers, but they seem willing to fight to the last."

The Archon stood abruptly and let her irritation show. "It would strike me, Mandrinn, that pinning a force down around the McKenzy Smelter was foolish. You had the wisdom to let the Skye Rangers' Second Battalion retreat to the mountains. Why are you forcing the Militia and the Rangers to die defending Port St. William?"

Tormano lowered his head for a moment. "First of all, your grand-aunt is directing operations on Coventry."

"From here, on Tharkad."

"Yes, but she is in command. Secondly, Duke Frederick Bradford requested defense of the metal works and of an ore refinery."

Katrina squinted slightly in thought. "Duke Bradford, as I recall, still professes some loyalty to my brother. His *requests* mean little as far as I am concerned."

"His requests are strategically sound." Tormano pointed at the map. "CMW is the second-largest 'Mech production facility in the whole of the Inner Sphere. We cannot afford to lose it. And the Second Battalion's retreat was not authorized. There appears to have been a mutiny in the unit. They obviously retreated to keep from getting killed by the Falcons, though their withdrawal will not have that effect. Our last reports indicated that the Clans have bypassed the smelter and are pursuing the Rangers into the mountains."

Tormano's eyes grew hard. "The defense of CMW and the

refinery are not nearly as important as the necessity of delaying the Falcons in achieving their objectives on Coventry. Every day they have to spend on that planet is one more day we have to prepare for the defense of Tharkad. If we can keep the Falcons tied up for another two weeks, we can have reinforcements there by then. If our people challenge the Clans when they arrive in-system, the Falcons could be trapped and never make it off to attack Tharkad."

Katrina considered what Tormano had said. The true objective for the Clans was obvious—they were coming for Tharkad because, as Vlad had pointed out, they needed to conceal their weakness behind a display of power. The need to stop them at Coventry was also obvious. If the Falcons progressed beyond that world they would violate the truce line and the terrible war with the Clans would be on again. That would be disastrous for the Inner Sphere and, as Vlad had also pointed out, disastrous for him because his Clan, in its weakened state, might not be able to take Terra.

"You are correct, of course, Mandrinn. I have reviewed and approve your use of the Eridani Light Horse and Wolf's Dragoons." Katrina smiled slowly. "I have also decided to send the Waco Rangers on to Coventry as well."

"But . . ."

"No buts, Tormano." She laughed aloud and waved away his protest. "You have more than enough loyal troops on their way to Tharkad to protect this world. Waco's Rangers will be more useful on Coventry, don't you agree?"

"Yes, Highness."

"Good." She smiled sweetly at him. "In my absence you have maintained open channels of communication with Thomas Marik?"

"I have, Archon. Negotiations on your behalf concerning his suit are progressing slowly."

Katrina nodded. "I wish to accelerate matters. If you will, ask Thomas if he would be so kind as to send the Knights of the Inner Sphere here to help defend Tharkad."

"What?"

"Oh, and see if he would forward a request to your nephew, Sun-Tzu, to make available to us one of his premier units."

"What?"

"I believe my requests are quite clear, Mandrinn."

Tormano snapped his mouth shut. "I applaud your forethought, Archon, but this invitation sets a dangerous precedent."

"Mandrinn Liao, the request accomplishes two goals. The first is that it makes Thomas aware that the safety of the Lyran Alliance is his first line of defense. It also suggests to him that if he wants my realm as a dowry, he had better be ready to defend it. While I share your reservations about Sun-Tzu, I hasten to point out that his troops will bleed as well as ours. Draining his strength means we make him less dangerous in the long run."

"Agreed. Your other goal?"

"Despite how well you've handled the news blackout on this deep probe into our territory, I know my brother is aware of it. By inviting League troops here I make any incursion by him into my realm a possible cause for the renewal of hostilities with the Free Worlds League. This will help curb his ambitions, and once we show we can weather a crisis without his intervention, he will have less justification to interfere with the Lyran Alliance in the future."

Tormano nodded curtly. "A sound plan, Archon, except for one thing."

"And that is?"

"What if we *do* need your brother in the future?"

"Victor will give me what I want when I ask, Mandrinn. He reveres our parents too much ever to act against their flesh and blood." She smiled in a most cold manner, aping the expression Vlad had used when speaking of Phelan. "I will ever be Victor's master because of that weakness. As long as he is never given leave to think about it, he will never escape me."

= 26 =

Cross-Divide Mountains
Coventry
Coventry Province, Lyran Alliance
30 March 3058

"Tony, get your ass back here or I'm going to shoot it off myself!" Doc swept the cross hairs of his *Penetrator* past the blocky form of Tony Wells's *JagerMech* and dropped them onto the humanoid outline of the green Falcon *Galahad* marching into the defile. The guns built into the arms of both 'Mechs came up, conjuring in Doc's mind duel scenes from bad holodramas set on ancient Terra. Behind Tony, between him and Doc, the last two 'Mechs of Tony's Strike Lance limped toward safety.

The roar of autocannons filled the canyon that had been carved from the rock years before by huge mining 'Mechs. A storm of metal sleet washed over the *Galahad*. The *JagerMech*'s autocannon shells chewed up over half the armor on the *Galahad*'s right arm and chipped away at armor on its chest and left arm. Two pulse laser shots from the *JagerMech*'s torso went wide, drilling neat lines of steaming holes in the canyon's rock walls.

The muzzles of the *Galahad*'s Gauss rifles flashed white as they fired. Two silvery balls streaked out and slammed into the center chest of Tony's 'Mech. Doc didn't see them hit, but he recognized the misshapen lumps of metal as they burst free of the *JagerMech*'s back in a spray of coolant and shower of armor scales. With two shots fired in just one salvo, the *Galahad* managed to reduce a 65-ton war machine to scrap metal and armor salvage.

As the *JagerMech* toppled backward, the top of its domed head popped off. Riding a flaming rocket, Tony Wells shot clear of the doomed machine and even managed to avoid slamming into the canyon walls. He quickly soared up and out of sight, and Doc had no idea where he was going to land.

"I wish you luck, Tony, but not all of it." Through the smoke from the *JagerMech,* Doc could see that the *Galahad* was down and that surprised him. Tony had hit the 'Mech hard, but the damage had hardly been overwhelming. *Let's hope our remaining luck hasn't been used up tripping that 'Mech.*

The *Galahad*'s fall had been the only verifiable bit of good luck since the retreat into the mountains. The fighting had been hard and largely unrelenting. The Jade Falcons had come after them with a regimental-size force and engaged them in shifts. The Falcons pushed them hard, then withdrew just before delivering the *coup de grâce,* or whenever the Rangers had somehow gained a minor tactical advantage.

Though the *Galahad* had only fired one salvo, the armor of Tony's *JagerMech* had already been reduced to tatters in the recent engagements. Everything Doc had read about the Clans indicated they preferred quick and decisive battles. Analyses of the titanic battle at Tukayyid had even pointed out that the Clans' downfall had been their profligate use of ammunition because of their frustration at having to fight long, drawn-out battles. By withdrawing into the mountains, Doc had hoped to give them just the sort of battle they hated, but the Falcons seemed quite content to grind down his unit.

Well, here's where I get to grind back. Doc thumbed the top triggers of his joysticks. The large lasers built into the *Penetrator*'s arms stabbed verdant beams through the smoke, and hit the *Galahad* as the manlike 'Mech came upright again. One beam melted a channel through the armor on the 'Mech's right thigh. The other struck the *Galahad* in the head, bubbling up all but the last bit of armor shielding the pilot.

The Clan 'Mech raised its Gauss rifles and returned Doc's fire. One slug went wide, striking sparks from the canyon's stone floor. The ricochet shot back between the *Penetra-*

tor's legs, but did no damage. The other slug slammed into the *Penetrator*'s right arm, sending a tremor through the whole 'Mech. Doc twisted himself and the 'Mech back around as a warning klaxon signaled him that the shot had blasted nearly a ton of armor from the *Penetrator*'s limb.

Enough sniping, time to hammer him. Doc sidestepped the *Penetrator* forward, putting the wounded 'Mechs behind him, and triggered the six medium pulse lasers built into his 'Mech's torso. Unlike the heavier lasers in its arms, the pulse lasers did not shoot a single, coherent beam of light. Instead they pulsed the energy out, with the targeting circuitry making random and minor changes between pulses, spreading the damage around and increasing its effect.

The hail of laser darts peppered the *Galahad*'s body left, right, and center. Vaporized armor wreathed the 'Mech with greasy gray clouds. While Doc had been hoping for another hit on the *Galahad*'s head, he settled for further damage done to the 'Mech's right leg. The 60-ton 'Mech wavered a bit and Doc thought it might go down, but the pilot recovered enough to fire back.

Doc braced for the impact of the Gauss projectiles, but both whizzed harmlessly overhead. *He kept the 'Mech upright, but he was rattled.*

"Doc, the stragglers are clear."

"Roger, Sharon. How about Tony?"

"Got him, but he broke his leg. Hurry up."

"On my way."

Backing the *Penetrator* toward the mine, Doc took one last shot at the *Galahad*. The pulse laser needles again burned armor over the 'Mech's heart and the right side of its body. Doc saw a gaping hole open on the *Galahad*'s right flank, a hole he knew he could exploit to kill the 'Mech with just one more exchange, but instead he pulled back.

As if to emphasize the wisdom of his choice, two Gauss slugs crisscrossed in front of his viewport and shattered rock on either wall of the artificial canyon. *One lucky head shot by a Gauss rifle and there wouldn't be enough of me left to get a DNA sample for identification.*

Doc turned the *Penetrator* and sprinted to the yawning black maw of a mine shaft. No one had been able to find Leftenant Copley—in fact, no one had seen him since Second Battalion had left Port St. William—but they *had* managed to pull mining records from the smelter president's computers. Examining the records closely, Sharon Dorne learned of a series of shafts that would take the Rangers so deep into the Cross-Divides that even the use of atomic weapons couldn't root them out.

More important, though, the chain of tunnels and caves ran all through the mountains, with a number of exits on the Veracruz side. If the Falcons came after them, Two Batt would be able to escape to the west and possibly link up with whatever forces were left at Port St. William. Of course, no one expected the Falcons to go after them in the mines because the close confines would make ambushes far too easy and potentially deadly. The necessity of moving single file through the tunnels left the first and last 'Mechs dangerously vulnerable to attacks.

Doc slowed the *Penetrator* as he brought it into the mine shaft and headed down. He switched the scanners over to infrared so he could pick out people on foot as well as other 'Mechs. Behind him, techs helped their security detail wire up explosive charges that could be used to seal the shaft if the Falcons did decide to pursue them.

"Sharon, report?"

"Get down here, go to vislight, and turn on your floods. It'll tell you more than I can."

The fatigue in her voice almost drowned the doubt, but Doc picked up enough of it to cause him concern. "Is it really that bad?"

"I'm not paid to be an optimist, Doc."

Down further and around a corner, Doc brought his *Penetrator* to a stop and turned on his external floodlights. Flipping his holographic feed over to visual light he found the wellspring of Sharon's pessimism. *This* is bad.

The two Support Lances had long since ceased to be support because they'd run out of long-range missiles. While most of the 'Mechs were still armed with lasers, those weapons were notoriously useless in anything other than a line-of-sight battle. And the missile boats tended to be slow, which made them a liability. Of the six they'd started out with, they were down to two, and both had been assigned to the Close Assault Lance to fill it out.

The three Striker Lances had been reduced to two, which wouldn't have seemed too bad if their 'Mechs hadn't been so beaten up. The pilots paired their 'Mechs up so they could use each other as "walking armor" to cover the places where their protection had been entirely shot away. The two limping 'Mechs that had entered prior to Doc belonged to the second Striker Lance, and the fact that the *Firestarter* had lost its left foot and right arm meant it would probably be scavenged for parts and abandoned.

Doc keyed his radio. "Isobel, what about the Titans?"

"Dings and dents, but we're all still here."

That report brought a big smile to Doc's face. The training he'd done with the recon company had paid off rather well. Within the tight confines of the mountain passes and gaps, the light, fast 'Mechs had proved adept at hitting and withdrawing. The company hadn't really done significant damage—only two kills—but their flanking maneuvers had apparently forced some of the Falcon withdrawals.

"I don't know why you're down on the unit, Sharon. Things look pretty good to me."

"Oh, have you finally found the wet bar there in Sarz's *Penetrator*? You must have because this group could only look good if seen after a few shots of whiskey."

"That's probably true, Sharon, but the fact is that the Clanners haven't killed any of our light 'Mechs." Doc sighed heavily. "That ain't much to hang hope on, but it's enough for the time being."

27

Tukayyid
ComStar Garrison District, Free Rasalhague
   Republic
2 April 3058

The Precentor Martial opened his hands in a gesture inviting both women to be seated. The brightness of the light reflected by the room's white walls all but banished the last of the gray weariness from their skin, though the dark circles under their eyes still betrayed their fatigue. "Again, I extend my welcome to Tukayyid. While you were resting up I had a chance to review the report you prepared in transit, Precentor Koenigs-Cober. I have found it most comprehensive and, alas, sobering. Still, I am gratified to see you were able to cripple or destroy most of the research facilities at Hilton Head."

Lisa pulled a chair out from the dining table and sat down at a place at the middle of the table. "I was doing what I'd been instructed to do. Had I been thinking correctly in the first place, we might not have lost Terra."

The Precentor Martial moved around to the head of the table and waited for the Primus to take a seat at the other end before sitting himself. "Even if the substitution had been detected, there would have been no way to prevent the capture of Terra, save abandoning Tukayyid and launching a preemptive strike against the Word of Blake forces. Information lately obtained from Terra and elsewhere seems to indicate the Word of Blake came into the system with three full 'Mech regiments."

Sharilar Mori stared at Anastasius Focht from the far end of the table. "How many regiments do they have?"

"Just those three, I believe, plus the pseudo-Lancers. They've all taken up positions on Terra." Focht shook out the linen napkins set on his plate and spread it on his lap. "The chef who prepares meals for our headquarters here is quite good. All the meat, grains, and vegetables are produced here. We've been very successful at rehabilitating the planet since the war and have production up to eighty percent of what it was before the Clans invaded. Normally the fare is a bit more meager, but the chef, Precentor Rudolfo, insisted upon giving you his best."

Lisa nodded gratefully, but Sharilar Mori frowned. "I admit I'm ready for something better after a month of eating flight rations, but shouldn't we be speaking about the reconquest of Terra? I agreed to delay long enough to rest, but I thought we would immediately be to business."

The Precentor Martial took a deep breath and wished there were an easy way to deliver the blow to the Primus. He exhaled slowly. "We would be immediately to business, Primus, if there were business to discuss."

"What do you mean, Anastasius?"

The Precentor Martial glanced at Lisa. "Primus, did you read the report Precentor Koenigs-Cober prepared?"

"You know I did, Anastasius. My comments are appended to the copy you were given. You read *them,* I assume."

"Yes, Primus." Focht folded his hands together and rested them on the edge of the table. "The Precentor's report provided an excellent analysis of what would be required to garrison and retake Terra. She suggested that six BattleMech regiments, with appropriate aerospace, artillery, armor, and infantry support, would be sufficient to garrison the world against an attack force roughly four times that large. I find her analysis quite accurate."

"You said Word of Blake had only four regiments on the planet."

"They will bring in mercenaries. Group W and the Legion of the Rising Sun have already refused contracts with them, but others are not likely to be so scrupulous."

"Anastasius, as I recall, we currently have about forty BattleMech regiments under your command. Use as many as you need." The Primus gave him a tight smile. "Precentor Koenigs-Cober's report also noted that a planetary bombardment of the sort the Clans visited upon the planet Turtle Bay would considerably soften up the defenses."

"As would jumping to the asteroid belt, strapping simple rocket motors to asteroids, and using them to pummel the planet." Focht shook his head. "The point is moot."

"Yes, bombarding Terra to save it is a less than satisfactory solution to the problem." The Primus frowned. "Your report about the Wolf Clan refugees on Morges indicated that they have an ample supply of OmniMechs. We'll use them to give us an advantage over the Blakists."

"I doubt Khan Kell will give them to us."

"Pressure him, Anastasius."

The Precentor Martial smiled in spite of himself. "Phelan Kell responds less well to pressure than I do, Primus."

"Everyone has his price, Anastasius."

"And you have forgotten the lesson Myndo Waterly learned just before you took her place as Primus: that price can be high indeed."

"Is that a threat, Precentor Martial?"

"Not at all, Primus." He looked over at an ashen-faced Lisa. "You will forgive us, Precentor. The Primus and I have, over the years, found baiting each other a useful way of dealing with frustration. She knows we cannot take Terra back, and I must pay the price for making her acknowledge that fact."

"I know nothing of the kind, Anastasius." The Primus fell silent as the door to the small dining room opened and two Acolytes rolled in a cart bearing a steaming tureen of soup and bowls. "That does smell good."

"It is a cream soup made with native black prawns." Focht waited for his guests to begin eating before tasting the soup himself. The onion and pepper in it added bite, while the hint of lemon complemented the taste of the prawns. "You should feel honored—Rudolfo is giving you the best I've ever had from him."

"Perhaps I will have him transferred back to Terra to serve me there."

"It is possible you could, Primus, for he is a very young man. He might live to see that day."

The Primus patted her lips with her napkin. "Why do you say it will take a long time to reconquer Terra? No matter how many mercenaries they bring in, we should have sufficient troops to defeat them."

The Precentor Martial saw Lisa's expression darken for a moment. "I don't mean to draw you into a battle between us, Precentor, but your perspective as a ground commander will be useful. How valuable is Terra to ComStar?"

"Except as a symbol, not very valuable at all." Lisa paused, then shrugged. "That's not to underestimate its importance as a symbol, but the Clans have been intent on taking Terra from the first. We know that if we can't stop them here on Tukayyid, we can't stop them on Terra. We had to garrison Terra because of the Clan threat, but now Word of Blake can take that duty."

Sharilar Mori set her spoon down. "The symbolic importance of Terra is incalculable. Because ComStar owned Terra the Clans accepted our offer to use Tukayyid as a site for a proxy battle. Does losing Terra mean we are no longer seen as a legitimate force in the minds of the Clans? Does Terra's loss mean the truce is null and void?"

A good question. "Were Ulric Kerensky still ilKhan of the Clans I would answer your legitimacy question with an unqualified no."

"And now that he's gone?"

Focht nodded slowly. "It's still a no, but largely because of a quirk in the makeup of Clan society. The warrior caste is at the apex of their system. I suspect they viewed Myndo Waterly as someone of a slightly lower caste—perhaps even as low as a member of their merchant caste. But the truce was negotiated with me, and that's why it held, despite her treachery. The agreement between warriors was far stronger than her attempt to undermine it."

Lisa looked over at him. "Then you think the fact that the Com Guards are still a force to reckon with means the Clans will respect the truce."

"They will for as long as they see us as a military force worthy of respect. The loss of Terra may begin to erode some of that respect. As we have no force positioned above the truce line, the Clans cannot test themselves against us. If we did, and they attacked and we defeated them, such a defeat would go a long way to reinforce our legitimacy."

The Primus nodded. "Perhaps you should arrange an expedition across the truce line. You could strike at the Wolves. Their weakness would guarantee a victory."

"Not guarantee, but it would weight things heavily in our favor."

Lisa winced. "Or convince the Clans we're hiding our own weakness by attacking their weakest Clan."

"True. And if a Clan that weak were to defeat us, everything would unravel." The Precentor Martial again dipped his spoon into his steaming bowl. "We do need to do something, but it has to be the right thing."

"What do we do now, then, Anastasius? Nothing?"

"Not nothing, Primus." He smiled and nodded to Lisa. "We do the hardest thing a soldier can do—we wait until there comes a time when we *must* fight."

Turkina Keshik Headquarters, Port St. William
Coventry
Coventry Province, Lyran Alliance

Galaxy Commander Rosendo Hazen stepped inside the doorway of Khan Marthe Pryde's office and snapped to attention. "Reporting as ordered, my Khan."

Marthe returned his salute. "You're prompt, Commander. That much at least can be said in your favor."

"I follow orders, my Khan."

"Do you?" She plucked a holodisk from the metal desk behind her and held it up. "Your report indicates that a significant number of the Tenth Skye Rangers' First Battalion escaped your force."

"Permission to speak frankly, my Khan." He let an edge creep into his voice because he was too tired and sore to put up with being reprimanded for events beyond his control.

Marthe stared at him without a shred of mercy in her blue eyes. "So granted, but do not waste my time with excuses."

"I have no intention of doing that, Khan Pryde." He watched her, knowing that their bloodlines had often been rivals within Clan Jade Falcon. He despised the Prydes for their height and slenderness, just as she despised him for his smaller, stockier build. While their Bloodname Houses bred Prydes and Hazens for divergent physical characteristics, it was with the same intention of breeding aggressive and resourceful offspring.

"My Khan, I did not think the purpose of this exercise was to kill our warriors."

"You belabor the obvious."

"And you overlook the obvious." Rosendo pushed one hand back through his hair, which was short and almost white-blond. "The commander of the First Battalion is very sharp. He is working with forces that, according to the records your people recovered here, are all substandard. Other information you gave me suggested that this commander is even a drunkard, and if this is true, I think fighting him sober would be a fascinating experience."

"You exaggerate ... you Hazens always do."

"We do not have among our number a legend like Aidan Pryde, so we are forced to compensate."

Marthe's expression sharpened, but he saw a trace of amusement tug at the corners of her eyes. "You should compensate by destroying your foes."

"I agree, and I will, but not yet. The Clusters I sent against this Kommandant Sarz learned a great deal. They suffered very few casualties, but inflicted few as well. They learned that maneuvering and position can be as valuable as tenacity and a bellicose attitude. Such were the lessons taught but not learned at Tukayyid."

Marthe leaned back against the desk and crossed her long legs. "The lesson your people will remember is that their quarry escaped."

"Hardly escaped, my Khan." Rosendo clasped his hands together at the small of his back. "They fled into a complex of mining tunnels and caverns east of here. There are a limited number of places for them to come out. I have initiated scouting operations that will help spot them when they do emerge. My Clusters are already preparing to respond quickly to the threat and eliminate it."

"Good. For all intents and purposes, resistance is ended here on Coventry."

"You eliminated all the forces here in Port St. William?"

The scowl that knitted her brows vanished quickly, but Rosendo caught it nonetheless. "The Inner Sphere forces are not complete dullards, Commander Hazen. Elements of the Militia and Tenth Skye Rangers broke out of our perimeter. According to the records we have recovered, they have no stores of weaponry or munitions, so we will wear them down."

Rosendo nodded and kept his expression serious. "I am pleased to see you found a way to teach your people the same lessons I taught mine."

"Indeed."

"So, how long before the Lyran Alliance sends more troops?"

Khan Marthe Pryde shook her head. "I have no way of knowing. I assumed they would move faster to intercept us."

"Were they worthy of possessing the worlds they claim, we would have ample enemies here." He shrugged. "You should have issued a formal challenge to some of their better units. That way we would be killing warriors, not killing time."

"I am content to let them choose which units to send here, Commander." Marthe smiled easily. "We are at the truce line. They know they must stop us here, or the war will begin anew and they will have to face all the Clans. Their troops are doubtless already on the way—and they will be some of their best units, too. We break them, and in doing so, break the spirit of the Lyran Alliance. And once we have done that, none will doubt the Jade Falcons, nor will they prevent us from taking whatever we desire."

=== 28 ===

Cross-Divide Mountains
Coventry
Coventry Province, Lyran Alliance
5 April 3058

This had better work. Doc glanced at the computer time-counter in the lower corner of his holographic targeting display. It showed the time as 1459 hours. *Which means they ought to be coming along very soon now.*

In the weeks since his people had become moles, Doc had learned to respect the speed and efficiency of the Falcons. The tunnels and caverns ran for a length of 160 or so kilometers beneath the Cross-Divides, and possessed enough side passages and chambers that at times he half-expected to find a minotaur come wandering through the labyrinth. Tunnels to the outside were rare, however, and the Jade Falcons had spotted all but a half-dozen of them. At these they had set up seismic monitoring stations that reported the heavy footfalls of 'Mechs in the area.

The Falcons had also set up a number of firebases about an hour out from the most distant of the monitoring stations, each base manned by a Star of 'Mech troops. When Doc sent out recon patrols the Clanners responded quickly, but so far the only combat had consisted of challenges and insults hurled back and forth over the radio as his people ran away.

Once Doc discovered the seismic monitoring stations, he decided to use them against the Falcons. Every day at precisely 1600 hours, for a duration of fifteen minutes, he had a tech take the seismic monitors offline. They simply reported no activity for that time. Using an unmonitored exit, a recon lance would slip out and move around until it was spotted, then it would return to the tunnels through an entrance that had been monitored.

While Coventry was not a seismically active planet, the Jade Falcons were using devices sensitive enough to pick up the footfalls of a tech approaching them. A total lack of activity for fifteen minutes was as significant a trace as having 'Mechs stomping a series of spikes into the data. The Falcons began to react to the lack of data and the Rangers' very predictable routine of sending a patrol out in the middle of the afternoon.

What the Clan commanders really couldn't know was that the seismic monitors, which had formerly been used to monitor the progress of borer 'Mechs underground, were programmable. Because they were intended for use in tracking the tunnel-makers' progress, the devices had a buffer that allowed for the storage of sample traces from other equipment and operations. Undesired traces were loaded into the monitors and when they detected one of these, that data was filtered out and discarded. While the monitors were offline, Andy Bick and a couple of techs loaded in traces for the non-recon lance 'Mechs still in the force, rendering them seismically invisible as far as the monitors were concerned.

Doc took the ten most combat-worthy of the heavier 'Mechs available and split them evenly into two lances of five 'Mechs each, modeling the organizational units used by the Clans. Then they set out on what they dubbed The Attack of the Mole-people, arriving unmolested at the most logical ambush point along the monitored route out of the mountains. The Rangers arrived two hours before the monitor would be shut down because Doc was expecting the Falcons to advance and prepare their own ambush. While his 'Mechs waited, the lighter recon company left the mountains through an unmonitored opening and got ready for their own mission.

The Clanners did not disappoint Doc, a fact that both scared and thrilled him. *For once, in the game of "Do they know that I know that they know . . ." we've come out ahead. We have to hurt them.*

The Clan Star came up over the hill and across the boulder-strewn incline in good order. Two *Vixen*s guarded the flanks, while a pair of *Peregrine*s held the point and back. The four light 'Mechs were centered on a medium-weight *Goshawk*. All five 'Mechs looked and moved like human beings in armor. The mottled green and black paint scheme contrasted sharply with the red rocks and clumps of the sparse yellow grass that grew on the plain.

Just a little bit further. Doc dropped his hands onto the joysticks for his targeting system. He'd assigned himself the task of firing the first shot, though all the other 'Mechs had their targets assigned to them. Once he fired, they would follow suit, and even though it was unlikely they'd take down all the Falcon 'Mechs in the first volley, they did expect to do some serious damage.

The dot in the center of his cross hairs glowed red, and Doc hit the triggers for his half-dozen pulse lasers. The laser fire hit the *Goshawk* solidly, liquefying armor on the 'Mech's right flank and over its heart. The lasers also burned two-thirds of the armor from the 'Mech's left arm and bubbled armor on its left thigh. One laser's energy darts played over the *Goshawk*'s small head, sending molten armor flooding down over the 'Mech's shoulders and chest.

The rest of the Ranger strike force opened up with all the weaponry they could bring on-line without frying their 'Mech's circuitry. In a flash of red and green laser beams, a *Phoenix Hawk* and the first of the Rangers' two *Ostsol*s nailed the first Clan *Vixen*. The lasers vaporized most of the armor on the left side of the 'Mech's protruding chest, then burned through the left arm's protection. Corded myomer fibers snapped, their smoking ends whipping furiously through the air as the beams filled the ferrotitanium bones of the arm with fire. They flashed white, then evaporated.

The other *Ostsol* hit the second *Vixen* with both of its large pulse lasers. The green beams sizzled into the 'Mech's heart, stripping away every bit of its protection. Doc's old *Centurion*, piloted by Tony Wells, blasted through the cloud of vapor armor with the autocannon mounted in its right arm. The depleted-uranium slugs ground through the internal supports in the 'Mech's chest, crushing the gyroscopes and shredding the fusion engine that powered the 'Mech. The *Vixen* collapsed in a heap. Then the cockpit faceplate exploded, and the pilot shot skyward in his ejection seat.

"Payback is grand!" Tony shouted over the radio.

The unit's *Vindicator* hit the *Goshawk* with its particle

projection cannon and a pulse laser. The PPC's cerulean beam stabbed into the Falcon 'Mech's right leg, plowing a molten furrow through the armor on the thigh. The pulse laser's ruby thorns tore at the armor on the *Goshawk*'s right arm, but failed to penetrate it.

The Rangers' only barrel-chested *Ostroc* used one of its large lasers to strip all but the last bit of armor from the first *Peregrine*'s right arm. The *Ostroc*'s other large laser combined with fire from the Ranger *Enforcer*'s large laser to disintegrate all the armor over the center of the *Peregrine*'s chest and melt some of the internal supports found there. Then the *Enforcer* launched an autocannon shot, scouring the armor from the left side of the *Peregrine*'s chest and leaving the 'Mech even more vulnerable to a second strike.

The final *Peregrine* fell prey to the Rangers' *Rifleman* and to the *Archer* Sharon Dorne piloted. Though normally considered a missile boat, the *Archer* became a deadly infighter with Sharon at the controls. The two medium lasers she fired from her 'Mech's forward arc converged and drilled through the *Peregrine*'s chest. Black smoke began to pour out, and the 'Mech wavered, telling Doc that Sharon's beams had cooked one gyro and had probably hit the 'Mech's engine. The *Rifleman* only hit with half its weaponry, but the large laser burned most of the armor from the *Peregrine*'s left arm while the medium laser slagged half the armor on the left side of its chest.

Doc kept his cross hairs on the *Goshawk*. He hit it again with a full salvo of pulse laser fire. The scarlet needles burst through the armor on the 'Mech's left arm, eliminating the last of the nearly exhausted armor and nibbling away at the artificial bones and muscle that made the arm work. Other laser fire scorched armor on the *Goshawk*'s torso, left leg, and right arm, leaving its ferro-fibrous flesh pitted and smoking.

The *Goshawk* struck back, but did not shoot at the *Penetrator*, choosing the *Vindicator* instead as Ellis angled for a better shot at the Clanner. The *Goshawk*'s large pulse laser spat out a stream of green darts that ripped into the *Vindicator*'s armor from left wrist to shoulder. The trio of medium pulse lasers struck the *Vindicator* in the chest, left flank, and leg, in seconds evaporating a ton and a half of armor that was worth its weight in platinum to the Rangers.

The *Vindicator*'s return fire sliced a blue bolt of artificial

lightning into the cratered armor of the *Goshawk*'s right
leg. The pulse laser's coruscating needles picked away at
the leg, freeing it of the last of its armor shell. More important, though, the sudden loss of so much armor shifted the
'Mech's balance point and the pilot lost control. Like an
unsteady child on wet ice, the *Goshawk* lost its footing and
went down.

The *Centurion* and *Ostsol* that had disabled the second
Vixen shifted their fire to the second *Peregrine* while the
other teams maintained their original assignments. Laser
beams crisscrossed the battlefield. One *Peregrine* spun down
hard to the ground while the remains of its arms whirled off
through air. The other *Peregrine* hit Bobbi Spengler's *Rifleman* with two pulse laser blasts and a large pulse laser shot.
The fire sliced through the armor on Spengler's right flank
and flensed most of the armor off the 'Mech's midline. The
one-armed *Vixen* went down, but not before its large pulse
laser pumped green needles into the right-arm armor of
Bell's *Enforcer*.

The return fire of the severely damaged Clan 'Mechs had
done little more than melt armor on Doc's people, and his
heart soared in elation. He wanted to shout with joy as the
Goshawk fell, but a green light flicked on in his cockpit. Beneath his position, the anti-missile system built into the *Penetrator* began to power up.

What? Why? No one launched missiles! Doc punched his
scanner over into magres mode, and the screen filled with a
legion of rising missile traces. "Incoming from over the
hill!"

The flights of long-range missiles arced up behind the Falcon 'Mech and created a fiery maelstrom on the incline and
into the gap where the Rangers had taken up their positions.
Doc watched a wave of explosions wash up and over his
'Mech. Kevin Smith's *Ostsol* staggered as missiles blasted
the 'Mech's left arm clean off. The other *Ostsol* fared
slightly better, losing all the armor of its left arm, but retain-
ing the fire-blackened limb.

A quintet of missiles slammed into the head of the unit's
Phoenix Hawk, but Brenda Pasek somehow managed to keep
the 'Mech upright. Doc's *Penetrator* shuddered as missiles
hammered its left hip, but he successfully fought against
gravity and kept the 'Mech on its broad feet. The rest of the

Ranger 'Mechs took damage and lost precious armor, but the missiles brought none of them down.

What surprised Doc about the missile attack was that the Jade Falcon 'Mechs took hits as well. Explosions bounced broken 'Mechs, tossing them rag-doll limp into the air before they crashed back down to the ground. Doc couldn't see what had happened to the pilot who'd previously punched out, but as the dust began to settle and the smoke thinned he saw two more pilots eject from their 'Mechs.

They must have expected us to close with them. That's the only reason they'd call fire in on their own position. Doc keyed his radio. "Pull back, Rangers. There's nothing left here for us."

"Roger that, Doc." The frustration Doc had grown used to hearing in Tony's voice had vanished. "We taught them they can't take us for granted."

"We did that, Tony." Doc slowly started his 'Mech working back toward the tunnels. *We also taught them to cover themselves, and I'm not sure that's a lesson I wanted them to learn so quickly.*

Two hours later they linked up with the ecstatic members of the Titans. While Doc's team had been shooting up the Clan patrol in the mountains, the Titans had staged a successful raid on the Falcon firebase. Once they'd neutralized the base's defenses, the drivers brought in on one of the Rangers' working hovertrucks liberated three truckloads of supplies and munitions, including the hovertrucks on which they'd been loaded. They burned whatever they couldn't carry, then screened the convoy from the Falcon 'Mechs returning from the ambush.

Isobel Murdoch briefed Doc on the operation. "It went very smoothly, Doc. And no one tried going after the 'Mechs limping home from your operation. There was one *Goshawk* surrounded by a Star of 'Mechs that my computer tagged as *Baboons*. They're very light missile boats and we could have given them a good run, but our mission was to get supplies back here before dark."

"And you just made it. The ammo and armor you pulled will be useful, if our guys can get the latter to work on our 'Mechs." Doc smiled, then stretched and yawned. "Good work, Isobel. Thanks for keeping the Titans together and whole."

"Yeah, well, you took the heat off us. Keep giving us missions like this and we'll do fine." She frowned. "There's just one thing that bothers me, but I can't tell if it's good or bad."

"What's that?"

She pointed back over her shoulder to the chamber where the liberated Clan loot had been stored. "Everything we got had already been loaded up on the hovertrucks. The storage bunkers there were clean. It makes no sense that they'd have set up those firebases just to abandon them at the end of the week."

"Agreed." Doc stood and stretched again. "I think I'm going to take a little walk. You might want to come along and bring some binoculars."

"Stargazing again?"

"Yeah. Having a hobby keeps me from getting bored." Doc gave her a wink. "I was thinking we might have something good to look at tonight, Bel."

"What makes you think it'll be any different this time?"

Doc shrugged uneasily. "There are two explanations for what you found. One is that the Falcons have decided to leave Coventry and we might see their DropShips blasting on out of Port St. William."

"And the other?"

"They're pulling away from us because they've found a more worthy foe." Doc smiled slowly. "If we're lucky, that means there are troops incoming and we just might be able to catch a glimpse of them as they burn their way in."

=== 29 ===

Victor Steiner-Davion swirled the brandy around the bowl of the snifter and let the sweet aroma fill his nose. The ComStar acolyte serving the brandy passed through the group, and everyone accepted a glass, including the Precentor Martial and the woman he'd introduced as former commander of the Terran Defense Force. *Had I been the one to lose Terra, I'd be drinking this stuff by the cask.*

The Precentor Martial held his glass up. "I offer a toast to those who have braved the fires of combat and yet are wise enough to see war as a most terrible thing."

Victor lifted his glass in response and touched it to Kai's, then to Focht's. He waited for a moment, then clinked the glass against both Hohiro Kurita's snifter and that of Precentor Koenigs-Cober. He drank and smiled as the brandy made its fiery way down into his belly.

The Precentor Martial set his glass on a mahogany side table and clasped his hands together. "I hope your attachés will not be upset that they were not invited to this dinner. It's true we'll all be seeing a lot of each other over the next month, but I wanted to speak with the three of you alone. Precentor Koenigs-Cober is here because she will liaise with you during the operations we've got planned, and some of those will be an outgrowth of this conversation. I hope you do not object?"

Victor shook his head. "Whatever you think best."

"You will forgive me, Precentor Martial, but I have a question." Hohiro Kurita, the son of the Coordinator of the Draconis Combine, bowed his head respectfully. "Unlike Victor, or even Kai, I cannot speak for my government. I will be most happy to bear your words back to my father, but if the purpose of this meeting is to craft a response to the conquest of Terra, I will be of little use to you."

"I appreciate your candor, Prince Hohiro, but it is not my intention to address that situation here." The Precentor Martial smiled graciously, which Victor found somehow reassuring. "I am not averse to discussing the attack on Terra, but ComStar considers it an historical event that does not require attention at this moment."

Victor glanced at Kai and saw his friend's barely hidden surprise at the announcement. During the trip to Tukayyid they'd discussed the chances that ComStar would suggest some sort of joint operation to retake Terra. Both had thought the request unlikely and believed ComStar might seek a pledge of neutrality in the matter. Victor knew he had to tread carefully, since Word of Blake had Free Worlds League connections and the war so recently ended could easily reignite.

"Precentor Koenigs-Cober and I have prevailed upon the Primus to maintain our current focus on the problem of the Clans. The operations we will engage in during the exercises will be directed toward honing our ability to deal with the Clans in a variety of situations." He opened his hands. "It will be our pleasure to share with you the opportunity to work against ComStar's Invader Galaxy."

"Invader Galaxy?" Victor arched a brow. "Would that be a unit configured to act as a Clan Galaxy?"

"That is it exactly, Highness." The Precentor Martial nodded toward the golden-haired Precentor. "Precentor Koenigs-Cober can give you the details since she is being installed as the unit's leader."

Koenigs-Cober smiled politely. "The BattleMechs are constructed mainly from salvage uncovered in the rehabilitation of Tukayyid. Over half the pilots are veterans of Tukayyid, and they've got more than two hundred 'Mechs and appropriate support personnel attached to the unit."

"It sounds impressive, Precentor." Kai smiled broadly and glanced at Victor. "Your intelligence people knew nothing of this unit?"

The Prince of the Federated Commonwealth frowned. "ComStar isn't considered hostile to the Commonwealth, so our assets aren't much focused in this direction."

"But you knew my wife was pregnant."

"Touché, my friend." Victor shrugged. "Perhaps if the Invader Galaxy had been pregnant we would have known about it."

"Calm yourself, Victor, my father's Internal Security Force didn't know about it either." Hohiro's mouth twisted up into a wry smile. "When Subhash Indrahar *does* learn about it, it may be his death."

From your lips to God's ears. Subhash Indrahar had been the director of the ISF since well before Victor's birth. He represented the old and reactionary forces within the Draconis Combine—forces that opposed the societal and military reforms that had enabled the Combine to adapt to the Clan onslaught. If Indrahar had his way, the Combine would slip back into the ignorant feudalism and rigid military that would crumble when the Clans came again. *The sooner Indrahar dies, the safer the Inner Sphere will be.*

The Precentor Martial nodded slightly as if he'd read either Victor's thoughts or his expression, and agreed with them. "The question I wish to put before you is this: would you prefer exercises that give us practice in defending against a Clan assault or exercises where we take the battle to them?"

Victor narrowed his eyes. "There's a subtext to those questions that needs to be addressed, I think."

"And that would be, Highness?"

"Are you advocating a shift in the way we deal with the Clans, including a change from defensive tactics to a more aggressive stance?" Victor took a deep breath. "And if you are, have you a target in mind?"

"Perhaps," Precentor Koenigs-Cober offered gently, "the latter question is premature."

"I hope like hell it isn't." Victor looked down and saw his reflection wobbling darkly in the liquor. "It's no secret to anyone here that the Jade Falcons are raiding fairly deep within the Lyran Alliance. My sister has declared that realm independent of mine, but I relinquish neither my claim nor my responsibility for the worlds and people of her Alliance. My last report indicated the Falcons have landed on Coventry, but that's all I know at this point."

Focht nodded as Victor finished speaking. "They've reached Coventry and have destroyed organized resistance on the two larger continents. Graf Joseph Mannervek declared himself ruler of the planet, accusing Duke Bradford of treason. It seems Mannervek has reached something of an accommodation with the Jade Falcons, so they've left him alone."

Victor felt a cold lump sucking the brandy's warmth from his stomach. "Any word on Duke Bradford or his family?"

"None, but we haven't heard word of their deaths either, which is a good sign." The Precentor Martial looked thoughtful for a moment. "I wish I could tell you more, but the Falcons have cut our people off from reaching the equipment that would let us communicate with them directly. All we've heard has come from simple radio broadcasts picked up by ships entering and leaving the system."

"I understand."

"The one good thing I can tell you is that four mercenary regiments have arrived and made planetfall. Two are Wolf's Dragoons. The others are the Eridani Light Horse and the Waco Rangers."

Hohiro shook his head. "Posting the Rangers and the Dragoons together on Coventry seems most unwise. They've been feuding for years."

Victor looked at Kai. "Your uncle Tormano is usually smarter than that."

"I'd have thought so, but his decision to become your sister's advisor has me wondering about his mental stability."

"Lunatics find comfort in company. Tormano and my sister are well suited to each other."

Focht adjusted the eye patch over his right eye. "You both know better than to think either Katrina Steiner or Tormano Liao insane or even foolish."

Victor nodded slowly. "We do know that, Precentor Martial. But it's hard to remember when they do things that defy what I define as logic. That's not to say there's not some method to their madness, but I don't trust their judgment because I can't understand it."

"I realize that, but to underestimate them is to risk being caught unawares by them." The Precentor Martial sighed.

"The Inner Sphere has long been home to intrigue, and members of the ruling houses are steeped in it. You three have each lost a parent or grandparent to an assassin, so I should think armoring yourself with caution is wise."

"Agreed, Precentor Martial." Victor upended his snifter and let the brandy's warmth relax him. "My question still stands, however: if we choose to operate with your Invader Galaxy as a defender, will we be using Coventry as a model for what we do?"

"We could choose worse examples, Highness."

Victor set his glass down and smiled. "And if we show ourselves to be adept at defeating Clan forces, how would you respond to the sovereign ruler of a nation inviting you to continue these exercises on a world in his realm?"

The Precentor Martial clasped his hands behind his back. "It is said the weather on Coventry is pleasant in the spring."

"The weather is *always* pleasant on Coventry." Victor's expression hardened. "Except when it's raining Clan 'Mechs."

"Perhaps, then, Victor, if our efforts are successful here," Hohiro said with a sly smile, "we should visit Coventry and see what we can do to clear up the weather."

═══ 30 ═══

Doc Trevena hoped that his ability to have his little force materialize inside the CEF's perimeter was not an omen concerning the Coventry Expeditionary Force's future or the success of its mission. The CEF had grounded at the northern end of the Cross-Divides, near where the mountains themselves ran down into the Central Sea. They'd chosen the mountain village of Leitnerton as their headquarters, then sent a task force southwest to help the remains of the Skye Rangers, Academy cadets, and Militia break out of a pocket around the town of Whitting.

The fact that Doc's recon lances found Waco Ranger and Crazy Eight patrols before they found his force made him proud, though it clearly did not amuse the leaders of the mercenary units sent to liberate Coventry. CEF security personnel ushered Doc into the Armitage Hotel's Grand Ballroom and marched him straight over to where the expedition's leadership stood studying the graphs, charts, and holograms being projected by the work stations that ringed the room.

The officers all turned and stared. Doc knew he looked a sight. His unit's deployment had been so fast that no one in his command had a sufficient change of clothes for the duration of the fighting. And they'd had more precious uses for fresh water in the mines than for washing clothes. The security police who'd brought him in let him wash his face and hands first, but without a clean change of clothes Doc was sure he looked more like a miner than a soldier.

He gave the officers a salute. "Hauptmann Trevena of the Tenth Skye Rangers reporting."

Of the officers present he had only previously met Judith Niemeyer, the Leftenant General in command of the Coventry Militia. The black jumpsuits with red trim easily identified two others as Dragoons. By process of elimination Doc also identified the black woman off to the left as General Ariana Winston, commander of the Eridani Light Horse. He'd read about her, and her presence made him think she and Alliance command took the current situation seriously.

Doc had seen enough of the Waco Ranger crests on the 'Mechs that escorted his people in to be able to pick out their leader, Colonel Wayne Rogers, from the group. It wasn't at all comforting that the man was dressed as casually as Doc. The only one who was missing was the commander of the Crazy Eights—a unit that had lived up to its name by becoming affiliated with the Waco Rangers.

The Waco Ranger leader squinted at Doc through thick glasses that magnified his eyes into huge brown reptilian orbs. "You're the idiot who brought two companies of 'Mechs into my occupation zone."

Doc pulled his right hand down from a salute and put himself at ease. "Those were my people, yes." He looked toward General Niemeyer. "We need repair and refit, but I have two companies that are operational."

One of the Dragoon officers, a man as tall as Doc, but a bit more slender, smiled carefully. "We appreciate what your people have gone through, and General Niemeyer *is* taking command of the Coventry Provisional Militia, but they will be serving in a reserve role at this point. We want to debrief you, of course, but we'll be handling things from here on out."

Doc frowned and looked at General Niemeyer. "What happened to General Bakkish?"

"Killed in a skirmish on the outskirts of Port St. William." Niemeyer glanced down as if she were uneasy with her position. He'd heard her described as matronly, and her look of defeat seemed to match. She seemed to Doc less a commanding officer than a grandmother disapproving what her grandchildren are doing, but who finds herself powerless to stop them. "As Colonel Tyrell has indicated, we're being held back as reserve troops."

"Reserve troops?" Doc shook his head. "I've got two-thirds of a battalion back there that's given as good as its gotten from the Jade Falcons in a month of fighting. While you guys were burning into this system, we were hitting the Falcons for supplies. My people went from green to seasoned fighters in short order. Not using them, especially when they have knowledge of this area, is foolish."

The dark-haired woman in a Dragoons uniform punched a command into a noteputer and one of the screens on the west side of the ballroom flashed up a copy of the Tenth Skye Rangers table of organization. "You speak rather possessively about a battalion led by Kommandant Horst Sarz."

"Not possessively, Colonel, proudly," Doc said. "Kommandant Sarz has a condition that rendered him unable to command. I replaced him."

"But you had no previous combat experience?" Doc read more curiosity in her blue eyes than recrimination. "The other two officers in the battalion had more time on the battlefield than you did."

"With all due respect, Colonel, I think the fact that we've survived as long as we have and maintained force integrity should speak for itself." Doc smiled despite the sour expression growing on Wayne Rogers's face. "Half my command is a scout company made up entirely of light 'Mechs. Aside from some armor damage, they've gone unscathed, yet they've engaged in more operations than my other 'Mechs."

Rogers exaggerated a shrug. "You were lucky. You should leave this to the professionals now."

Before Doc could answer, the woman from the Dragoons snapped at Rogers. "Hauptmann Trevena *is* a professional, Colonel Rogers."

"Yeah, I know that, Shelly dear, but a pro who had his butt stuck in a lousy unit in a worse assignment. They put him in charge of a recon *company*! Blake's Blood, woman, they *invented* a do-nothing unit for him." The way Rogers blinked made Doc think of him as a toad—a tall, bald, florid-faced toad, but a toad nonetheless. "The only way he could have been busted lower was if they'd put him in charge of a lance of simulator pods."

Tyrell stared laser bolts at Rogers. "What Colonel Brubaker is trying to get into your thick skull, Rogers, is that Hauptmann Trevena may not have the experience we do, but he's been trained and knows how to use his training."

Ariana Winston imposed herself between the Dragoons and Wayne Rogers. "With all that being true, my friends, I have no doubt that Hauptmann Trevena is merely espousing the wisdom of our working *together.* He's offering his experience here to help us, not to hinder us or steal any glory. He's been fighting the Falcons, and that's what we're going to do, too."

She looked over at Doc, her brown-eyed gaze searching his face for something. Doc blushed and she smiled. "Hauptmann Trevena, we're here to push the Falcons off Coventry. As you can see on the diagram over there, they've set up a perimeter around Port St. William. Their force is estimated at three Galaxies, which makes them roughly equivalent to our force. We intend to move them."

Doc looked up at the map. "Quite the task. When we last had radio contact with our regimental headquarters, it sounded like the Falcons were coming in from the north, through the lowlands, using the river as their right flank."

Niemeyer nodded haltingly. "Our forces pulled back into the Bradford Hills district, then escaped northeast to Whitting in the agricultural district. We barely had time to regroup before they enveloped us and started to squeeze."

Rogers adjusted his glasses. "So, what do you make of this ancient history, *Hauptmann* Trevena?"

Doc did his best to ignore the sarcasm, aided in this endeavor by a brave smile from Shelly Brubaker. "The Northlands approach makes sense. You put a screen force out to cover the river and another to cover the Hills, and you're clear to the center of Port St. William. It's definitely the easiest approach. And the one they'll be expecting. Now I may not have seen fire before this year, but it strikes me that an assault against entrenched Clan units is going to be pretty brutal."

General Winston nodded. "Agreed."

Doc pointed at the diagram on the wall. "What you've probably thought of already is bringing a force forward to fix the Clans in place along the Northlands and Hills area.

With a screen up along the northern reaches of the river you can prevent a Clan force coming up and rolling around your flank. They're still going to have to try that, though, which means they're going to head pretty far north until they find a good ford that will let them cross fast enough to secure the far bank."

Shelly's blue eyes sparkled warily. "That would put them in our rear area, threatening our supply lines from Leitnerton."

"True. The trick here, though, is that you'll already have a force that crossed even further north and is positioned in the Dales. Once your screen force reports contact, the Dales regiment pops on down and eats up the Clan flank. Then they shoot past it and take the west side of town. That puts them in the Clan rear."

Colonel Tyrell brushed a hand back through his closely cropped brown hair. "That's one plan we've considered, but we had to reject it. The geography in the Dales is too rough and wild for a force to get through fast *and* in good order."

Doc smiled. "Begging your pardon, sir, but that's not right."

Rogers scowled. "Any unit in there would break up quickly. It's a labyrinth. Getting caught up in there would be suicide."

"Unless you know the way through it."

General Winston gave Doc more than a once-over. "Do you?"

"My scouts and I held a month of exercises in that area earlier this year. We can get you through."

Brubaker hid her laugh behind her left hand. "Forgive me, Hauptmann, but you've provided a key to a puzzle we couldn't unlock."

"Glad to be of help." Doc frowned. "General Winston, you said the Falcons have three Galaxies in Port St. William."

"Yes."

"Where are the rest?"

That question brought him stares from everyone. "The rest?" echoed Tyrell.

"I saw DropShips coming and going the whole time we were in the mountains. I always hoped I'd see them just *going,* but no such luck. At the range I was watching from, I can't tell you what type of ships I saw, or what they were carrying, but there was a lot of traffic."

Wayne Rogers waved Doc's explanation away. "It doesn't matter—I handled the challenge and bidding myself. They're defending Port St. William with three Galaxies. That's our problem."

General Winston shook her head. "That's our *immediate* problem, Colonel. What Hauptmann Trevena has revealed is a bigger problem. We all knew this wasn't going to be easy." She hesitated for a moment and her eyes hardened. "I just hope we've not underestimated how difficult it will truly be."

Turkina Keshik Headquarters, Port St. William
Coventry
Coventry Province, Lyran Alliance
19 April 3058

Galaxy Commander Rosendo Hazen turned away from the holographic terrain table as the younger members of his strategic operations group stiffened to attention. He smiled casually at Marthe Pryde, saluting respectfully. "It is a pleasure to see you again, Khan Marthe."

"Of course, Galaxy Commander." Her long-legged strides shrank the distance from the door to the edge of the holographically-projected greensward. Displayed was a model of Port St. William from the north, looking south toward the bay. Small 'Mechs took up their places in the defensive positions manned previously by Inner Sphere troops, with a Galaxy in the Bradford Hills, another in the Northlands, and a third in the city held in reserve.

Marthe scanned the plan, then nodded. "Standard defense."

"Agreed, but Arimas here has noted a couple of flaws in the enemy that we had not previously suspected." Rosendo waved a hand toward a tall, slender soldier with a shock of red hair. "Tell us what you have discovered."

The youngster's blue eyes brightened. "In reviewing the action around Whitting, I noticed something we might be able to use. The Eridani Light Horse secured the Inner Sphere landing zone, then the Dragoons sent their regiments down, one heading west to cover the right flank, the second taking the center. The left, which was apparently an area where they were not expecting trouble, was covered by the Waco Rangers. The movement of the Rangers seemed not to be fully integrated with that of the Dragoons. Supplemental research on the Rangers reveals an institutional hatred for the Dragoons. This hatred appears to be mutual."

Marthe nodded. "All this is already known."

"Yes, my Khan, but I thought it would not be useful to review the advance of the lucrewarriors without noting this background." Arimas hit two keys on the noteputer he held. The holographic display shrank in scale, pulling back far enough to show the approaching Inner Sphere forces. Marching along like tiny toys came the Eridani Light Horse regiment sandwiched between the two Dragoon regiments. The Militia held the extreme west flank, and the Waco Rangers were shown back at Leitnerton.

"It is my belief, Khan Marthe, that the Dragoons would never trust the Rangers with securing their base. Moreover, I do not believe the Rangers would accept being left behind in the battle for Port St. William. The enemy knows that attacking prepared defenses calls for as overwhelming a concentration of firepower as they can amass. That means the Waco Rangers cannot be in Leitnerton."

Marthe looked at Rosendo and raised an eyebrow. "Your assessment?"

"I am reluctant to believe the Dragoons would leave Leitnerton vulnerable, but we would be hard pressed for the armor, infantry, and 'Mechs needed to take it, even without the Rangers present. Our bid forces really do not permit us to threaten their rear *and* adequately defend the city."

The Khan directed her attention toward Arimas again. "What is your estimation of how the Rangers will be used?"

Arimas hesitated for a moment, revealing a crack in his composure. "I believe the enemy intends to bring them through the hills of the area called the Dales and hit us when our reserves come out to threaten their flank. Having the Militia remnant acting as the western screen presents us with a tempting target. Moving out and trying to envelop the enemy's western flank is a sound strategy, one we would be expected to employ."

"Arimas, are you aware we considered such a strategy when we attacked Port St. William?"

"Yes, my Khan. It was abandoned because the Dales are considered a difficult area to transit. We did not have guides. I believe the Rangers do." Arimas pointed to the Cross-Divides. "According to records we have captured, the Skye Ranger battalion had a light element that spent time in the Dales. Their raids have stopped in the east, so I believe they have linked up with the mercenaries and can lead them on this sweep of our flank."

Marthe smiled slightly. "Rosendo, is he one of yours, or one of ours?"

"Neither. He is a Malthus, with some Nygren and Widow-maker mixed in."

"Remarkable."

"Just wait." Rosendo nodded to Arimas. "Present your plan to the Khan."

"As you wish." In response to the command Arimas typed into his noteputer, the display again shifted. The defending Galaxies had been stripped of a Trinary each, creating a light Cluster of fast 'Mechs. The reserve unit consisted mainly of heavy and assault 'Mechs, while mediums and heavies served as the garrison units in the city.

"What I intend is for our forces in Port St. William to pull back in the face of the initial onslaught. The enemy obviously intends their frontal assault to pin us in place, so the premature withdrawal will present them with a situation they can exploit before the Rangers are in place to strike. As our forces pull back, our reserve force begins its flanking maneuver. It will hit the screen force ahead of schedule and, given the strength of our unit, should rip through it.

"This will seriously threaten the enemy's rear area. The Rangers would have to advance more quickly than planned and will fall into disarray. In truth I *do* expect them to advance early because they do not want to let the glory of taking Port St. William go to the Dragoons alone. When they hit the reserves, the fast Cluster can pour through into the enemy rear and threaten Leitnerton."

"And if the Rangers do not advance in disorder?"

"The fast Cluster will speed out and engage them, allowing our heavy reserves to move into the enemy rear." Arimas smiled openly. "The enemy's movements into the city can be slowed by the use of Elementals so that before they have a solid foothold, their backs will be vulnerable. They will be obliged to withdraw."

"They will, indeed."

Rosendo looked at Marthe. "We make this plan operational, *quiaff*?"

"With one slight change, *aff*." Marthe pointed toward the enemy's Port St. William assault force. "The Dragoons were once part of the Clans, and the Light Horse claim their tradition runs back to troops who remained behind when General Kerensky left the Inner Sphere. Deceiving them this once will be permitted. After that I want them at their best, and I think we can use this operation to guarantee I get what I want."

ComStar Headquarters
Tukayyid
ComStar Garrison District, Free Rasalhague
Republic

Victor Davion sat back in one of the overstuffed chairs arranged around the fireplace in the study. The room looked ancient, as if it had been on Tukayyid since before mankind left the confines of Terra, but he realized it was a skillful reconstruction. With all the walnut paneling, the built-in shelves stuffed with leatherbound books, and the wooden furnishings, it reminded him of his own office on New Avalon—the office that had also been his father's. Those memories combined with the glass of single-malt Scotch whisky and the roaring fire in the hearth to make him feel very much at home.

Hohiro Kurita, seated across from him in another of the deep armchairs, took a sip of his brandy, then smiled. "These surroundings are far too cluttered to be considered restful by my people, yet I do somehow find this room inviting."

Kai Allard-Liao leaned forward toward the fire, his snifter cradled in both hands. "It's the brandy and the fire, Hohiro. They're dulling your senses."

"Not to mention the fact that we're all bone tired." Victor rubbed his eyes with his left hand. "However, it's a good tired. Your Genyosha really rolled up that Invader flank. Very nice envelopment."

"I will pass your compliment to Narimasa Asano. He directed our movements."

"Yeah, you merely led them." Victor had been amazed at Hohiro's boldness in driving his company into the edge of the Invader flank. The maneuver froze the flank, allowing the rest of the battalion to curl around and concentrate fire on the Invaders. As the Invaders began to retreat, the rest of the Genyosha regiment pushed forward and the Invader left wing collapsed.

"What I did only worked because the Invaders were fighting by Jade Falcon doctrine. They were concentrating on single combat between warriors. This is a tradition warriors of the Combine understand and, perhaps, like too much."

Victor frowned. "How do you mean 'like too much'?"

"Had they been fighting as Wolves I would have been blasted back. They would have enveloped me and destroyed my command." Hohiro smiled ruefully. "We would have demanded a great price from them, but I would have been yet one more samurai who met a glorious death in combat."

"As I recall it was warriors from the Draconis Combine who sent my Uncle Ian to just such a glorious end."

"Indeed, Victor, and his bravery is remembered among my people."

"Strange how the glory of battle, the displays of courage, somehow bleed over to color death." Kai took a sip of his brandy. "A hero dies a glorious death and even the warriors trying to kill him are somehow elevated by their participation in his demise. And if the person who actually does kill him praises the fallen warrior as brave, the death and the act of killing rise to an even higher pinnacle of nobility and grace."

Victor blinked, surprised at Kai's words. "You will forgive me, Kai, but hasn't your career as the Champion of Solaris been built on exactly such glorious combat?"

"True." Kai hesitated, and Victor could sense his doubt. "There is certainly death enough in the arenas of Solaris, but that isn't really the goal. I managed to win the championship without killing any of my foes. When someone dies in the arena, well, it's usually because of some stupidity or accident, and the death is mourned."

"We mourn those who fall in combat."

Hohiro held a hand up. "I think I know what Kai's driving at. The fights on Solaris are contests of skill. Because of the way they're waged and presented, others can enjoy the abilities of the MechWarriors involved. Solaris fights are to war what boxing is to a riot. Death is not the end-goal in those fights the way it is in combat."

Kai nodded in agreement. "And on Solaris we acknowledge the pity and tragedy of death. But we can't let ourselves do that in war, or we would never find the will to continue waging it. We have to elevate the slain to the ranks of heroes, or at least tragic figures, because doing that puts a benign mask on the ugly face of death."

Victor set his glass down on a side table. "I understand what you're saying, but I think you're operating from a false premise. Hohiro stated it when he said killing is the end-goal of war."

Hohiro frowned over the lip of his snifter. "If it is not, what is?"

Victor sighed, thinking that was a question that had provided historians and philosophers with fodder for generations. "I don't want to oversimplify, but the goal of war is to defeat the other side."

Hohiro nodded. "Which is best done by killing the enemy."

"Not necessarily, Hohiro." Kai sat back in his chair. "I have defeated my foes on Solaris without killing them."

"But those are games."

"And how different are those games from the way the Clans fight? To them war is a contest to see who is the toughest. On Solaris the toughest warrior wins money and fame. In the Clans the toughest warrior wins glory and a chance for his genes to become part of the breeding program. In essence, the Clan warrior wins immortality. The Clanners fight well and hard, so their prize is fitting for what they do. A warrior's death or survival is immaterial to his reward, so the death of one only makes room for more warriors to take his or her place in the immortality lottery."

Hohiro shrugged. "It's seductive to believe we could kill enough of them to stop them, but the battle for Wolcott proves that killing the Clans isn't the only way to defeat them. My father outmaneuvered them and they retreated, sparing each side unnecessary bloodletting."

Victor rubbed his eyes for a moment, then smiled. "I think, in removing death from the formula for defeating the enemy we've just hit on a lesson that has to be learned by each new generation of warriors—a lesson some generations never learn, and others pick up because their leaders failed to do so. That is, quite simply, that blood is not the only currency with which victory may be purchased."

Hohiro raised an eyebrow. "But can you win a war without killing?"

"Perhaps not, Hohiro, but that's not exactly the point." Kai brought his hands together, fingertip to fingertip. "No leader who is presented with defeat will march his men straight into the guns of his enemy, unless he's suicidal or stupid, or both. He'll pull back and wait for another opportunity. Flanking an enemy, isolating him from his supplies, forcing him to divide his strength so you can overwhelm bits and pieces of his force—those are superior means for winning wars because they minimize the blood-price your side pays for defeating your enemy."

Victor nodded emphatically. "That's it exactly, Kai. That may not sit well with you, Hohiro, but I think all of our martial traditions—including those of the Clans—have a double standard by which warriors are measured. Individual soldiers are judged on their lethal nature. Those who kill great numbers of the enemy are highly lauded. You yourself said my uncle Ian was praised for fighting valiantly and dying bravely, much as you would be for taking vast numbers of Clanners to the grave with you."

"I see your point. Go on."

The Prince of the Federated Commonwealth hitched forward to the edge of his seat. "Leaders are judged by how well they defeat the enemy, and the emphasis is placed on skill and cunning, not brute force, because brute force kills lots of the leader's own people."

"Even so, a leader who avoids war, yet still gets what he wants is somehow seen as less honorable than one who sheds blood to achieve his goals." Hohiro took a sip of brandy as he paused reflectively. "Why is that?"

"It's because no one trusts an individual who's skilled at deception." Kai shook his head. "He who wins through deception, though he does so without shedding blood, is not regarded as winning a true victory. The decision is not clear, though the results are."

"And yet, the leader who can win without killing anyone should be the example that everyone tries to emulate." Victor reclaimed his glass and drained it. "Winning without killing may be the final lesson one has to learn to become a truly great warrior. It's one I'm willing to try to master."

Hohiro nodded. "That has a rather intriguing Zen quality to it—becoming great in an arena without using the tools others resort to. If you wish a study partner for this lesson, please consider me for that position."

"I think it better to have a thousand living men think of me as a deceiver than one corpse to support my fame as a masterful warlord." Kai smiled thoughtfully. "I, too, would join this course of study."

"Very good, my friends." Victor held his empty glass aloft. "From this day forward our aim will be to forestall death instead of aiding and abetting it. Even if they don't want to call us great warriors, at least we won't be filling graveyards with the evidence to damn us."

═══ 32 ═══

The Dales
Coventry
Coventry Province, Lyran Alliance
21 April 3058

Had he still been piloting the *Penetrator,* Doc would have taken a shot at Colonel Wayne Rogers' *BattleMaster.* "Colonel, I don't care if the Jade Falcons are lining the streets with banners and handing cold beer to advancing Dragoons, we're not supposed to advance until General Niemeyer reports Buckler Force has made contact. We don't know where we're going or what we're going to run into."

"That's what your little scout company is for, Trevena." The *BattleMaster* pointed south with the gunlike particle projection cannon in its right fist. "The Falcons are collapsing in Port St. William. With you out in front of us, we'll know what's coming and be able to prepare for it."

But you won't stop. Doc had known Rogers would pull some bonehead stunt. The man wasn't stupid, but he just didn't think straight when it came to the Dragoons. At the time the Dragoons had revealed their true origins as former members of the Clans, Rogers and his people had tried to form a mercenary coalition to destroy them. While he'd calmed a bit on that score, Rogers was so obsessed with proving that his people were the equal of the Dragoons that his desire rolled off him like sweat off a fat man.

The Crazy Eights weren't much better. Their commander, Captain Symerious Blade, didn't really have any grudge with the Dragoons, but he seemed willing to be dragged along in Rogers' wake. The Eights stayed away from the Dragoons for the most part, but when they did run into them seemed almost as ready as the Waco Rangers to pick a fight.

Shelly Brubaker had laughed when Doc told her his concerns about Rogers. "Of course he'll do something stupid. That's why we refer to them as the Wackoid Rangers and why *they'll* be in the Dales while we do some fighting."

Doc sighed and keyed his microphone. "Colonel, let me ask you this: if I go out there and report back that every Jade Falcon on the planet is coming to nail your hide, you won't pull back, will you?"

"I don't deal in hypotheticals, Trevena," Rogers growled. "Get your people out there. Run the river and tell me what you've got."

"Get me an order from General Winston, and it's done."

The *BattleMaster*'s PPC swung into line with the *Centurion*'s cockpit. "You take your orders from me, boy. You're attached to my unit. Now, move out."

"Yes, *sir,* Colonel." Doc started his 'Mech forward. "I hope like hell nothing goes wrong out here because when this is all over, we're going nose to nose. And I'm gonna hit you so hard you'll end up lower than my opinion of you."

"Better men than you have tried that, Trevena."

"If they couldn't do it, Colonel, they weren't better men."

Doc and his people headed south along the banks of the Ridseine in a line approximately two kilometers long. The terrain through which they moved had the rolling hills for which the Dales were known, but gradually flattened out into wide meadows carpeted with the first green vestiges of Coventry's spring grasses. Tall stands of trees that had served as windbreaks and boundary markers in the past broke up their line of sight and limited them to only three or four kilometers of visibility in any direction.

Doc didn't like it at all. Because of the trees that grew parallel to the river out to a kilometer from the bank, he couldn't always see the furthest end of the line that he and Isobel Murdoch anchored with their heavier 'Mechs. Andy Bick had his lance at the far end, and though Andy had become a pretty good commander, Doc was afraid he might somehow miss something out there. *Of course, Andy has more variety of combat under his belt than I do at this point, so I guess I'm just going to have to trust him.*

Doc's radio crackled with static. "This is Buckler calling Dagger."

Rogers's voice came back through in answer, and was far stronger than Doc thought it should have been. "Dagger here, go ahead, Buckler."

"We have contact in sector 2843."

"Hang on, Buckler. Dagger is on its way."

Doc glanced at his auxiliary monitor. "Dagger, this is Scabbard. Sector 2843 is fifteen kilometers south of my present position. We'll need an hour to clear it."

"Buckler doesn't have an hour, Scabbard. My force will be there well before that."

Doc could already see Waco Rangers moving through the treeline in his aft arc, with the Crazy Eights grouped closest to the river. "Dagger, they just reported *contact*. We have orders."

"Yeah, well, battle plans never survive contact with the enemy. Move your people, we're going through."

"Be reasonable."

"I'd rather help Buckler."

Doc switched his radio over to the Titan tactical frequency. "Titans, on me. Speed to sixty klicks—repeat, six-oh klicks—when you link up, hold a line on the river. Murdoch, you have point."

"Roger, Doc."

The Titans moved forward, their line shrinking, setting their speed at just less than the maximum for their slowest member—Murdoch's *Hunchback*. The fact that the *Hunchback* packed a solid punch made it a good 'Mech to have when traveling into hazardous areas without knowing what was out there. Doc's *Centurion* could also hit hard in a tight battle, a trait he thought they'd need since a Clan force wasn't likely to travel far ahead of its scouts.

He punched up the radio frequency Mace force was using, but he couldn't raise either General Winston or Shelly Brubaker. *This is wrong, this is all wrong!* He could feel disaster looming up beyond the next woodline, or the one after that. His Titans—in their small 'Mechs with mottled and mixed colors—willfully and daringly burst past one barrier and plunged on into the next, and behind him the Waco Rangers came across a front nearly a kilometer wide. Uniformly painted in tan and olive, with blue and red stars on their torsos and arms, the Rangers were a sight to behold as they moved out at speed. Even the mismatched, gaudy 'Mechs of the Crazy Eights added to the majesty of the advancing 'Mechs.

The Falcons, I assume, are not going to be impressed.

"Contact, Doc." Andy Bick's voice had none of the doubt and hesitancy from when Doc had first met him. "Moving to speed."

Doc saw he'd been right: the Falcons did have a small scout Star ahead of their main body. Five *Baboon*s were launching salvos of long-range missiles at the Titans, but the burst of speed by the lighter 'Mechs ruined the Clanners' aim. The two that had targeted the *Centurion* and the *Hunchback* made hits, but the damage proved minimal. Doc cut his 'Mech to the left in reaction to the missiles slamming into the cockpit, then had to fight to avoid spinning full around as other missiles hit the 'Mech's left arm and leg.

"Bel, you okay?"

"Yeah, head and shoulders, but I'm okay. Got him in my sights."

The *Hunchback*'s shoulder-mounted autocannon vomited fire and metal at one of the squat, long-armed 'Mechs. The stream of slugs chewed the *Baboon*'s arm from wrist to shoulder, then blew through the joint. The 'Mech's twisted, broken arm whirled away as autocannon fire ate its way through the left side of its chest, leaving only an eggshell-thin layer of back armor in its wake.

Doc slid his cross hairs onto the outline of the 'Mech that had hit him, then triggered the medium lasers in the *Centurion*'s chest, slashing deep wounds into the armor over the *Baboon*'s heart. The *Centurion*'s right-arm autocannon also stabbed fire at the Clan machine. The rain of depleted-uranium shells struck the left side of its chest and peeled armor off in long sheets. The projectiles continued on into the *Baboon*'s chest, shredding internal structures.

Doc wasn't that surprised at how much damage he and Murdoch were able to do to the first two *Baboon*s, but the savaging his light 'Mechs gave the others left him completely astounded. Bick's lance picked its target apart, blasting open the *Baboon*'s chest, tearing up its legs and melting its left arm off. The other two lances dispatched their targets with equally ruthless efficiency, then circled around and tore the other two *Baboon*s apart before Doc and Isobel could close the gap with them.

The Waco Rangers thundered on past the Titans and entered a green field ringed on three sides by two-kilometer-long lines of aspens. The brief glimpse that Doc got through the trees before the Rangers dashed in there looked so peaceful and benign that he wanted to deny the evidence of danger that lay smoking at his 'Mech's feet. Even the glint of sunlight off metal in the far row of trees seemed as if it would have a harmless explanation, but deep down Doc knew it meant the Waco Rangers were doomed.

Colonel Rogers and his people reached the midpoint of the box approximately a minute and a half after entering the field. Somewhere back beyond the far tree line, Falcon missile boats began to launch hundreds upon hundreds of long-range missiles. Explosions created a wall of flame across the front of the Ranger formation. With all the smoke raised by the barrage, Doc couldn't really see much from his position, but he knew the Rangers had gone down.

"Doc, we've got company to the west."

"Roger, Julian." Pulling back around to the right Doc picked up movement and 'Mech outlines. He hit his radio. "Dagger, this is Scabbard, pull back out of there. It's a trap. Repeat, trap. 'Mechs are coming in toward you from the west."

Colonel Rogers did not reply.

"Doc, what do we do?" Concern overrode the trace of fear in Isobel's voice.

"Titans, pull back north. When we get to Shallot Ford, we go across and head back toward Leitnerton."

"We can't leave the Rangers, Doc," came Andy Bick's voice.

"Sorry, Andy, but the only thing we'll accomplish if we follow them is die." Looking back toward the Ranger position Doc saw the first of the Falcon 'Mechs moving forward from cover to engage. "We have to get to where we can let Mace know what's happening."

"But, Doc . . ."

"No protests, it's an order." Doc wrenched his *Centurion* around. "They wouldn't let us do our job before, and now there's nothing we can do for them. Dying with them won't help anyone, but alerting the others will. If any of the Rangers or the Eights straggle out, we'll help them, but that's the best we can do. Understand?"

Doc filled his voice with as much conviction as he could muster, and his lances turned and formed up around him. *They're good kids, they trust what I'm telling them. I just hope what I've told them is true.*

=== 33 ===

Tormano Liao found he could not read Katrina Steiner's expression, and that disturbed him. Not because he thought he'd lost any of his skill at sensing the moods of others and reacting accordingly, but because he was seeing Katrina in a new state of existence. *Never before have I had to deal with her when she is being . . .* thoughtful.

With the quick flick of a finger against a keyboard, Katrina put the holographic projection hovering above her white desk through a day-by-day shift. The diagrams showed the relative positions of Jade Falcon and mercenary troops on Coventry, with the Falcons in green, the mercenaries in red, and the remnants of the Lyran troops displayed in a light blue. Each day the perimeter shrank, pushing the mercenaries back toward the mountain hamlet of Leitnerton. On the 27th the mercenaries lost a third of the force, effectively dropping from three regiments to two, but the statistics running along the side of the diagram had predicted that collapse days earlier.

On the 28th of the month a fourth Jade Falcon Cluster was added to the Clan force.

Katrina, wearing her hair in a long golden braid tied with blue and red ribbons, looked up at Tormano. "The situation is indeed most alarming. How reliable are the identifications of the units attacking our people?"

"I would consider them all but unimpeachable, Highness."

She nodded slowly. "That means our forces have faced and fought elements from eight different Clan Galaxies during the campaign that's forcing our people back to their base. How is it possible for the Falcons to field so many troops? The war with the Wolves should have devastated them. It's a trick, *quiaff*?"

Tormano ignored the Clanism. "I don't know, Highness. In the ancient past, warlords were known to try to deceive foes by building more campfires than they had troops, or by marching the same troops past a spy in a great circle, so the same people were counted more than once. The purpose, obviously, was to make the enemy overestimate the size of the force. While that sort of thing would be of value if the Clans were truly outnumbered, we're seeing members from these different Galaxies in actual combat. There's no doubt they're there."

"Where?"

"The Chakulas continent. Graf Mannervek appears to be playing host to them, or at least tolerating their presence. Some of our intelligence analysts believe the Falcons are using the third continent as a staging area. Units are prepped there, then shipped to the Veracruz continent to fight. Letting us know how many troops they have available on Coventry is a mistake, but I'm not accustomed to being the beneficiary of Clan mistakes."

"Providing us that information does seem foolish, but the Jade Falcons aren't seen as intellectual giants by their peers." Katrina focused distantly. "Their inability to simply sweep our forces away points up their weakness. The crushing defeat of the Waco Rangers was one thing, but they haven't been able to duplicate that level of success again. Why?"

Tormano shook his head. "I don't know the answer, but pondering that question might be diverting us from more important considerations."

"Such as?"

"Such as the very real threat to Tharkad. Eight Galaxies are the rough equivalent of twelve Inner Sphere regiments. Fortunately, Thomas Marik has responded to your appeal, and his Knights of the Inner Sphere are en route now. Sun-

Tzu has also sent the Harloc Raiders to represent him." *And to anger me, for I would have destroyed the Raiders years ago had my plans not been ruined by his and Kai's meddling.* "Your Eleventh Lyran Guards are here, the other three Dragoon Regiments are inbound, and you also have the First and Second Royal Guards on Tharkad. If we call up the Militia and bring in the Reserve, that would put us roughly equal to the Clan force on Coventry.

"Of course, it would be prudent for us to keep up the pressure on Coventry to keep the battle being fought there instead of having it come to Tharkad. We need more time to collect troops sufficient to defend us here, but in the meantime we might actually be able to wipe the Falcons out on Coventry."

"To do that I would have to shove more troops piecemeal into the grinder the Falcons have created on Coventry. I would be trading lives for time."

"That would be the size of it." The old man shrugged and knitted his fingers together. "A most difficult decision, Highness."

Katrina arched one eyebrow. "Is it? I think the trade quite worth it, provided I'm trading someone else's lives for *my* time. Come now, Mandrinn, you didn't think I held some romantic view of combat, did you? Combat is where people die, and I would rather have my people memorializing the valiant foreigners who died in their defense than mourning their own dead. And, think of it, one of the first units I would consider using is your nephew's, so you will be rid of it."

The latter suggestion did little to warm the chill her voice had put into his bones. The image of innocent beauty that had lurked at his core conception of Katrina suddenly vanished, replaced by that of a woman with a razor's edge to her voice and a darkness in her soul. The image did not repulse him, but merely taught him again to be on his guard.

"Where is Victor?"

"Still on Tukayyid, Highness."

"Good."

"Good?" Tormano frowned. "That makes him close enough to threaten your border. If he wished, he could move down with his troops and amputate the Lyons thumb, consummating your technical loss of that area to the Combine. Having him this close is not good."

"True, idle hands are the devil's playthings." Katrina smiled, then tapped a fingernail against her teeth. "The only person I'd wish to bleed more quickly than Sun-Tzu is my dear brother. I think I shall give him a target for his attention."

Tormano held his hands up. "Perhaps you wish to reconsider drawing your brother into all this, Highness. It sets a precedent for him to bring troops into your space for the good of the realm. It wouldn't take much to stretch that into a need for military occupation."

"True, but I don't anticipate my brother continuing to plague me for much longer." Katrina sat back and stared at the holographic display. "What you will do is this, Mandrinn. You will have a report prepared on the operations on Coventry. You will note that the previous attacks were devastating, and that we have been blacking out news of it to hide our weakness. Go so far as to hint at some civil unrest and animosity toward me because of the deception. Indicate that I have taken personal charge of what is going on and that I am micro-managing every aspect of the situation on Coventry."

A smile grew on Tormano's face. "You will make it impossible for Victor to stay away from Coventry."

"And impossible for him to get away from Coventry. Your report will show the correct troop strengths for those we have on the ground, and suggest that their survival is doubtful. You will also indicate that elements of *four* Galaxies have been confirmed to be on the planet. Note that I am going to send the rest of the Dragoons, the Knights of the Inner Sphere, the Eleventh Lyran Guards, and the Harloc Raiders to Coventry to end this thing. You will time their arrival to be close to the time Victor could possibly get there."

The simplicity of her plan sent a shiver down Tormano's spine. *Victor will arrive under-strength and engage the enemy, facing defeat or death, or both.* "I was alive when your Uncle Ian died fighting against the Combine."

"Ian *is* Victor's middle name." Katrina leaned back in her chair. "He's already courted death at the hands of the Clans more than once. Perhaps out of guilt for having murdered our mother, hoping to redeem himself by preventing the Clans from leaping to Tharkad, he throws himself into combat and is killed. A tragic and heroic death."

"Though grief-stricken, you will accept the throne of the

Federated Commonwealth and unite the realm in memory of your parents and your brother?"

"I do suppose, Mandrinn, I would have to do just that."

"An interesting plan, Highness, but that still does not solve the problem of the Jade Falcons. Even if Victor hurts them, they may still come to Tharkad."

She shook her head. "That is not going to be a concern, Mandrinn. On this you will have to trust me. Even if it were a problem, my brother will weaken the Falcons enough that the troops we gather here can finish the job. Of this I have no doubt."

Tormano had to agree with her. *Victor isn't stupid. He won't follow in the footsteps of Colonel Rogers or his namesake uncle. Die he might, but many Jade Falcons will die with him. A wonderful plan—simple in execution and rewarding in result.*

His head came up. *But not a perfect plan.* "Highness, what if your brother wins and survives? He will have defeated your enemies and will have saved your realm."

"And so I will thank him profusely and send him home. His regiment couldn't hope to oppose the forces that will be gathered here on Tharkad." Katrina gave him one of her most winning smiles, one that showed off the perfect whiteness of her teeth. "We will honor those of the Federated Commonwealth who gave their lives to defend us, elevating the dead to the status of heroes, all the while leaving unvoiced the question of why, when so many had to die, my brother managed to survive?"

"His effort on behalf of your nation will contribute to his vilification." Tormano fought to suppress a shudder. "I think, Highness, that I'm grateful not to be the object of your attention."

Katrina sat forward again and killed the display with the press of a button. "It is well you are not, Mandrinn Liao. I would not like destroying you." She laughed and waved him on toward the door. "It would be too easy and, therefore, no fun at all."

34

"**P**retty depressing, isn't it?"

Doc Trevena spun around, lowering his binoculars. He smiled as he saw Shelly Brubaker step from the ladder leading up to the roof of the building the Titans had appropriated as their headquarters. "Depressing, yes, but more puzzling and frustrating than depressing, really." He handed her the binoculars and turned back and stared out to where the Jade Falcons had entrenched themselves in a big semi-circle around the Alliance position. "Things just don't add up."

"Such as?"

"The Waco Rangers."

Shelly reached up and rubbed a hand across his right shoulder. "What happened to Rogers and his people wasn't your fault. Even if he *had* let you do your job, you would only have found the heavy force, which happened to be where we expected it to be. The Galaxy that swung out and around still would have hit the Rangers from the side. An enfilade assault like that is impossible to defend against. Had you stayed, you and your people would be dead or captured right now. The Crazy Eight survivors were lucky you waited for them and helped them get away."

"Thanks." Doc sighed. "Part of my problem is that deep

inside I don't feel bad about pulling my people out. I feel more loyalty to them than I ever did or will to Colonel Rogers."

"Hey, you didn't owe him any loyalty. He didn't respect you or your people. You can bet that if things had gone the way we expected, the role of your Titans, as recorded in the Waco unit history, would have been reduced to that of 'indig guides.' And your people deserve your loyalty because they've done more to harass or hinder the Falcons than the rest of us."

Doc forced himself to scoff. "As I recall it, the Titans were running around warning of doom when you pulled your Delta Regiment out of the Northlands assault, wheeled to the northwest, and came up to hammer the Falcons. If you hadn't hit them and given the others time to come around and contain them, we'd have lost our base. The Falcons didn't expect that, and it sure as hell stopped them cold."

Shelly smiled as she handed him back the binoculars. "You're quite the flatterer, Hauptmann Trevena."

"It's not flattery to tell the truth, Colonel Brubaker." Doc flushed in surprise at his own glibness. "Forgive me. That didn't sound quite how I meant it."

Shelly shrugged, her blue eyes flashing playfully. "I liked how it sounded."

"Um, ah, um . . ." Doc felt his whole face burning red. "Why do I get the feeling I'm digging myself into a hole here?"

"I'll help you out." Shelly winked at him. "You're an intelligent man, Doc. You may have been green in terms of real combat experience—there's no substitute for it, of course—but you've not shied from battle. You've identified what your unit can do and you use its abilities and skills to accomplish what you can. You're realistic, yet willing to take carefully calculated risks. You're thoughtful, but not someone who worries a problem to death. I find these qualities attractive, and the package holding them isn't too bad either."

Doc squatted at the edge of the flat roof. "Tell that to my wife."

"Wife?"

"Ex-wife, I guess." Doc shrugged. "I imagine the divorce

papers are sitting in the Port St. William office waiting for me to sign them."

The Dragoon officer looked down at him. "Your wife is divorcing you? Why?"

"You think I'm thoughtful. I guess my thoughts weren't full enough for her, so Sandra found herself another friend. Moving here to sunny Coventry would have strained their relationship, so Sandy decided to save me the trouble of shipping most of my belongings here by keeping them."

"What a fool."

"Yeah, so much for me being intelligent."

Shelly cuffed him lightly on the back of his head. "Not you, *her*."

"That's the way to a man's heart—pointing out that his ex didn't know what she is missing."

"She clearly doesn't, Doc, and you're smart enough to know that." Shelly leaned over and gave him a quick kiss on the cheek.

Doc smiled. "You mercs don't have any rules against fraternization with indig forces?"

She straightened up and shook her head. "You know us, a conquest after every conquest. Besides, you're an officer. With you I wouldn't be fraternizing, I'd be *liaising*."

"That sounds almost respectable."

"I can assure you it would be nothing of the kind."

"So much the better." Doc sat back on his heels. "It would be best if we had a conquest to celebrate."

Shelly knelt down beside him. "I agree, but I don't think it's possible. Our munitions are low and we can't mass enough strength to break through the Falcon cordon without threatening the collapse of our whole line."

Doc's eyes narrowed. "The breakout isn't impossible." He pointed toward where the Clan line butted up against the Cross-Divides. "The chain of caverns and tunnels that runs under the mountains goes pretty far past their line."

"And well the Falcons know it. That's why they blew up the openings."

"They only hit the ones they knew about. We can make it past their lines and get into their rear area." Doc rubbed a hand over his mouth and set the binoculars on the roof. "Once we're there, if I'm right in what I'm thinking, we could shake them up a bit."

Shelly watched him closely. "So what are you thinking?"

"Okay, treat the attack on the Waco Rangers as an anomaly."

"Done."

"I've spent a lot of time studying Clan tactics, their philosophy, and all that, right? They're big on pride and honor in a fight—to the point where valiant fighting sometimes replaces prudent fighting. Now here, looking at the pattern of very simple attacks followed by a lack of exploitation of those victories, I think I'm seeing warriors who are out to prove something, but more to themselves than to us. Beating us a little bit now gives them a chance to beat us a little more later, heaping up the proofs of their bravery and skill."

Shelly's face went blank for a moment, then her dark brows arrowed toward each other. "Yes, and so the Rangers would be an example of them going a bit overboard?"

"Maybe, though I think it might have been some fairly confident warriors going out to set a high-water mark for the others to hit." Doc twisted around and rested both of his hands on her shoulders. "More than that. I think the Falcons eliminated the Waco Rangers so the rest of our force would be the best possible opposition available. The destruction of the Waco Rangers has been a motivating force for us, yet we're also kind of relieved they're gone. Little victories against the Dragoons have got to count for a lot more than even a big victory over the Waco Rangers."

Shelly slowly smiled. "I can see it. The reason the Falcons haven't wiped us out yet is because they need us to be the toughest people around."

"Right." Doc pointed off toward the Falcon cordon. "Right now they have us where they want us. They call the shots, they fight as long as they want, then they pull back to brag and analyze what they did right and wrong."

"I take it you have a plan that could foul them up?"

"I think so. Whitting, the town where you pulled the last of the Militia from, is a perfectly defensible position from which the line here can be commanded. If we go through the mountains with two forces, one that hits the edge of the line while our main body pushes along the front, a small, light, fast force could roar into Whitting and pop a bunch of the Falcon command staff. It wouldn't destroy them, but it might slow them down."

The Dragoon nodded emphatically. "Simple, clean, limited but achievable objectives. Nice work for someone who's previously been only a desk jockey."

Doc smiled at her. "More flattery. Makes me think I could get to like liaising."

"I'm sure you could come up with a good plan for that, too."

The sound of someone clearing his throat killed Doc's riposte as he and Shelly turned quickly toward the ladder behind them.

Andy Bick, his face almost as red as his hair, coughed lightly. "Begging your pardon, sirs, er, ma'am, ah . . ."

Doc gave Shelly a wink. "Go ahead, Andy."

"Sir, we've got someone below you'll want to see. Dragoon security picked him up. He's one of ours. He was AWOL."

Doc rolled his eyes. "You can't go absent without leave here in Leitnerton. There's no place to go."

"No, sir, but he went AWOL in Port St. William. They found him among the refugees."

"Who?"

Bick smiled broadly. "Leftenant Copley, sir. He's been asking for you."

The two Dragoon soldiers standing behind Copley snapped to attention as Doc and Shelly entered Doc's office. Copley, who sat slumped in a chair, flicked the barest sketch of a salute at Doc. "Glad to see you, Hauptmann. You can tell these guys to let me go now."

Doc frowned. "And why would I do that?"

"You forget our deal?"

"No. It's quite fresh in my mind, actually."

Copley glanced at Shelly. "I'm sure the Dragoons would love to know what you were up to."

Doc folded his arms across his chest. "Colonel Brubaker, I believe you will recall my telling you about a thieving quartermaster we had in the unit. I told you he was a pathological liar we'd not seen since we left Port St. William."

Shelly nodded. "I'd never believe anything he said, especially if it was self-serving."

Copley sat up a bit straighter. "Oh, that's good, Doc. You're sharper than I figured."

"There are blunt instruments sharper than you thought I

was, Copley." Something niggling began to worm its way up through Doc's consciousness. "Colonel, the leftenant here proposed to me a way to make money by stealing government property, then having it listed as destroyed in training exercises. It would be resold through the black market and be pure profit."

"He's lying, Colonel, it was his plan." Copley got a grip on himself and smiled smugly. "Not bad, but not perfect."

Shelly smiled at Doc. "It does seem a bit more brilliant than I would have imagined Mr. Copley capable of being."

"You'd be surprised," Copley laughed.

Doc's jaw dropped open as he replayed Copley's previous comment in his mind. Realization exploded in his brain. "My plan wasn't bad, but you perfected it, didn't you, you son of a bitch!"

Copley shrank back in the chair. "I don't know what you mean."

"Sure you do. I should have seen it before." Doc smacked the heel of his hand against his forehead. "The garrison units in Port St. William reported being short on munitions. You used *our* deployment to the smelter as a cover to duplicate supply orders. The Titans got what we needed, but the others got shorted because you moved a whole bunch of their stuff out, too. The only thing more believable than equipment and munitions being destroyed in training exercises is them getting destroyed during an attack by the Clans."

Copley's self-satisfied smirk burned through his innocent expression like acid through paper. "That would be a good idea. Maybe next time."

"What makes you think there's going to be a next time for you, Leftenant?" Doc stared down at the man and dropped his voice half an octave. "I think you know where there's a storehouse of weapons, munitions, and other supplies. You want a next time that doesn't involve reincarnation, tell me where it is."

Copley shook his head. "I invoke article three of the Lyran Alliance Code of Military Justice. Get me a lawyer."

"Fresh out of lawyers, Copley, not that one would be much help to you right now." Doc reached down and grabbed a handful of the man's tunic. "Try this scenario on for size. We last saw you in Port St. William. It is now a

Falcon stronghold. We understand captive officers are being detained in its prison facilities. The fact that you are here and out of uniform suggests to me that you have willingly chosen to give aid and comfort to the enemy. You're a spy. I can have you shot."

"That'll get you a lot of supplies, *if* they exist."

Doc released him. "That's your worst alternative, Copley."

"You gonna give me a better one?"

"Sure. We'll buy the supplies from you. We'll give you five percent of the black market value."

"Try five *hundred* percent over market value." Copley smiled. "Or you can buy elsewhere."

"I'd think again if I were you, Mr. Copley."

"Huh?"

"By bargaining here you've confirmed you've got the supplies squirreled away." Doc cracked his knuckles. "A little narco-interrogation and you'll be giving us a full inventory of everything, and directions on how to get it."

Copley's Adam's apple bounced up and down once.

"It's a buyer's market." Doc shook his head. "Five percent is more than fair."

"How do you figure that's fair?"

"It's five percent of *something,* not a hundred percent of nothing."

Shelly smiled. "Let me try. I think I could get him to pay *us* to take the stuff off his hands."

Something in her voice made Copley pale. "Five percent, okay, I can give you the coordinates. It's about a day from here in the caves."

"Yes!" Doc gave Shelly a quick kiss. "Andy, take Copley down to the map room, get a fix on the site, then get the Titans ready. We've got a run to make."

"Wilco, Doc." Andy snagged Copley by the shoulder and dragged him off, the two Dragoons following closely on their heels.

Shelly patted Doc on the back. "Well done."

"I set him up, you came in for the kill."

"Nice teamwork." She smiled easily. "I'll go convince the others that your little raid plan has a lot of merit. I'll pull my Delta battalion off the line and prep them to hit the Falcon line from behind while you go to Whitting."

"Sounds like a plan." Doc laughed lightly. "I look forward to our continued liaising."

"As do I, Hauptmann Trevena," Shelly said as she headed off, "and celebrations of victories to come."

35

DropShip **Barbarossa**
Nadir Recharge Point, Arc-Royal
Arc-Royal Defense Cordon
19 May 3058

Victor Davion wasn't certain he'd heard correctly. "What do you mean you won't go?"

Phelan Kell, tall and darkly handsome, wearing gray Clan leathers that covered his muscular form like latex flesh, shook his head. "I cannot go with you to Coventry, Victor."

"But didn't you just conclude a war with the Jade Falcons? Aren't they your enemy? Didn't they kill Ulric Kerensky and Natasha Kerensky?"

"Yes, Victor, yes, all of those things are true." Phelan's fists knotted and slackened rhythmically. "Had I a choice, I would go. I'd take all of my warriors and go off with you to Coventry. Unfortunately, I can't because there's another threat we must be prepared to deal with."

"What other threat?" Victor pointed at the holographic display of the data his Intelligence Secretariat had obtained from sources inside the LAAF. "The Jade Falcons have, according to this, four Galaxies on Coventry. They're four jumps from Tharkad. My sister is prepared to defend herself, but what she doesn't see is that if the Falcons jump toward Tharkad from Coventry, they'll break the truce line. They'll violate the truce and the war will break out again. There's no other threat to the Inner Sphere that's even close to this one."

"In *your* mind."

Victor looked around the room to see if anyone else thought Phelan's reply was ridiculous. Kai and Hohiro remained expressionless. The Precentor Martial's head cocked slightly in concentration, and Colonel Daniel Allard, leader of the Kell Hounds, frowned a bit. Only Ragnar Magnusson, once heir to the throne of the Free Rasalhague Republic, appeared to agree with the sentiments of the Clan Wolf Khan. *But he's been adopted into the Clan, so that's no big surprise.*

"Phelan, forgive me, but the Falcons aren't just a threat in my mind, they're a threat in reality."

Phelan's green eyes closed for a second, then opened again as he nodded. "I agree, they *are* a threat. Still, you have a formidable force gathered to meet them. The First Genyosha, the First St. Ives Lancers, your Davion Heavy Guards, this Invader Galaxy of ComStar's, and both Kell Hound regiments. Those units, along with those your sister is sending, should be more than enough to defeat four Galaxies of Falcons."

"I would agreed but . . ."

"But?"

Victor met his cousin's stare head-on. "But I can't trust my sister's data. That's why we diverted here instead of going straight to Coventry—to pick up more troops."

Phelan shook his head. "It's her realm at stake. Why would she not want it dealt with? Deliberately underestimating the strength of the enemy on Coventry threatens her nation, and she wouldn't do that."

"No?" Victor swallowed hard. "She already has."

"It wasn't her realm at that time."

Victor blinked. "What?"

Phelan folded his arms across his chest. "When she murdered your mother, it wasn't her realm."

Shock hit Victor with a jolt. Even though he knew to his own satisfaction that Katherine was complicit in his mother's assassination, he had almost a knee-jerk reaction to defend her—a member of his family—from such a vicious accusation. Every time he thought about Katherine, every time he reviewed in his mind the evidence for her guilt, part of him still hoped and wished she could somehow be proved innocent.

In the silence that followed Phelan's remark, he was glad to see that none of the others in the room had shown any sign of surprise at Phelan's statement. Victor was so used to the guilty finger being pointed at him by the scandal-vids and the conspiracy mongers that he thought Jerry Cranston, Agent Curaitis, and he himself were the only people who believed him truly innocent.

"How do you know Katherine did it?"

Phelan looked back at Colonel Allard. "Dan?"

The white-haired mercenary officer nodded. "We learned from Phelan's father, who heard it from your mother, that you'd asked her not to abdicate in your favor. You could have taken power any time you wanted it. You didn't need to murder Melissa to get it. Besides, killing her would also have deprived you of her popularity and influence in the troubled parts of your realm. Her death stole from you a powerful weapon to use against your enemies."

Victor looked at the others. "None of you believed I killed her?"

Kai shook his head. "You're a soldier first and a politician second. You deal with enemies ruthlessly, but you never saw your mother as an enemy."

Hohiro Kurita smiled. "My sister told me you were innocent. I consider her judgment unimpeachable in such matters."

The Precentor Martial tugged at his eye-patch. "The Davions, whom you most resemble in temperament, are not much given to deposing their flesh and blood. That is a Steiner trait—one that has flowered full in your sister. Foolishly she concerns herself with her position instead of focusing on the threat to the Inner Sphere as a whole."

Victor shook his head, again not believing his ears. "I feel as if I'm waking from a dream in which I was the only one who realized it was a dream. I'd always feared that you, my peers, would believe the rumors told about me. I never thought to ask."

Kai clapped Victor on the shoulder. "Victor, if we thought Melissa Steiner Davion's blood was on your hands, we'd not be here."

Phelan's voice hardened. "And you would be dead, Victor.

The same blast that killed your mother slew mine. That blood debt would have long ago been paid."

"Then come with us, Phelan. After Coventry, we can go to Tharkad . . ."

"No." Phelan shook his head vehemently. "You know as well as I do that to depose Katrina by force of arms would be to ignite a civil war that would destroy the Lyran Alliance and give the Clans a free path to Terra. As much as all of us might like to see her brought to justice as quickly as possible, that has to wait until we have proof of her guilt—incontrovertible proof."

The Clan Khan took in a deep breath. "It is for a similar reason I cannot go with you to Coventry. The Wolves—the *other* Wolves—are shifting troops around. Just as Vlad has spies among my people, so do I have spies among his. I do not know what he is planning, but he could easily be preparing a strike into the Alliance. My father made a commitment to the worlds in the Defense Cordon. While the Hounds go to help you, I must stay here to prevent my old comrades from attacking."

Victor nodded. "I understand your thinking, but I think you're being overly cautious. We need your help."

"I know. I am prepared to give it." Phelan looked at Ragnar, and the tall, blond man stepped forward. "I will send this warrior with you."

The Prince of the Federated Commonwealth frowned. "One warrior wasn't exactly what I had in mind."

"Don't discount the effectiveness of one warrior." Phelan slowly smiled. "In the invasion, one warrior took the world of Gunzburg all by himself. Ragnar has earned the rank of warrior among us. He knows the way of the Clans—how we think and how we operate. You will find him invaluable in dealing with the Falcons."

"Glad to have you with us, Ragnar." Victor raised an eyebrow at Phelan. "Sure you don't have a couple hundred more like him we can borrow?"

"No, Victor." Phelan shook his head. "You're trying to save the Inner Sphere from the Clans, and so am I. Our methods diverge, this time. In the future, perhaps not. I am a Wolf, Victor, but I am also a Kell. Arc-Royal is my home and my allegiance is with the Inner Sphere. Our goals are the same, and I hope we will both succeed."

"So do I." Victor offered Phelan his hand. "If you won't give us more warriors, at least wish us luck."

"You won't need it," Phelan said, shaking Victor's hand. "Bargain hard, bargain well, and what you want done will be done."

≡ 36 ≡

Whitting
Coventry
District of Donegal, Lyran Alliance
30 May 3058

Doc piloted his *Centurion* forward and to the right as the Clan *Hellhound* lumbered out into the darkened Whitting street. The pistol-like large pulse laser in the Clan 'Mech's right hand came up and tracked Doc's *Centurion*. Then a volley of gleaming green energy darts sizzled through the night, casting sickly shadows as they flashed past the *Centurion*'s left arm.

They continued on and passed to the right of the *Hunchback* Doc's 'Mech had been blocking. The *Hunchback*'s shoulder-mounted autocannon roared, shooting fire and metal out in a fiery burst that hit the *Hellhound* in the right knee. The joint locked as the depleted-uranium shells munched the ferro-fibrous armor on that limb. Unsated, the slugs devoured the ferrotitanium bones of the leg, severing them at the knee.

As the shin and foot careened backward down the narrow cobblestone street, the 50-ton war machine toppled to the right. The *Hellhound* crashed through the corrugated tin wall of a warehouse, then lay there helplessly as the structure slowly collapsed around it.

Doc centered his targeting cross hairs on the humanoid *Hellhound*'s broad back. One burst of fire from the autocannon in the *Centurion*'s right arm stripped all the armor off and nibbled away at the internal structures holding the 'Mech together. Doc's medium laser, joined by two beams from Murdoch's *Hunchback,* ravaged the rest of the *Hellhound*'s heart, exploding a jump jet and reducing the fusion engine to incandescent slag.

"Lead here, *Hellhound* neutralized." Doc turned the *Centurion* around and started back toward the center of town. "South end secure."

"One Lance here, Lead. *Peregrine* down, north secure."

"Roger, One. TRU, you are good to go."

"Roger, Lead. Incoming."

Doc took a quick look around the main square of Whitting. Built on a series of four hills, the town had an old-world alpine kind of look—the kind you saw in old hardcopy histories or in reconstruction villages and living museums. Thatched roofs over full or partial log construction marked most of the buildings in the core of the city. Warehouses and other uglier but more utilitarian buildings had sprung up as required, but even their presence hadn't kept the town planners from mandating cobblestone streets that wound here and there in a pattern that was as pretty as it was impractical.

Doc could see that the town had once been quite beautiful, but the various military occupations had taken their toll. Cobblestones did not fare well beneath the pounding feet of BattleMechs. Much of the land surrounding the town had also been churned up by vehicles, 'Mechs, and explosions, leaving muddy flats where greensward had once been. Some buildings also showed signs of war, from bullet holes to spots where a broad-shouldered 'Mech had scraped flowerboxes and shutters from both sides of a street as it passed by.

To the north Doc could see a lightning storm lighting up the horizon. *At least, from here, it looks like a lightning storm.* He knew those strobing flashes marked the point where Shelly Brubaker's force had come out of the mountains and struck at the rear of the Clan line. Her assault had pulled most of the Falcon garrison from Whitting and sent it toward the front, leaving behind a Star of 'Mechs and a Star of Elementals. Working together the Titans had managed to mop up the resistance without taking any losses. Doc attributed that to their having come in from the south themselves and to the Titans having become very good at hitting without getting hit.

The Dragoons' Tactical Response Unit—an infantry squad

cobbled together from security personnel and 'Mech pilots whose machines had been shot out from under them—sped into the center of town in a stream of hovercars and trucks. One small sedan swerved off toward the downed *Hellhound* while the rest headed in straight at the City Hall. The first people out of the vehicles shot concussion grenades in through the open doors, followed them with smoke, then the rest of the force surged on in.

Doc saw light flare explosively in the darkened windows of the upper floors. Though he had his external mikes up sufficiently to hear the blasts and the tinkle of falling glass hitting the street below, he heard no gunfire from within the building. Moving his *Centurion* forward, he brought it to where it could cover the western side of the building, and noticed the 'Mechs from his second lance covering the back.

"Force leader, this is TRU leader. The building is secure."

"Great, TRU Lead. Anything useful?"

"Lots of data and a handful of prisoners. We'll be loading it up to head back out."

"Roger, TRU Lead." Doc saw the hovercar that had headed toward the *Hellhound* come into the center of town with a man trussed up on the hood like a stag taken while hunting. *The more the merrier.*

Doc keyed his radio. "Titans, form up and secure our exit vector. We're going home. This is one in the win column for us, people. Well done. Mission accomplished."

DropShip **Barbarossa,** *Inbound from the Zenith*
  Jump Point
Coventry
District of Donegal, Lyran Alliance
5 June 3058

Sitting behind the desk in his cabin, Victor Ian Steiner-Davion studied the holographic projection of the Coventry system. Every fifteen seconds a neon-green plane would descend through the spherical display, refreshing the images as the DropShip's scanners presented new data to be factored in. Each ship represented in the sphere had a small alphanumeric tag trailing after it. By punching the code into the keyboard on the desk he could call up what the computers knew or could guess about any of the targets.

There's very little to guess about. The task force JumpShips had plotted themselves in at the zenith jump point, nearly 4.7 billion miles above the north pole of the Coventry system's sun. An equal distance below the sun sat the system's recharge station and, as expected, the Jade Falcon fleet of JumpShips and WarShips. Under most circumstances, possession of that location would have been contested, but the casualties and damage done to the Inner Sphere forces by fighting JumpShips would have made even a victory far too costly.

The DropShips that had come in with Victor trailed the *Barbarossa* as the wedge-shaped formation jetted in toward the third planet. Six hours behind them came a second formation containing the DropShips of Katrina's task force. Victor couldn't help but smile as he watched that second flight slowly catch up with his ships. Coming in at roughly two Gs of acceleration, they'd join his formation just as day dawned down on Coventry's largest continent, Veracruz.

Victor glanced at the chronographic displays at the bottom of the sphere. One showed landfall, at their current rate of speed, to be nine and three-quarters days away. The second showed less than an hour remaining before Hohiro, Dan Allard, and the Precentor Martial were due to rendezvous with the *Barbarossa* from their own DropShips to begin analysis and planning of the action down on the planet.

Victor glanced down at the screen of his small noteputer. "With three Dragoon regiments, the Eleventh Lyran Guards, the Harloc Raiders, and the Knights of the Inner Sphere added into our force, I show us with approximately twelve and a half 'Mech regiments. The Falcons are reported at a strength of four Galaxies on the planet, which would make us roughly twice their size. According to conventional wisdom that makes the two forces virtually equal."

Ragnar's blue eyes flicked from the display to Victor. "Remember, Highness, the Kell Hounds, the Dragoons, and the ComStar units have a great deal of equipment that originated from within the Clans. With the exception of the Harloc Raiders, the rest of the units in your force all have updated Inner Sphere equipment. A two-to-one ratio in favor of the Inner Sphere was necessary to achieve parity with Clan forces back when the invasion started, but by now your two-to-one advantage may be closer to a true advantage."

Seated beside Ragnar, Kai Allard-Liao nodded in agreement. "We can't forget the forces on the ground on Veracruz already. They may have another regiment or two down there."

"Or they may be gone altogether." Victor shook his head. "If we're lucky I think we can count on the mercs to keep our landing zone secure. Whatever their number, they won't bring us up to the three-to-one advantage normally suggested for a successful assault against a defender."

The Wolf warrior smiled. "That advantage you can gain through good bargaining."

"I don't follow. When we fought the Clans during the invasion, we put up all we had to offer and they decided how much they were going to send against us." Victor frowned. "Surely the Falcon commander would put up all available forces to oppose us."

"Not necessarily."

"Why not?"

Ragnar smiled indulgently. "If she has four Galaxies and bids two in the defense of the planet, she creates a competition among her own people to be included in the planetary defense. She will get the best effort from her warriors because, even if they die in the effort, their exploits will be recorded and their genes will become part of the breeding pool."

"What if she says she's defending with two Galaxies and I decide to attack with everything I have?"

"A Clan commander would never do such a thing. Too great a loss of honor."

"I'm not a Clan commander, Ragnar."

The Wolf nodded. "So I recall. In that case she would probably choose to fight you in a place that puts you at an extreme disadvantage. Now, provided the data sent out earlier is reliable and she's still alive, you're dealing with Marthe Pryde. Her line had been in disfavor, but was redeemed at Tukayyid. The Prydes hold themselves to high standards. She *could* declare that an attack using an overwhelming force makes our force *dezgra.*"

"Dezgra?"

"Disgraced. Hohiro would think of it as being unclean or dishonored." Ragnar hesitated for a moment. "Such a declaration would have repercussions for you if you were a Clansman. In this situation, it might allow her to withdraw her force, but she would be disgraced herself by retreating from an Inner Sphere attack."

"She'd prefer death?"

"Think about it, Victor," Kai began, "the reason *we* want to live is to stay with our families and raise children to inherit the future. Within the Clans the survival of the geneparent is incidental to that. With a valiant death a person might guarantee lots of progeny."

"Well, in the Clans we do prefer people to live through combat and work up into command positions," Ragnar commented, "but Kai's still right. Certainly the valiant death of Aidan Pryde on Tukayyid redeemed his line. The Prydes are all but worshipped by the Falcons."

"Great, I've got a Falcon-goddess defending a world against me." Victor smiled in spite of how he felt. "It's a pity my sister isn't here. I could do what Phelan talked about and bid her to take the planet. She could go one on one with this Marthe Pryde."

"Marthe would have to bid herself down to using only one arm." Ragnar laughed softly. "She'd still hand Katherine her head."

Victor's smile grew. "It's a plan."

Kai cleared his voice. "You'd lose the planet."

"Yeah, there *is* a down side to it." The Prince sighed. "I'll need help preparing for the bid."

"Are you going to bid the fight, Victor, or are you going to let the Precentor Martial do it?" Kai asked. "Given that ComStar and the Com Guards defeated the Clans before, the Falcons might consider that Focht has the most right to conduct negotiations. This is especially true if the Word of Blake conquest of Terra has this Marthe Pryde thinking about violating the truce line."

"That's a good point, Kai."

Ragnar nodded. "You'll have another seven days before Marthe challenges you. Of course, I wonder if any sort of consensus will have been reached by then."

"Meaning?"

The Wolf laughed abruptly. "Highness—Victor, I am not the kid I was on Outreach seven years ago. Even though I've spent a lot of time among the Wolves and I've become a warrior, I haven't forgotten how it is in the Inner Sphere. Dammit, my speech is deteriorating."

Victor looked at him. "Excuse me?"

Kai jerked a thumb at Ragnar. "Clanners do not use contractions."

"How would you know . . . ?"

"I've spent more time with Clanners than you have, Victor—in fact, I've spent more time with Jade Falcons than either of you, I'd bet." Kai rested a hand on Ragnar's shoulder. "Back to your point."

"Thanks. My point is this: in the second force you have troops from the Free Worlds League, the Capellan Confederation, the Lyran Alliance, and Wolf's Dragoons. Even at the conference on Outreach all those forces did not get along. The League supported the rest of the House leaders in the fight against the Clans because your father blackmailed

Thomas Marik. Romano Liao kept the Capellan Confederation's troops out of the fight entirely—the Harloc Raiders are breaking new ground here. The Eleventh Lyran Guards is a Steiner loyalist unit, and the Dragoons are probably going to be spoiling for their own fight just so they can get their own people out of the situation down there."

Victor thought for a second. Ragnar's point was well taken. The incoming forces had all the components of a coalition force, but the internal jealousies and conflicts among and between them could prove a greater threat to the task force than the Jade Falcons. *If I'm not careful, the whole mess could explode in my face. That would be bad for me, but worse for the rest of the Inner Sphere.*

"You're right, Ragnar, the situation is tense. I think I have a solution, but I'll have to run it by the Precentor Martial and Hohiro. If they agree, then we can present it to the others."

Kai leaned forward. "What have you got in mind?"

"We make the Precentor Martial the head of the task force. As you pointed out, he has the prior experience of defeating the Clans in a major series of battles. He is respected by everyone who's coming."

Kai nodded. "So, what role do you play?"

"Because the Kell Hounds are here under an agreement with me, *and* I also have the Davion Heavy Guards RCT, I have the most troops under arms coming in."

Ragnar shook his head. "The Dragoons have three regiments and had two on the ground."

Kai held a hand up. "I'll put the Lancers under your leadership and I'm sure Hohiro will agree to do the same with the Genyosha."

"Thanks. That should entitle me to be second in command. It avoids a discussion of who owns Coventry—well, the Falcons own it now—or who has a moral right to command. If we present it as an Inner Sphere effort to stop Clan aggression we might be able to sidestep some of the problems."

"It might work." Kai laughed, his gray eyes sparkling. "And if it *does* work, maybe we can reestablish the Star League and put you at its head."

Victor sat back and rolled his eyes. "One Herculean task at a time, please. After we get the Falcons off Coventry, then we can spin pipe dreams to our heart's content."

Leitnerton
Coventry
Coventry Province, Lyran Alliance

Ariana Winston looked the way Doc felt—tired and ready to keel over. She hit a button on the noteputer and Doc heard it beep, indicating she'd reached the end of the file. "You got a wealth of information from this Arimas. Do you trust it?"

"Yes, ma'am." Arimas was the *Hellhound* pilot. Doc thought of him as the man Andy Bick might have been if Bick had been raised on steroids and cruelty.

"As the report indicated, we used narcotics to interrogate the prisoner. What we did get out of him was corroborated by the files and disks taken from Whitting City Hall." Doc hid a yawn behind his right hand. "The Falcons have a pathological fear of being absorbed by another Clan. They're using people who have little or no practical experience at war to fill the ranks of their units. By inflating the numbers of people under arms, they think they'll appear formidable enough to scare off other Clans from attacking them."

"Very much like a cat puffing up its fur to look more threatening." Shelly Brubaker came into Winston's office and handed Doc a cup of coffee. "In this case, though, we're talking quills instead of fur because we can and have been hurt by the puffing."

Winston looked at her noteputer, then up again. "What's the reasoning behind all the in and out travel to this system?"

Doc shrugged. "Arimas wasn't very clear on that, but it would appear that warriors with promise are being sent out to fill garrison units on the planets the Falcons still control."

"Right." Shelly set her coffee cup down. "I've been trying to take the numbers we wormed out of Arimas and translate them into something useful. It looks like the Falcons have three veteran units here and five newly formed Galaxies. Two of the new ones now have enough combat experience to be considered veterans. One is still green and the other two are filled with warriors who've survived a week of fighting already."

Ariana Winston set the noteputer down on her camp desk and shook her head. "I can't believe it. I've only got a battalion of the Eridani Light Horse left. Shelly, your Delta Regiment is down two companies and Tyrell's Gamma Regiment may still be regimental in terms of personnel, but not operational equipment. All this destruction and death so some child-warriors can play soldier and prove their Clan is tough."

"There's more to it than that, General." Doc stared down into the steaming depths of the coffee. "The Falcons recently fought a disastrous war against the Wolves and were severely hurt. The Coventry operation is helping them recover the respect they lost. Apparently their old leaders had violated the customs and traditions of the Jade Falcons. Marthe Pryde needed to show that the Falcons *could* defeat the Inner Sphere's best without moving away from its traditions—and Coventry is the latest stop on their victory tour."

"But only a fool goes to war to prove a philosophical point."

Shelly shook her head. "Be careful, General. That's the first step down a very slippery slope. There's no way to argue that one person's reason justifies war and someone else doesn't."

"Colonel Brubaker, we're both mercenaries. We fight because we're paid to."

Doc sipped his coffee, then looked up. "None of us are in any shape to talk philosophy, but the fact is that the *only* justifiable reason for a fight is to preserve life and freedom. Yet even that is subject to interpretation. The Jade Falcons undertook this series of raids as a means of proving their traditions strong. It's also allowed them to blood new warriors to replace those killed by the Wolves."

The leader of the Eridani Light Horse rubbed her eyes. "I don't know about you, but I hate like hell being used as a simulator exercise that can bleed."

"It wasn't my choice of vocations either, but we did get some back." Doc smiled at Shelly. "The attack on the Falcons' western flank definitely bloodied one of their Clusters."

"And the Whitting raid has taken the pressure off as they try to figure out what we know and what we're going to do with that information." Shelly wrapped both hands around the barrel of her coffee mug. "So, you've seen the report, General. Any ideas?"

"I'll have to talk things over with Colonel Tyrell and General Niemeyer, but I think our only chance of surviving is to split into smaller units and carry on a guerrilla war, as Doc did before." Ariana Winston glanced again at the noteputer. "But if we do that I'm afraid they'll use aerospace fighters to bomb and strafe us back to the Stone Age."

Doc shook his head. "They didn't go after the Titans that way."

Shelly gave him a gentle elbow in the ribs. "The Titan 'Mechs are too small to hit in a strafing run."

"Yeah, but there's enough of us that you'd think they might hit some at random."

"Let's hope the rest of us can live up to the standard your Titans have set, Doc." Winston gave him a wan smile. "With luck we can hold out until reinforcements arrive."

"Reinforcements?" Doc sighed. "You're an optimist."

"Hey, Doc, we were sent here to reinforce you," Shelly Brubaker put in.

"That you were, Shelly, and that you did." Doc shrugged and raised a hand to block the first dawn rays slipping through the office window. "I'm tired and I've got a bad case of survivor guilt. Even knowing that, though, I don't think anyone is going to be stupid enough to toss more troops into this meat grinder."

Shelly's shoulders slumped slightly. "I have a feeling you're right. Sending more troops here would mean some politician had to admit a mistake was made earlier when they didn't send enough. No pol's going to do that."

One of the surviving Light Horse troopers tapped on the door jamb. "General, priority one message just came in over the radio." The man's smile instantly infected Doc. "We've got twelve and a half regiments incoming."

"Theirs or ours, Johnston?"

"Ours, General. Prince Victor is bringing them in. Ten days, give or take."

Ariana Winston thumped the table with a bony fist. "Best news I've had since we landed." She looked up at Doc. "So, which is he, Doc? Stupid, or a politician who can admit he's wrong?"

"Neither, General." Doc nodded solemnly. "He's a warrior and undoubtedly the best chance we've got of getting out of this in one piece."

═══ 38 ═══

Inbound, DropShip **Barbarossa**
Coventry
Coventry Province, Lyran Alliance
12 June 3058

As Victor looked around the crowded briefing cabin at the collection of military leaders hurtling toward Coventry, he sensed much less tension in the room than he'd expected. From the first he'd braced for opposition to everything, from designating the Precentor Martial as the leader of the expedition to his own appointment as second in command. That very little in the way of opposition actually did surface reinforced for him the gravity of the situation they all faced.

He'd expected the group to break along the line that marked loyalty to his sister and himself. That would have put the Free Worlds League's Knights of the Inner Sphere and the Capellan Confederation's Harloc Raiders together with the Eleventh Lyran Guards in one coalition. The three Regiments of Wolf's Dragoons would nominally have been part of that group, but General Maeve Wolf, the black-haired commander of the Dragoons, had more sense than to split the force heading in to relieve her people.

Wu Kang Kuo, commander of the Harloc Raiders, had gone beyond neutral to being supportive of Victor's suggestions. Wu also spent a lot of time speaking with Kai, which had surprised Victor until Jerrard Cranston reminded him that Kai had fought and defeated Wu's son in some matches on Solaris. Victor assumed there was some debt of honor there, which could only help things along.

Equally surprising was the position taken by Paul Masters, commander of the Knights of the Inner Sphere. He remained more neutral than Wu, but did enter debates on the side of unity. His only real concern involved direct command of the forces. While allowing that he respected Victor's experience, he didn't want to be placed in a position where Victor would be assigning dangerous missions to his unit, lest it look like the Prince was trying to pay back the Knights for their role in the recent invasion of Victor's Sarna March. That seemed logical to everyone involved, so the Knights were attached to the Dragoons, for the purposes of command.

The only true obstructionist proved to be the Eleventh Guards' Marshal Sharon Byran. Because Coventry was a Lyran Alliance world, she argued that, as the Archon's representative, she should be given a commanding role in the planning and execution of the expedition. She quickly alienated the mercenaries by implying that their commitment was suspect because they were being paid to fight. Colonel Dan Allard had pointed out that the Eleventh Lyran Guards had *fled* from the fight with the Free Worlds League and suggested that if the task force planned to retreat before a shot was fired, she would be consulted for her expertise in the matter. That shut her down, but Victor could tell she was still smoldering inside.

The Precentor Martial stood at the far end of the black table. "This is our last informational session before contact with the Falcons on Coventry. This first contact will be by radio only—we expect a challenge in which the Jade Falcons tell us how many units they will use to defend the planet against our force. Those of you who've fought against the Clans previously are familiar with this procedure. The Clans treat bargaining over the size and power of forces to be used in combat as something of a sacrament."

Focht pointed to Ragnar. "As you know, a large portion of Clan Wolf has defected from the Clans and is in residence on Arc-Royal. Khan Phelan Kell sent Ragnar to assist us in analysis and bargaining with the Jade Falcons. Prince Victor and I have complete trust in Ragnar. Bargaining will be our first engagement with the Jade Falcons, and a successful negotiation will be the first step on the road to defeating them."

Dan Allard levered himself away from the bulkhead he'd been leaning against and raised a hand. "Will some units get bargained out of the fight? If so, by what protocol will you decide which those are to be?"

Maeve Wolf glanced at the Kell Hound. "Dan, are you worried, as am I, about having your unit pieced out?"

"Exactly."

Victor held his hands up. "Unit cohesion is something we're going to keep, trust me. Maeve, you've got people already on the ground, so you'll be bid away only in the event that the bidding goes so low that we're talking a token combat. We don't expect that, but I've learned enough from Ragnar so far to know that we can't be sure exactly what we'll run into.

"Dan, as to your question, the protocol is simple: We've divided the assembled forces into two groups. The first group are those units with a tangential interest in the outcome here. I say that not to devalue your participation—and I know *everyone* in the Inner Sphere has a stake here—but it seemed the best way to break things down. The units in this force are the First Genyosha, the Kell Hounds, the Knights of the Inner Sphere, the Harloc Raiders, and the First St. Ives Lancers. If we bargain down units, they'll be selected by lot from this group for exclusion—and the Hounds will only be out if we're pulling two regiments."

The logic of the choices didn't seem to upset anyone in the room. Victor had hoped to retain the Genyosha and St. Ives Lancers in what he saw as the core group because their recent training on Tukayyid would make them invaluable in fighting the Falcons. Even so, the Precentor Martial had made an excellent case for the need to weight the exclusionary group in favor of units Victor had brought with him because the core group would be similarly weighted. The Dragoons, the Davion Heavy Guards, and the Com Guard Invader Galaxy could all be seen as residing in Victor's camp. The Eleventh Lyran Guards remained the only force loyal to Katherine that would be involved in the fighting. Even if the Harloc Raiders and the Knights of the Inner Sphere were added to the core force by random selection, the weight of the troops involved would still favor Victor.

Paul Masters rubbed a hand along his jaw. "So, when will we know if we're going home?"

Focht smiled confidently. "It will be a while yet."

"But the Falcons should be making contact soon. We have two more days before planetfall. Surely your selection will be made by then because your plans will have to be in place. If not, a contested landing could spell disaster."

Victor nodded. "It could, but it won't."

Sharon Byran stared daggers at him. "Overconfidence isn't a good trait in a warrior."

"Neither is a tendency to jump to conclusions." Victor folded his arms across his chest. "The Jade Falcons are the most tradition-minded of the Clans. In general the Clans tend not to contest landing zones. Whether they will or not is something we'll learn when they contact us for the preliminary bidding."

"But it's their choice to defend against our landing."

"True, but they won't attack until the bidding is done." Victor let the hint of a smile tug at the corners of his mouth. "The Jade Falcons have a tradition of granting the right of *safcon* to their enemies—guaranteeing free access to a battlefield where the fight will take place. According to Ragnar, this right was even granted to the Wolf force that attacked Wotan in the recent war between the Wolves and the Falcons. We shall avail ourselves of this tradition of theirs."

Byran's eyes sharpened. "And if they deny it?"

Ragnar stood at Focht's right hand. "They will not."

"How can you be certain?" Byran's anger twisted her features. "They would be stupid to let us land uncontested."

"They are the Jade Falcons, Marshal Byran. They value tradition and form more than logic. Losing does not frighten them as much as breaking with their own rigid code of conduct. *Safcon* allows warriors to enter a battlefield unharmed, *hegira* allows them to leave—there are hundreds of such rights and traditions to which the Jade Falcons enslave themselves. They are not unlike the warriors of the Combine and their code of bushido."

Byran turned toward Victor. "If you trust this Clan claptrap, I assume your Heavy Guards will be the first unit to ground?"

"Gladly."

"But that's not the way it will be." Anastasius Focht's voice dropped in register and his gray eye gleamed with fire. "The Falcons threaten the truce that ComStar won. The Com Guards will go in first."

Byran shook her head. "You'll bleed just as easily as any FedCom."

"Since it was Com Guard blood that won the truce, Marshal Byran, I see no sin in having Com Guard blood maintain it." The Precentor Martial looked from her to a small red light that pulsed at his end of the table. "Prince Victor, if you and Ragnar would be so kind as to join me. It is time we invoke *safcon* and begin the reconquest of Coventry."

Turkina Keshik Headquarters, Port St. William Coventry

Rosendo Hazen admired how lithe and proud Marthe Pryde looked standing there in the middle of the holotank. Her long dark hair fell over the shoulders of her cooling vest like a silken veil. The long expanse of flesh exposed between the tops of her boots and the hem of her 'Mech shorts might, at any other time, have been distracting, not to say inviting. Even more attractive was her intelligence. Indeed, since beauty and intelligence were both survival traits, it stood to reason that they should converge. In Marthe, both traits had combined with a vengeance. Underestimating her intelligence would be as deadly as misinterpreting her stance and attire. *Certainly the Inner Sphere's people will be overmatched.*

The smoke-gray walls of the holotank lightened slightly. What appeared to be the bust of a man appeared in the air before Marthe. Old, with a shock of white hair and a patch covering a missing eye, he regarded her without expression. "I am Anastasius Focht, Precentor Martial of ComStar, commander of the Com Guards and victor of Tukayyid. I apologize for appearing to you in so limited a capacity, but I do not have access to a holotank or its equivalent."

Marthe nodded indulgently. "I am Khan Marthe Pryde, warrior of the Jade Falcons and leader of this expeditionary force. I welcome you to Coventry-trey, though I would have thought you would be concerned with the events of Terra more than the events here."

"Terra stands well behind the Tukayyid line, while Coventry sits astride it. I find it preferable to oppose your desire to possess Terra by fighting you before you reach it. The

Blakist sect disputes this wisdom. My concern is preserving the truce won on Tukayyid."

"Then let your mind be at ease." Marthe opened her arms in a cruciform gesture of innocence. "Those who would have repudiated the truce for personal gain have been destroyed by their own dreams. I have no intention of taking my force beyond the truce line at this time."

"You honor those who fought and died on Tukayyid."

"I honor the warrior who won at Tukayyid." Her hands came together, pressed flat, palm to palm. "There are none among the Clans who will declare the truce void because Terra has changed hands. As you said, the truce was won on Tukayyid. It cannot be lost on Terra."

"Or Coventry."

"All that can be lost on Coventry is glory and life."

The Precentor Martial nodded and his image shrank slightly as he glanced to his right. "Khan Marthe Pryde, I would present to you Prince Victor Ian Steiner-Davion. He is my second in command and will serve as my spokesman in our negotiations."

Marthe turned and waved Rosendo forward. "And this is my second in command, Galaxy Commander Rosendo Hazen. He has been the architect of most of the fighting here."

The man the Precentor Martial introduced impressed Rosendo immediately because of the steely strength in his eyes. Few people could project their personality through holographic imaging, but this Victor Davion did. The Falcon sensed depths in the man that hinted at what he had to be as a leader.

Victor's face became an unfathomable mask. "Khan Marthe Pryde, I am Victor Ian Steiner-Davion. I am coming to Coventry with a task force to contest your possession of the planet. At this time I know I am supposed to ask you with what forces will you defend the planet, but I shall not. Instead I invoke the right of *safcon*."

Rosendo tried to smother his surprise, but he was certain Victor caught it in the way the corners of his eyes tightened. *He invokes* safcon, *which means he has been schooled in our ways. I do not think Marthe anticipated this turn of events.*

Marthe Pryde bowed slightly toward Victor's floating image. "Consider it granted, Prince Victor, well bargained and done. I shall assume you wish to ground at Leitnerton to relieve your forces there?"

"Provided they will still be there in two days, yes."

"They will be. Galaxy Commander Hazen will pull our lines back to Port St. William and give you ample room to ground. The troops of yours who remain are valiant and, I trust, will be allowed to continue to fight against us, *quiaff*?"

"I would not deny them that. I will inform them of your request."

"Thank you." Marthe half-turned from the two busts, then came back around. "Oh, and you should know that I will defend the world with *everything* I have. This is what your people did, and to do less would dishonor them."

"I understand." Rosendo thought he heard a bit of surprise in Victor's voice.

"Very well. I will have force reports available for you when you ground."

"And we shall communicate same to you at that time." Victor glanced away for a moment, then looked back at Marthe. "Shall we set the sixteenth as the day we meet to conduct formal negotiations, *quiaff*? Would Whitting be acceptable as a location?"

Marthe's voice rose, betraying surprise and curiosity. "You wish to negotiate in person?"

"I wish to get the full measure of you, Khan Pryde, and meeting you in person is the only way that can be accomplished." The Prince shrugged. "I will understand if you do not think this desirable."

"Whitting, on the sixteenth, then." The Khan nodded graciously. "Good grounding to you."

The two busts blinked out as Marthe severed the connection. "What did you think, Commander Rosendo?"

"They know something about us. That could make them more difficult to defeat."

"Influence of the Wolves, I have no doubt. When he looked away it was to see what his advisor had to say."

Rosendo nodded. "Khan Phelan Ward was related to this Victor."

"Doubtless that explains it." Marthe's eyes sharpened. "The part about meeting at Whitting was his own idea, however. He thinks I will underestimate him after I meet him."

"It is possible, Khan Marthe, but it was good that you accepted." Rosendo's face darkened. "I do question the wisdom of your declaration of what we will use to defend the planet. Since you granted them *safcon* you were not required to give them that information."

"I know." Marthe smiled carefully. "I did so to confuse them. By telling them I would defend the world with everything after telling them we would pull back to Port St. William, I have given them the impression I intend to keep the planet. They will think I want to do this because it denies them the 'Mech production plants. They will begin to plan for battles over possession of the factories. And while they are doing that, we will be making other plans of our own."

"You say that without knowing what forces they bring against us."

"True, Rosendo, very true." Marthe Pryde nodded slowly. "It is up to us, then, to make certain the same stone that hones our Falcons' claws will not dull them. Such glorious work is what gives birth to warriors and makes their lives worth living."

39

Leitnerton
Coventry
Coventry Province, Lyran Alliance
15 June 3058

Doc Trevena wasn't particularly surprised to hear the sound of footsteps on the roof behind him. Everyone in the Titans had become used to finding him up there staring out toward Whitting and beyond to Port St. William. Most often Shelly Brubaker joined him there on the "Captain's Walk," but she hadn't been his only visitor. *And with the rest of the Dragoons here, her visits have been far too infrequent.*

He glanced back over his shoulder, then spun around and snapped to attention. "Highness, I didn't . . ."

Victor returned the salute, then gently thrust his chin out toward the view. "Hell of a vantage point for watching everything."

"Yes, sir." Doc's heart hammered in his chest. "Is there something I can do for you, Highness?"

The Prince thought for a second, then nodded. "I apologize for interrupting your solitude. I noticed you up here yesterday. When I asked who you were, I learned the whole story of how you've been able to run these Falcons around in circles. I thought I might avail myself of your insight. Does such wisdom come from your time spent up here?"

"I don't really know, sir." Doc was suddenly feeling awkward and tongue-tied. "What I mean, sir, is that I've got no special abilities."

"Oh?" Victor looked him up and down. "You managed to take a company staffed with unskilled but eager troops and build them into a unit that's lost little more than armor and the odd actuator in three months of operations against a Clan enemy."

"When you put it that way, sir, it sounds like more than it is."

"Don't devalue it, Hauptmann Trevena."

"No, sir." Doc smiled slowly. "I don't want to devalue it, but I don't want to elevate my role, either. The Titans, they're full of heart. All I did was teach them to hit while not getting hit."

"You also planned and carried out the Whitting raid."

Doc shook his head. "The Dragoons carried the battle to them, Highness. We just got to Whitting and stole some data. It was a last act of defiance."

"But it means the last battle fought on Coventry was a Clan defeat."

"That's because they decided not to push things because you were coming in." Doc looked down at the Prince. "Begging your pardon, sir, but I'd imagine you've got better things to be doing than standing here making me feel good about the most lightweight unit on the planet."

"Perhaps." Victor's breath hissed in through clenched teeth. "The Falcons sent us data on their forces on Coventry. You won't be surprised to hear that it corresponds to the data you extracted during the Whitting raid. This presents me with a problem."

"Yes, sir."

The Prince frowned. "The information that convinced me to come here indicated the Jade Falcons had *four* Galaxies operating on Coventry. Because of my source, I assumed there might be as many as six."

Doc folded his arms across his chest. "We got information out to Tharkad that we'd seen elements of a dozen different Galaxies here. You should have known . . ." He fell silent for a moment as the implications of the Prince's *not* knowing penetrated his brain. "I guess you and your sister aren't exactly speaking to each other right now?"

"No, we're not." The Prince smiled ruefully. "Do you and your siblings get along?"

"Very well, but I've got an ex-wife, so I can relate."

"I suppose you can." Victor looked Doc over again. "Your people down below called you 'Doc.' May I?"

"As you wish, Highness."

Victor let out a little laugh. "For right now, why don't we make it Victor because what I want from you, Doc, doesn't involve titles or ranks or any of that. I want an honest opinion and direct answers. This is one soldier to another, nothing more. Don't tell me what you think I want to hear, tell me what you know and what you think. Got it?"

"Yes, sir."

The Prince raised an eyebrow at him.

Doc winced. "Sure I can't just go recon Port St. William for you . . . Victor?"

"Later, perhaps." Victor squatted down and plucked a rock from the building's tarred roof and launched it into the night. "Give me an assessment of the Clan forces here."

Doc exhaled heavily. "We've seen a lot of people and a lot of different styles of fighting. The Falcons have made some pretty basic mistakes. Everything I've gleaned makes me think they're desperate and sweeping up anything they can find who can fit in a cockpit."

The Prince's brows furrowed. "I've heard that assessment from others, but I'm reluctant to believe it."

Doc raised an eyebrow. "Why?"

"You're the first person who asked for my reasons. That's good." Victor smiled briefly. "Ragnar has taken a look at the numbers you've put together and a look at the prisoners who were taken. He's even reviewed some of the holographed interrogations. He suggests that if the Falcons were using a mass draft, you'd have a wider range of ages among the prisoners. Arimas, for example, is of an age to already be serving in a line unit but he shows no signs of having tested for such a position."

"It did seem odd that someone like him wouldn't already have been serving. What does Ragnar think the Falcons are up to?"

"He's got no solid idea, but the Clans have always had rumors about members of the scientist caste going rogue and producing their own cadre of warriors to oppose or forestall action by the warriors of their Clan. If such a clandestine breeding program had been begun two decades ago, you'd have a crop of candidates for the units we've been fighting here."

I should have seen it. Doc slowly shook his head. "I was seeing green troops and assuming their lack of experience was because they were as ragtag a band of fighters as the Titans. A crop of kids would be just as inexperienced. The Falcons bring them here, train them against us, and ship them home to fill the void left by their war with the Wolves. We're fighting for our lives and they're looking for playmates."

"We don't know that for sure, so don't be so hard on yourself, Doc. It's just a guess."

"But it feels like a good one. It explains a lot."

The Prince nodded. "Your data and Khan Pryde's reports indicate they've got eight Galaxies on this rock. Counting in what we have left here in Leitnerton, our force is at thirteen regiments. Figuring in all the adjustment factors for unit makeup and condition, we're at rough parity with the Falcons."

Doc stared out over the town. "Leitnerton *is* defensible. If they come, we can hurt them."

"Agreed. The problem is that we're going to have to be the aggressor here."

"Like you said, we've got a winning streak going."

"True, but I need to figure out the way to extend it." Victor reached a hand out and rested it on Doc's shoulder. "You've been here since they got here. You've fought against some of their best units and some of their most green. You were there when the Waco Rangers were wiped out."

"I was."

"So what I want to know is this, Doc: do the troops the Falcons have here possess the belly for a real fight?"

"They sure as hell shoot straight and generally hit what they aim at." Doc arced his own rock out into the darkness and heard it clatter into the street below. "I think the Falcons will give us the best they've got. The Titans managed to surprise them a couple of times, but that's because we were running up against green kids. You can bet the next troops we face will have vets stiffening the lines and directing actions. They'll be full of fight, Victor, no doubt about it."

"The question still remains, though, 'why?' " Victor pointed off southwest toward where the glow from Port St. William lit the horizon. "Fighting to train troops makes sense, but only because they were in control of things and could call an end to the fighting when too many of their people were getting hurt. I can also understand trying to prove your doctrine works, but simulator exercises could do that. If I were going to attack an enemy to hone my troops, I think I'd choose a place I could support better, one that was closer to my home so logistics wouldn't be that much of a problem."

"Like a world on the border."

"Exactly."

Doc smiled as the last piece of the puzzle slipped into place for him. "They came here because they knew we'd defend it."

"What?"

"Coventry is just like the smelter my battalion was sent out to guard when the Clans first arrived. We set up to defend it, but the only interest the Clans had in it was the fact that we were there. They wanted to train against troops. Out on the border they're not going to run into the Dragoons or the Eridani Light Horse. Only if their threat appeared credible and real to a place like Tharkad would we toss our best units at them."

"So it was never about hitting Tharkad. They just wanted to face off with the best we have." The Prince picked up another rock and bounced it from hand to hand. "You can't hunt tigers unless you go where the tigers live."

"And these are some tiger hunters, Victor." Doc gave the Prince a frank stare. "They're good and they get better. The eight Galaxies they've got here are going to be very sharp and ready to do whatever they must to beat you. They'll come at you from every direction. They might be a bit rigid in how they choose their targets, but I've always thought someone who lets you know he's going to knock you down before he does it has a lot of steel in his spine and courage to burn."

"Not always the expedient way to wage war, but certainly a bold way."

"Bold and proud, that's the earmark of the Falcons." Doc shrugged. "I don't really think there's anything else I can offer you by way of information. Don't know if I've been any help . . ."

The Prince nodded, then patted Doc on the shoulder. "You've given me more to think about, thanks. Plenty of tough decisions to make."

Doc brushed his hands off on his pants. "Figuring out how folks are going to die isn't supposed to come easy."

"True enough, Doc." Victor offered Doc his hand. "I'll have to see what I can do so it doesn't come to that."

Turkina Keshik Headquarters, Port St. William Coventry

Rosendo Hazen would have preferred something other than anger on Marthe Pryde's face when she summoned him. He had been reviewing the datafiles sent by the ComStar force and found them disturbing in what they predicted for the future. Facing the Falcons would be the rest of the Dragoons and the Kell Hounds. Those two mercenary units and the Genyosha had been critical in defeating the Smoke Jaguars and Nova Cats in their bid to take Luthien, the capital of the Draconis Combine, seven years previous. To them were added a ComStar unit and seasoned regiments from each of the Inner Sphere's Great Houses.

Save increasing the size of the force, it is difficult to imagine the Inner Sphere fielding a more formidable army. It was clear to Rosendo that the Inner Sphere task force would give as good as it got. The two sides were close to evenly matched, which meant whetstone and knife would grind each other away to nothingness.

"You sent for me, my Khan?"

"Yes, Commander." Marthe's blue eyes sparked with fury. "We are stuck fast on the horns of a dilemma and I fear there is nothing we can do to free ourselves."

"How so? The Inner Sphere force will present us a good fight, but we can still defeat them."

"Yes, and bleed ourselves white doing so, *quiaff*?" She swiveled her chair around and picked a holodisk up off the desk. "I just received this."

Marthe shoved it into the appropriate slot on her desktop and a full-sized holograph of Vlad Ward appeared in front of her desk, presenting his profile to Rosendo. The figure bowed toward the projector that was giving it form—looking somewhat silly in doing so—but even that did nothing to relieve the leaden sensation in the pit of Rosendo's stomach.

"Greetings to you, Khan Marthe Pryde. I wish you well on

the impending fight with the force the Inner Sphere has pulled together to oppose you. You have my admiration on striking so deeply into the Lyran Alliance. I am certain those you brought with you and trained there have learned enough to become valiant warriors, true heirs to the proud Jade Falcon traditions that set your Clan apart from the rest. You are to be congratulated on this strategy, and so I do congratulate you."

Vlad's hands opened. "Of course, you could never believe that I, the Wolf who slew a Falcon ilKhan, would stand in awe of your accomplishments. Words are simple, but actions—such as those you have undertaken here—are the true measure of intent. Therefore, so you will believe me, I will tell you that I look forward to meeting and testing the troops you have so recently trained. Appended to this message is a list of my current troop dispositions. You may be uncomfortable with them, but this is a matter that can best be discussed across a battlefield."

The Wolf's image exploded into a torrent of data. Marthe slapped a button on her desk, killing the glowing text. "Do you see?"

Rosendo's mouth tasted of decay. "He threatens some of our worlds . . ."

"Six. They were all hit hard by the Wolves previously and several have only recently been pacified again. He would cut our occupation zone in half."

Rosendo grabbed a wooden chair and swung it away from the wall, then seated himself with his chest pressed against its back. "Why warn us?"

"It was only half a warning, the other half was gloating." Marthe stood and began to pace. "Vlad is aware of what we are facing here and how gravely we stand to be hurt in this fight. He wants me to know that if I were to withdraw from Coventry I could block his strike against our territory. By threatening to strike at something I hold dear, he forces me to give up something about which I do not care: Coventry."

"But that tactic only makes sense if the Inner Sphere were doing it. What Vlad is doing helps them."

"He is returning a favor."

"I do not follow you."

She stopped and stared down at him. "For Vlad to put this pressure on us, he must know two things. The first is the makeup of the Inner Sphere force. He knew in advance that it closely matched our own strength, which is something even we did not know until two days ago. We have not sent that information out of Coventry, so the only source for it is from within the Inner Sphere.

"Second, he refers to units being trained here. We have not communicated that data to anyone. The Whitting raid, however, made enough information available to the Lyran Alliance that a knowledgeable person could conclude we were using troops that were the product of Elias Crichell's special breeding program."

"You are suggesting the Wolves have an alliance with Tharkad?"

"Khan Phelan and his people are at odds with the government. Even Vlad could see the benefit of establishing relations with his enemy's enemy." Marthe closed her eyes and lifted her face toward the ceiling. "From the message it is apparent that Vlad even knows I pledged everything I have to defending the planet. He tortures me with the fact that I will be *dezgra* if I evacuate Coventry and return home. I shamed him on Wotan and now he shames me."

"The disgrace is nothing, my Khan. Under the circumstances, retreating *is* the expedient thing to do."

She stared fire into his soul. "But it is not the *Jade Falcon* thing to do. Vlad resented his Wolves being made over in *our* image. The choice he gives me would force me to make the Falcons over in the Wolf image. I will not. I *cannot* do this. I will not destroy the foundation of what we truly are just to preserve some crippled form of ourselves in the future."

"There is no merit in compromise where compliance is coerced." Rosendo nodded slowly. "This leaves us only one choice, of course."

"The choice we have always had." Marthe smiled solemnly. "Meet our enemy, slay him, bind our wounds, and begin again."

Leitnerton, Veracruz
Coventry

Victor looked at the rainbow array of data disks spread over his desk. Each one contained the results of dozens of scenarios pitting the Falcons against the expeditionary force. The outcomes ranged from disastrous all the way up to depressing, with scant room in between. The only scenarios that appeared the least bit hopeful were ones in which the Falcons made hideous mistakes and the coalition forces somehow managed to exploit them perfectly.

"That's not going to happen." The Prince sat back in his chair and clasped his hands behind his head. The casualty figures for the scenarios had been uniformly glum, predicting better than fifty percent losses on both sides. That was utterly unacceptable, but the only way to avoid it was to retreat and leave the planet to the Falcons.

The problem with that idea is that it will be costly, too. If the Inner Sphere force were to withdraw from an even odds fight because the casualties would be too high, the Clans would push forward and continue their conquest of the Inner Sphere. It didn't matter that Khan Marthe Pryde had said her force would go no further—such a display of weakness by Inner Sphere leaders would be like dumping blood into a shark tank. The feeding frenzy would be incredible and the Clans would begin to gobble up worlds.

Victor knew the Clan reaction to a retreat would in some ways be the least of his problems. Katherine would accuse him of betraying the people of the Lyran Alliance, and he wasn't sure she'd not be right. Forces within the Federated Commonwealth—reactionaries who didn't trust the Combine and didn't lik Victor's ties to Hohiro and Omi Kurita—would begin to actively campaign against him. The recent loss of the Sarna March and other worlds the Federated Commonwealth had won twenty-five years ago had already begun to rankle with the people of his realm. Any act that could be branded open cowardice might set off all manner of problems, not the least of which was outright insurrection.

Sitting up, he tried to massage the muscles in his neck and ease their tension, but the pain persisted. Anger flashed through him as he thought of Phelan Kell, his cousin and the one person who might have turned the tide. *If you'd come with us, Phelan, we'd have had enough troops to send these Falcons packing.* The second that thought came, Victor dismissed it as unworthy. Even so, the thought of Phelan lingered and something about their meeting in space above Arc-Royal began to gain momentum as it moved into Victor's consciousness.

Damn, that has to be it. Phelan said to bargain hard and bargain well and what I want to be done will be done. I've been looking at battle plans, but all that is epilogue to the bidding. He realized that there was no way Khan Marthe Pryde was going to make a mistake, which meant she must also realize that the fighting would be as crippling to her force as to his. *If there is a loophole, some way that will let her lower her bid, then I can lower mine and neither of us needs to destroy our entire commands in a fight over a planet that means so little to us, but so much to the future of humanity.*

Victor stood and pulled on his jacket. "I hope you're a light sleeper, Ragnar, wherever you are. I'm going to need you wide awake if we're going to find a means to use the Falcons' own ways against them. It may not win us much of an advantage, but anything would be better than what I've got right now."

40

Whitting
Coventry
Coventry Province, Lyran Alliance
16 June 3058

Dust drizzled itself in a lazy curtain over the motionless hovercar's windscreen, muting the dawn light pouring into the vehicle, dulling colors and deepening shadows. For Doc everything looked unreal, as if warped by memories and hopes into a dream from which he could not escape. *Into a nightmare from which there is no escape.*

He found it impossible to believe he was truly sitting there, in the close confines of a hovercar, with the Archon Prince of the Federated Commonwealth, a Wolf warrior who was also heir to the throne of the Free Rasalhague Republic, the Precentor Martial of ComStar, and the FedCom Secretary of Intelligence. Being admitted to the councils of such powerful men was as foreign to him as had been war—and yet he had been able to study war to learn how to handle it. This was something for which he never could have been prepared.

Subtle tremors had been sending a vibration through the vehicle, but it stopped along with the faint echoes of what seemed distant thunder. *That silence means the Titans are in place here in Whitting. The last troops to fight here will be the first to die here when the fighting begins anew.* Doc looked up at Victor. "Did you truly want to honor the Titans by making them your honor guard, or are they here to guarantee my compliance with your wishes?"

Victor's gaze did not waver. "My father might have used your Titans as hostages, but I wouldn't. I do want them honored, which is why they're here. If you required coercion to do what I—what *we* want you to do—then we're the ones who need to be rethinking our strategy."

"And we lose nothing by trying it," Ragnar said.

Doc smiled nervously. "I've heard better endorsements of plans in my time."

The Prince chuckled. "And I've endorsed better plans than this. Unfortunately, in this case, our options are limited."

Doc slumped back in his seat. "If I'm being cast as the savior of the Inner Sphere, that much is obvious." A shiver ran through him made up of equal parts of fatigue and fear. His whole experience on Coventry had been surreal, beginning with command of a unit full of misfits that he'd had to transform into warriors to dealing for supplies to somehow keeping his command together during three months of a Clan assault on the world. Being awakened in the wee hours of the morning by Prince Victor and then subjected to an intensive debriefing somehow fit in with everything that had gone before.

What Victor and the Precentor Martial had suggested to him seemed sheer insanity and he'd almost refused to go along with them. He thought they'd gone mad and was about to tell them so, when someone knocked on the office door. When Jerry Cranston answered it, Andy Bick stood there with a pot of hot coffee. He explained that he'd happened to notice lights in the office, so he had gone to make coffee figuring whoever was up at that hour might need it.

It was probably the hour, and definitely the lack of sleep, but as steam from the pot curled up over Andy's face, all Doc could see was a shattered skull with empty eye sockets. In the whole time he'd been commanding the Titans he'd never let himself acknowledge the horror of what would happen to his command if he made a mistake. He couldn't because he was working too hard to make sure there were no mistakes.

It occurred to him that refusing Victor's request might be the biggest mistake he could make. As Andy set the tray down and retreated from the room, Doc thanked him, then told the Prince that he would do what Victor wanted.

Jerry Cranston leaned back from the driver's seat and showed them his chronometer. "0645 hours. They'll be here soon."

Victor slapped Doc's leg. "Let's go."

Doc cracked the door of the hovercar and immediately caught a blast of dust in the face. He coughed, then wrapped a muffler around his mouth and nose. The scent of the dust combined with the musty odor of the wool to fill his head with an earthy aroma. He tried to think of it as normal and healthy, but its lifelessness somehow brought the image of a desert filled with bleached bones to his mind.

He settled goggles over his eyes, then took his first daylight look at Whitting. The gentle winds once famous for rippling through endless fields of golden grain had long since sucked all the moisture from the 'Mech-churned topsoil in and around the town. The wind streamed and eddied over the broken ground, picking up dust and whirling it down the streets. Piles of dying sod formed spiky tan towers that quivered and toppled as the winds undermined them.

Someone—Doc cynically decided it was some member of the Eleventh Lyran Guards—had been up early stringing light blue and gold pennants from building to building in the town square. They fluttered and snapped, calling attention to themselves. Whoever had put them up must have thought they would add dignity to the momentous occasion of the bidding for Coventry, but Doc found them as appropriate as clowns at a funeral. They were a gaudy invitation to a holiday in a ghost town at the heart of what could quickly be transformed into a ghost world.

Having seen the town previously in the strobing light of muzzle-flashes and missile explosions, Doc had taken for shadows the black fire-stains on most of the buildings. Standing on the ground he could look into their charred interiors and see gray sky where roofs should have been. Even the tan dust clotting each crack and crevasse of charred beams and half-burned furnishings couldn't make things seem more benign. The fires might not still be burning, but Doc heard their crackle and snap in the sounds made by the pennants.

He looked over at Victor. "This is it, isn't it? Whitting is what Coventry will become if we don't succeed."

The Prince, wrapped in a cloak and also wearing a muffler and goggles, nodded slowly. "This is why we have to succeed." With each nod a little dust drifted down from his hair like smoke from the burning cockpit of a dead 'Mech.

New vibrations came up through the ground and grew stronger as time passed. Everyone on the Inner Sphere side of Whitting's main square knew that the sounds marked the arrival of the Jade Falcons. Doc glanced back over his right shoulder, past Victor and the Precentor Martial, to where the leaders of the coalition force stood in the lee of a canvas windbreak. The angle of their poses betrayed their tension and anxiety. Though trying not to be obvious, no one could keep his eyes from the southern edge of the town, waiting to see the shadowy silhouettes of war machines moving through it.

They're waiting for the first glimpse of the people who might be their death. Doc shifted his gaze to Victor. "They know nothing of our opening bid, do they?"

Victor shook his head. "You deal with the Clans, I'll deal with our allies."

Doc smiled under his scarf. "I guess if I have to have someone guarding my back, I don't mind if it's you."

The Prince nodded. "Just pray they shoot low."

"I think I'll pray you shoot first."

"Another fine option."

Doc saw distorted shapes through the edge of his goggles and turned to see the fearsome BattleMechs of the Jade Falcons approaching. Heavy footfalls pounded cobblestones into gravel and sent slate shingles sliding from partial roofs to shatter in the streets. The Clan 'Mechs had an alienness about them that had not fully struck Doc before he saw them lumbering ominously forward within the confines of the village. *On the battlefield they seem perfectly in place, but here, in a town that should be filled with the sounds of ordinary life coming and going, of children laughing, of men and women going about their day-to-day joys and sorrows, they just seem malevolent and malignant.*

The Falcon 'Mechs stopped one street before the central square, but Doc harbored no illusions that they did so out of fear of tearing down the pennants. The positions they took up were all behind cover. Unlike the way the Titans stood out in the open, arrayed for ceremony, the Jade Falcons were in place for war. Their presence mocked the pennants, the people who had strung them, and whatever frail hope could make anyone think they were appropriate at a time and place like this.

Doc first saw the members of the Clan contingent when they entered the alley between the town hall and the toasted ruin of the building next to it. In the darkened alley they were protected from the wind, so it was not the wind that gave a sway to their green cloaks but the purposeful strides of their strong legs devouring the distance to the street. Once they emerged, the fierce wind pushed their cloaks back away from their bodies, but the two Falcons seemed not to notice, their pace not slowed, their heads unbowed by the sting of blowing bits of dirt.

It is as if they're in league with something more powerful than the elements. Doc shook himself, spraying a cloud of dirt from the folds of his gray cloak. The wind buffeted him, wrapping the cloak around his legs. If he took a step forward he would go down in a tangle of cloth and limbs, not at all the image the Inner Sphere force would want to present before the Clanners.

The pair of Jade Falcons came to a stop in the center of the desolate sandpit that had once been the grassy emerald set in the heart of Whitting. Doc found himself entranced with the tall woman moving to the fore. The wind played with her cloak, revealing the green jumpsuit she wore underneath. While the garment was never intended to be revealing, it was cinched tight enough at the belt to give shape to her slender form. She walked forward with a commanding grace that summoned even more admiration than her beauty, and her continued resistance to the vagaries of the wind marked her iron will.

In her wake trailed a shorter man, though not so short when compared to the Prince of the Federated Commonwealth. Stocky and strong, the fair-haired man seemed to be taking in every detail of the square and the people gathered there. His easy, loose-limbed stride might have made Doc think the man viewed the meeting as a lark, but his sharp, hawklike gaze suggested otherwise. He took a position slightly upwind of the woman, and used his body as a bit of a windbreak for her.

The woman challenged Doc and the others to approach with an intense stare that the bubble-goggles she wore could not diminish. The Precentor Martial and Prince started forward, but the cloak still constricted Doc's movement. The woman oriented on him and waited, not impatiently but expectantly. *She will judge me by how I handle this. She pays the wind no heed, is somehow more powerful than it is. It holds me fast, making me her inferior.*

Keeping his eyes locked with hers, Doc shifted his right shoulder back and brought the other one forward. The wind slid along his body and into the opening of the cloak at the front. It filled the garment and billowed it out, freeing his legs. He let it peel the cloak away from the right side of his body, yet caught enough of it in his left hand so it would not fly away and carry him off with it.

I do not need to be more powerful than the elements, I merely need to be smart enough to turn their strength to my advantage.

The woman gave him a curt nod, then looked at the Precentor Martial as Doc closed the gap with the rest of the group. Both parties stood with but a few steps separating them. No one made any attempt to bridge the distance with a hand offered in salutation.

The woman bowed her head to the Inner Sphere contingent. "It is time for the bidding to be done. I am Khan Marthe Pryde of the Jade Falcons. This is Galaxy Commander Rosendo Hazen, my second in command on this world."

Anastasius Focht acknowledged Hazen with a nod. "I am Anastasius Focht, Precentor Martial of ComStar. This is Prince Victor Ian Steiner-Davion, my second in command." He held his left hand out to wave Doc forward. "And this is Hauptmann Caradoc Trevena. He has lately been attached to my staff. He has been here on Coventry since your attack began."

Focht waved his right hand around the square. "It is his handiwork you see here, and his unit behind us. Hauptmann Trevena was the planner, executor, and commander of the Whitting raid."

Doc felt color flooding his face as the Falcon Khan gave him an openly appraising look. He felt as if he'd been stripped naked and put on display before an audience that could not marry his image to whatever preconceived notions they'd formed about him. He forced himself to breathe calmly and he held her icy stare when her eyes found his.

"So, you are the leader of these light 'Mechs, *quiaff*?"

"The Titans, yes."

"The Titans." Marthe Pryde smiled, again giving him a nod. "The irony is not lost on us. Your actions slew many dreams of glory."

Focht brought his hands together. "In honor of all he has done, Hauptmann Trevena will present our bid."

"Very well." The Clan Khan brought herself to attention. "As I declared before, we bid all we have to defend the planet."

The Precentor Martial nodded gravely. "Yes, I recall the bid from when we were incoming. At that time we had misconceptions about your strength and you had no knowledge of ours. Given the circumstances, we see no need to hold you to that bid."

Doc leaned slightly forward as if broaching the distance between them would enable him to beam into Marthe's brain the message *Take the deal*. The talks he'd had with Victor and the Precentor Martial left no doubt in his mind that if she remained intransigent, the resulting battle would devastate both sides. The Clan casualty figures for Tukayyid, according to the Precentor Martial, were hideous, and the estimates here were running twice as high. *Not since the Terran wars of the twentieth century had mankind participated in the sort of slaughter we will see on Coventry.*

If Marthe Pryde was surprised by Focht's comment, she concealed it well. "I appreciate your consideration in this matter. I will not hold your statement as an insult, for clearly that was not your intention. In the past you have bargained with Wolves. You are now advised by Wolves. A Wolf might even accept your offer and modify his bid, but then Wolves have no shame and an anemic sense of honor. I am Jade Falcon. My bid stands."

Focht nodded. "No offense was intended, Khan Marthe. We are prepared to offer our bid."

She nodded. "Proceed."

"Hauptmann Trevena?"

Doc took in a deep breath, then pulled the muffler away from his mouth. He even pulled off his goggles and stood before the Clan Khan openly and unarmed, but not without pride and determination. He wanted her to know that he respected her strength. He wanted her to know that in combat he would give her a fight that, if she survived, she would never forget.

He saw all that in her eyes, and the promise of the same

in return. *We understand each other, then. Good.* He swallowed once, nervously, then offered his bid.

"In the name of the Precentor Martial, in the name of the coalition force assembled here, *I,* Caradoc Trevena, commander of the Titans, conqueror of Whitting, offer you *hegira.*"

=== 41 ===

Victor felt pain in his hands and it took a moment for him to realize it was from his fingernails digging into his palms. *You have to accept this offer! You must!*

The Jade Falcon Khan covered her reaction completely, but Rosendo did not. His jaw shot open, then clicked shut again. Surprise didn't leave his eyes until they began to narrow and the corners of his mouth turned upward. He clearly understood the import of the offer and the opportunity it gave them all for salvation. Had the decision to accept or reject been up to him, Victor had no doubt the Jade Falcons would be on their way off Coventry in a heartbeat.

Rosendo, silent, looked up at his Khan.

Marthe Pryde remained rock-still as if Doc's offer had combined with the wind to petrify her. She stared off distantly and Victor could discern no breathing, no movement from her save that of her wind-tossed hair and cloak. It was as if she had somehow moved outside of time to consider the words that had been said. All the while, as dust and sand blew around her face and body, she might have been a statue of an ancient war-goddess poised between life and death.

Her shoulders dropped a millimeter, then her icy gaze brushed Victor's face before she looked up at the Precentor

284 Michael A. Stackpole

Martial. "It appears, perhaps, that I was rash in dismissing the value of Wolf advisors, *quiaff*?"

Focht nodded. "Aff, Khan Marthe."

She turned to look at Doc. "I, Khan Marthe Pryde, conqueror of Coventry, accept the offer of *hegira.* Your generosity in the face of the losses we suffered here, in Whitting, is noble."

Relief rolled off Doc in waves. "The nobility is in your acceptance."

"Our battle here would never have faded from memory."

Doc nodded. "Better the scorn of armchair warriors than a font of blood and tears."

Marthe seemed to consider his words for a moment, then the steel in her voice softened slightly. "As is customary with *hegira,* we will release all bondsmen."

Victor nodded. "We shall have your people here by dusk, if that is acceptable. We can take ours back at that time."

"Excellent." Marthe Pryde turned to her second in command. "Galaxy Commander Rosendo, please make the arrangements."

"Yes, my Khan."

Marthe Pryde rested fists on her narrow hips. "This bloodless solution will anger some of my people."

Victor's eyes narrowed. "Anyone who desired bloodshed in this place can wallow all they want in their anger and frustration. It is not only the Clans who harbor such individuals."

Marthe looked beyond Victor at the Inner Sphere officers gathered outside the square. "They did not know what you were planning to do here, *quineg*?"

"They only knew what all of us knew—if we fought, many would die. Your honor trapped you here. Our need to protect our people trapped us here. Now you retain your honor and our people are protected." Victor shrugged. "We both win."

"But perhaps you win a little bit more. In the past, all three of you have defeated the Clans by force of arms. Here our nature was used against us—to our mutual benefit, agreed, but more in your favor than in mine." Marthe Pryde shook her head. "I shall remember that you know more than one way to fight."

The Khan of the Jade Falcons extended her hand to Doc.

"It is well bargained and done. The Jade Falcons are leaving Coventry."

Doc met her firm grip with one of his own. "Well bargained and done. The winners here are those who would have died. In that victory no one loses."

Both sides turned away and proceeded slowly out of the square. The Jade Falcons disappeared in a billowing brown cloud while the coalition's officers slowly became more real to Victor. Jerrard Cranston and Ragnar joined the trio as they exited the square, and paced them across the gravel to where the other officers were waiting.

Marshal Sharon Byran broke away and made straight for Victor. "How many of us have been bid away?"

"Don't worry yourself, Marshal, it's over."

"Over?" The amazement in her voice was echoed by the expressions on the faces of the others. "What do you mean it's over?"

"We offered them *hegira*."

"What does that mean?"

Victor looked to Ragnar. "If you would be so kind as to explain."

"Gladly, Highness." The young Wolf clasped his hands behind his back. "*Hegira* is a right among the Clans that allows a defeated enemy to withdraw with their honor intact. It is a celebration of their skill and a sign of mutual respect between enemies."

"What is this nonsense? When were they defeated?"

Victor pointed up at the Titan *Hunchback* standing above the group. "They were defeated here in Whitting, by Hauptmann Trevena and his Titans. He offered them *hegira* and they accepted. Once we exchange bondsmen with them, they will go away."

"They're leaving?" Paul Masters of the Knights of the Inner Sphere blinked with surprise. "Just like that?"

"Just like that."

"You're letting them *get away*?" Sharon Byran's face had become a mask of disbelief. "After all they did? After all the death and destruction, you're letting them walk away scot free?"

Victor started to answer, but the Precentor Martial laid a hand on his shoulder and stopped him. "What is it you're protesting, Marshal Byran? We came here for the purpose of driving the Jade Falcons off Coventry. That was our sole aim. That purpose has been accomplished. They are leaving in accord with the rights granted by the Clans to a vanquished enemy."

A smile spread slowly across Kai's face. "You had this planned for a long time. You specified Whitting as the place for the bidding when we were incoming."

Victor shook his head. "I'd like to claim to be that clever, but I can't. Whitting was just luck—I suggested it because it was the only town aside from their base or our base that I knew of here. That was well before the idea of offering *hegira* popped up. When it did, Hauptmann Trevena had to make the offer because he was the one who handed them their last defeat."

Byran turned angrily on Doc. "And you consented to be party to this? You were willing to let those who murdered your commanding officer go free?"

Victor would have replied for him, but Doc gave him no chance to do so. "I was a party to this because I spent the last three months fighting against these bastards. I've watched whole regiments of good and decent people get ripped apart, maimed, and killed. I've undertaken operations that I knew were risky, and the whole time thought the fear would eat me up alive . . ."

"So you take the coward's way out!"

"No, damn you, I'm not a coward. That fear I felt, the fear I fought through was fear of getting my people killed. My people, the people in your commands, even the Jade Falcons, didn't need to die here. Yes, every one of us is willing to face death to preserve our own freedom and our way of life—we're soldiers—but nowhere is it written that the only way to back that willingness is with blood."

"The people who died here cry out for retribution."

"Only *survivors* cry, Marshal Byran, the dead remain silent." Doc raked both hands back through his hair. "Honor and high ideals and all the moral justification in the world mean nothing when weighed against the value of a life. To commit troops to war for an objective that can be taken any other way is a crime that is an order of magnitude more serious than mass murder. If you want evil in its purest form, there it is. I want no part of it, and none of you should either."

His anger spent, Doc looked wordlessly at Victor Davion. The Prince gladly took up his fight. "Everything Doc has said is true. Fighting here would have been worse than murder because we'd have been killing Falcons and they'd have been killing us over an objective that meant nothing to them. They came to Coventry to train troops and show the other Clans that they're still a force to be reckoned with. That was the reason they couldn't retreat from us, though they might have wanted to. In letting them go, we all have a victory."

Byran shook her head. "We'll just have to kill them in another place, at another time."

Victor's eyes sharpened. "Are you speaking of *your* troops or *theirs,* Marshal?" He let her stammer for a moment, then burrowed in again. "We will face the Falcons in the future, there is no question of that. We'll face all the Clans again, without a doubt. The problem with that is, and has always been, that *they* have chosen the battlefields. They fight on worlds that we *must* defend. They force us to make decisions about what we value. If we continue to fight when *they* call us to battle, we will forever be at a disadvantage and we will never truly defeat them."

Wu Kang Kuo's quiet voice broke in. "What is your solution to this problem, Prince Victor?"

The Prince of the Federated Commonwealth looked around at the assembled officers, willing grim determination onto his face and into his voice. "The force we've gathered here shows me that we *all* understand the seriousness of the threat presented by the Clans. The solution seems equally clear. We need to build on the foundations we've established on Coventry and do what even the Clans would think is impossible."

Victor opened his hands to take them all in. "We need, my friends, to assemble a united force, search out the source of Clan power and, for the first time since we've met them, take the war to the Clans."

42

Leitnerton
Coventry
Coventry Province, Lyran Alliance
16 June 3058

Standing there on the rooftop of the Titans' headquarters building, Doc scratched at the back of his head. "That's a good question, Shelly. I guess I figured I'd stay with the Titans, or at least try to keep them together. I kind of doubt the Lyran Alliance Armed Forces are going to rebuild the Tenth Skye Rangers anytime soon."

Shelly Brubaker turned to face him, the setting sun reddening the right side of her face. "You've impressed a lot of people with what you've done here."

"I was just doing what Prince Victor told me to do."

"I don't mean that, though your stock will be considered quite high within the Clans for making the offer. They dwell a lot on things like that." She laid her left hand on his shoulder. "And I'm not just talking about your managing to keep a bunch of light 'Mechs operational during a three-month campaign. What's impressed folks is your ability to plan things out, your insights about the enemy, and the way you refuse to take unnecessary risks with your people."

"I hear you say that, and I appreciate it very much, but it doesn't seem that remarkable to me." Doc shrugged and watched hovertrucks returning with prisoners from Whitting wend their way up the road to Leitnerton. "I guess I have a hard time seeing anything I did as impressive because I just . . . did it."

"All the more impressive, Doc." Shelly smiled. "And that's why you need to think about the future. You know, after the way you spoke to Marshal Byran, your career is at a dead end in the LAAF."

"Yeah, but I've done that sort of duty before, so no big hardship."

"You make it sound like a sentence."

Doc snorted. "Yeah, I guess I do. My problem is that all this seems so unreal at times that I can't really get a handle on it. Objectively, I know that by keeping my people alive, I did a good job, but I don't know how much better I could have done. I'm into new territory and I have to tell you it's scary. Being sentenced to the same old thing is safe."

Shelly's hand fell from his shoulder. "Perhaps they'll return you to Calliston so you can settle back in with your wife."

"My *ex*-wife." Doc patted the pocket containing the holodisk with all the legal documents on it. "Save a planet, get a summons via ComStar. No, there'll be no Calliston for me, and she's history."

"So you *are* making changes."

"Yeah, but not radical ones. I really do feel an obligation to my people." Doc reached down and took her hand in his. "You *do* understand that, right?"

She squeezed his fingers. "Better than you think, Doc. What would you say if I told you I want your Titans in my rebuilt regiment? I've got clearance from General Wolf herself to offer all of you contracts."

"Most of the Titans still have obligations to LAAF."

"We can work something out." Her blue eyes sparkled brightly. "Think of it. You'll still have all your own people while joining the top-notch mercenary unit in the Inner Sphere. We've got the best training, best equipment, our choice of assignments, and even our own world. You'll be making more money than any Leftenant General in the LAAF and your people will see similar raises in their pay. Retirement benefits and family benefits are better than you'll find anywhere in the Inner Sphere."

Doc half-closed his eyes. "And how would you feel if I said yes?"

"I'm the one offering you the job, remember? I wouldn't make the offer if I didn't want you with us."

"But how would you feel personally?" Doc smiled and tightened his grip on her hand ever so slightly. "All this time I've felt there were sparks between us. I've missed you since the rest of the Dragoons arrived and you've had so many other duties taking up your time. I realize this is really a hothouse atmosphere, and we were tired and worn out emotionally, so I don't want to presume or assume or . . ."

Shelly pressed a finger over his lips. "My home on Outreach is really too big for one person, but I have no intention of moving. Does that answer your question?"

"Rather succinctly and directly, yes."

"Good." Shelly laughed lightly. "So you'll join the Dragoons?"

Doc smiled. "It's the best offer I've had all day."

"The day isn't over yet, Hauptmann Trevena."

Doc and Shelly whirled around to see Victor Davion coming up onto the roof. "Colonel Brubaker, I thought the Dragoons recruited from within."

"We do, Highness, save in cases when exceptional talent is available."

The Prince nodded toward Doc. "Hauptmann Trevena is in my employ. He's not available."

Shelly arched an eyebrow. "His commission is with the Lyran Alliance Armed Forces."

"It *was* with the LAAF. To have things in order for this morning's ceremony, the Titans were temporarily transferred to the Federated Commonwealth. Marshal Byran has evidenced no desire to reclaim the Titans, so I'm making the transfer permanent." Victor smiled. "You've been working for me since sunrise, Doc. I'm sure you could tell the difference."

"To tell the truth, sir, no."

"Then let me make amends." Victor held his hands up to forestall comments. "Hear me out, completely, then make your decision. If you don't like what you hear, you can resign and my loss will be the Dragoons' gain."

Doc looked over at Shelly and she nodded. "Okay, I'll listen."

"Doc, somewhere along the line you learned a lesson that separates commanders from great commanders. You learned that victory without bloodshed is better than victory that's blood-soaked. I know it seems like something every officer ought to know and keep foremost in mind, but most never learn it and even fewer actually try to work with it. This is a lesson that's only recently been drilled into my brain, so when I see someone else who understands it, I see someone I don't want to lose."

Victor walked to the edge of the roof and looked down as prisoners started filing out of the hovertrucks. "What I said earlier at Whitting is true—we have to take the war to the Clans. That's going to require everyone working together and working toward the same end. There will be a lot of killing during that campaign, no doubt about it, but I don't want any stupid surplus killing. I want objectives, not body-counts; I want missions that are sharply defined and completed, not Pyrhrric victories that bleed us white.

"To get that, I need people like you, Doc. I want to make you a Leftenant General—Chairman of the Coalition Committee for Operational Review. You and your staff will be the people who review every operation, every situation and find a way to do it better, with fewer casualties and more efficiency. If you say an operation can't go without modification, it doesn't go without modification. If you tell me a commander is overestimating himself or underestimating the enemy, I'll say he is."

Shelly nodded. "You want Doc to be the Coalition's conscience."

"Sure, I want that, but I also want him to be its brain. He took a motley collection of troopers and brought out the best in them. Maybe he can have the same effect on the commanders who'll be part of this coalition." Victor looked up at him. "Your job will be to save lives. The goal of breaking the Clans cannot and will not be used to justify using any and all means to achieve it. I think you're the man who can fill that position, so I'm offering it to you."

The Prince of the Federated Commonwealth glanced down for a moment. "One last thing. I didn't realize until I came up here that there was some personal involvement between you and Colonel Brubaker. I would never begrudge you a chance to be happy. In this line of work there's scant little enough of that sort of thing, as well I know. Before you turn me down on those grounds, however, realize that the Dragoons are going to be gone a long time from Outreach because they'll be heading out with the rest of us. Chances are good the two of you will see more of each other with Doc on my staff than if he's a Dragoon."

Doc nodded slowly and felt Shelly give his hand a quick squeeze. The position Shelly offered him with the Dragoons would allow him to oversee his people and keep them safe, but Doc knew that wouldn't go on forever. There would be a point where someone made a mistake, a critical mistake, and the Titans would be hurt, maybe destroyed. And the worst of it was that it need not be the Titans that made the mistake— someone on staff could order them to be at the wrong place at the wrong time, and they'd pay the price.

Victor's offer meant Doc would be the man in position to prevent that from happening. He realized that no matter how well he'd commanded his unit against the Falcons, he'd gotten by more on luck than on skill. Sure, his ability to think and plan had kept the Titans away from unnecessary jeopardy, but if they'd really stumbled into trouble he wasn't at all certain he could get them back out again. His strength lay in his ability to analyze weakness, to plan out strategies, and to put people into positions where they could make the best use of their own strengths.

And my strength means I can *do this job.* He glanced over at Shelly, and she gave him a half-lidded nod. Doc turned back to the Prince. "What will happen to the Titans?"

"You'll need staff. Pick out the folks you want to go with you. The rest can choose their own assignments and I'll make sure they get them." Victor smiled. "There are times when it's useful to be the Archon Prince."

Doc nodded. "Fair enough. I accept your offer."

Shelly gave him a quick kiss. "As much as it pains me to say this, you made the right choice."

"Thanks."

Victor extended his hand to Doc. "Congratulations, Leftenant General Trevena."

"Thank you, sir." Doc shook Victor's hand, then stopped as he saw someone in the street below. "If you'll excuse me, sir, there's something I have to do."

Victor blinked in surprise. "Excuse me, what did you say?"

Doc looked at Victor, then Shelly, and back again before pointing down at a burly man walking away from one of the hovertrucks. "That's Wayne Rogers of the Waco Rangers. The last time I saw him he recklessly endangered my unit with his irresponsible action. I promised him the next time we met I'd drop him. I thought the Clans had killed him, but I guess not."

Shelly shook her head. "He's too stupid to realize he was supposed to die in that ambush."

The Prince rested his fists on his hips. "And so now, Leftenant General Trevena, you're going down there to deck him?"

Doc nodded. "You'd not want an officer on your staff who didn't keep his promises, would you?"

"No, but you're a Leftenant General now, and in the Armed Forces of the Federated Commonwealth, not LAAF." Victor frowned at him. "You can't go around punching mercenary leaders just because they're stupid . . ."

"Sir . . ."

". . . at least not without orders to do so." Victor shrugged. "Go."

Doc blinked. "Sir?"

"Six months in the LAAF and you forget what an order sounds like?" Victor jerked his head toward the stairs leading from the roof. "Go keep your promise. That's an order, Leftenant General."

"Yes, sir!"

Doc faithfully executed his orders.

And with only one punch, too.

Epilogue

Tharkad City
Tharkad
District of Donegal, Lyran Alliance
17 June 3058

The hurled remote control bounced off the holovid viewer screen with a clank. Katrina noticed that her brother's smiling face didn't shift a whit. It oozed smugness. The thing that truly bothered her about it was that she knew Victor had escaped disaster by dint of luck and, unbeknownst to him, her intervention.

The intelligence about the Jade Falcons' operation on Coventry that she'd passed to Vlad had prompted him to send a message to Marthe Pryde informing her of his interest in acquiring several Falcon worlds. Katrina had wanted the pressure put on the Jade Falcons so they'd withdraw from Coventry or face being attacked by two enemies.

But I only wanted the withdrawal after they'd rid me of Victor. Instead the Wolf pressure had supplied the Falcons with a reason to accept Victor's offer of *hegira*. Marthe Pryde had accepted *hegira* to frustrate Vlad, but in doing so she'd frustrated Katrina.

"Shall I leave the picture on, Highness?"

Katrina wanted to snap at Tormano Liao as he held the remote up, but she controlled herself. "Please, kill it."

Tormano hit a button and Victor's triumphant face shrank to a glowing dot. "Simply done."

"Would that it were so easy. His death in battle would

have been perfect!" She gestured dismissively toward the dark screen. "Now he and that coalition show up, ask the Falcons to leave, and they do so. And most infuriating is the fact that since *you* blacked out news reports of the raids and have systematically drained the Falcons' predations of sinister importance, I can't even accuse Victor of being a coward. This looks as if he and his people just reacted swiftly to an emergency situation and were successful in their effort to deal with it."

Tormano bowed his head contritely, but she knew he had no regrets over his action. "I apologize for the difficulty I have caused you, but I was given little in the way of other options. I am fairly certain your people would not like to know you traveled to Clan space and have entered an agreement with a Clan Khan."

"Is that a threat?"

"From me, no, Highness, because I would be seen as complicit in this act of treason since I covered for you. While your efforts through Clan Wolf *were* instrumental in the Falcons making their decision to withdraw, your role in this matter must remain secret."

"I know that." Katrina pounded on her desk with a fist. "Not even a scratch! Damn him! Just when I need him to be a soldier and get himself killed, the little son of a bitch finds a way to avoid fighting. The story coming out of Coventry will play so well in the news that it will set my efforts to vilify him back for years. A true David and Goliath story, the diminutive Prince and a company of light 'Mechs drive *eight* Galaxies of Jade Falcons from Coventry! Even those who hate Victor will have to admire his cleverness at figuring a way out of this one. I'll never hear the end of it."

Tormano regarded her with a cautionary expression on his face. "That is, perhaps, true, Highness."

Katrina stopped. "I am not in a mood for inscrutability, Mandrinn, out with it."

"You noted you needed Victor to play the role of soldier, a role with which he is closely identified. Perhaps you should look to the role in which most people see you."

"Meaning?"

"Meaning you are the peacemaker who tried to mediate between your brother and Duke Ryan Steiner. You are the peacemaker who refused to join your brother in the prosecution of a war against the Free Worlds League." Tormano set the remote on top of the holovid viewer's case. "It was you who brought together half of Victor's coalition, for the Dragoons, the Harloc Raiders, and the Knights of the Inner Sphere would never have been present except for your efforts. This victory and what it portends for the future, as Prince Victor indicated in his statement, is a victory for the whole of the Inner Sphere. And it is, in great part, your victory."

Katrina sat back abruptly, making her golden hair dance over the shoulders of her blue jacket. "I am a peacemaker? How can I claim credit for this military victory without shattering my credibility?"

"You do not take credit for the victory, Highness, but you exert control over the juggernaut it has spawned." Tormano smiled in a way that Katrina saw as delightfully filled with deceit. "You will hail this victory. You will thank your brother and everyone else with the grace and wit that you alone possess. Best of all, being a conciliator and peacemaker, you will declare your intention of hosting the Whitting Conference here on Tharkad. You will invite all the parties to this coalition to attend, to formalize the unity of Whitting. It was in the face of this unity that the Clans retreated. What began with a retreat at Whitting can become a rout after your conference."

"I understand what you are saying, Tormano." Katrina felt a smile growing on her face. As the sponsor of the conference she could set the agenda. Working to bring the parties together, she could fashion the result she wanted. She would have everyone in her web and be able to bring them together to further her goals. "This will give me great power, but I fail to see how it will rid me of Victor."

"Surely, Highness, you are not that blind." Tormano tapped the screen with a knuckle. "Your brother has already stated what will become the goal of this conference. Through it a force will be assembled that will go to war against the Clans in their own territory."

"Of course." Katrina nodded solemnly. "And my brother, Victor, the warrior born of warriors, will be the only logical choice to lead this force."

"Exactly, Highness." Tormano's grin became a reflection of her own. "The war will carry them far from here, to the worlds that spawned and sheltered the Clans. Only when the

Clan homeworlds have fallen will their threat to the Inner Sphere be eliminated."

"And while Victor and his people are away," Katrina purred, "I shall do all I can to prepare the Inner Sphere properly for their return."

ABOUT THE AUTHOR

Michael A. Stackpole, who has written over fifteen novels and numerous short stories and articles, is one of Roc Books' bestselling authors. Among his BattleTech® books are the *Blood of Kerensky* Trilogy and the *Warrior* Trilogy. Due to popular demand, the *Blood of Kerensky* has recently been republished. This trilogy has also been adapted for television, and is currently one of the highest-rated animated series on Saturday morning, featuring state-of-the-art computer animation. Three other Stackpole novels, *Natural Selection, Assumption of Risk,* and *Bred for War,* also set in the BattleTech® universe, continue his chronicles of the turmoil in the Inner Sphere.

Stackpole is also the author of *Dementia,* the third volume in Roc's Mutant Chronicles series. In 1994 Bantam Books published *Once a Hero,* an epic fantasy. *Rogue Squadron,* the first of Stackpole's four Star Wars® X-wing® novels, has recently been published.

In addition to writing, Stackpole is an innovative game designer. A number of his designs have won awards, and in 1994 he was inducted into the Academy of Gaming Arts and Design's Hall of Fame.

Baboon

Peregrine

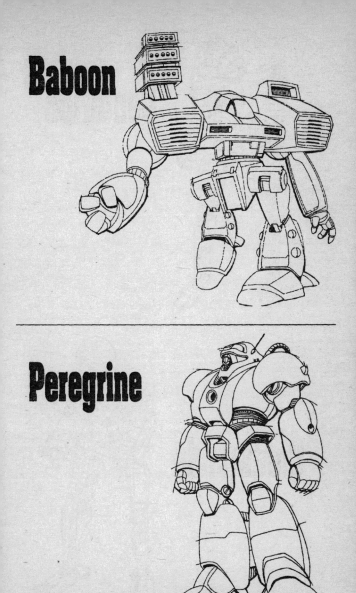

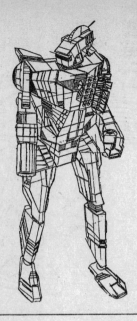

Centurion

Commando

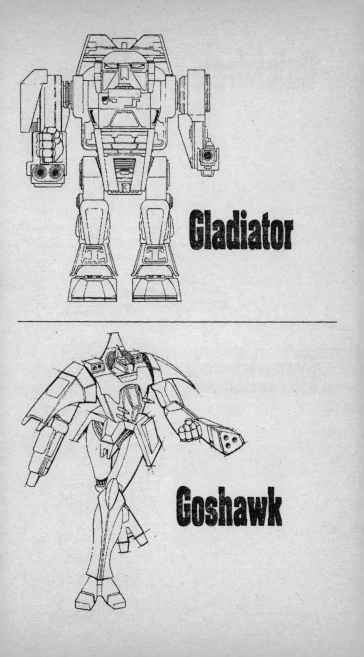

Gladiator

Goshawk

Quickdraw

Hunchback

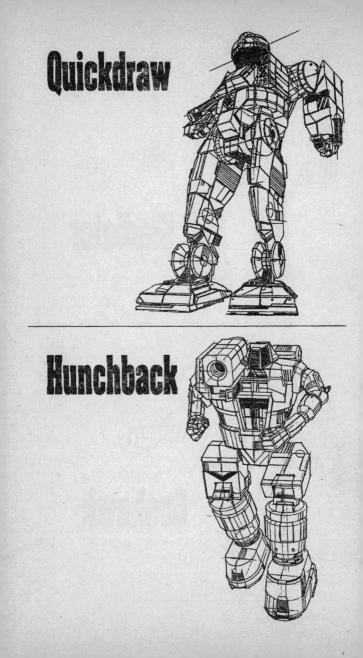

Penetrator

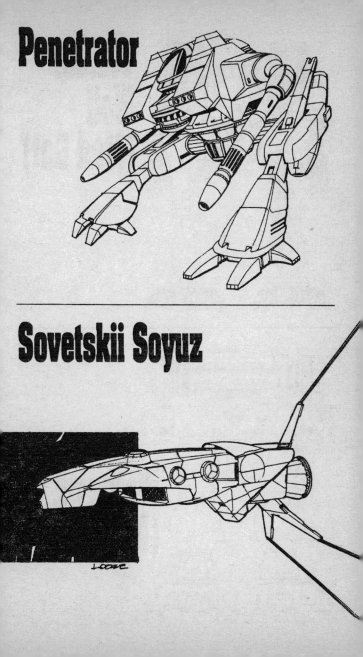

Sovetskii Soyuz

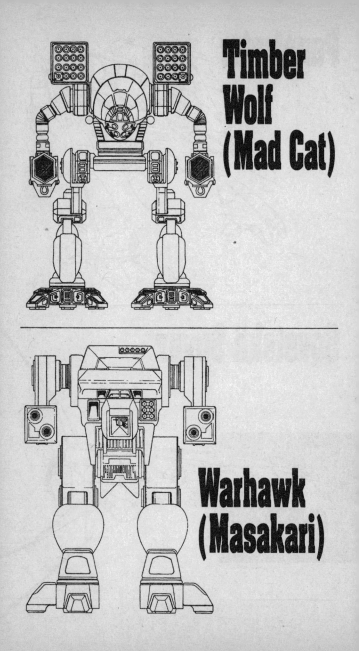

Timber Wolf (Mad Cat)

Warhawk (Masakari)

Transit Fighter

Leopard Class DropShip

WOLVES ON THE BORDER

by Robert N. Charrette

Batan Airspace, Quentin IV
Draconis March, Federated Suns
13 June 3023

The primal violence of the planetary storm was a threat even to so tough a craft as Lieutenant Hamilton Atwyl's *Lucifer*. The AeroSpace Fighter bucked and pitched as it plowed through the turbulence of howling winds. The storm was bad enough without having to worry about the enemy DropShip out there, somewhere. That huge spacecraft would be less disturbed by the winds and pressure shifts that buffeted his own sixty-five-ton LCF-R15.

The Davion DropShip that he was chasing had broken away from the fight in the orbital space above Quentin IV. Atwyl's Blue Flight had been detailed to hunt it down. Even damaged, a *Union* Class DropShip was still a threat.

Days ago, the JumpShips of Wolf's Dragoons had flickered into existence at the system's nadir jump point. They had come for their first mission in the employ of the Draconis Combine, a raid on the Davion planet of Quentin IV. Officially, they had been in House Kurita's employ for three months, time spent crossing the volume of space from the realm of their former employer, House Steiner, to their new employer's border with the Federated Suns of House Davion.

When the Dragoon JumpShips had unleashed their cargo of DropShips for the in-system trip to Quentin, the Davion ship had abandoned its own course toward the jump point and had fled from them. Flight Colonel Jason Carmody had suggested that it could be carrying cargo that might prove troublesome. It had also been close enough to get good data on the strength of the forces the Dragoons had brought to the Quentin system, something Colonel Wolf did not want revealed so soon. Carmody had advocated the immediate destruction of the Davion ship, and Colonel Wolf had agreed. Carmody's AeroSpace forces had mounted a pursuit, but the DropShip's Captain had been skillful enough to elude their fighters in deep space. Reaching Quentin IV, the DropShip had joined the hastily organized defense that the Federated Suns had mustered to oppose the sudden Dragoon raid.

When a DropShip had pulled away from the battle and headed planetside, the main battle computer aboard Wolf's *Overlord* Class DropShip, the *Chieftain,* had identified it as the one that had run from the raiders earlier. The orbital fight was still undecided, and all Carmody could spare was the hastily organized Blue Flight. Lieutenant Atwyl's aerolance of two *Lucifers* and two aerolances of SPR-H5 *Sparrowhawks* had orders to chase it down.

Against an intact *Union* Class DropShip, they would not have had a chance, but Colonel Carmody had informed him that six AeroSpace Fighters would be sufficient for a ship estimated to be seriously damaged. Carmody had not counted on the severe storm that caused the flight to lose track of its quarry.

With the way the *Lucifer* was being tossed about now, Atwyl was glad he was not in a *Sparrowhawk.* The thought of that tiny, thirty-ton ship that was little more than a cockpit strapped to an engine reminded him to check the formation. This was his first mission as a flight commander, and he was still getting used to having to worry about more than just himself and his wingman.

Atwyl's radar screen was fuzzed with junk readings, but showed several intermittent blips that should be the rest of his flight. His visual scan of the airspace outside his cockpit only picked out AeroPilot Gianni Bredel in the other *Lucifer,* glued to his left wing tip as usual. Raising power to punch through the interference, he called over the channel reserved for Blue Flight, "Let's close it up a little, children. There's a big, bad DropShip out there. Crippled or not, it can swat a *Sparrowhawk* out of the sky. I don't want anyone finding it by himself."

He received acknowledgment from Gordon, Hall, and Reischaur, but not from Morris. Shifting more power to the comm circuit, he tried again. "T.J., you out there, girl?"

"Sure am, boss man. What you want?" The words were distorted and barely audible, but T.J.'s jaunty tone came through. Hamilton was surprised at the relief he felt. AeroPilot T.J. Morris had just graduated from the Dragoon AeroSpace pilot program and was on her first mission. Her high scores and outstanding simulator performances did not keep him from worrying about her, however. Enthusiasm and training often counted for little in the field, especially with conditions as bad as they were now.

"Close up with Reischaur and the rest of the flight. Can't have you taking down that DropShip all by yourself, hotshot."

"Roger, boss man."

Atwyl looked for the closing fighters. Off to the right, he could see the shapes of Beta Lance's craft break through the clouds. The bright yellow paint jobs of both fighters made them easily visible against the storm clouds. The dark, anodized metal sheaths of the Martell lasers that jutted forward on either side of the fuselage gave a _Sparrowhawk_ the profile of a winged bullet. It took a lightning flash to reveal the dark wolf's-head against a red circle that decorated the tall, vertical stabilizer rising behind the cockpit of each ship.

Unable to see the fighters of Gamma Lance, Atwyl switched his communicator over to the band he shared with his wingman.

"Yo, Gianni. I don't have a visual on our little Gamma birdies in this soup. My scanners show them off to the left, I think. Can't be sure what's a real echo and what's a ghost. This storm has really screwed things up. Hope it's as bad for the groundpounders holding this rock."

"I'll give it a look-see, Ham." The speaker crackled and popped in accompaniment to his wingman's voice, which was calm and steady as ever. It took more than a bumpy ride in a wild storm and playing hide and seek with a hostile DropShip to fluster AeroSpace Pilot Gianni Bredel.

"Not too far, Gianni. Don't want to lose you in this murk, too." Atwyl watched as the other ship vectored thrust and shot away from his side. In the patched and cross-wired technology of the Successor States, things had a too-common tendency to break down. Even in the long-ago era of the Star League, *Lucifer*s had been notorious for the fragility of their communication and sensor systems. Fearing that the recent communication problems might be due to more than the storm's interference, Atwyl didn't want his wingman out of sight.

"You and me both, boss man," said Bredel, but the rest of his words were drowned in a burst of static. Atwyl fretted while the other *Lucifer* moved out 200 meters, then pulled up even with him. As it did so, Atwyl's visual angle changed, making it seem as though he were being paced by a flying skeleton. The other *Lucifer*'s wings, both the canards under the cockpit and the main vee, had disappeared against the midnight blue of the ship's color scheme. The dark fighter's shape blended with the stormy sky, leaving only the white bars and shapes of highlighted panels and structural elements.

"Got 'em, Ham." Bredel's call snapped Atwyl from his musings. "Safe and sound."

"Roger, Gianni." Switching over to the flight frequency, he said, "All right, children. Let's keep it this way if we can." Resolving to hold his own attention on the job at hand, Atwyl returned to watching his sensor sweeps.

Minutes crawled by while the tempest tossed the flight's fighters about. Twice, Atwyl had to call for the young pilots to quit grousing about the rough ride and keep the comm frequency clear. During a brief lull in the storm, AeroPilot Friedrich Reischaur was the first to pick up the DropShip's readings. "Big mark on MAD sensor, Lieutenant," he reported.

"I've got it too, Friedrich," Atwyl said. The Lucifer's bigger computer had been even quicker at registering the target, but he revealed little of his excitement in finding the quarry. "Reading matches the Davion DropShip, and comp places it on the surface just shy of the Batan spaceport. If that's our baby, she'll be an easy target as long as we keep clear of the port's guns."

Atwyl punched in some numbers and waited for the fighter's battle computer to confirm his estimated flight plan. When it did, he laid out his plan to the flight. "We're going to go down on the deck and come in low. That should put us under the spaceport defenses. Comp says there's a forest that will screen us most of the way to the DropShip. Beta and Gamma, when we're down, stretch out your lead on us. I want you in fast with your eyes open for hostiles. Recon only on the first run. Bredel and I will come in hard and rip up the sucker after you give us the all-clear. After we've softened it up, it's an open turkey shoot. Questions?" Morris's channel lit up.

"What's a turkey, boss man?"

Atwyl laughed. Intentionally or not, T.J. had broken the tension that had been rising in him since he'd first caught the readings on the DropShip. He hoped her words had loosened up the others, too. "Never mind, T.J. What it means is that after Bredel and I hit the ship on our first pass, you guys can make your own attack runs."

"Roger, boss man. You crack the shell, and we take the turkey." That got laughter from Bredel and Hall. Atwyl quieted them down.

"Let's all go down together. Make it a six-eight degree glide slope down to three-zero meters off the deck. Then open throttles and go in. Got it?" Five voices chorused acknowledgment, while Atwyl keyed the final figures into his battle computer. It set up a countdown timer in the left corner of his head-up display.

"O.K. Recorders on. Three. Two. One. Punch it!"

Acceleration pushed Atwyl back into his flight couch. A small whine came from behind him as the pressure equalizer cut in. The system was supposed to inflate bladders in his flight suit to prevent blood from pooling in his limbs under the weight of the tremendous gee forces of dives and high-speed maneuvers. If he lost power in the system, he could black out and lose control. Though the equalizer was noisy, it did seem to be working.

A sudden drumming announced the end of the clouds as waves of rain hit the hurtling ship. The water sheeted over the canopy, leaving everything gray and dim beyond it. Ahead of him, Atwyl could see the flames of the *Sparrowhawk*'s afterburners as the fighters leveled out and accelerated. Easing back on the control stick, he came out of the dive smoothly. Checking on Bredel, he saw his wingman following cleanly behind. Ahead, the lights of the smaller fighters' engines winked out as they reached attack speed. He vectored all thrust aft to bring his own ship up to speed.

The Dragoon fighters broke through the front of the thunderstorms. Under the clearer sky, the open, rolling hills of the countryside were visible around them. The roads Atwyl could see were deserted. In places, he spotted the rubble of towns and industrial complexes, highwater marks of the Succession Wars battles that had swept over this planet time and again. Right on schedule, the forest loomed ahead, its trees rising to almost a hundred meters high. The fighters roared up and over the forest.

When they reached the edge of the woods nearest Batan, a path of newly broken trees appeared. It was as though a giant, flaming hand had swept across them, splintering and burning them despite their sodden condition. As the last trees fell away, the cause became apparent.

Half-sunk in the fields outside the city was the immense sphere of the Davion DropShip. The pilot must have been making for the spaceport when disaster struck. The ship had gone down, skimming the trees and plowing into the open fields west of the city. Seven kilometers short of its goal, the DropShip had foundered.

A huge hole gaped on the upper surface, the edges blackened and warped outward. Debris was strewn in a trail from the forest's edge to the crash site. High on the elevated side, one of the great unloading doors was open to the sky, its protective armor crumpled and torn. Across one edge, limp as an unconscious man, was the shape of a BattleMech. The giant machine seemed small against the bulk of the transport spacecraft. Even as Atwyl registered the carnage, the *Sparrowhawk*s were zooming over the wreckage, two on either side of the ship.

Just then, a startling twin flash of laser pulses split the sky, followed by the stuttering light of tracer fire from autocannons. The lead fighter of the left-hand pair crossed the streaks of light and disintegrated in a ball of fire. No sound reached Atwyl over the roar of his own engines. Reischaur was gone.

The author of the *Sparrowhawk*'s destruction emerged from the shadow of the downed DropShip. It was a *Rifleman* BattleMech. The wing antenna of the Garret D2-j targeting system was rotating as the machine's torso swiveled to bring the paired autocannon that made up each of its arms to bear on a new target.

Atwyl felt paralyzed, stunned by the sudden loss of his pilot. His hands were rigid on the *Lucifer*'s controls, but the other members of Blue Flight went into action. Beta Lance split and began jinking to throw off the enemy machine's tracking. Morris threw her *Sparrowhawk* into a steep climb, thereby avoiding the lethal streams of coherent light and armor-piercing shells that filled the air where her fighter would have been. Even Bredel was reacting. He launched a flight of missiles that impacted far short of the DropShip. The *Lucifer*s were still too far away to do any damage, but Bredel's attack had roused Atwyl from his shock at the loss of Reischaur. He took command again.

"Overthrust, Gi! We've got to get in there." Atwyl's voice was shrill with emotion. He had lost one man. He didn't want to lose any more.

"Roger." As always in battle, Bredel's voice was emotionless. "I'll take the 'Mech."

"No! He's mine. Strafe the DropShip." Atwyl wanted the killer for himself. He knew that wasn't a professional reaction, but he didn't care. Arming his missiles, he threw his craft into an evasive roll. Ground and sky flashed alternately across his cockpit. Once, he glimpsed Bredel's *Lucifer* in the midst of a similar maneuver.

Before they could close to firing range, Atwyl caught a flash of sunlight on metal high above the fields. A check of his IFF scanners revealed it to be Morris's SPR-H5 diving down on the crash site.

"No, T.J.! Abort!" Atwyl's fear for the young pilot came through in his strained voice. The small fighter was too light to go against a BattleMech that excelled at antiaircraft work.

No reply came from the AeroSpace Fighter weaving a crazy corkscrew path as it dove. All four of its lasers were blazing. Some of the beams caught the *Rifleman* and sent chunks of blistered armor spraying from its torso. The 'Mech's own fire cast a deadly net around the fighter, but the small ship darted like the winged predator of its name. A burst of fire from the *Sparrowhawk* caught one of the twin guns on the 'Mech's right arm, shearing it clean away. Then the fighter cut sideways and roared over the field, miraculously untouched by the *Rifleman*'s weapon fire. Now shielded from the 'Mech by the bulk of the DropShip, T.J. sped her craft toward the onrushing *Lucifer*s. Atwyl shook his head in amazement at this virtuoso display.

"Not to worry, boss man." T.J.'s voice was clear, though the words were slightly spaced as she caught her breath. "Those tin men are too slow to catch this—"

T.J.'s comment was cut off as missiles arcing up from a

concealed position struck her fighter. One hit her port wing. Its explosive warhead and the speed at which she was traveling were enough to rip the wing away from the body of the craft. As the *Sparrowhawk* began to roll, the turbulence tore more pieces from the stricken craft. Trailing flames, it dropped lower. Morris's screams lasted until the fighter plowed into the ground and exploded.

With those screams echoing in his ears, Atwyl hit the firing stud. All of his forward-mounted lasers raked the ground at the point where he had seen the killer missiles rise. Clouds of steam rose as kilojoules of energy flash-heated the ground, then flame erupted as the launcher's ammunition exploded. The infantry team who had fired the SRMs ceased to exist. A savage smile split Atwyl's face. It vanished just as suddenly when his *Lucifer* rocked under autocannon fire from the *Rifleman,* which had now cleared the side of the DropShip.

A swift shift of thrust vectors let him sideslip the fighter away from the 'Mech's searing energy beams and pounding shells. Banking the *Lucifer* around, he came in from the other side of the DropShip.

The *Rifleman* was waiting for him, its remaining three guns brought to bear on the Dragoon fighter. Atwyl, lost in his fury, bore straight in. His craft's armor was vaporized by the hellish energy of the 'Mech's lasers and the pounding of its autocannon shells. He didn't care. Flight after flight of missiles roared out from the Holly LRM launcher beneath his cockpit. His aim was poor, and most of the shots went wild streaking past the BattleMech or striking the ground beside it. Some burrowed into the heavy plating of the crashed DropShip to send scraps pattering harmlessly against the 'Mech and the scorched dirt around it. Some few others found their target, repaying the BattleMech some of the punishment it was dishing out.

Atwyl's lips were skinned back, baring his clenched teeth. Sweat rolled down his face, puddling under his eyes and blurring his vision.

The shutdown alarm shrilled, warning of heat burden above acceptable limits. His hand stabbed out to hit the override, silencing it. Another stab launched the last of the Holly's ammo.

The *Rifleman* loomed larger and larger. Atwyl cursed the heat, then loosed all of his lasers. Red fire lanced out.

As fissures opened in the 'Mech's armor, a small explosion came from within the machine, followed by a string of larger ones. The BattleMech rocked and toppled backward as its torso ripped open. The *Lucifer* screamed through the fireball where the *Rifleman* had stood.

Now Atwyl had to pay the cost. The heat burden had risen too high for the fighter's cooling unit to handle. The automatic cutoff had shut down the fighter's reactor. The ship was going down, and him with it. To correct a flaw in the LCF-R15's design, the engineers had created a new one. The fighter had no emergency ejection system.

Fighting the sluggish controls, Atwyl thought that it was lousy to die now after he had wasted the 'Mech. Struggling with controls, he thought that the *Lucifer*'s nose did finally come up, a little. *Enough?*

No.

Maybe.

He was glad he was in a ship that had at least minimal atmospheric streamlining. Some AeroSpace Fighters relied almost exclusively on their engines for lift. Lift that the *Lucifer* would need. To avoid crashing . . .

Crashing . . .

YOUR OPINION CAN MAKE A DIFFERENCE!
LET US KNOW WHAT *YOU* THINK.

**Send this completed survey to us and enter
a weekly drawing to win a special prize!**

1.) Do you play any of the following role-playing games?
   Shadowrun ———— Earthdawn ———— BattleTech ————

2.) Did you play any of the games before you read the novels?
   Yes ———————— No ————————

3.) How many novels have you read in each of the following series?
   Shadowrun ———— Earthdawn ———— BattleTech ————

4.) What other game novel lines do you read?
   TSR ———— White Wolf ———— Other (Specify) ————

5.) Who is your favorite FASA author?
_____

6.) Which book did you take this survey from?
_____

7.) Where did you buy this book?
   Bookstore ———— Game Store ———— Comic Store ————
   FASA Mail Order ———————— Other (Specify) ————

8.) Your opinion of the book (please print)
_____
_____
_____

Name ———————————— Age ———— Gender ————
Address ————————————————————————————
City ———————————— State ———— Country ———— Zip ————

Send this page or a photocopy of it to:
FASA Corporation
Editorial/Novels
1100 W. Cermak Suite B-305
Chicago, IL 60608